The Hall of the Wood

SCOTT MARLOWE

Umberland Press
IMAGINATION RULES

THE HALL OF THE WOOD

Second Edition

scottmarlowe.com

Published by Umberland Press

umberlandpress.com

First Edition: March 2008
Second Edition: August 2013

OTHER WORKS BY SCOTT MARLOWE

<u>The Alchemancer series</u>

The Hall of Riddles (An Alchemancer Prequel)

Engines of Alchemancy
The Nullification Engine
The Inversion Solution
The Alchemist's Forge

<u>Assassin Without a Name series</u>

The Assassin's Blade
The Assassin's Cunning

<u>Standalone</u>

The Hall of the Wood

NORTHEASTERN FRONTIER OF VRANNA

UGULL MOUNTAINS

GRETH

CAVERN OF THE WELL

SOLLIN·KEL

HALL OF THE WOOD

HIGHPASS TRAIL

EAGLE'S NEST

TOMB OF DELBIN KINKAED

STONE EYE TRAIL

HUNTER'S LODGE

CRIMSON TRAIL

FELLER TRAIL

CRYSTAL FALLS

RELL

HOMEWOOD

GOLD OR

KETTLING WAY

CIMMARON WOODS

HOLDEN BRIDGE

N

THE PLAYERS

Aliah Starbough: Half-dryad. Daughter of Vadeya Dawnoak.

Ash: Jerrick's (sometime) faithful canine companion.

Aurum: Kayra's horse.

Billard: Mayor of Homewood.

Bostan the Quick: Company commander, King's Patrol.

Delbin Kinkaed: Arch-druid.

Evar: Eldest of the Elders of the Simarron Hall of the Wood.

Graewol: A citizen of Homewood.

Gral: Goblin lord of Greth.

Holly: A bard. Kayra's herald.

Holtz: Company commander, King's Patrol.

Jasper: Retired trapper. Old friend of Jerrick's.

Jay: Dwarven proprietor of Jay's Tavern.

Jerrick Bur: Patroller of the Simarron Hall of the Wood.

Jezebel: An inhabitant of Homewood.

Kayra Weslin: Knight-Esquire of Kallendor, Daughter of the House of Weslin.

Murik Alon Rin'kres: An eslar sorcerer.

Nohr: Gaugath warrior in the service of Lord Gral.

Parthen: Priest of Sarrengrave.

Relk: Trapper.

S'nar: Evar's owl.

Saress: A sitheri witch.

Sarrengrave: Immortal. Lord of Rot.

Skave: Haurek stalker in the service of Lord Gral.

Speck: A grekkel in the service of Saress.

Thomas Drake: Company commander, King's Patrol.

Ushar: Undead eslar sorcerer. A prisoner of Murik's.

Vadeya Dawnoak: Dryad. Mother of Aliah Starbough.

Zokore: Haurek captain.

THE HALL OF THE WOOD

CHAPTER ONE

A WARNING

J ERRICK BUR STARED IN DISBELIEF at the green haze
emanating from the creek. Blinking away sleep, he thought
it a remnant of a dream until, with uncanny deliberateness,
it wafted, rose, then billowed over the banks, transforming
from oddity to potential threat in the span of a breath. Jerrick's
mind cleared as patroller instinct took hold. Grasping the
sword he always kept close, he scuttled back. He'd only just
managed to stand when the fog engulfed him.

Jerrick!

The voice echoed from the walls of the narrow canyon,
making it impossible to tell from which direction the speaker

called.

"Who's there? Show yourself!"

Jerrick . . . please . . .

Jerrick crouched, waiting and watching, but he saw nothing but smoky emerald in all directions. The canyon grew deathly quiet; even the sound from the rush of the stream had disappeared. Jerrick counted ten heartbeats before curiosity tugged at him. He rose, and padded toward the source of the fog. His bare feet were sloshing in the water before he realized he'd reached it. Immediately, he saw why the noise from the stream had grown quiet: the water was completely still, as if time itself had stopped. Mesmerized by the stillness, Jerrick looked deep into the now mirror-like surface. The reflection looking back at him was not his own.

The delicate, feminine features were familiar. Her eyes, the color of jade, and the smooth, emerald hair brought back many memories. He struggled to say something, but found no words adequate to greet the impossibility of the face looking back at him.

Jerrick . . . please . . . you must help me!

The tears streaming down her cheeks shook Jerrick from his trance.

"Aliah! What—how is this possible? Help you with what? What do you mean? Where are you?"

Dead. They're all dead. She was sobbing.

"Who's dead? Who—"

You must return to the Simarron. There is so little time. You must help me!

"I'm on my way to the Simarron now. Who's dead, Aliah?

Help you with what?"

I cannot go on alone. You must return. Together— She stopped to look over her shoulder. When next she spoke, her face loomed large on the still, watery surface. *They're coming!* Anger gave strength to her voice. *I will not allow them to take me.* Then, with renewed urgency, *There is so little time, Jerrick. Please hurry!*

"Aliah, wait! What of the King's Patrol? What—"

Her visage faded. As it disappeared completely, the mist contracted, sucked back into the water from which it had sprung. Jerrick, frustrated, interrupted the surface with his hand, but there was nothing there. Then, the last of the mist disappeared, the water's flow started again, and all returned to normal.

Jerrick sat back to find Ash standing next to him.

The dog had disappeared sometime during the night, and must have only now returned. Absentmindedly, Jerrick put an arm around him as disbelief and confusion warred with each other. *Dead. They're all dead.* Aliah's foreboding words echoed in his mind. Was she talking about the patrollers? How could they all be dead? The notion struck Jerrick a heavy blow, and he found the need to rise. *They're coming.* Who was coming? There was no telling. But Jerrick had seen the fear in her eyes. It was not something he'd seen there often.

Jerrick shook his head clear. He was sure of only one thing: there'd be no more sleep tonight. Best he break camp and get moving. Whether coincide or fate, the Simarron was already his destination. Aliah couldn't have known that, yet still she'd sought him out. They'd been friends—still were—so of course she had. But that she'd enlist his aid and not the patrollers already in the forest . . . There was no answer. Better to reach the Simarron than waste time speculating.

It took only a moment to kick dirt on the last of the glowing embers of his campfire and gather his things. With weapons at his belt, pack slung securely over both shoulders, and his bow held in one hand, Jerrick motioned to Ash to get moving. The dog took off running, disappearing into the darkness. Ash was a solitary creature, a frontier dog. He'd pick his own path, only remaining close when the terrain or the path made doing otherwise impossible. Theirs was a relationship built on tolerance.

Partial moonlight allowed Jerrick to maintain a solid pace. Already, he was deep in the foothills, his home of recent years behind him, with the rising slope of the mountains underfoot after only an hour of walking. The familiarity of the trail afforded him time to ponder not so much the warning his friend had delivered, but the deliverer herself. Aliah Starbough. A creature of the woods if ever there was one, but one who ultimately had wanted to experience more than her own little corner of the world. She'd left the Simarron even before Jerrick had. He hadn't seen her since, and so didn't know when she'd come back to the woods. Jerrick himself hadn't been back for just over four years now. Like Aliah, he'd sought something more, but returned now because that life was no more.

As if to remind him of what might have been, Ash popped out from the brush ahead. Tongue lolling, the dog sat, and waited. The look he gave as Jerrick approached suggested a singular desire: food. The sun was rising now, and Jerrick supposed it as good a time as any to break his fast. He found a fallen log to sit on and ate in silence, tossing Ash his share of their jerky. Jerrick hadn't packed for two, but the dog had insisted on following him. He didn't know why. Ash didn't like him. Jerrick's introduction those years ago had caused a reordering of the hierarchy. Most dogs adapted to such change. Not Ash. The dog's loyalty belonged to the one and only person who had raised him from a pup. There was no replacement for her. Ash would never understand how much Jerrick agreed with him on that point.

As soon as Jerrick began stowing the remainder of the food, Ash stood, bounded down the trail, and disappeared from view once more. Jerrick followed at his own pace. Only when the trail grew steeper and more rugged did he see Ash again, for then the dog chose to stay in view as he blazed the way more slowly. With evening drawing near and the fringes of the mountain's cold already touching them, Jerrick stopped and made a patroller's camp: a small fire for cooking, with a bedroll laid out next to it. A comfortless arrangement for most, he found the simple efficiency of it settling. He tried not to think of the green mist and Aliah's plea as he warmed a meal of porridge sweetened with sugar. He shared more of the jerky between them and let Ash eat the remainder of the porridge. The dog licked the pot clean, leaving Jerrick to clean it more properly. Jerrick had already fitted himself with fur leggings, an undercoat of deerskin, and a jacket to help stave off the growing chill. The mountains were cold at the best of times, so he'd sleep dressed as he was now for the next several nights. Sleep came, but only fitfully. Morning began with a quick meal, and then they were moving again.

Evergreens were thick until they surmounted the tree line. What remained was a barren landscape moving ever upward to the great, snowy peaks of the Ugulls. They'd stay below the worst of the snow and ice by making their way between those peaks. They found shelter that night in a low spot nestled amongst a jumble of boulders either exposed by wind or brought here by a landslide of old. There was no wood for a fire, so they ate a cold meal and retired immediately. Ash remained in camp, sleeping close for warmth more than anything else, Jerrick figured. They started out early the next morning, nearly reaching the trail's highest point close to nightfall. Knowing better refuge lay ahead, Jerrick pushed them on a little farther, until Eagle's Nest came into view.

Eagle's Nest was a place of old. Once called Eagle's Tower, soldiers and patrollers alike had stood at its crenellated top to watch in all directions for the goblins and gorgons once infesting this part of the mountains. That duty, if it had ever been truly needed, was no more, as was the Eagle's Tower of the past. Now, the only portion remaining of the roofless structure was its uneven stone walls and, leading up to them, the chipped and cracked remains of a staircase carved from the very rock. The only purpose Eagle's Nest served now was as a wayfarer's station, a bivouac for travelers seeking a temporary respite from the wind and the mountain cold. Most times, the ruins were empty. The trail over the Ugulls was infrequently traveled, less so this late in the year. Another month, and with the first snowfall, the trail became impassable. So it was with some surprise that Jerrick smelled the smoke from a fire. No lighted emanation greeted them from behind the walls of the ruins as they closed the distance, but Jerrick's closer proximity confirmed the smoke, as he saw it now, rising lazily. Eagle's Nest was already home to one visitor this night.

"Hello, there!" Jerrick called out.

It was customary—and good sense—to announce one's presence in such circumstances. When the way across the mountains was traversed, it was most often by merchants, missionaries, or the occasional patroller. Given the present lack of wagons and pack animals, Jerrick ruled out the first. The second, perhaps. The third . . . No reason to get his hopes up.

No one had replied, and so Jerrick called out once more. He waited another few seconds, and when he still heard nothing, decided to mount the stairs and try again. Ash went ahead. Once, the stairs must have led to a sturdy door. Now, there was only a dark opening. Jerrick was about to call out again, but, slightly annoyed, he wondered if he ought to step forward and throw caution and courtesy to the wind. Ash made the decision moot. One moment the dog paused before the entrance, the next he was gone from view. Jerrick swore under his breath. There being nothing else to do, he went in after him.

Inside was the expected fire burning at the center of the circular room. On one knee, facing the flames, was a man wrapped in a dark cloak. Busy warming his hands, he seemed at first to take no notice of either Jerrick or Ash, who stood halfway between Jerrick and the stranger. But then the man's head turned ever so slightly, and the fire's light revealed skin neither black nor white, but whose exact color was indeterminate from his silhouette alone. The stranger spoke

7

with a tone of welcome. "Ah, other travelers walking the weary road. Please join me at the fire and warm yourselves."

Jerrick kept his distance. He saw no sign of weapons, though the stranger's cloak might conceal any number. Jerrick figured the man had to be alone; there was nowhere for anyone else to hide. That, and he saw only one leather pack and a gnarled walking stick propped up against the wall. Hanging from the stick was a trio of conies, dressed and ready for skinning.

"Are you alone?" Jerrick asked. Despite the signs, it seemed worth confirming.

The man's hands stopped their motion. "Hmm? Why, yes. I am alone."

Ash glided forward, his attention fixed more on the rabbits than the stranger.

"Perhaps you should stand, and turn around. Slowly."

"Hmm . . . Oh, yes. Never can be too trusting, after all. Very well." The man rose and turned, empty hands extended away from his body.

Jerrick saw right away the man was an eslar, who dwelt far to the north and east and who rarely trafficked beyond their own borders. Jerrick had seen their kind only a handful of times, when merchants of theirs ventured to the Hall to trade goods and knowledge of the forest. This one was much like those others, with blue-black skin and russet-colored hair cut short. He had a hawkish look to his face, a nose which tapered at the end, and, most unusual of eslar traits, eyes stark white and devoid of color. Those eyes were unreadable, but the tilt of his head and the beginnings of a smile on his dark lips suggested something between curiosity and amusement. Clad in worn leather breeches, high boots much like Jerrick's, and a cuffed white shirt beneath a fur-lined leather vest, he stood taller than Jerrick, but by his posture seemed to favor one leg more than the other. Forearms were covered by metal bracers, and his traveling cloak—dark blue and much too thin to provide adequate warmth at their current elevation—shimmered in the light of the fire like no other material Jerrick had ever seen. At his belt hung a short sword and dagger, both resting in jeweled sheaths. Though his age was indeterminate, the eslar's demeanor suggested the callowness of youth had been left behind long ago.

Ash, whose attention remained on the conies, now looked at the stranger. The eslar held his hand out, a gesture Ash accepted as he padded in to sniff. The hand wasn't enough; Ash took his leisure sniffing boots, legs, and crotch. Jerrick admonished him for the last. The eslar remained unperturbed other than to let out a short burst of laughter as Ash performed the last part of his inspection.

"We're a long way from Panthora," Jerrick said. "What business brings you to Eagle's Nest?" Once, demanding such answers was well within his rights. Now, he supposed patroller instincts died hard.

The eslar lowered his arms. "Is that what this place is called? Eagle's Nest? How intriguing . . ." Still facing Jerrick, he looked about, taking in the high, empty walls as if constructing in his mind what the tower must have looked like in its former glory. Finally, he answered Jerrick's question. "I am but a simple traveler, come through these mountains on my way to the

Simarron Woods to the east. My final destination is a place called the Hall of the Wood. Perhaps you've heard of it?" The eslar did not wait for an answer. "I came across these ruins and, as it was getting dark, thought it a good place to stop for the night."

The answer satisfied Jerrick, and Ash as well, who took it upon himself to lie down by the fire.

"My name is Murik Alon Rin'kres, of Isia."

Jerrick stepped forward to clasp the eslar's outstretched hand. "Jerrick Bur, of Rell."

"Rell . . . I'm afraid I've not heard of it. And your dog?"

"His name is Ash. But he's not mine."

Murik moved back to the fire, where he knelt next to Ash and rubbed his side in long, even strokes. Ash closed his eyes in ecstasy. "He is a beautiful animal, though a tad dirty. Not yours, you say? Is there someone else with you?"

"No. I meant only that Ash has a mind of his own. He calls no one 'master.'" *Once he had, but not since* . . . Jerrick left the thought unfinished. "Accept my apologies for the reception."

Murik waved a hand in dismissal, then gestured toward the modest blaze. "Please."

Jerrick moved closer to the fire, readily absorbing its warmth.

"I was about to indulge in a small repast. You and Ash are welcome to join me." Murik gestured toward the conies. "Though I fear the meal may prove rather meager."

Jerrick removed his pack, setting it and his bow against the wall as he moved to inspect the rabbits. There were three, all of good size. "These will do just fine. Thank you."

"Think nothing of it."

"One rabbit each, then. I have bread and some vegetables in my pack."

Murik looked confused for a moment. "Yes, of course! One rabbit each. I'm afraid I forgot about Ash here."

At the sound of his name, the dog plopped himself into Murik's lap.

"He certainly is friendly," Murik said, "though I had my doubts when I first saw him. He's quite big."

"He's friendly enough," Jerrick said, "especially when he knows there's food coming."

They said nothing more as Jerrick saw to skinning the rabbits. While Murik kept the fire up, Ash licked his chops in anticipation. With the rabbits cooked, Jerrick retrieved the promised loaf of bread and what remained of his stock of carrots and turnips from his pack, and they ate. Ash tore into his meal, gobbling the whole affair down in minutes. Jerrick and Murik took their time, savoring each greasy bite.

While they ate, a biting wind kicked up, creating a persistent howl which swept over and around Eagle's Nest. The trio was protected well enough within the ruined tower, but a harsh chill still embraced them, and they took turns keeping the fire up. With their bellies full, the two men settled into an easy silence. Ash had already dozed off near the fire. Every once in a while, one of his legs jerked out or he softly whined before growing quiet again. Murik showed a genuine interest in the history of Eagle's Nest, so Jerrick related what little he knew of its former glory as a scout post. Eventually, the conversation died away and the two bid each other good night. Jerrick, his sword and knife close, lay listening to Murik's soft breathing as thoughts of Aliah filtered through his mind.

They're all dead.

Jerrick remained awake a long time, thinking on the words and the fearful expression of the woman who had spoken them. The Hall wasn't far now. Soon enough, he'd have an answer.

CHAPTER TWO

STONEY CREEK

J ERRICK WOKE JUST PRIOR TO dawn. Rubbing sleep
from his eyes, he found himself alone. The fire, its surviving
wood charred and cold, had not been rekindled. He listened
for last night's wind, but heard nothing. Still, it was cold, and
as Jerrick draped his heavy cloak around him, he heard a laugh,
lighthearted and cheerful, resounding from outside the tower.
The laugh was followed by a succession of barks.

Jerrick walked down the tower's outside stairs to find Murik seated upon the Looking Stone, an elevated, oblong-shaped rock so named because it provided the best perch from which to observe the surrounding landscape. Ash sat next to the eslar, his ears perked, tail wagging, and tongue hanging unceremoniously from his mouth. They each sent visible breaths into the frigid morning air. As Jerrick shuffled to the base of the Looking Stone, Murik smiled down at him.

"Good morning, friend."

Jerrick grunted a reply.

"I tried not to wake you. Do you wish to join us?"

"Me and Ash need to be on our way."

"I see. But the dawn will be here momentarily. I'm sure it shall be a spectacular sight. Surely the road can wait a few moments longer."

Looking to the dark sky, Jerrick saw the first colors creeping over the horizon. Murik was right about the view being spectacular. How many years had it been since he'd witnessed it? Too many, he decided. This journey was one of recovery and restitution, not urgency and haste. The road wasn't going anywhere. Jerrick clambered up to join them, pushing Ash aside as he sat. The dog padded to the other side of Murik and seated himself once more.

The sun's rays touched the western peaks first, morphing them from dark, hulking mounds into majestic, snow-covered mountains. As the sun continued its inexorable rise, the great shadow cast by the eastern range receded to reveal a wide, wooded valley far below. At its center, Jerrick saw a meandering river carving its way through a sliver of a canyon.

Densely packed pines spread out in waves from either side to climb the surrounding mountains before giving way to barren, snow-capped peaks. To the distant north, misty clouds floated over the horizon as they gently brushed the mountaintops. Snow covered all, the sunlight casting a heavenly sheen of orange across valley, mountains, and trees alike.

Jerrick thought of Kendra, who had enjoyed waking before dawn most mornings to witness the rising sun and the splendor it brought. It had been her favorite way to start the day. That morning, she had been sitting on the porch with her morning tea when her water broke. From the very start, they knew something was wrong. Kendra had screamed such awful sounds. He'd been in the barn. When he heard her, he ran to the house, thinking to do he didn't know what. In the end, he was helpless to do anything other than hold his wife's hand and watch the life drain slowly from her eyes. Their child was dead before it ever left her. The ruin it left behind became his wife's doom. *You killed her.* He remembered those words more than anything else. There were things he should have told Kendra. Secrets he buried, thinking they no longer held weight. He'd been wrong.

Jerrick found his admiration of the morning's beauty replaced by an acute sense of loss. He sat there for a time, staring out into the vast expanse, trying to think of nothing but always coming back to his wife, their child, and what could have been. Beside him, Murik remained silent. Finally, Jerrick stood, descended from the Looking Stone, and reentered the ruined tower without a word. Shortly thereafter, Ash came bounding in after him followed by a slower-moving Murik.

Jerrick had been right about him favoring one leg; the man walked with a limp. Jerrick cast him a sidelong glance, but otherwise ignored him as he packed his belongings in preparation for his and Ash's departure. It was Murik who broke the silence.

"I don't recall if you mentioned your destination last night."

"I didn't," Jerrick said, more brusquely than he intended. He took a breath, and said more evenly, "The Hall. The Simarron Hall of the Wood."

Murik's face lit up. "Then our destinations are identical. Perhaps, were we to travel together, the journey might be safer, and the time pass more readily. What say you?"

Jerrick halted his packing for a moment. Companionship, aside from the four-legged kind, might help keep him distracted from darker thoughts. But the eslar, with his handicap, might slow Jerrick down. For Aliah's sake, haste was paramount. On the other hand, leaving Murik out here alone was not an option. Duty, if not decency, had its demands. With that, the decision was made, and so he accepted Murik's proposal.

The pair set off immediately. Better to leave the cold behind than to tarry about in it, or so they reasoned. They ate their breakfast—Jerrick's jerky along with dried fruit and nuts provided by Murik—while on the move. Jerrick set a torrid pace; he felt he had to. He was pleasantly surprised as Murik, who made heavy use of his gnarled walking stick, not only matched it, but did so with no complaints. As they hiked, they conversed little. Occasionally, Murik asked a question about local history or made a comment concerning the geography they traversed. Those times, the two settled into a brief conversation, but that was all. They stopped once at midday to rest and eat a small meal. Jerrick had them up and moving again in short time, though, as he hoped to reach Stoney Creek before nightfall. Ash spent much of his time around Murik or wandering ahead by himself, ignoring Jerrick altogether except to shove past him every so often as he made his way from Murik at the rear to the point position. The first glancing impact only mildly annoyed Jerrick. After the second, however, he was irritated enough that when Ash next attempted to pass, Jerrick intentionally blocked the narrow path. Ash glided happily past him regardless of his efforts, which only annoyed Jerrick all the more. Ice and snow slowly gave way to naked earth. The air was mostly still. Here there was plant life once more: prickly bramble bushes surrounding clusters of pines becoming denser the farther they descended. Soon, the tall pines were all around them, their needles covering the ground like a blanket. Then the sound of rushing water reached their ears.

"We'll need to cross," Jerrick explained once Stoney Creek was in sight. "Once we're on the other side, we can make camp for the night and pick up the trail in the morning. There are two ways to cross the creek. The first is closer, but requires a surer foot." He emphasized the location of the crossing by pointing his finger across the expanse of trees still separating them from the waterway. "The other will take us out of our way a bit, but not by much. We'll have to backtrack a little once we reach the far shore, but it has the advantage of being the easier crossing." Jerrick paused. "I mean no insult, but with your leg, perhaps the second—"

"If you deem the first crossing the quicker of the two, then, by all means, let us cross there." Murik held his walking stick across his body as he spoke. The eslar's face was lit by an odd smirk.

Jerrick lifted his brow. "It's wider than you might think."

Murik only stood there with that amused look upon his face.

Shrugging, Jerrick said, "Come on, then."

While the two were talking, Ash had gone ahead. They found him running back and forth along the creek's narrow shoreline, splashing through the water.

In girth, Stoney Creek was more river than creek, with an aggressive flow and a plethora of rocks of all shapes and sizes jutting above the surface. Water moving between these created a myriad of small waterways and diminutive falls. In the distance, they heard the crash of Crystal Falls. They remained at high elevation, and the water was fatally cold. Ash was protected from cursory splashes by his waterproof undercoat, if not a brief soaking. Jerrick had made the crossing more times than he remembered. But Murik, with his leg . . . Jerrick did not look forward to building the fire big enough to dry him should he fall in.

"The rocks form a sort of natural bridge," Jerrick explained. "I've done this a hundred times, so if you just follow me from rock to rock, you'll be fine."

Murik nodded his understanding. If he was worried or

concerned, he gave no indication.

Jerrick looked him up and down once more, then started across. Ash followed with excitement. The initial part of the traversal was easy, as the rocks were low and flat. But these quickly gave way to large, irregular boulders separated by wide gaps of rushing water. One such opening had a fallen tree trunk spanning it. Jerrick shuffled lithely across, reaching the other side. With one leap, Ash bounded across behind him. Jerrick came to another gap, this one without a bridge. Even worse, the rock on the other side sat higher than the current one. Confident in his ability to make the leap, he backed a few paces, started running, and jumped across. His knee hit the rock, but he managed to pull himself to the top. He turned just as Ash, who had barely waited for Jerrick to get situated, made his own attempt. The dog landed off the mark, in a precarious position, his upper half held in place only by rear claws which scrambled for purchase. He started to slip backward when Jerrick reached out and grabbed him, heaving him the remainder of the way up. Rubbing his knee, Jerrick looked for Murik, who he expected to see close behind. Instead, he saw him exactly where he had left him. Jerrick was about to yell, to find out when he planned on following, when he was stunned into silence.

The eslar held his walking stick before him with both hands. Jerrick swore, for the staff glowed with golden fire. Murik just touched the tip of that staff to the surface of the water. Jerrick watched, fascinated, as the creek hardened and froze, the effect spreading from the point where Murik's staff had touched all the way across to the far bank. Without hesitation, Murik stepped out onto the frozen creek. In moments, he had closed the distance between him and Jerrick. Ash barked as the eslar drew near.

Murik gestured at the dog, who floated from the rock down to the icy floor. Ash whined, but only until he was set down. Then his tail wagged so fast Jerrick heard the whoosh of it parting the air.

"Shall you join us as well?" Murik smiled, quite enamored of his demonstration. "It's quite safe." He tapped the end of his wizard's staff, whose glow had dissipated, on the ice in emphasis.

"No!" Jerrick's reply offered no opportunity for rebuttal, as he turned away and sought out the next stepping stone.

Murik shrugged. There was a certain measure of joviality in his blue-black face, a hint of mirth in his pure-white eyes. "Suit yourself." While Ash ran circles around him, the dog's barking eliciting laughter from the eslar, Murik crossed the remainder of the creek.

Back on his rock, Jerrick felt misled. Murik had said nothing about being a sorcerer. Jerrick didn't like magic, if only because he didn't understand it or trust it or think anyone sane should have anything to do with it. It was dangerous, and unpredictable. Given the choice, he'd prefer to have nothing to do with it. If Murik had said something sooner, he might never have agreed to accompany him. With nothing to do for it now, Jerrick shook his head and completed his crossing in his own time. Never once did he step on the creek's icy surface.

At the other side, he found Murik and Ash lounging upon

a flat rock. Murik tossed pebbles onto the frozen surface as Ash lay quietly at his side. Jerrick sat, refusing to meet the eslar's stare. He noted that, in places, the surface of the creek had already started to break apart.

"You didn't say anything about being a wizard," Jerrick said. "You said you were a 'traveler.'"

"Well, I am a traveler, and a wizard. I am a traveling wizard, if you like." The eslar smiled, quite pleased with himself.

Jerrick rolled his eyes and glowered, deciding to wait for a more thorough explanation later. "Come on," he said, standing. "We can make camp for the night up ahead." Without waiting, Jerrick headed downstream, toward the top of Crystal Falls.

They made camp amidst a thicket of pines a short distance from the creek where the cascading falls provided a pleasant backdrop. With just over an hour of daylight remaining, Jerrick immediately set about catching their dinner. First, he gathered a series of stout pine boughs, which he instructed Murik to trim of all smaller branches. The eslar pulled out his dagger without a word and got started. While Murik kept busy, Jerrick walked to the bases of several trees. At each one, he cleared away the layer of pine needles and dug about a foot into the ground. He returned to camp with a small handful of wood grubs. Pulling out some rolled fish line from his pack, Jerrick used his knife to cut long lengths, which he then tied off at the end of each of the branches. Producing a hook for each, he tied these to the lines. Then, he stabbed the poles at regular intervals into the soft shore, making sure the hooks drifted within stagnant pockets where fish most likely sought refuge. In no time, Jerrick had caught enough trout for dinner, with some left for morning. Meanwhile, Murik took the liberty of starting a fire. They ate in silence as the last of the sunlight disappeared behind the mountains. Once they were done, Jerrick took out a pipe, from which he soon blew puffs of smoke into the crisp air. The leaf—Rell's best—managed to dispel some of his earlier annoyance at the eslar.

"I apologize if I frightened you at the creek crossing," Murik said. "Such was not my intention."

"You didn't frighten me. Just surprised me, is all." Jerrick took a long draft from his pipe, blowing a trail of smoke into the air on the exhale. "You should have said something sooner about being a wizard."

"You're right. But I felt caution was needed, just as you no doubt did. Sorcerers—especially ones who are eslar—are sometimes looked upon with undue . . . suspicion, shall we say?"

I wonder why, Jerrick thought. "So why reveal yourself at all?"

"If we are to journey to the Hall together, we will need to trust one another. Keeping such a thing from you for all that time might have the opposite effect, don't you think?"

Jerrick nodded. The eslar was right about that.

"So, tell me," Murik said, "what takes you to the patroller's Hall?"

"Just visiting old friends." It was true enough, and seemed to satisfy the eslar, for he nodded, sat back, and did not press

Jerrick further on it.

"The Hall is a place of learning, is it not?" Murik asked.

Jerrick nodded. "That, and more. The Hall of the Simarron is one of two halls. The other is Merrow Hall, deep in the Merrow Woods. There was a third in the Alzion Mountains, but it was destroyed long ago during the Second Great War and never rebuilt. The Alzions are still patrolled, just without the benefit of a patroller base."

"Are you, then, a patroller?"

"At one time. Still am, I suppose. I was a squad leader for a time, then a rover."

Murik settled into silence. Jerrick studied him for a moment, seeing, for once, the eslar without his usual mirth.

"The night will be dark one last time this evening," Murik said.

The sorcerer's words were so soft Jerrick barely heard them. Looking heavenward, Jerrick confirmed the statement.

"Another, say, eight days," Murik said, "and we shall see the moon full again."

Uncertain what direction the eslar's conversation was headed, Jerrick nodded. He supposed that was right.

"Forgive me," Murik said, his gleeful demeanor returning. "A sorcerer's whimsical nature throws even myself askew sometimes."

Jerrick raised a brow, but accepted the explanation. Then he said, "I've told you my reason for traveling to the Hall. What is yours? I don't recall any visits by sorcerers during my time there."

Murik took his time answering. When he did, his words came out slowly, as if he chose them with care. "I am seeking an associate. One I have not seen in some time. Word reached me that this person dwelt at your Hall, so I set out to see for myself."

The Hall was a way station of sorts, home to many more than just patrollers.

"What if this person is not there? What if he's moved on already?"

It happened often enough. Life at the Hall was not for everyone.

"Then my search will continue elsewhere."

Neither spoke much the remainder of the evening as they settled in for the night. Ash was already asleep by the fire. Murik soon followed as he bid good night to Jerrick, who stayed up a while longer to finish his smoke. Soon, his own drowsiness caught up to him. The fringes of the Simarron were only a day away now. After that, one more to the town of Homewood, and then, finally, on to the Hall. Jerrick's mind drifted away into the mist of dreams, and he slept.

CHAPTER THREE

A CALL
OF HEROES

THEY BROKE CAMP EARLY. THE trail started steep, but lessened once they made their way down to the waterfall's base. From there, they followed the creek until snow on the ground faded to patches and then nothing at all, and evergreens yielded to great, billowing willows; white-barked birch adorned with leaves of yellow, orange, and red; and, closest to the creek, needle-straight aspens. The afternoon grew increasingly warmer until dark clouds settled in and began to emit a light rainfall. Jerrick stopped at one point to wring water from his cloak and to announce, with little fanfare and a sour expression on his face, that they'd reached the Simarron.

"Will the trail take us directly to Homewood?" Murik asked.

Jerrick gave up on his efforts with his cloak. He was soaked through, and likely to remain that way until they reached shelter. "Not directly, no. It turns south some miles ahead and eventually intersects Bandits' Way. If we leave the path and head east once the trail turns, though, we'll still reach the road and save some time in the process. Once at the road, we'll head north to Homewood. We'll be there by tomorrow afternoon."

"What is this Bandits' Way?"

"Its proper name is Belkin's Way. It's named after Lord Belkin, a knight of old. The last I heard the tale, Belkin held off a force of a hundred goblins come down from the Ugulls while refugees in the area fled to safety. The battle took place somewhere along the path of the road, down near Holden Bridge people think. In Lord Belkin's honor, and because the bridge already had a name, it was decided to name the road after him."

"Interesting, but I still do not see—"

"There used to be a significant bandit problem south of here, down near Brinnok. The bandits—thieves and murderers to the last—became a big enough problem Vrannan regulars were called in to root them out. The bandits held their own well enough against caravan guards, but they weren't much of a match for Vranna's finest. Most fled north into the Simarron. The soldiers, figuring they'd done their duty, didn't pursue.

Eventually, the bandits regrouped and started plying their trade again. Only now they preyed on those traveling Belkin's Way. The road's name was never officially changed, of course, but locals just started calling it Bandits' Way after that.

"When I was with the King's Patrol, we tried dealing with them, but the effort proved difficult. We mostly issued warnings, set traps, denied them food and other resources. Made their lives miserable, in other words. Some took the message to heart and left. Others stayed. But, unless the Hall came up with a way to finally deal with them, they're still a danger. By traveling east instead of waiting to intersect the road farther south, we may avoid being robbed or worse. This is all assuming we don't just run into them out here somewhere, of course."

As Jerrick indicated, once the trail began to turn, they left it behind to make their way deeper into the forest. Lesser trees vanished, for the great blackwood oaks of the Simarron ruled here. The oldest of them were hulking, intimidating specimens that spoke of potent Earth Power culminated over a lifespan of more than a thousand years. Jerrick had been just shy of seventeen when he'd first walked under their boughs. He remembered looking up, the branches so intertwined he barely saw the light of day. Their trunks, thicker than the span of his arms held outright, stood higher than the tallest of man-made towers. Their leaves were larger than his hand splayed out. Never before had he been in such awe. The feeling returned as even Murik felt compelled to pause and pay silent reverence.

They were both staring upward when they heard someone

approaching. Murik and Jerrick exchanged glances. Highwaymen, or more travelers? Whoever they were, they made no attempt at hiding their approach: neither voices nor heavy footsteps were kept low or held in check. Jerrick identified at least two voices. In between bouts of arguing, he also heard the distinctive neigh of a horse.

Two women came into view from around a blackwood oak. At the sight of Jerrick, Murik, and Ash, they both stopped. One made no further movement. In fact, she froze. The other narrowed her gaze and lowered a hand to the hilt of a sword.

"Hello," Murik said, his voice full of greeting and cheer.

The one with her hand on her sword looked from Murik to Jerrick. She wore armor: a blue surcoat over plate and chain. From her shoulders hung a fine, blue cloak so long it almost touched the ground. Her other hand held the reins of her mount. Her gaze was not friendly.

"Hello, friends," Murik said again. "My name is Murik Alon Rin'kres. You are?"

The other one, the one who had frozen up, managed to move her lips in a greeting of her own. "Well met." This one wore no armor, but a shirt which was dirty and torn, leather breeches, and a simple jerkin. A plain, hooded cloak, soaked through, hung heavy from her shoulders. She wore a dagger at her belt which Jerrick doubted she'd much skill with. She looked about to add to her terse greeting, but stopped to clear her throat and take a deep breath first. "Well met, Murik Alon Rin'kres."

She looked a girl in Jerrick's eyes—not yet a woman, but

not a child either. That she had been spooked or frightened was obvious from the way her hands trembled, though she must be cold as well, given that her hair and clothes were plastered to her skin from the rain. Though she was no worse off than any of them, some simply weren't cut out for the wilderness.

The girl gestured at her armored friend. "May I present to you Kayra Weslin, of the House of Weslin and Knight-Esquire of Kallendor."

The other's lips remained sealed in a tight, firm line, but the woman nodded at each of them.

"My name is Holly, Herald and Balladeer." Then she looked at Jerrick and waited.

Only when Jerrick saw all eyes on him did it occur to him to offer his own name. "Jerrick Bur, of Rell."

"But once of the Simarron Hall of the Wood," Murik said.

"Yes, once of the Simarron Hall."

"And your dog?" It was Kayra who spoke. The woman had yet to relax her stare.

"Ash," Jerrick said. "His name is Ash."

"So," Murik said, "what brings a knight of the Order and her . . ."

"Herald," Holly supplied.

Murik smiled. "Yes, of course, and her herald. What brings the both of you this far from the road? We are still far from the road, aren't we?" The last question was directed at Jerrick.

Jerrick pointed in the direction from which the two women

had come. "An hour or so that way."

Holly and Kayra exchanged glances.

"We thought the road was in that direction," Holly said, pointing another way entirely.

"Afraid not," Jerrick said.

Kayra's expression turned into a scowl, while Holly emitted a slight sigh. The two women exchanged glances again. Holly tried smiling at the other. It was met by a tight-lipped stare that, after a heave of the woman's shoulders, finally relaxed.

"Might as well tell them," Kayra said.

Holly turned her attention back to Murik and Jerrick, took a deep breath, and blurted out, "We were robbed!"

Jerrick had never heard anyone so excited about having been victimized. Then, as she began her tale, Jerrick realized it was not the act itself but the telling which had the woman so excited.

"We were traveling Belkin's Way," Holly said, "heading north from Brinnok. Though it was morning, the woods all around were dark as night. Suddenly, bandits plunged from the woods from all sides, surrounding us. There were at least twenty of them—"

"There were six," Kayra interrupted.

"There were twenty," Holly insisted, "though only six confronted us. The others waited in the forest. They were rough, unshaven men, hardened from a life of thievery. Their leader, a bald man with only one eye, demanded we turn over our goods. Kayra laughed from Aurum's back, drew her sword, and engaged the leader. Two other brigands moved to stand against her. Kayra beat them back, thrusting and parrying their every move. Finally, they grew tired of the fight, turned, and ran back into the woods." The delight in Holly's voice faded as she went on. "Unfortunately, while Kayra held off the three bandits, the others made off with my horse and most of our supplies. But Kayra wasn't ready to admit defeat." She picked up the tempo again. "So we plunged headlong into the forest in pursuit and—"

"Wound up hopelessly lost," Kayra said in conclusion.

"Yes," said a dejected Holly. "We left the road, failed to find the bandits or my horse, wound up lost, and, well, here we are." She threw her hands up. "They stole nearly everything we had, including my mandolin. We've been trying to get back to the road ever since."

Her story complete, Holly took a moment to run her hands through her chestnut hair, using the dampness already there to slick it back. It was short, and didn't hold well.

Ash, who had been eyeing Aurum since the horse's appearance, chose that moment to slink forward toward him. The destrier made no reaction at first, huffing but otherwise seeming unconcerned. Still, Jerrick knew the trouble the dog might cause. Just as he was about to warn Ash away, the knight's steed stamped its hooves on the ground and made to rear. The motion was enough to startle Ash, who scrambled backward. Kayra grabbed hold of the horse's bridle, controlling the animal and staving off any further mayhem. Ash barked once, but he did it from a safe distance.

"Well," Murik said, "perhaps we can at least get you back

to the road. From there, your journey is your own. Unless, of course, our destinations happen to be the same?" He looked expectantly from one to the other.

"We go to Homewood, and then to your Hall," Kayra said, nodding at Jerrick, "to answer a Call of Heroes."

"A Call?" Jerrick asked with some alarm. He thought of Aliah's words again.

"Yes," Holly said, "one was issued by the Hall." Holly looked with surprise at them. "Neither of you know about it?"

"This is the first I've heard of it," Jerrick said. "If Murik knows anything, he's said nothing to me."

Murik admitted his own ignorance before he asked, "What can you tell us about it?"

"Unfortunately, not much," Kayra said. "We received word of it just a week ago when we arrived at Brinnok. The Call had already been issued and answered numerous times by others before us. No news had returned to say how they had fared, though. The Call itself said little enough, only that strange happenings had occurred and they required assistance from all willing and able." She paused, gathering her thoughts before continuing. "As a knight-esquire, I travel in search of a deed worthy enough to justify my promotion to the rank of knight. When I saw the Call's proclamation, I knew we needed to respond."

This new information gave Jerrick much to think on. Coupled with Aliah's warning, it gave him no peace. But without any further knowledge, he was unsure of what questions, if any, to ask. It surprised him when Murik posed a question of his own.

"This Call," he said, "when was it issued?"

"I don't know for sure," Kayra said, shaking her head. "Maybe four or five months ago."

"Nothing was said regarding the 'strange happenings'?"

"No. The Call was vague on the exact threat."

Murik chewed on his lip for a moment, then, with head lowered, he strolled away, lost in thoughts of his own.

"We'll take you to Homewood, if you like," Jerrick said. "We're going there anyway, and four will travel safer than two."

Murik was agreeable, and so Jerrick led them all to Bandits' Way. It took only the hour he had estimated. The road was revealed as a crude, narrow strip of dirt meandering from the outlying farmlands of Brinnok all the way north to Homewood. Trees lined its either side and, through the drizzle, they found the way deserted as far as the eye could see.

"Homewood isn't far," Jerrick said. "We'll be there before nightfall."

Thoughts of a dry roof and a warm bed drove them on with no breaks. Only Kayra did not last long on her feet. Her armor was heavy and not suited for such travel. But she'd Aurum, and no one took issue that she rode while they walked, though Jerrick wondered aloud why she wore the armor at all.

"You'll be up half the night drying and oiling it to keep the rust away," he said.

"I know," Kayra said, a note of dejection in her voice.

"Today was supposed to have been my grand arrival in Homewood. The knight in shining armor riding in to save the day, or some such thing." She let out a mocking laugh. "Little did I realize it was going to rain most of the day, or that we'd be waylaid by bandits, or that . . ." She sighed. "Let's just say this has not been my best day. Nor have things gone my way of late."

Jerrick was surprised at her frankness. He didn't know this woman at all, but something told him she did not reveal chinks in her armor often. That she had weaknesses, Jerrick had no doubts. Everyone did. But if she admitted those weaknesses to herself, or let others see them, was another matter entirely. Jerrick cast a sidelong glance at her. She wasn't much older than Holly, he realized. It was sobering to think he was twice their age. Once, he'd been young too, arriving in the Simarron wide-eyed and full of ambition. Perhaps his goals were not as grand as a knight's, but he'd wanted to prove himself. He supposed he had. He was always well regarded as a patroller. As squad leader, he'd earned the respect of his men. But he'd chosen to leave that life and begin another. The decision still haunted him. "I know what you mean," he said, more to himself. "I know what you mean."

The rain never stopped, but it did lessen. Once, a train of wagons three deep hove into view, heading south from Homewood. Kayra and the others yielded the narrow road to them. As they passed, Holly issued a greeting. Neither the wagon masters nor the stone-faced guards, who walked beside the caravan with halberds in hand and broad swords at their hips, acknowledged her. Then, the wagons faded from view and were gone.

"Well," Holly said, "they certainly weren't very friendly."

Jerrick just shook his head, remembering past encounters along this road as pleasant exchanges of news and local gossip. Shaking his head some more, he gestured at Kayra to take the lead again.

Jerrick's thoughts drifted back to the Call. Patrollers prided themselves on self-reliance. It was a good thing, too, for there were few willing or able to lend them assistance if and when they needed it. Brinnok, the closest major city, lay several weeks away. Though they possessed a contingent of soldiers, mercenaries, and no doubt a wizard or two in their employ, offers of assistance from them were few and far between. Brinnok relied on the patrollers of the Simarron Hall to guard their frontiers, to warn of goblin activity, and to slay any creature violating their lands. But when the patrollers required aid, like when the bandits took up residence in the forest, the dignitaries of Brinnok had invented one excuse after another why they couldn't help. Jerrick didn't understand all the politics, but he knew the relationship the Hall maintained with Brinnok was tenuous at best. He also knew the situation must have become dire for the Hall to have issued such a plea.

The forest to either side of the road gradually opened up as the travelers approached several farms. Smoke drifting from chimneys and a few dim lights shining through drawn drapes were the only signs of life. They left the solitary farms undisturbed, reassurances from Jerrick that Homewood was not far urging them onward. Then, the frontier town came into view.

Like so many other border settlements, Homewood began as a place of safety amidst an inhospitable and often dangerous wilderness. The first settlers, a hardened lot of trappers, hunters, backwoodsmen, and farmers, often congregated at the early settlement seeking provisions, shelter, and protection from the night's denizens. Even in those early days, Homewood enjoyed the protection of the Simarron Hall. The King's Patrol had been there for as long as anyone remembered, guarding Vranna's frontier against goblin invasion while maintaining a vigilant eye for other dangers. As Homewood grew from a seldom-visited way station into a burgeoning community, the comforting presence of the patrollers and their Hall helped attract additional permanent residents.

Now, approaching the woodland outpost, they spotted flickering torches shining through the afternoon's gray like beacons guiding wayward travelers. The entirety of the place was ringed by a wooden palisade so high not even the roofs of the buildings on the other side poked over it. The only entrance was a single, large gate sealed shut. The road led directly to the gated entrance.

Jerrick thought it strange the place was so tightly shut, and he related as much to the others. Homewood always welcomed travelers, whether they were frequent visitors or newcomers. At night, the gate was closed. But never during the day as it was now.

Jerrick led the others the remainder of the way to the gate.

Torches, the ones they had spied from a distance, were lit to either side of it. The others looked to Jerrick, unsure if a challenge from inside was forthcoming or if they needed to announce their own presence. Jerrick shrugged, walked up to the gate, and pounded on it with his fist. There was no immediate indication anyone had heard him. Jerrick was about to knock again when the door's spy-hole, located at eye level, shot open with a sharp creak. In its open square was framed a man's unshaven and scared face.

"Welcome ta Homewood." The words were spoken in a bored, routine manner. "State yer business."

Holly politely stepped forward and said, "We have come to answer the Call sent out by the Hall of the Wood. We travel in the company of a knight of the Order, and request a night's— oops," she said, giggling, "stay in your good town."

Jerrick thought Holly's answer a bit overdone, but he let the knight's herald have her say.

The guard's eyes became slits as he took in each member of the group. "A knight, ya say?" His gaze lifted to the mounted woman.

"Yes," Holly said. "May I introduce Kayra Weslin of Kallendor, Knight-Esquire of—"

The peephole slammed shut, leaving Holly with her mouth open and the wet and weary travelers with bewildered expressions. Jerrick was just wondering if he needed to pound on the gate again when they heard an inside latch drawn. Moments later, the gate creaked inward. Without hesitation, the group entered Homewood. At the wall's other side, they watched as the guard latched the gate tight once more. When he was finished, he turned to address them. The man wore a chain hauberk with leather pants and boots. A short-bladed sword whose leather-wrapped hilt was tarnished and worn hung from an equally tattered belt.

"The market's closed fer the day, but you'll find food and a hot bath at Jay's Tavern. 'Tis straight ahead and ta yer left." They saw the man was missing a few teeth. Those remaining to him were stained yellow and black from chew. The habit was confirmed as the guard paused long enough to eject a stream of saliva from his mouth. Wiping the spittle from his stubbled chin, he went on. "Yer horse," he said, nodding toward Kayra, "can be stabled at the livery, if it pleases yer knightship. End a' the road and ta the right, past ol' Varg's blacksmith shop." He started to walk away without further comment, but then stopped and said over his shoulder, "The Call a Heroes came from here, not the Hall. Naught's been heard from them patrollers fer some time now." Before any had a chance to respond, the man shambled off, entered a small guardhouse which shared one wall with the town's palisade, and slammed its door shut. The door creaked back open of its own volition, then slammed again, this time staying shut for good.

"So now what?" Holly asked.

Jerrick knew his own plan. "I'm for Jay's Tavern for a hot meal, a room, and a bath."

"I think we all shall join you," Murik said.

"I'll see to Aurum," Kayra said, "then meet you there." She

motioned the horse onward, and they trotted off.

"Shall we find the tavern?" Murik asked. "I, for one, am eager to be out of this constant drizzle." He shook the rain from his cloak for emphasis. No one mentioned that he somehow had stayed the driest.

Strolling down the muddy street, they saw few crisscrossing the main thoroughfare. Those who did wore coats with hats pulled low or cloaks with hoods drawn, and all moved with a hurried step. Not one of them paid any heed to the newcomers, though Ash encountered his own greeting party in the form of three mangy mutts. All outgoing caravans had left for the day, though they saw a series of wagons being outfitted for the morning. They passed these by, noting the wagon master, a rough-looking man, and the caravan's owner, a snout-nosed, long-necked raspel merchant chittering directions to his lead worker. Both looked their way briefly, but neither offered a greeting. Such unfriendliness came as no surprise to Jerrick given their experience on the road in. Still, he was taken aback by the contrast between the folk he remembered and those he now encountered. Shaking his head, he at least found comfort in the familiarity of the town itself as he looked from place to place.

There was Homewood's guard station, Blek Thunderaxe's carpentry shop, and Rupert's Trading Post. Across the street was Davlin's Fur and Tannery and, next to it, Homewood's abattoir, where a third-generation butcher plied his trade. Cabins lined a road which branched off from the main street. Some were occupied by year-round denizens of Homewood, while others stood empty until some well-to-do merchant came along needing privacy and a place to stay free from the noise of places like Jay's. Farther down, more shops, houses, and other dwellings lined the main street. The group came to a halt before reaching them, though, as Jerrick gestured toward a rare two-story building, whose sign read, in big, faded letters, *Jay's Tavern*. Next to the lettering were two frothy flagons of beer carved into the sign, both nearly tipped over and spilling their contents. Under cover of the tavern's awning, Jerrick and Holly took the opportunity to remove their wet cloaks and stomp some of the muck from their boots. Murik kept his cloak about him. His boots needed no cleaning, for they were as if new.

"Jerrick?"

The voice, low and grizzled, came from a slight figure seated in a rocking chair in a shadowed corner of the porch. Jerrick took a few steps toward him.

"Yes, my name is Jerrick. Who are you?"

A balding and grayed head stuck out from the shadows. One of his eyes was closed permanently, while the other scrutinized the patroller. "Why, Jerrick, it is you!"

Instant recognition dawned on Jerrick. "Old Man Jasper!"

The patroller strode forward and embraced the still-seated oldster. Jasper returned the hug with enthusiasm.

"How have you been, Jasper?"

Old Man Jasper pulled a quilted blanket closer about him. "Oh, fine, just fine."

Jerrick looked to Holly and Murik. "Jasper's been a

permanent fixture around these parts for longer than I've been alive. He's the best trapper the Simarron's ever seen."

Jasper cackled. "Oh, I mighta been the best, but not no more. Age has crept too far inta these ol' bones."

"Nonsense." Jerrick smiled at the man.

"How long has it been, Jerrick? Four, five years?"

"Something like that."

"Why, I haven't seen the likes a ya since ya ran off fer that girl. How is that wife a yers?"

The question gave Jerrick pause, but he answered before the silence grew too heavy. "She's well."

"So, what brings ya back ta these parts?"

"The Hall. We've heard some things. Perhaps later, if you've the time—"

Jasper leaned close. "If yer wantin' ta know what's goin' on, Jerrick, best talk ta Relk."

"Relk?" Jerrick remembered his old friend, a hunter and trapper much like Jasper, only younger by many years. Relk spent most of his time outside the walls of Homewood, living amidst the outback of the Simarron. When he did venture into town, it was usually for very brief stints. "He's here?"

Old Man Jasper nodded, gesturing with his thumb toward the interior of Jay's. "Inside. Been here a couple a nights. Brought in quite a catch this time around, too. He'll no doubt be headin' back out sooner rather than later."

The two spoke a moment longer before Jerrick excused himself and the others. Leaving with a promise to catch up later, Jerrick herded the others, including Ash, who'd shaken off his greeters, into Jay's.

⁂

Jerrick, Murik, and Holly were just in the process of paying for two rooms and dinner all at once when Kayra, her horse settled for the evening, entered and offered to pay for everything as a gesture of thanks for leading Holly and herself out of the wilderness. Jerrick and Murik, while appreciative, refused to accept. Kayra's insistence won out in the end, however. Then, with a time close to early evening set for them to meet up again, they all retired. Jerrick, Murik, and Ash shared one room, while Kayra and Holly took another. Hot baths and a change of clothes were the first priority for all. Since all of Holly's belongings had been on her stolen horse, including extra clothes, Kayra sent out for a clothier, who provided the woman with new, clean garments. Kayra again insisted on paying, feeling responsible for their ill-fated encounter on the road. Holly protested, but the knight's persistence was without equal.

As the designated time arrived, Jerrick emerged into the hallway dressed in a clean shirt and breeches, with the worst of the road's dirt wiped from his boots. He left his bow and sword behind in the room, but kept his hunting knife at his belt. He opted not to shave, but had thoroughly washed and combed his hair so it looked much neater than it had throughout the journey thus far. The others promptly joined him. Murik remained garbed in his usual clothes: a leather vest worn over a long-sleeved shirt, a pair of leather breeches, and his eslar cloak. He kept his wizard's staff close and housed his sword and dagger in their jeweled sheaths at his side. Holly's new garments consisted of leather woodsman's breeches and a simple tunic tied at the waist by a leather belt. Kayra emerged last. She had removed her armor and, in its place, wore cotton breeches dyed brown with a blue tunic. Her hair, previously woven into a single braid, remained so. Ash emerged the same mangy dog he had been upon entering the tavern.

Once they descended to the common room, they each saw a scene not unlike the one they had found upon arriving. A subdued tone hung over the place as people sat huddled about round tables, conversing in muttered whispers or not at all while they nursed drinks and picked at food. Soft music greeted them as a journeyman balladeer played a melancholic tune from the corner of the room, while barmaids quietly strolled about, carrying drinks and food to the sparse crowd. A dwarf with a braided beard manned the bar. Requests for drinks being light, he spent his time sucking on a pipe and blowing lazy puffs of smoke into the thick air. A healthy blaze, the only warmth in the room, burned in a hearth set at one side of the room. Holly wondered out loud if the people were preparing for a funeral. A few patrons shot her irritated looks, but they turned away and went back to their business when Kayra's stare met theirs.

They found Jerrick's friend Relk seated at a table large enough to accommodate them all, and so they joined him after the proper introductions had been made. Jerrick and Relk immediately slipped into an easy conversation, while the others sat in silence, taking in the sights and sounds of the place as they listened to the woodsmen's conversation. When a barmaid strolled up to their table, they ordered food and drinks. Before long, the table was covered with dirty plates, spent ale mugs, and a trio of empty spiced-wine cups before Kayra. Beneath the table, Ash chewed merrily away on a massive soup bone.

The music stopped as the traveling minstrel called for a break. Relishing the strong ale, Jerrick took a long draft, only to find himself staring at the flagon's bottom once more. About to call for another, he paused instead as the tavern door swung open and four unshaven men wearing a patchwork of clothes and armor entered. Their weapons were equally diverse: axes, short swords, and hunting knives hung from thick belts. They were a clamorous lot, loud and boisterous as they galumphed their way to a table and yelled for drinks.

Holly followed Jerrick's gaze as she looked over her shoulder. Her head immediately spun back around for a quick moment before she shot her gaze back toward the men once more. "That's my mandolin!" She gestured at one of the men, who'd such an instrument hanging over a shoulder.

"How can you be sure it's yours?" asked Murik.

"Trust me, I know. That's definitely mine."

"She's right," Kayra said. "Two of them were amongst the bandits who robbed us." The woman rose. "All of you, stay here. It is my honor alone which demands satisfaction."

"Need I ask if you're sure it's them?" Murik asked.

"It's them. I never forget the face of someone I've crossed

swords with."

Holly put out a hand to touch her friend's forearm. "Kayra, don't. There's too many."

"Worry about them, not me."

The knight strode directly up to the quartet of bandits. Though her sword leaned within easy reach against the nearby wall, she chose to leave it behind. When she reached the men's table, she planted both feet apart and waited for their attention. One took note of her immediately, motioning to his fellows, who were too busy drinking and laughing to notice themselves. When all four eyed her, Kayra spoke.

"I am Kayra, of the House of Weslin and Knight-Esquire of the Order. Yesterday, on the road into town, you and some of your fellow thieves robbed me and my friend."

One of the men looked Kayra over with a critical eye. "So what? Ya want yer stuff back or somethin'?" He laughed. "Too late fer that! We sold it all already!" His cohorts joined him as he broke out into a series of loud guffaws.

"Except for the instrument, it seems."

"What instrument?" asked the thief, who had unslung the mandolin and now held it.

"The one in your hand, you sot."

"Who ya callin' a sot?"

The man rose. As he came around the table to stand before Kayra, his eyes appraised the woman's figure and a broad smile played out across his face. "Here now, lass, yer a fine-lookin' one. Mayhap me and you can head on up ta one of Jay's rooms and discuss this like—"

45

Kayra slammed her fist into the brigand's face. Blood spurted, and the thief yelped in pain as he stumbled back and fell onto the table. His friends laughed as blood streamed from underneath a hand he held to his nose. They grabbed his arms, shoving him back up as they verbally prodded him back into the fight. Indignant, his eyes took on a wild look, and still holding the mandolin in one hand, he swung it at Kayra's head like a club. "Why, ya stupid—"

Ducking beneath the clumsy blow, the knight turned about and grabbed the man's outstretched arm. She pressed her fingers into his wrist, forcing a cry of pain from him as he released the instrument. Kayra snatched the mandolin out of the air, then smashed her elbow into the thief's stomach. He doubled over in agony. She disentangled herself from her assailant just as a second brigand lunged at her from behind. Sensing his approach, she sidestepped his charge. Moving too fast to stop from ramming into a neighboring table, he sent plates and flagons flying everywhere, and as he attempted to right himself, he slipped, hitting his forehead hard on the table's end. The thief slumped to the ground, unconscious.

Kayra turned just as the first brigand, ready for more, took a vicious swipe at her with a knife he'd pulled from his belt. She backed from that first attack, then backed some more as the man slashed at her. Then she butted up against a table and could go no farther. A look of delight crossed her attacker's face as he brought his arm back for the kill. In that instant, Kayra sent one, then two quick jabs into the man's broken nose. His howl of pain was silenced as Kayra launched her boot into his groin. He doubled over in agony, his mouth opening wide to issue a silent scream. Kayra grabbed a flagon from the nearby table and crashed it down on the back of the thief's head. Knocked senseless, he fell flat to the ground.

Kayra looked at the two remaining brigands, both of whom had remained seated throughout the conflict. Neither of them dared meet the knight's stare.

Leaning over each of the prostrate men, Kayra removed their purses from their belts. She opened each, performed a cursory inspection of their contents, then said to the two seated men, "Take your fellows and be gone. I'm keeping these," she said, holding up the purses, "as compensation. Now, be off!"

Kayra turned and walked to the bar. Behind her, she heard the men's chairs slide back and their booted feet stomping on the wooden floor as they gathered their fallen comrades and made for the exit. She reached into one of the purses, and a flash of gold sailed toward the dwarven bartender.

"For the mess."

The barkeep caught the coin in midair, bit into it, and smiled. "Any time, dame knight!"

Jerrick, along with everyone else at the table, had stood the moment the second brigand had risen, ready to jump into the fray if necessary. Holly urged them not to, however, as Kayra's honor demanded she handle this herself. So they hung back, relieved when Kayra finished off both the ruffians. Now, the knight returned to their table and sat. The tavern's other patrons, who had paused to watch the outcome of the confrontation, returned to their own business. Ash, who had taken no notice of the commotion, continued to gnaw away at his bone.

Jerrick looked at the woman with grudging respect. He'd heard enough tales about those of the Order and their prowess in combat, but never thought to see one lay out two much-larger men with nothing but her bare hands.

Kayra handed the undamaged mandolin to Holly, who squeezed her friend's arm for a moment and offered a thank-you. The knight smiled a moment—the first such gesture of kindness Jerrick had seen from the woman—then drained what remained of her spiced wine and ordered another. A moment later, they heard the barkeep shouting it was on the house.

Holly, delighted at the return of her instrument, slipped into her own world as she held the mandolin close and plucked and tuned the strings with practiced fingers.

With the excitement over, Jerrick thought it best to get to business. "Relk, I need to ask you about the Hall."

"Aye, the Hall." The man's eyes dropped and his expression took on dour seriousness.

"It's been more than four years since I've been to Homewood or the Hall," Jerrick said. "The gloom I see everywhere is not how I remember this place. What's happened to bring this darkness down on these people? More importantly, what news of the patrollers?"

Relk took a gulp of ale. "Folk are scared, that much ya no doubt can tell. That's the reason fer the doom and gloom. They've got good reason to be frightened, too."

Murik chimed in. "Perhaps if you start at the beginning."

Relk took another swig from his tankard, wiped the froth from his beard, and then, after releasing a healthy belch, said, "I can't tell ya much a the Hall itself, only 'cause I haven't been there a late. But I've heard and seen things aplenty in the forest. In times past, I'd cross paths with a patroller or two every so often. Not that my business was ever anything ta concern them, mind ya. I'm just a simple trapper, after all." He flashed them all a grin, then lowered his voice as he went on. The others were forced to lean in to hear. "A while back, maybe six or seven months ago, they stopped checkin' in. I thought maybe they figured I didn't need lookin' after, but then I ran inta some other woodsmen who told the same tale. Just like that, poof!" Relk's hands came up in balled fists, then he spread his fingers wide in emphasis. "What's stranger, 'twasn't just the wood-folk who no longer ran inta them. 'Twas everyone! No one's—I mean, no one's—heard from them patrollers fer a while."

"The guard at the gate said as much," Murik said.

"Aye, but there's more," Relk said. "I stopped here in Homewood fer a night or two after that, ta catch up on news and such. Well, when I ventured back out ta the Simarron, somethin' was different." He paused to take another drink. "The woods had grown dark, and I'm not talkin' about from the sun goin' down. Oh, 'twasn't sudden, but as I traveled north toward the Hall—not my usual direction, mind ya, since I do most a my trappin' ta the east—the whole time I swear somethin' was watchin' me from the shadows. The oaks didn't even look right. I dunno how ta explain it, but they almost looked . . . sick. Well, with those eyes on me, I decided it'd be best ta stay clear a the Hall, and I turned east back ta familiar ground. It wasn't until then that the feeling left me, and things returned ta normal." Relk took yet another draft from his flagon, this time a long, deep one.

Jerrick knew Relk was a hardened man who did not spook easily. But he was a woodsman, and prone to their superstitions. Jerrick wondered in the back of his mind if perhaps some of those fears had taken hold, leading his old friend down a road of false manifestations.

Kayra asked, "What of the Call? What can you tell us about it?"

Relk nodded knowingly. "The mayor a Homewood issued it after contact with the patrollers grew stale. Oh, he sent some people up there before issuing it. Jaslin's husband, that fella Rodal, Kert, the tanner's assistant, and a few of the town's guards. All I know is not a one a them returned."

"None at all?" Holly asked, with widened eyes.

"Well, one, but the poor man's mind's gone. 'Twasn't like that before he left. But he's a stark-raving-mad lunatic now, if ya get my meaning."

"What's his name?" Jerrick asked. "Perhaps he can tell us something."

Murik added his agreement.

"I reckon he won't say much. Nothin' you'd understand anyway. The fella's name is Graewol. Ya can find him at the blacksmith's shop most times."

"Perhaps in the morning we can talk to him," Kayra suggested.

The others agreed.

"And what of Greth?" Jerrick asked.

"Ah, now ya be gettin' ta the heart a what's got the good people a Homewood so worried, my patroller friend."

"What is Greth?" Kayra asked.

Jerrick was about to explain when Holly beat him to it.

"Greth . . . I've heard that name before." Her features narrowed in concentration for a moment before her face lit up. "Oh, I remember! There's a brief reference to it in a story my bard master used to tell. The entire story is rather long, but the part mentioning Greth goes something like 'and so the goblins—'"

"Goblins!" Kayra said, too loudly, as the surrounding tables took notice.

Holly shot Kayra a look of reproach, raising her voice as she went on. "'—were driven back to their dark mountain fortress, Greth, where they plot and wait for the King's Patrol to wither, die, and forget their duty so they might one day emerge anew and cast a shadow of Darkness over all.'"

Relk nodded approvingly. "Aye, 'tis the tale a the Battle a Brakken Pass ya tell. 'Twas the goblin filth's last stand, and one they sorely lost. Their few survivors fled back to Greth, where 'tis said they remain ta this day, waitin' and watchin'."

"Which is what they'll continue to do as long the patrollers stand ready," Jerrick said.

"Yes. But now, people are beginnin' ta wonder, and worry. If somethin' has happened ta them patrollers . . ." Relk just shook his head.

The group fell into silence, each lost in their own thoughts. Relk took the opportunity to finish off the last of his drink and excuse himself.

"I'll be here till mornin' if ya need me fer anything."

"You're actually going to sleep in a bed?" Jerrick asked, smiling. It was unusual for the trapper to sleep on anything but dirt and leaves. Even more unusual for him to remain within Homewood overnight.

Relk laughed. "No, more likely the floor. The guard won't open the gate after nightfall. Not without a bribe, anyway. Mayor's new rule. Yer lucky ya arrived when ya did, otherwise you'd be stuck out in the cold. Speaking a the mayor, I reckon he's heard a yer arrival and will be wantin' ta talk ta ya. The fat slug's probably been sleepin' all day, otherwise he woulda come sooner. Ah, well, when ya see 'im, give 'im my regards fer keepin' me trapped in his town all night."

Jerrick rose and extended his hand, which Relk shook with vigor. "I'm afraid you leave me with more questions than answers, my friend," Jerrick said. "I thank you, nonetheless."

Relk said his farewells to the others, wished them well, and made his way to the stairs leading up to the tavern's rooms.

Jerrick watched his friend go, then, returning to his seat, cleared his throat and said, "There's something else. Something I haven't told any of you yet." He looked around the table, seeing their full attention upon him. "When I started this journey, I didn't know anything about any of this trouble. I meant to return to the Hall to visit old friends, nothing more. But now . . ." Jerrick paused, taking a swig of ale. He swallowed hard before continuing. "The first night I was in the mountains, before I ran into Murik at Eagle's Nest, something happened. Several hours before dawn . . . I was woken, by a mist—a green mist—rising from a nearby stream. When I went to investigate, I found the current still. The surface looked like a window. When I looked into it, I saw the face of a woman, an old friend. Her name is Aliah. She was here in the Simarron. She spoke to me. Cried for help, actually."

"Was she in danger?" Kayra asked.

"Not at first, I don't think. But she said someone was coming, that she wouldn't allow them to take her. She was frightened. Then her face vanished from the water and everything returned to normal."

"Did she say anything else?" Murik asked.

Jerrick swallowed again. "She said they were all dead. I don't know who she meant."

"The patrollers?" Kayra asked.

Jerrick shook his head. "I don't know. Maybe. She disappeared before I found out for sure."

"The means by which you communicated with her is known to me. Is she a sorceress?"

"She's a half-dryad, the daughter of a forest sprite."

"Ah, a friend to water faeries, then. That explains much," Murik said, though he offered nothing else.

Kayra took a long pull from her wine cup. "If your friend—this half-dryad—did speak of the patrollers, then we could be walking right into occupied territory. Possibly right into a trap." She looked at Jerrick. "I'm sorry, but this must be said:

The goblins may have overrun the Hall, killed everyone, and even now plan an attack on Homewood."

Jerrick had already thought that particular scenario through. He had hoped to find news proving such speculation wrong, but everything up to this point only corroborated it.

"If the Hall has been overrun," Holly said, "then maybe we should head back to Brinnok to let the governor know about it. At the very least, he can send the city garrison—"

"No," Kayra said. "If we go back now, with no proof, they'll do nothing, and we will have wasted precious time, for we'll just have to come right back here to find it. By then, it might be too late."

"Agreed," Jerrick said. "I'm for the Hall, to see for myself. If it has been taken over and the patrollers are . . . gone, then I'll head to Brinnok straightaway and let Vranna's soldiers deal with the goblins."

"What is this sudden talk of 'I'?" Kayra asked.

"The patrollers are my business, and I will not ask—"

"You have no need to ask. We were all committed to this journey before this night. I, for one, plan to follow through on my commitment. While I will not speak for Holly, I know she is as resolute as I."

Holly's lips formed a nervous half smile, but she nodded her affirmation.

"I am also committed to the stated course of action," Murik said. "I will complete my journey to the Hall and see what has happened there."

"Are we all in agreement, then?" Kayra asked. "We travel

to the Hall of the Wood together to discover what fate has befallen the patrollers?" She waited for each of them to agree. "I don't know what destiny has in store for us, but we've been brought together for a reason. Of that, I have no doubt."

Jerrick opened his mouth to say something, but then just shook his head, took another drink, and stayed quiet. He put little stock in destiny or fate, but let the others think what they liked. If nothing else, he did feel better for the company.

Murik stood. "With that, I take my leave of you. The rain has stopped, and I think I shall take a brief walk about town before I retire for the evening." Murik gathered his cloak about him, picked up his knotted staff, and walked outside.

Those who remained barely had time to take another drink before Relk's prediction concerning the mayor proved true. As Murik exited the place, a balding man with a short beard and a round waist entered. His arms waved about enthusiastically as he spotted the newcomers and proceeded directly for them. Without pause, he introduced himself as Billard, Mayor of Homewood, before greeting each of them in turn. Kayra rose, informing him they answered the Call of Heroes and pledging to help in every way possible. Billard bubbled with excitement as he expressed his immeasurable gratitude, ordered them all another round of drinks on him—or, more likely, out of the town's purse—and pledged all the resources at his disposal to their cause. He even went so far as to offer them a modest reward, but all joined Kayra in turning it down. They readily accepted provisions and other supplies, though.

As the drinks Billard had ordered arrived, Kayra asked the

mayor quite pointedly, "Relk mentioned others who had ventured to the Hall. What happened to them?"

Billard's jovial manner disappeared. "I'm afraid none have returned, including our own who were the first to journey to the Hall. Of them, only Graewol came back. We issued the Call only because we knew not what else to do. As you no doubt know, the nearest city is Brinnok, and they've always some excuse for sending aid. We might appeal to the duke, but that takes time. In the meanwhile, if something has happened to the patrollers, we wish to help them."

"How many other heroes have answered the Call?" Holly asked.

Billard's face contorted as he thought for a moment. He started counting on his fingers, then finally said, "Twenty-three others. In fact, three dwarfs left just a week ago. Said they'd be back in no time."

The three party members stared at the mayor, waiting for him to relate their fate.

Billard squirmed under their scrutiny, then, his lips curling into a half smile, he said, "Their definition of 'no time' must be different from our own, for there has been no sign of them . . . yet." He emitted a chuckle, which faded into a sigh. "But I have a feeling good fortune has come upon us this time. You, good knight, are the first of the Order to answer our Call. That, combined with a patroller returned home and a bard whose songs I must no doubt hear before you leave, and . . ." Billard looked about, his plump cheeks jostling back and forth. "Wasn't there another with you? An eslar, if rumors are true.

Oh well, no matter." The mayor of Homewood rose. "I shall see that all of your needs are met and waiting for you in the morning. Good night to you."

Without further comment, the Billard shuffled off, leaving them to look at one another with befuddled expressions.

"Strange man," Holly commented.

The two women excused themselves for the night, leaving Jerrick alone at the table. He ordered another ale, and as soon as it arrived, took the drink outside to the tavern's porch. Ash, his soup bone devoured, followed in silence. Jerrick found an empty chair, lit his pipe, and smoked.

CHAPTER FOUR

THE SUMMONING

URIK KEPT TO THE SHADOWS as he hobbled his way down Homewood's main avenue. This late, few people were out and about, and after he had left the vicinity of the tavern behind, he found himself alone. High above, a break appeared in the drifting clouds, revealing light from the crescent moon. Murik paused a moment to study it. Returning his gaze to the street, the eslar used his staff as support for his lameness as he headed deeper into town. He gripped the gnarled thickness of the staff tighter, sensing the invisible power coursing up and down its length as he passed darkened shops closed for the night. Despite the absence of rain, the night air remained cold, and Murik wrapped himself tighter in his cloak. Immediately, he felt the garment's ambient temperature rise to make him comfortable. The road was littered with patches of mud; the sorcerer inevitably sank into several of them. As he lifted each foot from the muck, though, the mud slipped away, leaving his boots unsoiled.

The fella's name is Graewol. Ya can find him at the blacksmith's shop most times.

The sorcerer meant to speak with this Graewol tonight, even if the man had been made into a gibbering idiot by whatever he had encountered on his sojourn to the Hall. What Relk had said about the forest, about what he had felt, disturbed Murik too greatly. But he refrained from drawing conclusions until Graewol's secrets were his own.

Homewood was not a large town, and Murik soon found himself at the blacksmith's shop. He slowed his pace, peering through the night's darkness for others who might be out taking advantage of the rain's respite. Seeing no one, he continued past the shop and wound his way around to the building's rear. There, he found a locked door. A whisper and the lock fell open. He pushed on the creaky door, stepped into the shop, and closed the door behind him. Darkness greeted him, though the eslar moved through the place with little pause, exploring quickly as he passed by the smith's racks of tools and materials. He heard a soft snore coming from the other side of the cold forge. As Murik stepped around it, he spotted a man curled into a ball on the floor, sleeping. The sorcerer lay his staff aside and crouched down next to him, tapping him lightly with a finger. The man stirred a little, but did not wake. Murik prodded him harder. His lids blinked open this time as he raised his head just enough to look upon the wizard. His eyes went wide with fear.

Murik raised a finger to his mouth. "Shh."

The man trembled as he sat up and pushed himself backward. There was nowhere for him to go. Murik knew he had found Graewol, for the man looked every bit the crazed lunatic Relk had described. He wore only pants, with no socks or shoes, and his hair was a greasy black and gray with no order to it. His untrimmed beard shot in all directions.

Murik held his hands out to the man. "I mean you no harm." The sorcerer's voice soothed him, and his trembling lessened. "Are you the one they call Graewol?"

The man's chin rose, then went back down. He repeated his nod over and over, stopping only when Murik spoke again.

"My name is Murik. The citizens of this town say you are a wise man who knows many secrets."

Graewol smiled. "Ah know many. Secrets, secrets ah know. All the secrets."

"I need to know of only one this night, my friend. Can you tell me a secret about the lands around Homewood?" Murik tread lightly, not wanting to unduly upset him.

"Secrets, secrets, ah know the secrets . . ."

"They say you are a traveler who has ventured far. Some time ago, you went on a journey with some others. Do you remember?"

"Ah remember a journey." His voice was low, nearly a whisper.

"Can you tell me what happened? You journeyed to the Hall of the Wood, did you not?"

Murik saw the glistening of tears in his eyes. "Ah remember. They took them. They took them all."

"Who took them?"

"*They* took them." Graewol went silent, then suddenly started shrieking as some buried memory took hold. He started to rise, his arms flailing about in all directions.

Murik shot a hand out, touching the man's forehead as he willed his magic to life. Graewol sank back to the ground, silent and motionless.

"I am sorry, my friend, but you have provided me with little information and I have no more time for subtleties." The sorcerer moved his hand to cover Graewol's forehead. "This experience will not be pleasant, but I assure you, it is necessary."

Murik shut his eyes. He felt power well up within him, invoked by his thoughts. Then, with a mental gesture, Murik allowed the magical energy to flow from him into Graewol. The man's body convulsed once, then did not move again. Murik let himself go as he entered Graewol's mind. At first, the sorcerer felt like he was at the forefront of a mudslide descending into oblivion, but the feeling diminished as he found both feet firmly planted on the ground and the tall oaks of the Simarron all around. In the distance was a dark, towering structure.

The Simarron Hall.

Murik traveled through Graewol's memories. The absence of any others told the sorcerer he was at the end of their journey. All the others were gone. Taken. The sense of dread to befall Graewol came unbidden to Murik. He felt eyes on him, watching. But they did more than just observe. They beckoned. Jerrick's friend, the half-dryad Aliah, had said they were coming for her. The sorcerer now knew both Graewol and the half-dryad had spoken of the same thing.

Murik exerted his will over Graewol's, dispelling the rising terror threatening to overwhelm them both. The task was nothing, for the sorcerer's mind was a thousandfold more disciplined and powerful than the simple woodsman's. But Murik knew if he pushed too hard or too fast, he might never retrieve the information he sought. He suffused Graewol's mind with comforting thoughts until it settled and the danger of his breaking had passed. Then, with a delicate touch, Murik probed the surrounding woods, searching for the telltale sign he hoped was there. All around, eyes—crazed orbs of white set in the dark—closed in, and Murik felt the fear strangling Graewol on that day rising again already.

Then Murik sensed it.

In the blacksmith's shop, Graewol's body convulsed. Within the man's mind, Murik recognized the distinctly evil sensation brought forth by the memory. His fears confirmed, Murik withdrew. The thread delicately woven about Graewol's mind unwound, and he was free. The sorcerer opened his eyes, taking in long, deep breaths as he sat back against the smith's forge. At his feet, Graewol lay sobbing. Murik felt a deep pang of regret for what he had done. But there had been no other way. Tired, the eslar picked himself up and leaned over the woodsman. He held his hand to Graewol's forehead once more. The man's crying stopped, and he settled into a silent slumber.

"When you wake, my friend, you shall remember nothing of our encounter. Further, from this point onward, you shall forget the events transpiring at the Hall. Your mind may never be the same as it was, but you may at least find some peace."

Murik retrieved his staff and exited the smithery. Staying to the shadows once more, he headed for the main gate. If any saw him, they paid the eslar no heed. He took special care to avoid Jay's Tavern, in case Jerrick or either of the women ventured out into the immediate vicinity. Minutes later, he stood before the gate. It was locked. Magic was not the answer here. In order to avoid raising suspicions, he needed someone to close and bar the gate behind him. The eslar tapped on the door to the guard's station. There was no answer. He knocked harder. This time, a weary-eyed guard, different from the one granting them entrance earlier, stuck his head out.

"Whatcha want? The gate's closed fer the night—"

Murik summoned forth his magic, and the man halted in mid-sentence as the spell took hold.

"You will open the gate now."

The man obeyed instantly.

"Close and lock the gate behind me. I shall return in one

hour's time, whereupon you shall allow me admittance."

The gate swung open and Murik walked through, not waiting for the guard's confirmation of his orders. The man had no other choice. Walking off the road, Murik headed deep into the forest. Low-lying fog embraced him as the nighttime sounds of the woods resounded around him. He walked for some time, looking back every so often to gauge his distance from the settlement. When the eslar no longer saw the torches at the town's gate, he slowed, finally stopping as he entered a small, grassy copse nestled amidst the great oaks.

Murik fell to his knees, allowing himself a brief moment of rest before reaching to his neck and grasping the golden links of a chain lying hidden beneath his shirt. At the end of the chain was an intricate gold amulet. The sorcerer placed the amulet upon the ground, allowing the deep cerulean gemstone at its center to stare heavenward. Uniformly etched around the stone were strange, cryptic symbols, black in color.

Using his staff to rise, Murik took a few steps back to distance himself from the amulet. Closing his eyes in concentration, he lifted his arms to the dark sky as he grasped his staff of power with both hands. Murik focused his thoughts as he summoned forth the staff's energy. The nocturnal sounds of animals and insects vanished, the copse left quiet but for the rising hum emanating from the sorcerer's staff. Murik brought it down before him, willing its magical energy forth to surround him like misty ringlets. The rings spun around him before breaking off and descending toward the amulet where they were sucked into the cerulean stone. As more of the energy was absorbed, the words etched around the amulet's stone flared to life. When it required no more, Murik cut off the flow. Shoulders sagging, the eslar slumped against his staff for support.

A burst of light exploded from the amulet's stone. Murik momentarily shielded his eyes from the brightness. When it had faded, the eslar's gaze returned to the amulet and to the ghost of the great eslar wizard Ushar, whom Murik had once called master, floating just above it. The vegetation all around the apparition, unable to abide the undead presence, wilted and died before Murik's eyes. The spirit's thick, flowing robes, so colorful in life, were gray and wraithlike. A long beard, braided and dark, hung motionless from his ethereal face. In place of eyes were empty sockets, for the dead had no need for vision as the living knew it. Sunken cheeks and a narrowed brow lent a sullen expression to his ghostly face.

Release me.

Though the wraith's lips did not move, Murik still heard Ushar's flat, lifeless voice. Murik sighed. They were the same words every time. He did not dignify them with an answer.

"At long last, I have found her. She is here." A rush of excitement sent a shiver through him. He drew his cloak tighter around him, as much from the sensation as from the cold emanating from the wraith. Murik's words were visible puffs in the chilled air.

The apparition's expression remained unchanged.

"Patrollers from a place called the Hall of the Wood have vanished, evil approaches the nearby town, those I have come with—"

Are of no consequence to me. I desire only release. You have it in your power. I have done all you have bid. Now, it is time.

"Time for you to be silent," Murik said.

Ushar obeyed. He had no choice.

"I sensed something this night. Incredible power. More power than . . ." It defied quantification. "What can you tell me of it? What do you see?"

I see only . . . Darkness.

"There must be something else! Tell me what you see!"

The specter's robes billowed about him in defiance, but it was a command he could not deny. *I see deception and lies, secrets held close, and another betrayal ahead.*

"I grow tired of your games, Ushar."

What will you do, then? Kill me again?

The apparition laughed, a horrible wailing chuckle which sent new chills down Murik's spine.

"Tell me of the witch!"

The laughter stopped, and Ushar fixed the living eslar with a stare which caused even Murik to take a step back. *I will tell you of the witch. She* is *here. She has found a source of Darkness, more powerful than . . .* Words defied even him. *You will find her. You will face her. At long last, you will join me, if not in this prison, than at least in death.*

"You lie. Tell me the truth!"

I do not lie. I cannot lie. Again, the laughter, followed by a lessening of Ushar's already vaporous form. The magic was fading, the summoning weakening.

"Tell me the truth!" Murik tried and failed to keep the desperation from his voice.

I already have . . .

The apparition said nothing more as it continued dissipating, drawn inexorably downward and back into the soul gem trapping it in the domain of the living. Then he was gone. The lettering on the gold device shone for a moment more before fading completely. Soon, the amulet looked as it had before the summoning had begun, and the sounds of the forest returned.

Murik went to the amulet. Though the apparition was gone, the cold its presence had created lingered. He stared deep into the amulet's soul gem. "This prison is of your own making, my master. I shall not join you in it. Not ever." Taking up the amulet's chain with the end of his staff, for it remained deathly cold to the touch, the wizard stumbled back to Homewood and the warm bed awaiting him there.

CHAPTER FIVE

OLD STORIES

HOLLY WOKE ESPECIALLY EARLY THE next morning, rising from bed just long enough to see Kayra was already up and gone before the pounding in her head forced her back beneath the warm covers. She groaned as her head sank back to the pillow, memories of last night's ale filling her mind. She remembered feeling fine as the contents of her third flagon disappeared, and so she had ordered another. But as soon as she had risen from the table to follow Kayra to their room . . .

Holly rolled to one side too quickly, the motion nearly making her sick. Then, as she lay still, the nausea faded, her splitting headache subsided, and she slipped back into blissful slumber.

When she woke for a second time, she found her headache replaced by the poignant grumbling of her stomach. The pangs demanded she rise and find sustenance; after another few minutes, Holly grudgingly did as they wished. She washed herself with fresh water from a basin, then quickly dressed. Heavy drapes were drawn across the room's only window, and as she peeked behind their folds, she discovered the morning gray and dreary. She sighed, already feeling the melancholy of another rainy day taking hold. But then she spied her mandolin and a smile crossed her face as she lifted the instrument and strummed a few strings. At least she'd have her music with her on the road ahead.

Thoughts of what lie ahead soured her mood and caused her to sit back down. She didn't know what she was doing here. She felt so small. Small and—despite Kayra's presence—alone. She wished she could go back and undo the commitment she had made to her friend, but it was too late for that. Holly had accepted the knight's proposal: to chronicle her heroic deeds and return with her to Sword Citadel, Keep of the Knights, to stand as witness to Kayra's accomplishments. She was grateful to have been chosen for such a high honor. But she couldn't shake the feeling her friend might have been better off recruiting someone more seasoned. Holly knew it wasn't the traveling itself that bothered her, for she'd spent the better part of recent years traveling the open road under Brayton, her bard master. But those roads had been heavily trafficked and patrolled. Now, they were preparing to leave the last bastion of civilization behind and plunge headlong into the wilderness. If they did discover the patrollers missing, or worse, they were on their own, with no one to turn to for help. She sighed again, holding her mandolin close until her stomach started complaining again. Swinging her instrument over a shoulder, she headed down to the tavern's common room.

She found the early-morning crowd—if there had even been one—already cleared out. An older couple sat at one of the benches, conversing lightly with each other, and a lone man wearing a wide-brimmed hat sat at the other side of the room reading a book. The dwarven barkeep from last night was still at his post, presumably after a night's sleep, washing mugs and arranging bottles. A moderate blaze burned in the fireplace, and as Holly descended the last of the stairs, she moved to warm herself by it for a time. A serving girl who didn't look much older than Holly's own eighteen years appeared from behind the kitchen doors and, upon spotting the young bard, told her to make herself comfortable and that breakfast was on its way. The barmaid spun about and disappeared before Holly had time to utter a thank-you. True to her word, Holly's breakfast—hen's eggs, runny but edible; bacon; biscuits and butter; and tea—was brought out a short while later.

When she was nearly halfway through the meal, the tavern's front door swung inward with a bang and in strode Kayra, resplendent in her shining plate mail. The knight held her helmet beneath one arm, and her long sword hung at her side. Spying Holly in the near-empty room, she walked straight for her, the knight's plated sabatons clacking against the wood floor with each step. Without so much as a good morning or hello, Kayra threw her helmet onto the table. As soon as she unbuckled her sword, it followed. Holly's plate jumped from the impact; she saved her cup from spilling only at the last second. Holly knew what those pursed lips beneath the woman's hard stare meant, and she steeled herself for the barrage she knew was coming.

"The patroller and I just got back from speaking with the madman at the blacksmith's shop. He told us nothing." Sitting, Kayra reached back to her braid, brought the end of it forward, and started twirling it around her finger.

Wonderful. She's really irritated about something.

"The supplies Billard promised are nowhere to be found. Neither is the mayor, for that matter. The dwarf at the bar said he's probably still sleeping." She stopped twirling the end of her braid. "I'm half-tempted to go find his house and knock that fat—"

"Bacon?" Holly said, offering her a piece.

Kayra removed her gauntlets and snatched it without comment, munching away as she continued to glower. "Did you see the water I brought up for you?"

Holly nodded. "I'm sorry I overslept, I—"

"It's nothing." Kayra helped herself to Holly's tea. "When I found out we weren't going anywhere anytime soon, I figured you'd do best getting some extra sleep. Yesterday was harrowing, for both of us." She paused for a moment to drink. "I didn't think we'd set out right in the morning, but I did think we'd at least have things ready by now. All this idle time—"

"Is driving you crazy?" Holly laughed. "It's only been a couple of hours since dawn, Kayra."

The knight sighed, and the briefest hint of a smile played across her lips. "I know. But this is serious business." Kayra sighed. "I feel we should be doing something. If Sir Devon was in charge, I know he'd find something better to do than sit around idly sipping tea."

"I don't know about that. I've heard Sir Devon quite enjoys his morning tea."

Kayra smiled at that.

"Perhaps," Holly said, her voice more thoughtful, "you shouldn't consider what Sir Devon, Lord of Napool, might do in this situation, but what Kayra, Knight-Esquire, would."

Kayra raised an eyebrow. "You're probably right. 'Wise beyond your years.' Isn't that what my father always said about you?"

Holly's face lit up. "I don't know, did he?" Holly had performed before the Weslins more than once, and Kayra's father had always seemed delighted with her performance and wit. But she didn't recall ever hearing any such compliment from the man.

Kayra shrugged. "I don't know. Perhaps I misheard, and he spoke of someone else."

The smile faded from Holly's features, but it returned when Kayra's own lips curled into a grin and the two laughed.

Kayra stood then, grabbing her helmet and sword. "I suppose I'll go check on Aurum one more time. You know what they say about idle hands, after all. I'll see you in a little while." Then, more firmly, "When you're done here, get yourself ready. One way or another, we are leaving for the Hall today." She smiled again. "I hope." The knight made for the tavern's doorway, and then was gone.

Holly finished the remainder of her breakfast, took a few last gulps of tea, then gathered herself and followed Kayra's footsteps outside.

Morning on the main street of Homewood was only slightly more active than it had been when the group had arrived. One wagon loaded with crates of produce and another with chicken pens clattered by in opposite directions. People walked to and fro, keeping mostly to themselves. Holly was just about to walk out onto the street, her intent to explore the town a bit, despite Kayra's more immediate instructions, when she heard a voice address her.

"Yer one a them heroes come ta answer the Call, ain't ya?"

Holly looked over to see the old man Jerrick had spoken with yesterday. The bard remembered his name; Holly prided herself on her ability to remember the names of people and places.

"Good morning, Jasper," she said, approaching him.

Ash, who lay at the foot of the old man's chair, poked his head up at her arrival, wagged his tail, then plopped his head back down.

"I travel with those who answered the Call, but I'm hardly

a hero. My name is Holly. May I join you?"

The old man, seated in the same chair as last night with the same blanket covering his legs, gestured with his lit pipe for her to pull up a chair.

"You a bard er somethin'?" Jasper asked, pointing at her mandolin.

"What gave it away?" She smiled, then rested the instrument on her lap and strummed the strings a few times, humming as she did so.

"Hey, that's pretty nice. Ya got a cute smile, too." He winked as he flashed Holly a toothless grin.

She smiled back. "Jerrick said you knew your way around these parts. I bet you know all sorts of stories."

"On account a me bein' so old?"

"No," Holly said, stammering, "that's not what I—"

Jasper let out a hoarse chuckle, which deteriorated into his doubling over in a fit of coughing. Holly leaped out of her chair to assist him, offering to go inside to get him a drink, but Jasper waved her away.

"I'll be all right. It's just this damn pipe." He stuck the pipe's end back in his mouth and continued smoking. "But, ta answer yer question, I reckon I do know a lot a tales. Been here in these parts fer a long time."

Holly sat again. "How long has Jerrick been around these parts?"

"The patroller? Oh, he's been here since . . ." Jasper screwed up his face. "I reckon around eighteen years if he hadn't left fer those four er so. So, fourteen."

"You said he left to marry someone?"

"I said that?"

"Last night."

"Oh! Reckon I musta." Jasper grumbled something under his breath as he chewed on his pipe. "Yep, he sure did. I never met her, her livin' in Rell and all, but Jerrick told me once 'fore he left she was the prettiest thing he ever had seen. You from Rell, too?" Jasper eyeballed her with his one good eye.

"No. I'm from all over, really. I grew up in Scilya. It's in Kallendor."

Jasper returned a blank stare.

"Kallendor? Fiefdom of the Horse Lords? Not that I know much about horses. That's more Kayra's area of expertise. But, anyway, I've never been to Rell, and only met Jerrick yesterday on the road into town. You two are good friends?"

"Yep. Least, I always thought we were." Jasper took a long draw from his pipe. "Jerrick's always been a loner a sorts. Most a those patrollers are. But he's a good, honest man." Jasper blew out a trail of smoke. "First came ta Homewood from the other side a the Simarron, from out past Twin Boulders Crossing."

Jasper's weathered lips curled into a smile, then he let out another hoarse chuckle. Holly winced, expecting the old man to succumb to another fit. Thankfully, his amusement remained undisturbed this time.

As Jasper continued to snigger to himself, Holly asked, "What's so funny?"

The old trapper rocked back in his chair, his smile wide. "Oh, just thinkin' 'bout the first time I ran inta ol' Jerrick. He was 'bout as old as you are now. Maybe a little younger. He'd been trainin' with them patrollers fer a few months by that time. Not that it did him much good. Boy knew next ta nothin' 'bout survivin' in the woods. He sure thought he did, though."

Holly leaned in, intrigued.

"Never did learn why he was out in the Simarron all by his lonesome in the middle a the night. But there he was, cold, shiverin', miserable. Only reason I ran across him that late in the evenin' was 'cause I was checkin' on some traps. Seein' how bad he looked, I invited him back ta my camp. Said some nonsense 'bout patrollers bein' self-sufficient and not needin' any help. Ha! I just waved some jerked squirrel I had with me in front a his face and he came a-runnin'! Well, I shared my camp with him that night, and he decided ta stay fer several more. Nice boy. Respectful."

Jasper leaned back in his chair, his gaze straying upward as he lost himself in the memory. Then, he leaned forward so fast he nearly leaped from his chair.

"Respectful till it came time fer me ta see ta my work! Now, girl, ol' Jasper knows his business. I've been trappin' fer, well, fer a long time, and there ain't no one knows it better. But then here comes Jerrick, fledging King's Patroller so-and-so, tryin' ta tell me there's a better way ta hunt wild boar than with traps! Ha!

"What had me laughin' a bit ago was this: I tell Master Jerrick if he thinks there's a better way, why, he should go 'head and show me. So there he goes, takin' out his bow and tryin' ta flush out one a those ornery, wild brutes from the brush. I tried ta warn him, told 'im Simarron boars ain't like anything he mighta hunted back home, but he musta had too much wax in his ears. Damn fool kept goin' along, a-lookin' and a-lookin' till he finally finds himself one. Only this boar was already on ta him! Wily bastard had been watchin' Jerrick the whole time, just waitin' ta pounce! Jerrick catches sight a that ol' brute, tries ta level an arrow at 'im, but it's too late ta do anything but turn tail and run fer his life! Ha! Here I am, sittin' on a stump, waitin' fer the mighty huntsman ta bring back his catch, when, what do I see, but the great hunter himself runnin' full speed and the boar chasin' *him* down."

Holly laughed, delighted at the story.

"Now, I saw the mess the young fool had got himself inta, so I lent him a hand. Darn pig was wild all right, but nothin' special about its size. Together, we got the wild bastard. Tricked him inta one a my traps in the end. Let me tell you, there was some good eatin' that night. Fool patroller never tried ta tell me my business again, either."

Holly laughed some more while Jasper took a long draw from his pipe. The old man leaned back, a wide grin on his face.

"Nothing special about its size?"

Holly and Jasper looked to the porch's steps, seeing Jerrick standing there with his arms crossed. Unlike the oldster and the bard, his face was without humor.

"Your version of the story," Jerrick went on, visibly

irritated, "grows less and less accurate with each telling, old friend. As I recall, the boar was the largest either of us had ever seen." Jerrick raised a hand to stop Jasper's protest. "I should know, seeing as how I was the one running for my life from it." Jerrick did smile then, and the three of them burst into simultaneous laughter. When their mirth subsided, Jerrick asked, "What other crazy stories has Jasper been boring you with?"

"Oh, just that one so far."

"I've got plenty more where that one came from," Jasper said.

"I'd love to hear them," Holly said, looking expectantly at Jerrick, "if there's time."

"I'm afraid there isn't," Jerrick said. "We found the mayor, and true to his word, we'll be provisioned within the hour."

Holly stamped her foot on the ground, disappointed. The sound caused Ash, who slept, to sit up. He studied the others with interest.

"I think it best we leave as soon as possible," Jerrick went on. "Kayra agrees."

Holly stood. "Where is Murik?"

"He was still asleep when—"

The door to Jay's swung open and out came the eslar. "Why, it's turned into a beautiful morning, has it not?" The sky remained overcast, the town shaded in gray. "Did I hear someone say we are leaving?"

"Yes, you did," Jerrick said.

"I suppose I'd best get ready quickly then."

CHAPTER SIX

INTO DARKNESS

K AYRA LED HER DESTRIER ON foot to the front of Jay's Tavern where a sparse crowd of Homewood's folk gathered to see the would-be saviors off. People stood back as she passed, giving the knight and her steed a wide berth. As she walked through their midst, Kayra studied many of their faces, trying to catch a glimpse of what went through their minds. She sensed more than saw the fear gripping them. There was no doubt they knew the stakes, for if goblins had overrun the Hall, Homewood was their next destination. Kayra would have wondered why they stayed if she did not see the answer right there in their faces. These people had made a life from the wilderness, toiling and suffering to make something from nothing. They had made homes for themselves here within Homewood and in the outlying farmlands, raising families and carving out their own niche in the world. Picking up and leaving was not an option. Not without a fight. Kayra both admired and pitied them their courage, for she knew if the goblins came in force, the citizens of Homewood didn't stand a chance.

Ahead, Kayra saw Jerrick, Murik, and Holly. The sorcerer sat on the porch steps, his staff held close as he watched Jerrick checking over the pack mule Billard had procured for them. Jerrick's dog was playing with a group of children who found great sport in trying to grab the poor animal's tail. Ash handled himself well enough as he stayed one step ahead of the young miscreants. As Kayra drew nearer, a soft tune filled the air, and she saw Holly strumming her mandolin with a delicate touch. The bard accompanied the melody with a common song of well-wishing and good luck for those about to embark from home and hearth. Kayra was thankful she had been able to recover the instrument for her friend and herald. It was good seeing her happy and smiling. The bard was her charge, her responsibility, and she had felt immeasurably bad about the robbery. She knew the journey thus far had not been easy on her, and Kayra had found herself more than once wishing she had not asked her friend to join her. Holly was a competent song-spinner and well-traveled, but she was untested under pressure and possessed no weaponry skills. Holly hadn't led an easy life. That much Kayra knew if only because the two had been fast friends for so long now. But neither had she led a hard one. Kayra knew the road ahead might prove more challenging than Holly's ability to cope. There was little to do about it now, though. Holly was as committed as the rest of them.

Kayra brought Aurum to a halt. Holly ceased her playing, smiled, and gestured to the knight's left. Kayra returned a quizzical look before turning to find a nervous young girl standing there before her. The girl was slight, probably no more than six years old, and dressed much like the other womenfolk of Homewood in a homespun blouse, long skirt, and toed sandals. She stared up at the knight with fragile eyes framed beneath thin eyebrows and bangs in need of trimming. Kayra sank to one knee.

"Hello, little one."

The girl's gaze dropped to the ground.

"My name is Kayra. What's yours?"

"Jezebel." The sound was a whisper Kayra strained to hear.

"Hello, Jezebel. What can I do for you?"

Still staring downward, the girl raised her arm. In her small hand she held a simple bibelot. Simple in design, the charm consisted of woven grass made into a square pattern surrounding a tiny, blue gemstone. Kayra did not know what special meaning it held for the child, but thoughts of other favors given to knights on the eve of battle filled her mind. She bowed her head for a moment before accepting it.

A woman, the girl's mother based on their resemblance, came forward to stand behind her daughter. Kayra rose to hear her out.

"I gave the charm to me daughter, dame knight, ta protect her from the evil. But she wanted you ta have it."

Kayra nodded to the woman. Then she said to the child, "Thank you, Jezebel. I shall keep it with me always. And you shall have it back when I return."

Kayra looked at the woman once more, seeing there was something else.

"'Tis a family charm ya hold, milady." The honorific came out in a stammer, as if the woman was unaccustomed to its use. "I was hopin' . . . that is . . ." The woman's face went flush, and she almost went silent if not for Kayra's gentle urging. "'Tis me husband, milady. He was one a the ones who went ta the Hall and never came back. Yer the first knight ta answer the Call. Please, find him. If any can, surely yer knightship is the one. Fer me daughter's sake. Please."

Kayra straightened. "Rest assured, we shall discover the whereabouts of your husband." Then, louder, so all heard. "We shall discover the whereabouts of all your kin, as well as the fate of the king's patrollers." Kayra touched the child's nose, and was rewarded with an embarrassed smile from the girl as she withdrew to the comfort and safety of her mother. Kayra mounted Aurum. "We will set things right. We will return." With that, she signaled to the others, kicked Aurum into a trot, and rode off toward the town gate.

They headed north for the Hall of the Wood by way of a narrow, leaf-strewn road meandering lazily through the woods. Kayra led riding Aurum, followed by Holly, Murik, and, finally, Jerrick, who held the mule's lead. Ash, who had taken an interest in the pack animal, brought up the rear. They moved at a moderate pace, wary and watchful above all else, for much of what lay ahead at the Hall remained unknown to them. The only thing they knew for sure was that many others had traveled this very same road in the recent past. None of them, with the exception of the crazed Graewol, had made the return trip back to Homewood.

The familiar gray haze gave way for a time. In its wake was a forest still heavy with shadows but lit by rays of sunshine filtering through the woodland's canopy to touch the lichen-embellished forest floor. There, chipmunks scurried about, popping their heads up briefly before dashing off in search of food. Ash made a play for them several times, but came up short each time. The Simarron's great oaks, their thick, ancient trunks marked with green and brown moss, spread their leafy branches in wide circles above them, wrapping the travelers in a feeling of serenity and security. Birds flew back and forth across the road. There seemed nothing untoward about the woods, and they each wondered if the strange stories and happenings were all some sort of misunderstanding. But as they traveled into late afternoon and the light from the sun began to dim, they noticed a subtle change in the forest. The wildlife disappeared, and an unnatural silence took hold. The trees grew gray and spotted, as if diseased. Even the air seemed thicker, somehow palpable and foul, as if they swam through rank water.

"What do you sense, sorcerer?" Kayra asked from atop Aurum.

The group stopped, and Murik moved to the head of the line. He paused, concentrating for a moment as he moved his hand in a wide arc before him.

"I sense . . . Darkness. Its flagrant taint is plain."

"Can you tell how—or what—has happened?" Jerrick asked, pointing to the unhealthy trees.

"No. But I am confident what we see here will only grow worse as we move closer to the source this corruption springs forth from."

"Do you think . . . Could the Hall be the source?" Holly asked.

Murik shook his head. "There is no way to tell presently."

Standing in silence, they each studied the forest, as if reluctant to continue.

"Perhaps a break is a good idea," Kayra suggested. "We can pick up the road for another hour or so afterwards."

All agreed, and they unfastened packs, sat, and pulled out waterskins and rations. Billard had provisioned them with dried fruit, nuts, salt pork, cheese, goat's milk, and bread—enough food to last them a good two weeks or more. Holly unstoppered a skin filled with goat's milk and took a long draft. The cool liquid had only just poured into her mouth when she spit it out, her face contorting in disgust.

"It's sour!"

Everyone looked at her.

"The milk—it's sour!" she repeated, louder this time.

Murik unstoppered his own supply and sniffed. He took a turn displaying his own displeasure, then said, "Mine, too."

Kayra checked hers also and concurred. "That's not possible. I had some before we left. The milk was fine."

Jerrick drew his sword in a smooth, quick motion, then handed the mule's lead to Holly. "All of you, stay here." He looked to the knight, whose hand was already at the hilt of her sword. "I mean it."

Without another word or gesture, Jerrick plunged into the forest, disappearing behind the wall of trees. Ash followed in silence. Only a few minutes passed before both he and Ash returned. The fur on the dog's back stood on end, and his eyes drifted back into the forest on more than one occasion.

"Grekkels," Jerrick said as he returned his sword to its sheath.

"How many?" Kayra asked, her own sword drawn now. "Did you see them?"

"No, but I saw their tracks. Couldn't have been more than a handful. The spot where the tracks ended reeked of brimstone."

"Teleportation," Murik said. "Line of sight only, but they could be anywhere by now."

"Agreed. I took a look around, but there was no sign of them. No way to tell what direction they headed, either."

"At least we know why the milk soured," Kayra said.

"Yes," Murik said. "That is just one of the ill effects of their presence."

"What—what do you think they were doing here?" Holly asked.

"Just watching us," Jerrick said. "Seeing what we're about. One thing's for certain, though. If grekkels have made it this far into the Simarron, then others of their kind—imps, haureks, and gaugaths—won't be far behind."

Kayra suggested they get moving. Holly dumped all of the sour milk out but kept the skins. As they continued toward the Hall, their gazes were fixed more on the surrounding woods than on the road ahead.

They watched in pairs, keeping the fire burning until the first rays of morning light pierced the forest ceiling. Sleep came sporadically for each of them. Thankful for a night without incident, none complained. They munched on a cold breakfast in silence. Then, having unpacked only the essentials, were soon underway. The forest looked no better than yesterday. The trees, in fact, looked worse. Just as Murik had warned, whatever hold Darkness had here seemed to tighten the farther they ventured. The morning was misty and dank, and the group spent much of it trudging ahead with little conversation and only an occasional break for rest and food. The gloom of the forest seeped into them, progressively dampening their spirits until, having had enough, Holly started strumming an upbeat traveling tune she called "The Wayfarer." The song was well-known enough even Jerrick knew its words, though he refrained from singing along with Holly and Murik. Kayra also chose not to participate, though she turned to smile every once in a while, as if to show she enjoyed the melody. Either that, Jerrick thought, or she wanted to show them the murk had failed to diminish her resolve or her spirit. Like a general leading her troops. Jerrick scoffed, but he let the knight demonstrate her fortitude as she chose. It didn't lessen the very real danger Jerrick's instincts told him they walked into. What if the Hall was overrun? The knight herself had asked as much. Though the grekkels' presence from yesterday corroborated the possibility, there was still a chance the ones who were spying on them were acting on their own. If that were the case, then perhaps their presence was not indicative of a larger goblin presence at all. Even still, there remained a single question swirling in Jerrick's mind: Where were the patrollers?

With dark approaching and the woods still enveloped in an ominous mist, they decided to stop and make camp for the night. They agreed to keep the fire burning till dawn once more. Jerrick scouted the immediate vicinity around their camp, but found nothing out of the ordinary beyond the sickness wasting away at the forest. If there were grekkels about, the patroller did not find them.

As they settled in, each dipped into the supply of rations and ate in silence. Holly strummed a soft tune on her mandolin, and Jerrick lit his pipe. The oaks, that earlier had seemed so magnificent, now stood like bare, skeletal simulacra. Those leaves not chased off by the inexorable march of fall had been leeched away by whatever poison infiltrated the trees' roots, and their branches now hung over the visitors to these woods like spindly fingers ready to snatch them up at any moment. Thinking to lighten the gloom, Holly suggested Jerrick tell them of the Hall and its history.

"I'm not much of a storyteller," Jerrick said, as he took the end of his pipe from his mouth and blew out a puff of smoke.

"Then tell us of its defenses, armaments, and anything else of strategic value," Kayra said. "If the goblin warriors of this Greth have taken it—"

"Then, come morning, we'll be hightailing it back to Homewood as fast as we can," Jerrick said as he flashed the knight a look of irritation. "The Hall is a woodland fortress, not a castle. It's solid enough, but there are no walls or moat. The Hall is a refuge, a place of learning. It is—" Jerrick sighed. "What exactly do you want to know?"

They talked into the night of it, of the man named Severan Ashtok, First of Patrollers, and of the compact he made with King Selus Braygin of Oslo: that any man who served Severan was exempt from the King's Call. These men, these patrollers, answered to no one but themselves. In return for such magnanimity, they were charged with a singular duty: protect the frontier at all costs. Kayra voiced her distaste at such a bargain. As a knight, her duty was ever to her duke, and all others second. Jerrick kept his peace, saving the argument for another day. Drowsiness overcame them in time, and Jerrick and Holly, with first watch duties, bid good night to the others. The darkness around them sank beneath their skin, and they each hoped silently the light of morning was not far off.

Jerrick felt a hand on his shoulder and heard the soft call of his name, indicating it was his turn to watch. He hadn't really been sleeping anyway, and so he rose quickly. Murik moved on to Holly and woke her. She sat up and rubbed her eyes. At least she had slept some, for Jerrick knew the girl needed it. Kayra was already bedding down, as she wrapped herself in her cloak, her back to the fire. Murik nodded a good night to Jerrick, then took his own spot on the ground. Ash slept on, oblivious. Jerrick took no comfort in the fact that even the dog had no desire to wander this part of the forest.

Jerrick stood and fixed his cloak about his shoulders. Grabbing his sword and knife, he walked to a fallen log just outside the light of the fire. Holly joined him, her own cloak wrapped around her like a blanket as she winked away the last of her drowsiness. The two sat close on the short log, both silent. Jerrick glanced at Holly several times, seeing her eyes open and alert. They reminded Jerrick of the look of a frightened doe. He was surprised when she broke the silence.

"Why did you join the patrollers?" Holly asked, her voice a whisper.

Jerrick looked at her for a moment, studying her face. Then he picked up a stick and started running its end through the dirt. "It seemed like something good to do with my life, instead of herding sheep. Not that there's anything wrong with being a shepherd. My foster father has made a good living from it."

"Your foster father? What happened to your real parents?"

Jerrick continued to run the stick through the dirt.

"I'm sorry. I didn't mean—"

"It's all right. My mother . . . grew sick and died, and my father left when I was still very young."

"I'm sorry," Holly said again. "It must have been difficult."

"Not really. I was young enough I don't really remember either of them. I feel bad for my mother, though. She was dealt an unfair hand. I suppose I was lucky in a way. My foster parents took me in as if I was their own. They didn't tell me about my real parents until I was older. By then, they were my real parents, so it didn't matter."

The forest was unnaturally quiet, even for the dead of night.

"It sounds like we have something in common," Holly said.

"Oh? What's that?"

"I never knew my real parents, either."

Jerrick dropped the stick to the ground. "Who raised you, then?"

"Well, after my parents left when I was seven—I think I was seven, at least—I was on the streets for a while. It wasn't easy, but I managed."

Jerrick looked upon the girl with new respect, for he knew the difficulties and dangers of such a life, especially for one so young.

"I was also lucky, though. I was taken in by a woman named Gracilla. She runs an orphanage in Scilya. Gracilla takes in a lot of strays from the street and does what she can for them. It was she who introduced me to Brayton, my bard master."

"Kayra," Jerrick said, gesturing at the sleeping knight. "Is she from Scilya as well?"

"No. Her family's estate lies outside Massfin Hold, not too far from Scilya. Both lie within Kallendor's borders."

Jerrick nodded. He knew of the Fiefdom of the Horse Lords, though he'd never visited it.

"Scilya's a water town," Holly continued, "located next to the Usarian River. Kayra and I traveled from the city, along the Usarian into Vranna, and eventually made our way to Brinnok, where we first learned of the Call."

"If Kayra's nobility, how did you two meet?"

"Well, Kayra is and isn't nobility. What I mean is, she really considers herself no different from anyone else. That's probably why we became such good friends. We met at an engagement hosted at the Weslin Estate, where Brayton and I had been commissioned to provide entertainment. I wasn't far along in my tutelage at that time, and Kayra had yet to enter the knighthood." Holly smiled. "She wanted nothing more than to leave, to get back to her horse riding and sword practice. Seeing her now, it's hard to imagine her in a dress. She approached me, said she liked my playing and such. We got along well and just sort of became friends from there."

They fell into silence, each lost in their own individual musings for a time. Holly had a hard time sitting still, as Jerrick watched her rise several times to stretch or to perform some other whimsical chore. Jerrick noticed the change and, figuring the girl was calmer while they talked, said, "It helps to think of other things, to keep your thoughts off of . . . well, off of out there." He jammed a thumb toward the surrounding forest.

"It's hard to keep my mind off it," she said, sitting. "I can't shake this feeling that something out there is pressing down on us, drowning us. It just doesn't feel right."

Jerrick nodded his agreement. "It used to be different. The Simarron was full of life and beauty. Whatever happened here . . ." Jerrick shook his head. "Just keep your wits about you, and you'll be fine."

Holly pulled her knees up underneath her cloak and wrapped herself tighter in its embrace. Then she asked, "What do patrollers think of when they're trying to chase the gloom away?"

"Oh, different things." Jerrick thought a moment. "For some, places or things of beauty. A quiet brook, a secluded glen, a new doe learning to walk. Others, perhaps, think of family, friends."

"And you?"

Jerrick didn't say anything at first. He looked at Holly for a moment, then looked back down. "I think of my wife the most."

"You left the Hall to be with her."

Jerrick remembered Jasper saying as much in front of both Holly and Murik when they first arrived in Homewood.

"Yes, just over four years ago. Almost seems like another lifetime."

"What's her name?"

"Kendra."

"Tell me about her."

"Very well. Anything specific?" That she died because of me and the child I gave her? Jerrick banished the thought from his mind.

"How about the first day you met her?"

Jerrick thought for a moment, smiled, then suppressed a laugh. "I suppose that will do. Our first meeting was rather humorous, after all."

"Tell me." Holly stared at him with those wide eyes of hers, which told Jerrick he'd have her complete attention until he finished his tale.

"This was, oh, six or so years ago. I'd been with the patrollers a while by then, mostly patrolling the Simarron. I had a squad underneath me, and none of us got many chances to go very far outside the forest. But I had the opportunity to return to roving. That's what we call lone patrollers. Pretty much go wherever you want, within reason, always on the lookout for any signs of trouble. I was given the Regdale Keep patrol. It runs from the Hall west over the Ugull Mountains, through Rell, and on to Regdale Keep a bit south of Thesia. I'd been running the route for about a year when, through my own shortsightedness—and stupidity, I suppose—I got stuck in the Ugulls, trapped in a cave for a week because of a storm. Though I'd known it was coming, I figured to outrun it. Well, it caught up to me. I thought surely I'd drown or starve to death. The rain stopped eventually, of course, and I was able to get out of the mountains and make my way down to Rell.

I'm sure you can imagine what I looked and smelled like after a week of being trapped in a cave. I wanted nothing more than a bath and a hot meal. So I headed for the first cottage with smoke coming from the chimney. I must have been so intent on the house I didn't even see Kendra come out from behind a stand of trees until I was nearly on top of her. I don't know which one of us was more surprised.

"I remember feeling . . . stunned. She was beautiful, like a woodland sylph. Me? I looked like hell and so my wife's impression of me was not quite so memorable. She'd had a basket of clothes under one arm, and as soon as she laid eyes on me, she threw it at me. I was standing there like an idiot, mesmerized, when the basket, which hit me in the face, nearly caused me to fall over. By the time I recovered, Kendra was running like the very hounds of Barathrum nipped at her heels. By the time I shook off my surprise, she was already too far away for me to tell her I meant no harm. So, I ran after her. Only later did I learn that, a few weeks prior, there'd been reports of marauding bandits who'd come down from the mountains, and Kendra thought I was one of them. The moment she disappeared into the same cottage I had been heading toward, a man emerged from the nearby barn—her father, Rusar. He had a pitchfork. The expression on his face told me he planned to use it if he had to. Fortunately, I was able to explain myself before he stuck me.

"I apologized to Kendra for startling her, she apologized for throwing her laundry at me, and everything was fine after that. Rusar offered the use of his home for the remainder of the day and that night. I repaid him by helping about their farm.

Then, the next day, I said my farewells and went on with the business of the Hall. As you can imagine, I returned on my way back. Made up some stupid excuse I know Kendra never believed for having to stop at their house again. We became good friends over time. About two years from the day we met, we married."

The space between Jerrick and Holly grew quiet as Jerrick finished his telling. Jerrick caught Holly's lingering gaze, though, and he looked down, pretending something at his feet was of interest.

"You love her very much."

"Yes. She's waiting for me back in Rell. Once all of this business is over, I'll return to her."

They spoke little after that, both waiting for the coming dawn in silence.

CHAPTER SEVEN

THE WITCH

S KAVE AND NOHR STEPPED FROM amidst the gray, withered oaks into the misty expanse surrounding the witch's home. Stopping well short of the place, Skave narrowed his gaze at the hunting lodge turned shanty as he ran dry, leathery fingers over his sword's hilt. Just behind him, he heard Nohr clacking the bones of his necklace together.

"You go first," Nohr said, his grizzled voice resounding through the stillness. Nohr was a towering mass of bristled hair and rock-hard muscle. A gaugath, largest and fiercest of goblinkind, whose appearance was made slightly ridiculous by the huge beer keg he wore strapped to his back like a pack. He purposely took one step closer to the house than Skave had, then set his legs into a stance even a giant couldn't dislodge him from. Resting the head of his warhammer—a weapon whose haft measured longer than a man was tall—on the ground between his feet, he waited for the other's response.

Skave spat in his direction, missing the gaugath's bare, fur-covered foot by inches. Then, curling his dark lower lip in derision, he shook his head. "I'll venture no closer."

Nohr emitted a deep, guttural laugh. "You're scared."

Skave peered at Nohr, who stood nearly two feet taller than his own six and a half feet. Thoughts of slipping his sword into the gaugath's unprotected back crossed his mind for a moment, but only for a moment. If he failed to hit a vital organ, things might go badly for him.

"If you're so brave," Skave said, "why don't you go knock on her door?"

"Not I!" Nohr rumbled back as he continued to fidget with the bone necklace he'd made from the skulls of mountain wolves. "The house stands accursed, and I'll go no farther."

"Then shut up!"

Nohr snarled a response, which Skave ignored.

Skave normally suffered such insults from no one, even if they came from eight-and-a-half-foot gaugaths. But he also prided himself on an unusual sense of tact. He chose his battles carefully, and always in his own time. For now, Nohr remained an able cohort, a capable warrior, and his current ally, and so he let the exchange go no further. This time.

Even still, Skave knew the gaugath was right about the

witch's house. It was hoodooed, and he'd be damned if he'd step any nearer to it. Even from his present position, the place sent a chill crawling up and down his spine. He shook it off, though, forcing himself to look upon the shanty. It appeared no different than before: timbered walls pockmarked with termite-bored holes, a shingled roof riddled with thatched plugs, and rotted slats nailed over paneless windows. The ground all around the place was charcoal black and devoid of life. Above, gray smoke rose into the night sky from a simple chimney, erasing any doubts Skave might have had about the shanty's current vacancy.

The haurek was just wondering how to go about announcing their presence when the door, a rickety, splintered thing, creaked outward partway. Teetering on its rusty hinges, it looked as if it might fall to the ground at any moment. But then it swung open the remainder of the way, crashing into the wall. The shock reverberated throughout the structure, sending shingles and thatch sliding off one side of the roof. Ignoring the growing cloud of debris and dust, Skave kept his eyes on the doorway, seeing nothing but a few candles glowing amidst the dark until a lone grekkel emerged from the dim interior and into the pale moonlight.

The smallish creature strutted a few paces before his slanted gaze fell on Skave and Nohr. Eyes sick with yellow went wide as he jumped back and emitted a high-pitched screech. The cadaverous creature's long, perked ears flattened, and he thumbed a curved nose at the two larger goblins before dashing headlong into the woods. In the next instant, he was gone.

"What tidings?" hissed a voice.

The words snapped Skave's and Nohr's attention away from the fleeing grekkel and back to the house, where, at first, they saw nothing but the scant glow of candlelight shining from within. But then a dark mass slid into view, blotting out the light. The witch remained hunched within the doorway for a moment, a dark amorphous shape whose eyes Skave felt boring into him. Nohr must have felt those eyes, too, for he surrendered his ground, taking a step backward so he stood even with Skave. Both goblins stood transfixed as the witch stepped outside the house.

Dark wool robes concealed every inch of her, from a face lying hidden away within the garment's hooded aperture to hands buried deep within the expanse of its sleeves. Free of the confines of the doorway, she straightened to a height greater than Skave's but not nearly as tall as Nohr's. Then, settling into motionlessness, she waited for a response.

Skave tore his gaze away, mindful of what ill effects might be inflicted upon him if he looked at her for too long. Instead, he fixed his eyes just below the hem of her robes. Next to him, he knew Nohr did the same. Skave removed his helm, gathered himself, and said, "We have returned."

"You state the obvious, stalker." The witch's voice was a reptilian hiss.

Skave licked lips gone dry. "It is as you told us. The Hall of the Wood," he said, unfurling a brown-and-black banner, which he casually let drop to the ground, "lies empty. The way is clear for invasion. Even now, my runners return to Greth with word of this. Soon, our armies shall march upon the Simarron." Skave smiled. "I myself shall watch the patroller's Hall burn to the ground once and for all."

"You may do whatever you wish to the Hall," the witch said, still unmoving, "*after* the next full moon has passed from the night sky."

Skave shrugged. This was not the first time the witch made mention of the moon. Then, as now, he had no idea what she spoke of, nor did he care. His duty insomuch as the witch was concerned was over. Should be over, he corrected himself. If not for the orders given to both he and Nohr by their damnable liege, they'd be on their way to meet the army soon to depart from Greth. If not for their orders . . .

Skave didn't like orders, and, not for the first time, he thought of lying to the woman or simply telling her nothing at all. But he knew what happened to those caught lying to a witch, and if there was one thing Skave feared about this one, it was her wrath.

"There is something else?" the witch asked.

Rising fear extinguished all other thoughts, and Skave answered. "Gral, Lord of Greth, has asked myself and Nohr to offer our services to you until his armies arrive."

"Your lord 'asked'?" The witch laughed, a terrible, mocking hiss that echoed throughout the lifeless glen.

Skave's expression soured, but he voiced no protest as the witch's laughter subsided. Next to him, Nohr shuffled his feet, the mead in his keg sloshing from the movement.

"That is well," the witch said, "for I have a task for both of you. Now, listen."

Though they moved no closer, they lent her a collective ear.

"A group has entered the forest. These trespassers must be stopped."

Skave took measure of the news, then asked, "What of your devils? Why not let them work their buggery on them?"

"The spirits work in their own time, in their own ways." The witch went silent for a moment, lost in her own thoughts. Then she said, "These trespassers are different. They may prove too able for the . . . devils, as you call them, for they keep company with a sorcerer. His power is of particular concern."

Skave spat on the ground, for he cared as much for wizards, with their mumbling and hand waving, as he did witches. The last sorcerer to cross his path had found a crossbow bolt in her throat before a word, magical or otherwise, had escaped her lips. He never knew if the woman had been ally or adversary, nor had he cared. Sorcerers were a dangerous lot, and Skave preferred to strike first and ask questions later. The same went for witches, though their kind safeguarded their lives with lecherous death pacts and baleful curses, making their killing a bit more difficult. Who knew what evil might plague him if he killed one? He didn't care to find out. Turning his thoughts back to the matter at hand, he asked, "How many of these intruders are there?"

"In all, four: the sorcerer, a simple girl, a knight, and a patroller."

"A patroller?" Skave's gaze narrowed with suspicion, and for once, he looked upon the witch's dark, robed form without wavering. "You said they were all dead. I have already sent word of this to Greth."

"He is the last."

Skave let the words sink in. The last patroller. Here. Now. Just waiting to be found and slain. Suspicion melted away as morbid excitement took hold. Long had he wanted to cross swords with one of their kind. Now, it appeared he might have his chance. Skave smiled. "If you wish them slain, only say the—"

"All in good time, stalker. Let the devils take the girl first, for I have need of her alive and untouched. After that, you may do as you will with the others."

"As you wish," Skave said, bending at the waist in a partial bow. "Once your devils have done their work, the patroller shall die by my hand."

"And the knight by mine," Nohr said, finally joining the exchange, as he flexed arms lacquered with muscles and bristled hair and lifted his gargantuan warhammer before him. "His armor will be his coffin." The gaugath warrior chuckled with glee.

"That is well," the witch said. "But know that the knight is a woman, and mark well the sorcerer. Underestimate his power at your own peril." The witch paused as her tongue, a slender, serpentine streak of red, flicked out from the darkness of her cowl. "Know this also, goblins." The witch's form seemed to grow larger as she leaned nearer. Skave and Nohr shrank back. "If you fail me by allowing any one of the three to survive, I shall rip the skin from your flesh, add your extremities to my collection of ingredients, and use your own stinking innards to hang your rotting torsos from the Tree of Despair. Do you understand?"

Skave and Nohr nodded in unison.

"Now, go!"

The two goblins scrambled to obey. Skave broke an oath he'd made to never turn his back on this witch or any other as he bolted for the relative safety of the forest. Behind them, they heard a door slam. Neither goblin looked back even once.

CHAPTER EIGHT

THE HALL OF THE WOOD

ONCE EVERYONE WAS AWAKE AND ready, Jerrick gathered the group around the fire pit, where a few remaining embers continued to smolder. Before he spoke, he kicked some dirt onto the cinders. Their light flickered for an instant, faded, and then was gone.

"We were watched last night."

The quiet of the forest seeped into the camp as they each digested the patroller's statement while casting wary glances into the surrounding woods.

Murik was the first to break the silence. "Watched by what? Grekkels again?"

"Hard to say. I took a look around. There weren't any tracks. No brimstone in the air like before, either. I meant to wake you once I—"

"Why *didn't* you wake us?" Kayra asked, the same unpleasant expression on her face as when she had faced down the bandits at Jay's Tavern.

Jerrick met and held the knight's stare. "I left that to Holly, unless I got back before. Or didn't come back at all. As I was saying, there wasn't anything to see. No tracks, no broken branches, no smell of brimstone, nothing. Even the forest floor looked undisturbed." Jerrick shook his head. "Even if I'd seen anything, with this damn haze obscuring everything . . ."

The mist had returned during the night, limiting visibility as, now, it created suspicious shadows and shapes where it lay thickest.

"So what do you think they were?" Murik asked.

Jerrick seemed not to have heard the eslar, as he continued to hold Kayra's stare. Neither patroller nor knight showed any signs of wavering.

Murik made a show of clearing his throat, then asked his question once more.

Jerrick's glance flickered over to the eslar, and the standoff, interrupted, came to an end.

"I don't know what they were," Jerrick said. "If I didn't

know any better, I'd say they were wood sprites. There are— or, were—enough of their kind roaming the forest in the past. But now . . ." He gestured to the diseased forest. "Not much point trying to chase them down. Be like running after shadows."

"Do you think they're still out there?" Holly asked, her eyes darting into the woods.

Jerrick shrugged. "Probably."

The bard's gaze drifted downward as hands hanging at her sides busied themselves twiddling the hem of her cloak.

"But as long as they remain lurking in the shadows," Kayra said, shooting Jerrick a disapproving look, "they are no threat."

Jerrick wasn't so sure about that, but he recognized the agitation he'd caused Holly so he kept quiet on the subject. "We'd best get moving. We'll reach the Hall by midday. When we do, I think it best I go ahead myself. We've seen no signs of a goblin presence other than the grekkels so far, but that doesn't mean they aren't out there." Jerrick waited for them all to agree. "We can decide our next step once I return."

Jerrick took a turn leading the group as Kayra, astride Aurum, and the others followed. Holly led their pack mule, which she had affectionately named Russ, while Ash padded along near Jerrick. The patroller cast several inquisitive glances Ash's way, but voiced no objections to his sudden desire to remain near him. While the condition of the forest did not worsen, it still closed in, dampening their moods and stifling conversation. Holly's mandolin remained silent, the bard possessing neither the will nor the spirit for her music.

Jerrick's raised hand stopped their progress several times. In each instance, Kayra brought her destrier alongside and the two conversed for a few moments, while Murik and Holly kept watchful eyes on the forest. One time, they consulted Murik, but the sorcerer was unable to perceive anything more than the others. Something had eyes on them. They all felt it. But whatever it was remained just out of reach and almost imperceptible. Though the feeling wore on their nerves, they did their best to ignore it for the time being. The only other alternative, as Jerrick had said, was to chase shadows. None of them were inclined to leave the road to attempt such an endeavor. Settling into a steady, watchful march, they traveled all of the morning and just into afternoon before Jerrick called a final halt.

"The Hall is not more than a half-hour from here," he said. "I suggest you settle in until I return." Jerrick removed his pack and cloak, handing both to Holly, who still led Russ. "Give me, say, two hours to get there, investigate, and return. I'll come back sooner if I see anything right away. If I'm not back after those two hours, best head back to Homewood."

They all wished him good luck. Only Holly questioned him further.

"What do you think you'll find?" she asked.

Ash sat next to her and looked up at Jerrick.

"Hopefully, the patrollers." Jerrick tried to smile, to offer her some reassurance, but the gesture felt awkward and was short-lived.

"Do you really think so?" The girl squared her shoulders for once, making a point of looking Jerrick in the eye. "You don't have to lie to me."

Jerrick met her gaze, studying her for a moment. Her fidgeting and nervous eyes, which never stopped probing the woods except for now, reminded Jerrick all the more of her fragility. The gloom of the forest was affecting them all, though. Kayra had grown more irritable, while Murik's jovial nature had been replaced by an unusual sullenness. Jerrick wasn't immune, either, though he took things in stride, as patrollers were wont to do, keeping his mind focused on the task at hand. Let them reach the Hall first. Other decisions came later. Jerrick supposed some part of him still held to the slim hope Aliah's warning and the Call were both somehow just misunderstandings. Taking another look at the dying forest, he felt that shred of hope fading.

"Whatever's happened at the Hall," Jerrick said, "whatever did this to the forest, we'll get to the bottom of it. We'll make things right."

Holly's lips curled into a slight smile, but she said nothing. She backed away, wishing him good luck again before leading Russ off the road to a grassy area where Kayra had already situated Aurum. Ash remained where he was, looking up at Jerrick.

"You coming?"

Ash wagged his tail several times, but it was a subdued gesture. The dog let out a series of short whines.

"This place has you spooked, too, doesn't it?" Jerrick patted his head, remembering those times back in Rell when a thunderclap from a passing storm sent Ash scurrying to Kendra for protection. She was gone now, though, and Jerrick supposed, with family and friends on the other side of the mountains, he was the only one truly familiar for the dog to turn to. "It'll be all right. C'mon."

With his bow in one hand, his quiver slung over one shoulder, and his sword and hunting knife at his belt, Jerrick, shadowed by Ash, made for the Hall.

They followed the line of the road, though they stayed a good distance away from it. Jerrick stopped often, crouching, listening, and watching. But there was nothing to see, hear, or even smell besides the pungent odor of decay permeating the forest. Jerrick saw none of the usual animals that usually crossed his path on such treks through the Simarron. No white-tailed elk, no spotted deer, no raccoons or chipmunks, no red jays or night sparrows. Curious, Jerrick halted their progress at one particularly large oak that looked to have resisted the rot slightly better than its neighbors. Peeling back a layer of bark, he expected to find some sort of insect life: beetles, termites, ants, wood grubs, anything. But there was nothing. He shook his head and threw the piece of bark to the ground. Next to him, Ash, whose eyes stared deep into the woods, started at the sound. Jerrick patted his side, then ushered them onward.

As the pair drifted through the mist and trees, Jerrick felt more and more that the same something that had watched them overnight now followed his and Ash's trail. It was an odd feeling, one that unsettled the patroller more than he cared to admit. Never before had he felt such a sensation, especially while walking within a place he considered home. Though the Simarron was populated by all manner of creatures, not one of them had ever shadowed Jerrick so closely without eventually being revealed. Even in those instances, Jerrick had never truly felt hunted like he did now.

Ash stayed close, submitting to Jerrick's authority as the animal looked to his every move for direction. Jerrick frowned more than once at the dog's behavior. Never before had he seen Ash so docile, this odd disposition of his altogether unsettling in its own way. Jerrick told him to stay as he ascended a small, rock-strewn hillock. At the top, peering through the trees and mist while on his belly, he got his first good look at the Hall. He saw only the tops of the watch towers and part of the stone exterior, but it was enough. The Simarron Hall still stood. Jerrick ran the back of his hand across his forehead, wiping away droplets of sweat and realizing for the first time his skin was drenched despite the coolness of the air. He took a deep breath, closing his eyes and allowing his mind to relax. When he opened them, he realized the sensation of being watched had dissipated. He remained cautious, though, descending the small hill to find Ash exactly where he had left him. Ash wagged his tail at his approach, going so far as to lick his hand in a gesture of welcomed relief. Jerrick rubbed behind Ash's ears, then he settled into a slow pace not toward the Hall but around it. Despite the silence and lack of activity, the patroller was still not ready to walk up to the front door. Instead, he started to make a wide circle of the place, intending to complete a full turn around the structure before moving any closer. Ash followed in silence. They crept foot by foot, tree by tree, remaining vigilant for any signs of movement or sound. Several times, when the mist parted and the Hall came into view, Jerrick stopped to study the place. His inspections revealed nothing untoward.

Once the pair had gone halfway around, Jerrick decided his overcautiousness was unwarranted. Crouching nearly opposite from the hillock where he had made his first visual inspection, he pulled an arrow from his quiver, fitting it to his bowstring. Creeping around toward the front of the Hall, he felt Ash's presence right behind him. They descended a moderate slope, then hiked up a small rise, and as the trees fell away and the fog parted, Jerrick caught his first unobstructed glimpse of the Simarron Hall since his departure those many years ago.

Built into the side of a hill, the Hall was wood and stone rising three stories high in most places and five at each of its three towers and single belfry. Though trees had been cleared around the structure, it was so nestled in the casual passerby might miss the place completely if not looking for it. Jerrick moved in close enough to spy the front, where a wide set of stairs led up to a long, covered porch and twin doors standing some dozen feet tall. Jerrick knew one of the towers served as a lookout post. It looked unmanned. The two pennants always hanging there—the simple brown-and-black flag of the patrollers and the other, the standard of the Simarron Hall, with its green backdrop and oak tree in the foreground—were missing.

Ash came up to Jerrick's side, pausing as he lifted his nose. Jerrick waited and watched, looking to see if the dog might detect something his own senses had not. Ash stayed like that for a moment, then lowered his nose to the ground before looking to Jerrick.

"C'mon, then."

Creeping their way to the foot of the porch, they mounted each creaky step at a snail's pace until they stood before the Hall's main doors. These were an elaborate affair, hand-carved by ancestral woodsmen whose names Jerrick had known well when he was younger but which he now forgot. He'd always appreciated their workmanship, and so it unsettled him perhaps more than usual to see a hatchet buried smack in the middle of one, right at eye level. He recognized the telltale signs of its maker instantly.

Goblin.

They had been here. Might even still. It was so quiet, though. Far too quiet for their kind. Unless they waited in ambush. Unless—Jerrick took a deep, silent breath, calming his mind and his nerves. Moving closer, he studied the hatchet. A black, wedged head scored by deep scratches and nicks was jammed onto the top of a splintery shaft of mountain graywood. Too big for a grekkel, the weapon was crude by any standard except a goblin's. Jerrick knew what the hatchet's presence meant: it was the mark of Greth, left here at the doorstep of the Hall for a specific reason. It was more than an indication they had been here. It was a promise they'd return.

One of the doors was ajar. No light shone from within, no sound rang out. He approached the gap, his boots making far too much noise on the wooden floorboards for his liking. When he stood just to the side of the opening, he paused for a moment to listen. Hearing nothing, Jerrick stepped into the Hall. Ash entered right behind him.

He immediately dropped to a crouch, directing the point of his arrow in all directions as he made a visual inspection of the interior. The Great Room, as it was called, was draped in shadows and faint light entering from windows lining the wall high above. The chamber, smelling musty and stale, was not unlike a king's audience hall in size, but only in size, for here all people met as equals. A full forty paces deep and twenty-five wide, the floor was level across; no raised daises or other platforms existed to afford any one person prominence over another. Here, visitors were welcomed, public matters discussed, and festivals and celebrations held. The layout of the room changed to fit the occasion. More often than not, though, great high-backed chairs surrounded thick-legged tables laden with food, wine, and ale. Now, however, the room was a shambles. Some of the regal chairs and long tables were there, but they lay in splintered ruin: legs had been broken or hacked off, and all were marked by wedged indentations indicative of axe blows. Wooden dining plates and flagons, large food trays, utensils, and refuse were strewn about in a haphazard fashion. In between a series of doors on either side of the chamber, oil lamps rested upon wall sconces. Several of the sconces had been ripped from the wall, the shattered glass of the lamps scattered on the floor. The oak walls, just like the chairs, were littered with axe marks. Ahead, at the far side of the chamber, two staircases led up to a balcony overlooking the entirety of the Great Room.

Ash remained at Jerrick's side as the patroller traversed the chamber, sidestepping piles of refuse and other clutter. At either side of the room were four doors. One stood open to Jerrick's left and two to his right. Jerrick checked each. He saw nothing down their shadowed halls, though, and he quietly shut each one tight. Then he walked to the far end of the room, where a fireplace of monolithic proportions lay situated beneath the upper balcony. The great, hulking thing was constructed of rough stones, each three feet across and a foot and a half tall. In Jerrick's mind, the hearth had always represented those things embodying the very patrollers themselves: strength, warmth, friendship. Now, it lay cold and unlit.

Jerrick let the tension slip from his bowstring as he sat on the hearth's edge. Ash took a position next to him, as they both looked upon the remains of the Great Room.

What happened here?

Jerrick looked again at the broken furniture, the scattered dinnerware, the smashed lamps, and the defaced walls. It looked as if a battle had been fought. By all appearances, it was a battle the patrollers had lost.

Dead. They're all dead.

Aliah's words repeated in his mind. This time, he felt he

knew who 'they' were. His friends, those who had been brothers and sisters to him, were gone. Dead. The Hall of the Wood was abandoned. Jerrick had hoped he might find Aliah here. She'd most likely come, witnessed this chaos for herself, and left, probably warning Jerrick right after. He remembered her distraught state, and understood now. She probably hid somewhere deep within the Simarron. And what of Evar? What fate had befallen his oldest, dearest friend? Jerrick might never—

The hairs on the back of his neck rose as a chill ran down his spine. Just like in the woods, he felt something watching them. Only this time was different. This time, the watcher was so close Jerrick felt its eyes searing into him. Its very presence weighed upon his shoulders, pressing down on him. His heart pounded in his chest. It was here. Now. *Right above him.* Jerrick returned his arrow to his bowstring. Ash felt the presence also, for he emitted a low growl that sprang from the deepest part of his throat until he exploded into a fury of barking.

Jerrick lunged, turning and taking in the length of the balcony in a glance.

It was empty.

Then a metallic clang resounded from above, as if something—a lamp, perhaps—had been knocked to the floor. Ash, whose barking had faded to a persistent growl, started at the noise, then launched into another tirade.

Jerrick took three long strides, then plunged headlong up the rightmost staircase. He had had enough. First, Aliah and her foreboding warning. Then, the people of Homewood, frightened as he had never seen them before. And now, the Hall, a place he had called home, ransacked, the patrollers gone. Whatever was up there was part of it all. He'd his fill of mysteries and questions. He wanted answers.

They took the stairs two and three at a time. Halfway up, Ash bounded past the patroller, the dog gaining newfound courage from Jerrick's own boldness. Seconds later, they reached the balcony. Halls immersed in shadowed gray greeted them to either side. Remnants of lamps normally mounted along both sides of the hallways lay scattered across the floor. Though Jerrick was uncertain which direction the watcher had fled, Ash was not. The dog hesitated only a moment as he picked his way through the debris, then he was off, bounding into the dark.

"Ash, wait!"

But the dog was already gone. Jerrick cursed and ran after him. The inner passages of the Hall were a maze, with other hallways branching off the main passage, additional staircases leading to upper floors, and doors everywhere. Even in the dim light, though, Jerrick ran with a sure foot, for this was his home and he knew it with intimate familiarity. Some part of his mind screamed for caution, but it went unheeded. Ash was lost ahead somewhere, his pace too fast for the patroller. Jerrick made the best of what clues were available to him, though. Several times, he heard a growl or bark. Other times, he stopped long enough to inspect the floor, noting a disturbance in the dust accumulated there. Darkened halls and doors, some open and others closed, whirled past. Then, as he rounded a corner, exiting one hallway only to find himself in another, he slowed his pace and stopped.

Just ahead, cloaked in murky shadows offset by dim light from several windows, Jerrick heard Ash launch into a furious torrent of barking. Then, he heard a yelp and all went silent. Beads of sweat fell from his forehead as he steadied his bow. He stood transfixed as the hazy shadows before him coalesced into a black cloud of darkness. He blinked hard, thinking it a trick of his mind, but the effect remained. The floor beneath him started to tremble. Something was coming. Drawing his bowstring back, Jerrick waited. Then, the shadows swirled like smoke curling from a fire and the thing appeared from the dark. There was a glimpse of wild hair and yellow, baleful eyes, and then Jerrick's arrow flew. Though he saw the missile strike home, it did nothing to stop the watcher's forward momentum. Jerrick threw his bow aside and was just reaching for the hilt of his sword when it plowed into him.

There was a flash, as all the stars in the heavens danced across his vision, right before he was propelled backward through the air. He came down hard, landing flat on his back, and the air was forced from his lungs. Struggling to breathe, the patroller caught a glimpse of metal rising above him. His eyes went wide as he recognized the wedge end of an axe.

Jerrick pushed to one side, feeling a whoosh of air and hearing a hard thunk as the weapon embedded itself in the floor where his head had just been. He tried to rise, but was shoved back down hard enough to knock the wind from him again. Hot, fetid breath caressed his cheek, and he lashed out with his elbow, hitting nothing. There was a grunt as Jerrick heard the axe come loose from the floor. He knew what came next. But then a flash of gray streaked overhead, and Jerrick felt the thing's presence lifted from him. Rolling to one side, Jerrick used the wall to steady himself as he rose and took in great gulps of air.

The watcher—a dark, hulking thing, manlike but hunched over like some beast—stood between him and Ash, its back facing the patroller. Ash was doing his best to keep the creature occupied, but it wielded its axe with great effect, easily holding the dog at bay.

Jerrick shook the last of the disorientation from his head, then drew his hunting knife. Still a bit unsteady, he spun it about so his fingers held the blade. Then he let out a high-pitched whistle that startled the watcher. It spun around and, for one instant, their eyes met. Jerrick saw wildness and death, and then he let his knife fly. The blade spun end over end, finding its target.

The knife was not enough, as not even a cry of pain escaped the thing's lips. It ripped the blade free, tossed it to the floor, then raised its axe high as it hurled itself at the patroller. It moved with such speed, it was on him in an instant. Jerrick managed to draw his sword, blocking the first of the creature's axe blows as it attacked him in wide, forceful swipes. He had no choice but to waver under that assault. Behind the creature, Jerrick saw Ash, fangs bared as he padded forward, waiting for his opportunity to strike. Jerrick gave it to him. Feigning an attack, he acted as if he meant to lunge blade first at the creature, but instead leaned in, then darted back. The watcher leaned away from his pretended lunge, stepping right into Ash's maw. The dog's teeth sank deep into its leg, and the thing screamed in agony.

Jerrick pressed the advantage. He attacked once, then twice, swiping his blade from side to side in alternating patterns, in order to throw the creature off-balance. Behind it, Ash snapped. The watcher maneuvered itself so both patroller and dog remained in sight. Caught between them, its eyes went wild, for it knew it was trapped.

Jerrick thrust his sword at the thing's chest. It used the head of its axe to knock the blade aside, then raked inch-long claws at Ash, driving the dog back. Jerrick's sword slashed back and forth, but the creature somehow avoided or blocked each strike with surprising quickness. It played a loser's game if it thought it was going to fend off strikes from both sides forever, though. As Ash moved in with a snarl, Jerrick jabbed with his sword. The beast kicked at the dog, then moved to avoid Jerrick's blade. But the patroller, in anticipation, used his free hand to push the creature's weapon-bearing arm away, then brought his sword down on the thing's elbow. This close, the beast's smell—something akin to the rotting smell of the forest—threatened to overwhelm him, but he clenched his teeth and bore it as he felt his blade sink into flesh. An agonized shriek tore into his mind, forcing Jerrick to release his hold on the creature as he stumbled back. Then the world around him exploded as the creature raked a clawed hand across his face. The impact lifted him from the ground and sent him hurtling backward. Groaning and dazed, he fought to rise. He lifted his head, but that was all. It was enough to see the damage he had wrought.

Hot, sticky blood sprayed from the stump of a severed arm. The arm itself lay at its feet, the fingers still clutching tight to its axe. The creature drew its lips back into a snarl. Through foggy vision, Jerrick watched it pick up its arm. Ash made one final lunge, but the watcher was too fast as it leaped forward toward Jerrick. The patroller fumbled for his sword, but the blade must have fallen from his grasp sometime between being knocked senseless and impacting with the floor. His knife was gone as well. Balling his hands into fists, he waited for the creature.

It was almost on Jerrick when, instead of attacking, it leaped right over him and, running down the hall, disappeared. Ash started to pursue, but then stopped when he reached the patroller. Jerrick tried to stand, but dizziness and the pounding in his head forced him back to the floor. He struggled to put his back to the wall, and failed in that endeavor as well. Lying there, he tried to call to Ash, but the words came out unintelligible. His face burned. He moved a hand to his cheek, feeling the cuts and the blood welling around them.

Poison!

The realization flooded his mind just as he blacked out.

CHAPTER NINE

SKAVE AND NOHR

"HOW LONG WE GOING TO sit here?" Nohr asked for the umpteenth time as he gnawed his way through yet another piece of tree bark. Half-eaten specimens, gray with disease, lay piled at his feet. Inhaling deeply, he spat out the latest to grace his mouth with a curse. "Tastes stale."

Skave rolled his eyes, for he'd listened to that very same conclusion more times than he cared to remember over the course of the morning. Now, as the day wore into early afternoon, he fought a losing battle trying to contain his irritation.

"How long—"

Skave, glaring at the gaugath from his side of the log, finally conceded victory to his temper. "We'll sit here until I say otherwise!"

Nohr bared his fangs, but made no move to challenge Skave's authority. Instead, he went back to gnawing on his bark.

Skave knew Nohr didn't want to be here; the gaugath had made that clear from the very start. But his lord—their lord—had so ordered it. The two of them, unwilling to disobey a goblin known the Underland over as the Meat Peddler because of the manner in which he sliced off and then pretended to sell portions of his victims, had selected a small contingent of goblins to accompany them into the forest and to the home of their longtime enemy. The witch herself had prompted this expedition. Come up from the Simarron, she had traversed the tangled forest of graywoods surrounding their fortress and, at its very gates, requested an audience with the Peddler himself. Gral had granted it, listening as she made her bold claim of having driven the King's Patrol from the forest by way of her skullduggery. Lord Gral knew if the woman spoke truthfully, then here lay an opportunity there was no ignoring. Skave, Nohr, and the others had traveled into the Simarron at the Peddler's behest, their task to verify the witch's claims. At the Hall, Skave was surprised when they found it deserted. Convinced of the witch's claims, and relishing this stroke of luck, Skave had dispatched his goblins back to Greth to inform Lord Gral of what they had seen. Skave had buried his own hatchet in the Hall's door as a warning of his intention to return. Visions of himself at the forefront of the advancing army had sprung to life, and waned just as quickly, for he next remembered the other orders given to him and Nohr.

The two goblins were to put themselves at the witch's disposal until such time as Lord Gral arrived with his army. The Peddler, seeing a powerful ally in the witch, wished to keep up relations with her and to demonstrate his own importance to their arrangement. Skave cared little for Gral's political maneuvering, but he'd also known the day to defy the goblin lord was not that one. He'd call Gral "lord" for the time being, but only for as long as it took to fulfill his own objective. Long had Skave desired to see the people of the Simarron driven from the forest and, more importantly, the patrollers broken, beaten, and slain, bereft of their lives and their precious Hall once and for all. While the witch's magic may have already stolen the patrollers from him, Homewood and the Hall itself still remained. Skave planned to tear down the latter piece by piece. Then, with the host of Greth at his back, Homewood would fall, its people taken back to Greth as food and slaves.

Skave's gloved hand absentmindedly went to the scar zigzagging across one cheek. He almost wished a patroller had left the mark to better feed his vindictive nature. But, no, one of Skave's own kind was responsible for this particular reminder of his bravado and overzealousness. Skave's wagging tongue had started the fight. His adversary's knife carving into Skave's face had ended it. In between, Skave had made his boast to bring the patrollers to their knees. Single-handedly, no less. He was young and stupid, and the other stalker had laughed at him, telling him he'd never survive an encounter with a patroller, let alone slay one. They fought. Skave lost. Leaving Skave defeated and humiliated, the other had turned his back and walked off as if Skave's presence was no longer of any consequence. Skave had made a pledge then and there to destroy the patrollers and , even more gratifying, to flaunt the accomplishment before his rival right before driving a knife into his gut.

A short while after that fateful day, Skave began slipping into the Simarron, evading the much-vaunted vigilance of the patrollers with ease. Skave was a stalker, a master of subterfuge, stealth, and skulking. Trained in the dank, subterranean halls of Deep Hollow, the stalker refuge buried in the depthless dark of the Underland, Skave was one of their best. Over time, he became so skilled at evading the patrollers' watchful eyes, he moved about the Simarron at will. Just a few years before, Skave had even ventured undetected to the very doorstep of the Hall. Never once had he regretted his bravado when he had risked all for that one glimpse of the place. Nor had he regretted it more recently when he had explained to the Peddler himself how he was ready to do it again. Of course, Skave had not been aware the Lord of Greth planned on ordering him to do just that.

"I'm hungry," Nohr stated.

Skave, interrupted from his thoughts, threw up his hands in frustration. "What must a goblin do to get some peace and quiet around you?"

"I care not for peace and quiet," Nohr said. "I say we go do something."

"Oh really? What do you want to do?"

"Find this knight, and bash her puny head in!" Nohr smacked a clawed fist into his open palm as he let out a deep chuckle which shook his body so hard it sent vibrations into the log. Nohr was huge, even for a gaugath. At just under eight and a half feet tall, with a massive chest and broad shoulders to match, his stride alone set the ground shaking. His roar caused lesser men to drop their weapons and flee the battlefield. Coarse, brown fur, whose lightened tips gave the gaugath a grizzled look, provided enough protection from the elements for Nohr to wear only leather hides even in the coldest of caverns. His eyes were strong and dark. His ears, large and pointed except one had its top torn off. A maw ringed with yellow, jagged teeth was set beneath a black nose and narrowed slits. Leaning against the log was his massive warhammer, a dreadful weapon the gaugath warrior had only recently renamed *Knightcrusher*.

Lord Gral had summoned Nohr from Desolation Peak, where his mountain tribe laired, commanding him to take part in this venture because of his reputation as a formidable warrior and because, in his younger days, he alone had fought an entire patroller squad and survived to tell the tale. Despite being past middle age now, Nohr remained amongst the strongest of his tribe. Before, while still behind Greth's walls, Nohr had expressed his displeasure with their assigned mission to Skave. The gaugath considered himself too old for such adventures. Too comfortable, Skave had replied. Nohr denied it, but Skave knew it was true. The gaugath had left the mantle of warrior behind long ago to become, of all things, a brewmaster. Mead was a staple of all goblin diets, and of gaugaths in particular. Nohr had inherited his family's renowned brewing recipe years before and, capitalizing on its popularity, gained much favor and reward from his own tribe as well as from neighboring ones. The only reason he had been coaxed from his home at all was because the brewing season had drawn to a close, and all which remained was to trade the last kegs for those necessities his family and fellow tribe members might still need before beginning their winter hibernation. Nohr had handed those last duties to his mate prior to his departure. Tradition, however, dictated the last few casks remain reserved for the brewmaster, his family, and those tribe-mates considered closest. Nohr didn't trust his own family to save any of those last ones for him, and so the only plausible thing to do, or so Nohr had reasoned, was to strap one of those last, precious kegs to his back. Now, the half-empty, gaugath-sized keg, of which Nohr partook of several times a day, lay near him on the ground. The barrel was dark and weathered, but none the worse for wear.

"Find the knight, and bash her head in," Skave said, repeating his comrade's words with a mocking tone. "Why don't you then?"

"Huh? Why don't I what?"

"Go find the knight. Bash her head in. Then, when the

witch's spies return to her—"

"Spies?" Nohr's head spun all around. "I see no spies!"

"—and tell how you defied her by going after the intruders before her devils had their way with the girl . . ." Skave looked the gaugath up and down. "You're so big, I doubt she has jars large enough for your organs. No matter. She can cut them up and boil them in a stew. She ought to get several weeks of eating out of you."

Nohr swallowed hard, then shook his head. "I'll not become witch food. I'm staying here." He looked around again and whispered, "I still see no spies."

"Trust me, they're there. Why do you think we've been sitting here for so long?" Skave took up his sword—a short, broad-bladed weapon—and waved it in front of him. "I've half a mind to go stick the little grekkel rodents, but it's not worth the effort. They'll grow bored soon enough and leave, and then we'll be on our way."

"On our way to where?"

Skave sighed. "To find the knight! But especially the patroller."

Nohr chuckled. "You're going to crush his head."

Skave smirked. "Something like that."

"But what about the witch? She won't like it if she finds out we killed them before the devils—"

"To Hell with the witch and her man-eaters! By the time she learns of anything, Lord Gral and his army will occupy the Simarron, and that filthy crone can scurry back to whatever hole she crawled from."

Skave grinned, and soon both goblins laughed and spoke of the slaughter to come as they waited for the witch's spies to wander off. Skave was right: her minions grew restless in short time. Once Skave had scouted the area just to make sure, the two gathered their things and, with Nohr hefting his beer keg onto his back, set out for the Hall.

CHAPTER TEN

TAKEN

MURIK WATCHED HOLLY DAB AT Jerrick's wound with a damp cloth. As she ran it across the patroller's forehead, he stirred, half opening groggy eyes.

"What . . . was that thing?" the patroller whispered, his voice gone dry and hoarse. Jerrick tried to rise, but the effort proved too much as he fell back onto his makeshift bed. Looking from Holly to Murik, he started to question them, but the words faded as his raw throat seized up.

Murik handed a waterskin to Holly. "Help him drink."

When Jerrick had drunk his fill, Holly tried to make him comfortable. Ash, sitting at Holly's side, barked once. Jerrick winced as he held a hand to one ear.

"See he sleeps," Murik said. Though the poison was gone from Jerrick's system, drawn forth by the sorcerer's magic, Jerrick still needed rest. Murik made sure he got it, hovering over him until he saw the patroller's eyelids droop and then finally close. Satisfied, he said to Holly, "I shall venture outside to see if Kayra has found anything." As he walked from the Great Room, he encountered Kayra coming up the porch steps.

"I found nothing," she said, her armor looking dull and shabby in the afternoon gray. She still carried the gray-hafted hatchet they had removed from the Hall's door. They hoped Jerrick might shed some light on its presence once he recovered.

Murik nodded, already looking past her, his white eyes fixing on the forest beyond. "Perhaps I shall have better luck."

Walking past Kayra without further comment, he used his staff as support for his crippled leg as he headed into the surrounding woods. Murik cast neither detection dweomers nor any spells, though, for the eslar was quite certain Jerrick's attacker was gone. He considered telling Kayra as much, but, for now, it was best the knight and the others believed he knew as little as they about Jerrick's encounter, the missing patrollers, and the corruption of the forest. Now, more than ever, they looked for answers. If they thought him privy to secret knowledge, the eslar might find himself surrounded by suspicions he neither wanted nor needed. In truth, much still baffled him. The mystery of the missing patrollers remained such, as did the exact cause of the forest's deterioration. But the sorcerer felt comfortable in his ability to trace all of it back to one commonality.

Saress.

The witch's name had haunted Murik for over thirty years now. It had been that long since her betrayal had been realized and thwarted. Their relationship had always been one of convenience; she had possessed knowledge and an understanding of processes of which he had been ignorant. In exchange, he'd offered her secrets of his own. It seemed a fair trade in Murik's mind, and might have been so if Saress had not purposely fed him incantations and eldritch knowledge which had almost gotten him killed. At first, he'd wanted vengeance. But, as the years had passed, such desires had fallen by the wayside, for Murik's purpose was not driven by such things. His was the thirst for knowledge. Power, as well, but he'd no ambitions beyond mastering a long-forgotten magic or discovering a bit of eldritch teaching. That Saress had denied him this did more than anything else to fuel the forces which drove him. He'd given her truth. At one time, he had wanted no more or less in return. Except, now, it was too late for bargaining or fair trade. He'd take what she should have given him all those many years ago and kill her if she tried to deny him. He'd probably kill her anyway. He might have no need for vengeance, but she did. Better to end it than to spend the remainder of his life looking over his shoulder.

The others needed to know nothing of this. He'd no desire to see them harmed. It was not beyond possibility they might solve the riddle of the missing patrollers as well as the corruption of the forest without ever having to face the witch. Alone, he'd return to his task of finding and destroying the crone. Murik looked upon the forest's decay and wondered about that. While such a task had never been trivial, it had always lain firmly in the realm of the possible. But now it seemed the witch's power had increased beyond anything imagined or anticipated. How else could she have sent an entire forest on a slow but steady march unto death? That both troubled and intrigued him more than anything. Saress had always been a powerful witch, but this spoke of something else. Something here, in the forest. Something that had kept her rooted in place long enough for Murik to catch up to her. This wasn't the first time he'd done so. Other times, she'd discovered him and fled. One time, they'd fought. His crippled leg served as reminder of that particular confrontation. But Murik believed in new possibilities. Even now, some hereto-unknown element may have tipped the scales back in his favor. Murik hoped so, for he saw nothing around him but decay, death, and the triumph of his enemy.

Jerrick drifted in and out of sleep most of the afternoon. While he did so, the others worked at bolting or blocking all of the Great Room's entryways so only the main doors remained unobstructed. The Hall was larger than any of them had anticipated. Given the increasingly late hour and mindful of the possibility Jerrick's attacker might return, they decided to postpone a more thorough inspection of the place until morning. Still, they couldn't help but look around for any immediate signs of what had happened here. A cursory examination told them no one had called the Hall of the Wood home for some time. Second-floor bedrooms looked as if their last occupants had risen from slumber, thrown sheets and blankets aside, and never returned. The surviving oil lamps were empty of fuel, their keys turned up all the way, as if left burning until exhaustion. The kitchen, which was just a short distance from the Great Room, had not been used in weeks, if not months. Cupboard doors were flung open, the shelves mostly barren. What little scraps of food they found were either stale or rotten. Dusty counters were covered with a mismatch of earthen jars, iron skillets, and pans, some of which were caked with rotting, half-cooked food. In the Great Room, they found empty packs, a few traveling cloaks, pieces of armor, and even an assortment of weapons, presumably left behind by the others who had answered Homewood's Call of Heroes.

Outside, Kayra discovered clotheslines on which shirts, gowns, pants, and socks still hung. Behind the Hall, she found the stables and a series of work areas, including those of the blacksmith, leather tanner, and furrier. Though the shops were devoid of life, there was evidence in each of projects started but left incomplete. The stables themselves were empty but for one donkey Kayra found standing quiet and subdued in the dark. It looked famished, and she provided the poor animal with what hay she found as well as oats from their own supplies. She also introduced him to Aurum and Russ. The donkey's spirits lifted just for the company.

Holly and Kayra had gathered an ample supply of wood earlier, and a comfortable blaze in the Great Room's hearth provided the travelers with light and much-needed warmth as night arrived. The pungent smell of burning wood pushed away the room's cool staleness, as the flames cast long, dancing shadows upon the walls. Jerrick, feeling better, woke long enough to pick at some food. While he did, Kayra requested he provide them an accounting, even a brief one, of what had happened. Jerrick obliged, providing a slow but detailed retelling of his arrival at the Hall. When Kayra held the graywood hatchet up, Jerrick explained what it meant. He went on, detailing his encounter with his wild-eyed assailant, but offering only a vague description of it before he drifted off to sleep once more.

The others used what remained of the evening to plan their next course of action. A more thorough search of the Hall was their first order of business come morning. One of the missing patrollers or someone else may have left behind some written clue—a journal or diary, perhaps—telling of their fate. In the meantime, however, they remained vigilant in case Jerrick's assailant decided to return. They each took a watch. Murik volunteered for the first, with Kayra and then Holly taking the next. Though the knight was confident the chamber was secure, Murik took the extra precaution of casting a dweomer to alert him should anything enter. With that, the eslar bid them all good night before he moved off to find a chair to sit in until his watch was concluded.

The gatherer spider watched all of this from one corner of the Great Room. Only when afternoon had turned to night and the dark-skinned one slept did the spider stir to life, leaving its perch to scurry upside down along a ceiling beam. Its multi-ocular vision focused upon only the one as it positioned itself directly above him. Then the gatherer lowered itself from the end of its web line. When it hung suspended just above him, it severed its tie to the silky strand and plopped down onto the man's clothing. The spider's prey felt nothing as it scurried up and down and across his shirt, moving to his waist and then to a shoulder before it spotted the single follicle of hair. Picking its way to it, the gatherer's mandibles latched on to the errant strand. The spider wasted no time effecting a getaway, returning to the rope of webbing and pulling itself back up to the ceiling with its prize. From there, it was nothing to return to the outside where the gatherer headed straight for a series of webs connecting the Hall to a nearby tree's branches. It scurried across the web and onto one particular branch, stopping when it came face-to-face with a grekkel who sat picking at the fur on his belly in silence.

Speck saw the spider and grinned.

"What tidings, little one?" the goblin asked, emulating the greeting of his mistress.

The spider held the single piece of hair out to the grekkel, whose chin curled and ears perked at the sight of it.

"Ah, little one," he said, "you have done well."

He took the hair from the spider's mandibles and, holding it tightly between forefinger and thumb, inspected it with one of his slanted, yellow eyes. A spindly tail peeked over his shoulder to curl about the strand. His fingers released their grip, and both hair and tail disappeared behind his back.

"Now, for your reward."

Speck reached for the small pouch at his side, but then stopped as a new idea popped into his head. Why give the gatherer its due when he could smash the puny thing and keep the reward for himself? Speck grinned as he envisioned his fist landing on the spider's body, its puss-like innards splattering across the branch and oozing out from beneath his hand. Something in his eyes must have warned the gatherer spider, for it started backing away from the grekkel. Speck suppressed a screech of glee as he moved to head off the small creature. "Don't leave yet, little one. Your reward awaits you."

But then Speck remembered something.

Months ago, his own mistress had also wanted to smash him after he had accidentally knocked over her special potion. Though she drove Speck out of her house, hissing all the while about how long it had taken her to gather the exact ingredients in the exact quantities and how she now had to begin the process all over again, she had not killed him. Speck knew he had been spared only because of the invaluable service he provided her. In the same way, the gatherer spider provided its own dutiful service. Speck decided to follow his mistress's example. He'd not kill this spider after all.

Speck's three-fingered hand grabbed at the drawstrings of his pouch. Reaching in, he fumbled around inside it for a moment. Then, his hand emerged. Enclosed in his balled-up grasp was a mass of black, twitching flies. He spread the winged insects out on the branch, then licked his hand clean of those which had stuck there. The grekkel smacked his lips. "Delicious!" As he backed away, the spider moved in, packaging bunches of the flies into web sacks which it then attached to its abdomen with sticky web strands. A powerful arachnid despite its small size, the gatherer had the strength to carry many of the fly sacks back to its home.

"Yes, yes," Speck said as he hopped up and down, "take all you can carry. That was our deal, little one." Speck snatched up one of the flies and plopped it into his mouth. He chewed for a moment, then swallowed. "They're only stunned, and will wake just in time for your feasting!" Speck, aware of the sleeping enemies nearby, suppressed an urge to clap. How he desired to be there when the spider sucked the life from each and every one of these poor, helpless insects! But his mistress had other chores for him to perform, and he needed to hurry back to her. "Tell all your spider friends about Speck." Speck wasn't sure the gatherer had any friends, but he went on anyway. "You tell them Speck honors his bargains, and that Speck always has tasks in need of performing. You tell them that."

Speck sat back against the tree and watched as the spider gathered the last fly sack, fastened it to its abdomen, then scurried away.

"Well, not even a good-bye!" Speck's face took on a look of feigned disappointment, then his lips curled back to reveal yellow, jagged teeth and he bounced forward on gangly limbs to lick the last of the remaining flies from the branch. "Delicious!" he said again. Then, with the sorcerer's hair securely held in the grip of his slender tail, Speck went—poof!—and reappeared on the ground. He immediately set out in search of his mistress.

Pain.

White-hot, it lanced through Kayra as if she burned. Her armor offered no protection; the metal was molten steel, searing the flesh from her bones as it cast her mind into pure agony. Her lungs heaved, desperate for air, but the motion only fueled the flames further and the pain increased. Looking down the length of her torso, her mouth opened in a silent scream, for where her stomach had been was now a great, gaping rent, oozing red blood and pink guts.

Kayra woke with a start, sitting up and groping at her stomach with both hands to feel for the wound which wasn't there. Surprise and relief flooded her mind all at once as she realized it had only been a nightmare. Kayra leaned back and closed her eyes. It had all seemed so real. The battlefield soaked red with blood, the agonized neighing of felled horses, the screams of the maimed and dying littering the ground in broken heaps of armor and flesh. She had been the last knight standing, ringed in by a horde of screaming, taunting goblins.

One came too close, and she had disemboweled him. That kept the rest at bay until their leader, a brutish ogre whose bared chest was crisscrossed with scars, plowed his way through their ranks, his nightmarish battle-axe held before him. Without so much as a challenge, he batted Kayra's shield aside and knocked her to the ground. Kayra screamed for quarter just before the brute buried his axe in her.

But it had only been a dream. She was safe.

The knight opened her eyes again at the sound of Ash's whining. Following the dog's stare, she saw one of the great doors open.

Then she noticed Holly's absence.

Kayra threw her blanket aside and rose, shouting at the others. "Wake up!"

Jerrick mumbled something, then rolled over and continued sleeping. Ash, who lay at his side, looked intent on staying there. Only Murik heeded her.

"Holly's gone."

Kayra grabbed her sword, whipping the blade free from its sheath. She tossed the scabbard aside as, barefoot and clad only in a loose tunic and leggings, she ran across the chamber, toward the open door. She stopped outside at the topmost of the porch steps, scanning the night for her friend. She saw nothing but gray mist and darkness. The night air was cool, and she suppressed a shiver.

Behind her, she heard Murik's staff tapping on the floor. "Where did she go?" he asked.

"I don't know."

Where in Barathrum *did* she go? And why did she leave without saying anything? Kayra balled her free hand into a fist and, with her other, clenched the hilt of her sword so hard her hand throbbed as the blood fought its way through the constriction. "I just woke from—I woke, and she wasn't there. Damn this fog!"

Murik brushed past her, picking his way down the steps and into the gray mist. Kayra followed, the damp earth cold on her bare feet.

Once they had walked a good thirty paces, Murik stopped. Lifting his staff to the sky, he willed his magic to life. His staff flared into white brilliance as it lit up the clearing from the Hall all the way to the tree line. Much to Kayra's surprise, the magical light penetrated the mist, revealing all. They spotted Holly immediately. She stood with her back to them, just at the edge of the trees. She was not alone, for a smattering of yellow eyes burning in the night's darkness looked back at them.

There was a moment of shocked surprise, then Kayra acted. There was no time for fear, no time to strategize. The knight shouted to her friend and, brandishing her sword, ran toward her.

Holly paid her no heed as ragged hands reached out from the darkness to take hold and draw her into the trees. The bard made no move to resist. In moments, as Kayra looked on in frustration, Holly was gone. Then, one by one, the yellow eyes blinked out until none remained.

"Holly!"

Kayra plunged into the woods after her. There was no

144

immediate trace of her. Nor was there any sign of the yellow-eyed fiends which had taken her. Kayra ran headlong in the direction Holly had faced, flying by trees which, at times, she avoided only by scant inches. Murik's light vanished behind her; Kayra knew the crippled sorcerer could not maintain her pace. The knight bit her lip and ignored the sharp twigs and thorns stinging her bare feet, running until her breathing became ragged and she felt as if her lungs might burst. She continued to call out to her friend as she ran, though her voice grew less and less audible as exhaustion steadily overcame her. Finally, unable to run any farther, she stopped, her chest heaving as she took in great gasps of air. Looking in all directions, she saw nothing but the dead and dying Simarron oaks standing amidst the cursed mist. But for Kayra's breathing, the forest was silent. The knight let out a cry of frustration as she sank to her knees. Tears welled in her eyes, and she felt as if she might be sick. Holly was gone. Taken right from under her nose. Kayra beat the ground with her fist, anger and frustration overwhelming her as the tears, no longer held in check, streamed down her cheeks.

Kayra sat like that for a few seconds, but only for a few. She blinked away the tears, wiping them from her cheeks. Refusing to surrender to despair, she beat back a rising tide of emotions. She took a deep breath and centered herself. Under her breath, she muttered the words which bound all knights: "Courage, Truth, Honor." The Three Merits. They were Kayra's foundation. Everything she did, everything she had learned, stemmed from their principles. They provided the knight with guidance and strength. Adherence to their values separated the knight from the knave, the chivalrous from the scoundrel, the true soldier fighting for duke and fiefdom from the mercenary fighting only for money and greed. Kayra felt she hung over a precipice, her hands clinging to a rope that dangled over the edge. If she let go, if she succumbed to her anguish, it meant Holly's death. She refused to let that happen. Wiping away the last of her tears, she pushed herself from the ground. She had sworn to keep Holly safe. A lack of resolve or courage or inaction was not acceptable. Not to her, not to the others, and certainly not to Holly, who needed Kayra now more than ever. Kayra's honor—the last and most important of the Three Merits—demanded she put forth every effort to find and protect her charge, even if it meant searching behind every tree and under every leaf. Blinking away the last of her tears, Kayra set off back toward the Hall. Her search might take hours, days, or even weeks, but no matter what it took, she'd find and save Holly.

As she emerged from the forest, she discovered Murik standing where she'd left him.

"Holly's gone," Kayra said.

She passed Murik without stopping, climbing the porch steps where Jerrick, half-dressed with his cloak wrapped around him, stood. Ash, his ears perked and head cocked to one side, was next to him. The patroller leaned against the door for support.

"What happened?" he asked. He sounded better than before, but still weak.

Kayra said nothing right away, brushing past him as she

headed straight for her belongings. As she started to don her armor, she explained what had occurred. She made no mention of her emotional episode.

"How did they get to her?" Jerrick asked.

Kayra shook her head. She didn't know. "The main door was open when I awoke." She placed her hauberk over her shoulders, letting the bottom of the chain shirt fall to her thighs. "It was locked from the inside, though, and there was no sign of forced entry."

Murik stepped into the room, the light from his staff still glowing, but subdued. "My spell did not alert me to anyone entering the room. Holly must have gone to them."

"Why would she do that?" Kayra asked.

Murik didn't answer right away. His brow narrowed in concentration. "She was entranced. There is no other explanation. We both saw how easily she went to them. Jerrick, do you know of any creature in the Simarron to possess such power of suggestion?"

Jerrick thought for a moment, but shook his head.

"So," Kayra said, "they have some sort of magic."

"It seems so," Murik said.

Jerrick looked at the knight. "You saw nothing else of the creatures but their eyes?"

"No," Kayra said, fastening pauldrons and vambraces to her shoulders and arms, "nothing."

"If the eyes are any indication," Jerrick said, "they must be the same thing which attacked me. I never considered there might be more of them." Jerrick threw his cloak aside. "I'm coming with you." Though his steps were unsteady, he reached his things and started to dress.

"You won't find her." Murik's voice caused both of them to stop. "Not easily, at least."

Kayra turned on him. Feelings of despair may have disappeared, but in their stead remained an intense anger just waiting for release. The knight had little patience for doomsayers. Not now. "What do you mean?"

"She has passed beyond my perception. If these are indeed the same creatures as the one who attacked Jerrick, there will be no trail to follow."

"Then we'll search every inch of the Simarron for them." Kayra returned to her armor, fastening her greaves to her legs.

Murik sighed. "Where do you propose we start? It's a very large forest. Without some direction, you'll never—"

"Damn it, wizard!" Kayra threw the greaves to the ground, then strode right up to Murik. "Holly is my charge, and I will not just abandon her to those things! If you have something to add, something that might help, then do so. Otherwise," she said, turning her back to the wizard, "shut up."

Kayra busied herself with her armor again, though her mind was only half on the task. Part of her refused to accept the eslar's words. But part wondered if he might be right. If Holly was truly lost, then so was she.

"Do not blame yourself, Kayra," Murik said, his voice calm, "for it is I, and I alone, who must accept the blame for Holly's abduction."

Kayra stopped what she was doing and looked at the sorcerer.

Murik's shoulders slumped under her gaze, and he sat back down. "It was my spell which failed us this night." He sighed and shook his head. "It never occurred to me to guard against someone leaving."

"Hoo! Hoo!"

Through the still-open door flew an owl. It circled the room once, then ascended toward the ceiling to perch amidst the shadows of the latticed rafters. The owl was the first native denizen of the forest any of them had seen since departing Homewood.

"It's a horned owl," Jerrick said.

A great brown-and-gray-feathered bird, it possessed the characteristic black bill, large yellow eyes, and white throat patch of its kind.

"There's something . . ." Jerrick narrowed his gaze at it. "I think I've seen this owl before."

The light given off by Murik's staff intensified as he stood and held the gnarled shaft higher. "I see nothing to distinguish this owl from any other."

"I know it looks like any other horned owl," Jerrick said, "but . . ."

Kayra, who had finished with her armor, moved to stand between the two men. "Who gives a damn about an owl?" She had to tear her own stare away. After so many days without seeing any wildlife, it was odd seeing the bird. "Have you both forgotten my friend has just been taken by . . ." She pointed to the outside. "Those things? Even now, they could be doing . . ." She didn't want to think about it. "We need to go. Now!"

She strode toward the great doors, not looking back to see if either Jerrick or Murik followed.

"Hold, knight!" Murik said. "I think the owl is trying to tell me something."

Kayra stopped, not sure if she had heard the sorcerer correctly. "The owl is what?" She took a few steps back toward them. "Are you insane, wizard?"

Murik kept his attention on the bird. "No, I am not insane. He's trying to tell me something, but he's very frightened. We need to try to get him down—"

"That's it! I know where I've seen him before. S'nar!" Jerrick called to the owl.

The owl looked down, but made no other movement.

"Jerrick, what are you—" Murik said.

"S'nar!"

The owl remained disinterested.

"Does anyone know how to call to a bird, to make him come?" Jerrick asked.

Ash barked.

"Shut up, Ash," Jerrick said.

Murik arched a brow. "A horn, whistle, or even a hand gesture typically works." Murik demonstrated a sign. "But I must warn you, even if this bird has been properly trained, precautions must still . . ."

Jerrick used the described gesture, calling again to the owl. This time, the great horned bird responded, leaving its perch with a hop as it spread its wings and swooped straight down at the patroller. But it came down too fast, with no perceived intention of landing on his arm. Jerrick just ducked beneath the owl's talons, stumbling from the effort and landing flat on his face. Kayra was too far away to do anything, but fortunately for Jerrick, Murik was not. The eslar wrapped his cloak about one arm, creating a makeshift perch which he held out. The owl flew straight for him, hovering for just a moment before touching down on his outstretched arm. Murik calmed the animal with soft noises as his other hand drifted closer and closer, until, finally, he was able to run the back of his fingers across the bird's feathered chest.

"Well now," Murik said, "it seems he has indeed been trained."

Jerrick rose, taking a few steps back from the owl. "Oh, he's trained. Trained to kill. That's S'nar, all right. I wasn't sure at first, but now . . . His handler is Evar, Eldest of the Elders, and the friend I came here to see." Jerrick scowled at the bird. "Stupid owl never did like me."

Murik fought to suppress a smile.

Kayra appeared next to Jerrick. "Tell us what is going on, Murik."

The eslar held up a finger. "Wait just a moment."

Kayra exchanged a look with Jerrick.

As S'nar purred and occasionally hooted, Murik responded with clicks and low noises of his own. Finally, the eslar turned back to the others. "I know it seems strange to you, but I can communicate with S'nar. Not in exact words, of course, but I can approximate the sounds and gestures he makes, and respond to him in like fashion."

Still suspect, Kayra asked anyway, "What's he saying?"

"That he knows where our friend has been taken."

Kayra's expression did not change. "The owl knows where Holly is? If this is some sort of a joke—"

"I make no jest."

Kayra stared at the eslar a moment longer, then threw up her hands. "Fine, then. Can he take us there now?"

"Yes. In fact, he has already offered to do so."

"There's more, isn't there?" Jerrick asked, studying Murik's expression. "What else did he say?"

"He says Holly has gone to the same place the others were taken. The place, he says, where they went but never returned from."

"Which means what?" Jerrick asked. "What 'others'? Does he mean the patrollers? Does he know where they are?"

Murik clicked a few noises at S'nar, who responded by shifting his weight from foot to foot before taking off from the sorcerer's arm. The owl flapped its wings in broad swipes, lifting itself back up to the rafters. Murik's gaze followed him up. "He only repeats what I have already told you. One thing is for certain, however: something about the place Holly and the others have been taken frightens him."

The leather straps of Kayra's armor creaked as she shifted

from one foot to the other. "If we have to follow an owl to find Holly, then that's what we'll do. We leave as soon as we can."

The others nodded their agreement. As Murik went about his own preparations, Kayra, concerned about Jerrick's ability to participate in Holly's rescue, asked him how he felt.

"I'll manage."

"Good." She made to turn away, but then paused and said, "I'm not the best with words, but I wanted to say . . . You know the forest the best of all of us, and your assistance is appreciated. I only want Holly back."

"We all let our guard down tonight. Holly's absence is all of our faults, not just yours."

Kayra nodded, then left the Great Room and headed for the stables.

They set out a short while later. Once Murik had coaxed S'nar outside, the owl flew from tree to tree, stopping often to allow the three to catch up. Though a nearly full moon shone overhead, heavy fog and mist blocked most of its light. They used the illumination cast by Murik's staff instead, plodding their way through the woods and into the night.

CHAPTER ELEVEN

THE CURSE
OF THE HALL

THE SOUND STARTED AS A murmur. Though Holly heard it, she thought it nothing more than the breeze touching the exterior of the Hall. But then the murmur became a gentle whisper floating across the Great Room, flowing into and permeating every part of Holly's being so that, all at once, her mind and body relaxed, her doubts were silenced, and the fear plaguing her since their departure from Homewood dissipated until nothing of it remained. How strange the voice woke no one else.

Thoughts of the others vanished, leaving only the sweet sigh repeating the same simple utterance over and over. Enraptured, Holly strained to comprehend it. The moment she did, she was lost.

Holly.

The sound of her name sent images and sensations fleeting through her mind. She saw herself running amidst the great oaks of the Simarron. The forest was beautiful, free of the evil taint. The dread of the past few days was gone, replaced by an exhilarating, carefree sense of freedom. Others ran with her, but they were nothing but shadows striding just beyond her range of sight. Voices called, beckoning her forth from the Hall. Through the fog eclipsing her mind, she felt her feet step forward of their own volition as she meandered past those continuing to sleep and to the great doors. She undid the heavy bar latched tight across them, swung one open, then walked out into the night.

The forest's mist no longer harbored shades and shadows for Holly, and she allowed it to engulf her without hesitation as she descended from the porch, moving farther from the Hall toward the whispered calling of her name. She paid no heed to the damp air chilling her skin. There was only the melodic voices and the thought that, just ahead, they waited for her. When she reached the trees, she stopped. Behind her, Holly thought she heard a voice—a new voice—call her name, but the summoning ahead grew louder, drowning out all else. The clearing lit up then, and she saw the eyes. Pacifying orbs of yellow, they reminded her of candles shining in the dark. Soft hands beckoned her into the forest. Holly, welcoming their invitation, offered no resistance. Behind her, a voice cried out again, but then she was surrounded, and all else slipped away.

Holly felt herself lifted up. Stars peeked through the haze above and trees swept by on either side as she floated through the forest as if in a dream. She closed her eyes and must have slept, for when she reopened them, the hands were setting her down. Leaves rustled as her booted feet touched the earth, and the hands released her. Her own weight was too much for her. Her knees buckled and she collapsed. The ground felt hard and cold against her face. She tried to rise, but didn't have the strength. None of the hands moved to help her.

Holly peered into the darkness, searching for the comfort of the yellow eyes, but they were gone. The air, already cool, grew colder still, until it chilled even the skin beneath her clothing. She shook involuntarily. Then, as if someone pulled away a veil, the fog lifted from her mind. In its place was a steady throbbing which caused Holly to wince in pain. She lay on her side, and she drew her knees closer as one hand went to her temple. She tried to wet her lips with her tongue, but her mouth had gone dry, her throat, raw. Slowly, she pushed herself to her knees. The throbbing in her head intensified, and she almost fell back to the ground. She steadied herself, though, closing her eyes as she sat still for a moment. When the pain had lessened, she opened her eyes and, through the mist, saw the robed apparition.

It stood no more than five paces from her, just at the edge of a ring of moonlight which illuminated the small glen Holly found herself within. All dark robes, its size dwarfed Holly's own. Its visage, buried deep within its cowl, was indiscernible, as were its hands, which were joined together within the folds of the robe's wide sleeves.

Holly shrank back from the specter. Some part of her mind screamed for her to stand and run, but the best she managed was to scurry backward on all fours. Fumbling with her mandolin, which somehow remained slung over one shoulder, she immediately butted up against something she thought at first must be a tree. Her hand recoiled when, instead of rough bark, her fingers brushed against thick hair and tight, quivering muscles. She looked up, her eyes locking on twin orbs of yellow. Whatever magic-induced comfort she had previously found in those eyes was gone. Now, they instilled only horror, and she recoiled from the evil she saw in them.

She lunged away from the fiend, inadvertently moving closer to the robed figure, which stood exactly as it had when Holly had first glimpsed it. Her heart leaped into her throat as she somehow managed to stand. She ran from both specter and fiend, but still weak and unsteady, slipped on a patch of wet moss and fell back to the ground. Footsteps and the rustle of robes told Holly the apparition was coming for her. She scampered forward, somehow gaining her feet again, but something whipped her legs out from underneath her and she landed flat on her back. Something cracked—her mandolin, which she had taken up just before . . . just before . . .

How did I get here?

She struggled to scream, but her breath had fled from her

lungs. As she struggled to recover, coarse, powerful fingers ran through her hair, tightening about the short tresses. Sharp pain stabbed into her scalp as she was hoisted up bodily from the ground. This time, she did cry out. She hung from the specter's grasp, her feet dangling in midair while it turned her slowly one way and then the other. Another hand shot out from the black robes, and Holly glimpsed, for only a moment, mottled, gray-black fingers covered in scales and tipped with claws. One of the claws scratched across Holly's forehead, and she cried out as it cut a line in her skin. She flailed and kicked at the monster holding her fast, as blood welled from the cut. Then the scale-handed creature slapped something mud-like and sticky onto her forehead, and Holly screamed in pain. It felt as if the flesh around her skull disintegrated away.

The hand holding Holly prisoner at last let go, and she toppled to the ground. The burning remained, though, and thinking nothing of the damage the substance's contact might do to her bare hands, she flailed wildly at her forehead, wiping it away. Her hands remained free of pain, and soon the burning lessened from her forehead as she scraped the last of it from her palms. She collapsed to her side, tears streaming from her eyes as she lay curled up, hoping the fiends forgot her and left.

"Her blood is pure," the robed being said, the voice a hiss. "You have done well, my minion."

The yellow-eyed creature bowed its head in acknowledgement.

"Return to your brethren," the reptilian voice said. "Leave the girl to me."

Though Holly heard nothing of the beast's departure, she knew it was gone.

Hot breath assailed the bard then, as clawed fingers wrapped about her throat. Holly was lifted to her feet, her chin thrust upward so she looked directly into the dark aperture of the specter's cowl. A serpent's tongue flicked out from the darkness.

"Know that I am a powerful witch. To trifle with me is to risk certain death."

A scaled hand grabbed hold of each of Holly's wrists and held them together while the witch bound them with a cord. Holly winced in pain as the knot was pulled tight.

"My slaves have taken you far from your friends this night, but we travel farther still."

The witch stepped back and drew the cord out, intent on pulling Holly along like an animal.

"Who—what are you?" Holly screamed at the witch, despite the rawness of her throat. "What do you want with me?" It was a struggle to keep from crying.

"Time enough for talk later," the witch said. She looked heavenward for a moment. "Now, time is short. Come, we must be away. Come!" She tugged on the cord, nearly jerking Holly to her knees. As the witch continued forward and the length of cord separating them grew taut once more, Holly dug her feet in and tried to hold her ground. It was a futile effort. Either the witch was too strong or Holly too weak. Left with no other choice but to follow, Holly stumbled after the witch. Together, they disappeared into the forest.

CHAPTER TWELVE

PATROLLERS
OF THE HALL

JERRICK AND THE OTHERS FOLLOWED S'nar for hours as he flapped his way through the dark, mist-enshrouded forest. Whenever the owl paused long enough for them to catch up, Murik traded indecipherable croons and clicks with him. Satisfied with their exchange, the sorcerer, who remained the most comfortable having S'nar as their guide, then sent the owl forward once more. Jerrick took note of every tree and rock they passed, creating a mental map of their route as they went. They had neither been led astray nor passed through the same section of forest more than once. For all of his own reservations about S'nar, it seemed the owl was leading them *somewhere*.

Jerrick remained on the lookout for signs of either Holly's or her abductors' passing. There were none, though. He found his lack of success disconcerting, for he was a skilled tracker. Only great natural ability or magic had hopes of foiling him so effectively for this long. Jerrick was still tired, though, his skills dulled. The poison might be gone from his system thanks to Murik's magic, but some of its effects still lingered. There were times when, if he moved too quickly, his head swam and he felt as if he might lose his balance. Other times, he just felt sick. He told the others nothing of these aftereffects lest they think to leave him behind. Jerrick knew he shared in the blame both Kayra and Murik had claimed for themselves. The truth was he felt responsible for not just Holly but all of them, even Murik, who was his superior in many ways, including age, wisdom, knowledge, and—as Jerrick possessed none of his own— magic. But the Simarron was Jerrick's home. In some strange way, despite their current predicament, he felt as if he were their host. This feeling extended even more so to Holly, who he knew was the most ill-equipped of all of them. It did no good to try to lay blame at Kayra's feet for bringing Holly along in the first place. The girl was in trouble, her life in danger. Jerrick was a patroller; protecting was his business. It didn't matter that he had walked away from that life, for it remained a part of him. No such thing as an ex-patroller, many of them were fond of saying.

Behind him, Aurum clopped across a series of rocks while Kayra questioned Murik on their progress. The eslar communicated the knight's inquiry to S'nar, who replied, through Murik, that they were close.

But close to what?

They had no idea what the fiends had planned for Holly, or how long they had to reach her. S'nar had spoken of "others" who had gone to their doom. Who else could the owl have referred to besides the patrollers? If S'nar's recounting, as told through Murik, held truth, Evar had also gone down this road. The Eldest of the Elders was the reason Jerrick had returned to the Hall. Perhaps not the only reason, he mused, for Jerrick had other friends and acquaintances here he looked forward to seeing again. But Evar's counsel was, first and foremost, the reason he'd left Rell. Years ago, Evar had freed Jerrick of his duties and given him his blessing to leave the Hall. Evar had been the best of friends, a father figure to him in many ways, and Jerrick had thought to return to the Hall to seek out his wisdom. If, somehow, Evar was still alive, he swore to do everything possible to help him. Jerrick's thoughts continued to preoccupy him until S'nar swooped onto a low-hanging branch and refused to go any farther.

"It appears we have arrived," Murik said.

Though he did his best to peer through the dark and mist, Jerrick saw nothing to distinguish this part of the forest from any other. Murik let the light from his staff fade as he thanked S'nar for his service. S'nar, making no pretense of his fright at what lay ahead, ruffled his feathers and hooted a response.

Keeping his voice low, Jerrick said, "I'm going to scout ahead to see what's about. If I see either the creatures or Holly, I'll return—"

"I think not," Kayra said. "We tried that once already, and look where it got you. I say we stay together."

"I don't think—"

"I must concur with Kayra," Murik said. "The creatures have already demonstrated an abnormal amount of stealth and ferocity, and though we remain unsure of their exact disposition, we do know they outnumber us. We should remain together."

Jerrick weighed their argument, finally shrugging his acceptance. "You'd best leave your horse behind, then. You're going to be loud enough walking around in that armor of yours."

Kayra hesitated as she considered the request. But then, in agreement, she dismounted, gathering her helmet and shield before giving Aurum a slight pat on the rump. The horse moved off and soon stopped. "When we find the creatures," Kayra said, "Murik and I will distract them. Jerrick, you locate Holly. When you have her, signal to us and we will withdraw. This plan relies on quick execution. As the sorcerer has pointed out, we will no doubt find ourselves outnumbered." Kayra looked at Jerrick. "How do you feel?"

"I'm fine."

Jerrick met Kayra's stare for a moment. Her message was clear to him: *you had better be.*

"Our first and only priority," Kayra said, "is Holly. Do what needs to be done to ensure her safe recovery. Murik, once we find them, we'll need light."

"I shall do what I can," Murik said. "But be warned: the same light which allows us to see will shine like a beacon to our enemies."

"Noted," Kayra said. "Now, let's go."

Jerrick, bow held ready, took the lead. Ash, silent as a shadow, padded at his side. Kayra—Jerrick clenched his jaw but said nothing about the audible creaks and groans her armor made—followed with her sword in one hand and her kite shield in the other. Murik brought up the rear.

Jerrick picked the best path possible, avoiding beds of dry, crinkled leaves and roots threatening to trip the more careless of them. The trees and shrubbery here were as tainted as elsewhere. The still air, heavy with fog and mist, obscured their scent, else the first of the creatures Jerrick saw might have detected his and the others' presence immediately. As it was, the creature had no inkling they approached as it crouched low to the ground, its back to them. Almost a shadow lost in the mist, it was alone. Long, wild tufts of dark hair shot out from its head in all directions, and its back was covered in dried mud and bristled, animal-like fur. Lean arms were folded at its sides. Its hands worked at something in front of it. It wore no clothes or armor, nor did it appear to possess any weapons. Thinking of the cuts on his face, Jerrick realized these creatures had no need of weapons.

The others stopped behind Jerrick. Despite the noise of Kayra's armor, the fiend was so preoccupied with its chore it remained unaware of their presence. Jerrick ventured a quick glance over his shoulder. Though Murik had dropped into a crouch, Kayra obstinately remained standing. Murik held one arm around Ash, who seemed nervous as he sniffed at the air.

Returning his attention to the creature, Jerrick pulled back his bowstring and took careful aim. Blinking away a moment of dizziness brought about by the last lingering effects of the poison, he let the arrow fly. The missile struck true, hitting the creature square in the back of the neck and sending its body to the ground with a muffled thud.

Jerrick motioned for the others to follow him as he approached the felled creature. Rolling it over with his boot, he got his first good look at one of the things. It was a lanky beast with gaunt arms and legs, a thin neck, and long, narrow fingers tipped with blackened claws. Its eyes and mouth were wide-open, its stiffening face reflecting the shock and surprise it must have felt when Jerrick's arrow had pierced its throat. There was a distinct unwashed odor about the thing, and its body was covered in tufts of hair clumped together by dried mud. In one hand it clenched a rock soiled with brown plant juice. The creature had been in the process of mashing roots. Surprised by its level of domestication, Jerrick still noted the wildness in the creature's unnatural, straw-colored eyes, in its lack of clothing, and in its wild hair and blackened teeth. He shuddered with distaste. "Let's get moving."

Kayra brushed past Jerrick and took the lead. Jerrick waited for both Murik and Ash to pass before he joined them. As he moved to follow, a glint of metal at one of the felled creature's fingers caught his eye. Jerrick bent and lifted its hand. Filth and mud were caked onto its skin, caught between the fingers so the object—a ring—was hardly visible. Jerrick wiped some of the muck off, revealing a simple gold band etched with the familiar oak-tree sigil of the Simarron patrollers. A ring bearing such a mark was given to newly promoted recruits once indoctrinated into the patroller fold. There was no way to know which patroller the thing had taken it from, nor exactly how the fiend had come to possess it. Jerrick was reasonably sure the patroller to whom it belonged had not simply handed it over, though. Jerrick removed the ring from the creature's finger and slipped it into his belt pouch.

Kayra spotted the next of the creatures, the knight having enough sense to duck behind the thick trunk of a nearby oak before she was spotted. The others did likewise, Murik finding a place behind another tree with Ash, while Jerrick went down to a crouch behind some leafless shrubs. Raising his head above the top edge of his hiding place, Jerrick peered through the mist. His eyes went wide as, all around them, yellow eyes lit up the gray night.

Jerrick cursed himself for a fool. They were surrounded.

"By Chaeick's bloody axe!"

Nohr smashed a balled-up fist down upon one of the few chairs remaining intact in the Great Room of the Hall. The high-backed seat fell to splintered pieces at the impact.

"The devils got them! Got them all!"

Skave shared in both Nohr's disappointment and his anger, for they had reached the Hall only to find it empty except for the presence of two donkeys in the stables.

"The devils did their work too well," Skave said in confirmation, as he wrought his own destruction on some of the Hall's furniture. "They've already been taken. Not just the girl but, as you said, all of them."

Nohr crushed another chair, took a few great breaths, then asked, "What we gonna do now?" When Skave did not answer, he leaned his great warhammer against the wall, swung the beer keg from his back, and, lifting it high, took a long draft. He restoppered it, then wiped his mouth with the back of his arm and emitted a belch which echoed from the chamber's high walls.

Skave walked about the chamber, studying the packs and equipment their prey had left behind. The witch had wanted the girl to fall under her devils' spell. For what purpose, Skave cared little. But the others—the sorcerer, the knight, and the patroller—were supposed to have been left behind for him and Nohr to deal with. Skave felt betrayed. But why had the witch sent them all of this way for nothing? What did she hope to gain by tricking them?

Nohr placed his warhammer and keg upon one of the long tables and, not seeing a chair large enough for his great bulk, satisfied himself by leaning against the wall. "I say we go back to Gral and forget all about knights and patrollers."

Skave held up a gloved finger. "Wait." He moved to the great hearth and sifted through the things strewn upon the floor there. Someone had left in haste. But not so fast they'd left everything behind. He grabbed one of the packs, taking in its contents with a glance. "Their weapons and armor are gone. Some rations remain." He waved his hand over the intruders' belongings. "But not many."

Nohr narrowed his brow at the haurek. "So?"

"Perhaps the devils did not take all of them after all."

Nohr's head tilted sideways, his ear—the one not missing the top half—arched forward. "Huh?"

Skave groaned in frustration. "The girl was supposed to be taken, right? She was. When the others discovered her missing, perhaps they decided to follow, to try and save her." Skave moved toward the great doors, talking all the while, but now more to himself than Nohr. "The devils worked their hoodoo on the girl, who rose and left the chamber. The others woke. Perhaps the door creaked or some such thing. Seeing their friend gone, they went outside to investigate."

Skave walked outside and down the porch steps. Behind him, Nohr hoisted his keg to his back, grabbed his hammer, and followed.

"These prints here are small, a woman's," Skave said, looking at the ground now. "She wore boots and walked with an even stride. But these . . ." Skave crouched low, cursing his own stupidity as his eyes passed over his and Nohr's boot prints. He only hoped enough evidence remained. Then he saw it. A single, barefoot print, indented deep in the soil. Skave ran a gloved finger lightly across the deep indentation of the heel, across the rising sole, then into the crevasse created by the toes.

169

The person had been running, and the size, while not petite, was too small for a man.

The knight!

Skave knew it was no other. He followed the prints as they led away from the Hall and toward the forest. Some were trod upon by booted feet going both the same and opposite directions. The stalker, focusing on the knight's footprints for the time being, saw they went both away from and toward the Hall. He followed them to the wall of trees and, motioning for Nohr to stay put, crept forward. He walked a few more steps and saw where the barefoot and booted prints diverged. He smiled knowingly, then returned to the patio, where the gaugath remained.

"The knight pursued her friend and the devils into the forest. She is either very brave or very stupid. She came back, though, empty-handed, at which time her friends joined her. They provisioned themselves with food, weapons, and armor. The knight put something on her feet." Skave laughed. "Then they set out together."

"You think we can find them?" Nohr asked.

Skave laughed again. "Of course! Their tracks are as plain as day, and they couldn't have gotten far. If we hurry . . ."

Nohr, needing no further prompting, gestured for the stalker to lead the way. Skave obliged, and the two set off in pursuit.

Jerrick rose, not caring that he put himself in full view as he pulled his bowstring as far as his strength allowed. He let fly one arrow and then another, the familiar swish of their flight filling his ears as each found their mark and two of the creatures fell dead. Meanwhile, Murik also stepped out from his place of concealment as globes of light too numerous to count sprang forth from the sorcerer's hands and moved upward in all directions. Then, one by one, each of the globes exploded into a luminosity so bright it was as if the morning sun had risen. The extreme change from misted shadow to near daylight momentarily blinded Jerrick, but it did worse to the creatures, who recoiled from it as if in pain.

Pausing only a moment for his eyes to adjust, Jerrick shouldered his bow, then drew his sword and hunting knife. He spotted a number of newly formed gaps where before a solid line of yellow eyes had been, and he wasted no time in exploiting one of them. As he plunged forward, he heard Kayra issue a challenge.

Two of the fiends leaped in front of Jerrick. There was time only for a quick slash with his sword. He heard a wail of pain as his blade bit, then nothing as he was past them and moving away. Another of the creatures, this one armed with a woodsman's axe, leaped at Jerrick. The patroller ducked beneath the axe's blade and, his desire to locate Holly overriding all else, launched himself forward. He thought he might have fought his way clear of the worst of them, but the unblinking eyes all around squashed such hopes. His only chance of finding Holly had been to locate her before all hell had broken loose. Now, Jerrick knew they'd be lucky to get out alive themselves.

Despite the sense of hopelessness rising within him, Jerrick kept up the search. Looking in all directions as he ran, he saw the eyes closing in around him. Then, something latched on to his shoulders and he was pulled backward. Unbalanced, he fell. But instead of damp earth, he felt the firmness of muscle and bone as the mephitic smell of unwashed body odor threatened to overcome his senses. Realizing he had fallen onto one of the fiends, Jerrick launched an elbow at it, the creature's grasp loosening as the patroller rolled away. He whipped his sword around to keep it at bay while he scrambled to his feet. Though the fiend lunged at him, Jerrick's sword warned it back as it retreated beyond the weapon's range.

The naked creature was much like the others, though taller, limbs a bit more lanky, and body more sallow skin than hair. Its primal eyes possessed the same wildness, though, with lips curled into a snarl as it circled Jerrick. The creature kept clawed hands extended from its sides, its fingers curled and claws pointed at him. Then it lunged again. Jerrick swung low with his sword, then followed with a backhanded slice of his knife. His sword hit nothing. But the knife slashed into the beast's arm. Far from pressing the attack or even delivering a counter, the creature retreated, holding its wounded arm close to its body as it flashed Jerrick a hurt look, as if the patroller had done something wrong. For just an instant, the madness left its eyes, and something in them looked—impossible as it was—familiar.

It can't be . . .

As the chaos continued all around him, Jerrick examined the creature more closely, looking past the unnaturally colored skin, the wild hair, and the madness already returning to its eyes.

"Evar?"

Impossible.

The creature lunged again. This time Jerrick sidestepped the attack and brought the hilt of his sword down hard on the back of its head. The creature slumped to the ground, unconscious. Jerrick crouched next to it, peering about through the wizard's light for any others. Behind him, he heard Ash barking and Murik working his magic. Jerrick returned his knife to his sheath and, while he kept one eye on the other fiends, parted the hair covering the face of the unconscious one. He tried to imagine its appearance without the sallow skin and caked-on dirt. The line of the jaw, the bridge of the nose . . .

How can this be?

With none of the sense of triumph he had expected, Jerrick realized as he looked upon the face of his mentor and friend that he had discovered the fate of the missing patrollers.

Everything fell into place then. The patrollers were not dead, but *changed* into something horrible. And he had slain with his own hands more of them than he cared to think on. If only I had known. But he hadn't. He thought of the patroller ring stowed away in his pouch. Somehow, he had been unable to put two and two together. But it was such an impossible thought that even now he struggled to find some other explanation. There wasn't one, though. His eyes and his instincts did not betray him. Evar and the other patrollers had been made into devils.

Jerrick wrapped his cloak around Evar's naked form and hefted the bundle over his shoulder. He was never going to find Holly in all of this. For all he knew, she was already one of them, something which made locating her all the more difficult. Jerrick and the others needed to leave, now, before more of the creatures—the patrollers—were killed. Jerrick retreated back whence he had come, finding the way clear. He reached the others shortly.

"Time to go!"

Kayra slashed into one of the patrollers-turned-fiends, disemboweling it before Jerrick could stop her. It grabbed at its gut for a moment, then fell. The moment Kayra saw the body slumped over Jerrick's shoulder, she fell into line beside him.

One of Murik's hands burned with crimson flames. The other held his staff, which burned with fire of its own. All around him, bodies and the lowermost branches of the surrounding trees were charred and blackened. The eslar held a dozen of the patroller-fiends at bay.

"Do not harm them!" Jerrick shouted.

Murik flashed him a quizzical look, then he said, "Go! I shall cover our retreat!"

Kayra and Ash, whom Jerrick kicked as he passed to force him to join the retreat, withdrew. Jerrick glanced over his shoulder and saw Murik backing away. Then, with one last burst of flame, which was more warning than anything else, the sorcerer ran to join them.

One of the patroller-fiends jumped out in front of the knight, who moved to engage it. Jerrick shouldered past Kayra, knocking her sword astray. Then he felled the patroller-fiend— a woman with long, streaming hair—with a glance from his sword's hilt.

"What are you doing?" Kayra asked.

"Leave her! Let's go," Jerrick shouted over his shoulder.

Their retreat came to a dead stop as more of the creatures emerged ahead of them.

"It seems we are again surrounded," Murik said.

Jerrick watched as the patrollers-turned-fiends drew closer, tightening the noose about them. Murik's magical flame had extinguished. The sorcerer looked haggard: his body was bent, his shoulders slumped, and even the weight of his staff looked too much for him. The globes of light he had summoned earlier faded rapidly now, and already the area plunged back into mist-enshrouded darkness. Despite the energy his spellcasting had drained from him, though, something in Murik's eyes told Jerrick he was prepared to summon his magic once more rather than surrender to their adversaries. Next to Jerrick, Kayra lifted her sword. Her face remained unreadable behind the cover of her helmet. The creatures were coming now. Jerrick had to stop the others before any more of the patrollers were killed.

"Don't harm them!"

"What?" Kayra said. "They killed the patrollers! They're about to do the same to us!"

"They didn't kill the patrollers! They *are* the patrollers!"

Jerrick missed whatever reaction Murik and Kayra displayed, as the patroller-fiends closed in on them. There was a sensation of warmth as Murik brought his magical fire back to life. At his other side, Kayra held sword and shield ready. Ash growled from somewhere behind him. Frantic, Jerrick tried to think of some way to prevent the continued bloodshed. There was no reasoning with the patrollers-turned-fiends. Yet Jerrick refused to raise his sword against them.

But then the great, withered oaks all around them started to shake and quiver, the few remaining leaves upon their branches falling like rain from the sky. The rattling gave the patroller-fiends pause. They started to back away, but it was too late as the sickened oaks came to life. Branches, bent and twisted, reached out for them. Driven into a panicked frenzy, the patroller-fiends bolted in all directions. Only some managed to get away. The rest were lifted up, grasped by limbs, torsos, and necks, and held tight. Though they squirmed and clawed away at the bark-covered appendages, there was no freeing themselves.

A single figure walked amidst that twisted carnage. Wrapped in a hooded brown cloak, the newcomer moved with urgency. "The trees are weak," the stranger said, "and will only hold them for so long. Best you come with me." The voice was feminine, even-toned, and calm. She gave them no time to respond as she turned and, without waiting to see if they followed, walked back the direction she had come. Left with few other choices, they followed.

She led them through the tangle of trees and patroller-fiends unscathed, offering no opportunities for explanations or conversation as they left the lair behind. Traveling without pause, they traversed many miles before the woman finally stopped them within a secluded thicket.

"We will rest here," she said, turning. "But only for a moment." She started to move off, then stopped. "I believe others of your group await you."

As if on cue, Aurum pushed his way through the thick bushes and pranced right up to Kayra. Perched on the pommel of his saddle was S'nar. The knight, shooing the owl away, took Aurum's head in her hands, rubbing his nose in greeting before she turned her attention toward Jerrick and his sleeping burden.

Jerrick saw the expectant look in the woman's eyes as he set his old-friend-who-was-not-Holly down. Steeling his nerves, Jerrick prepared himself for the coming confrontation.

It only took Kayra a moment to realize the person they had rescued was not who she expected. Throwing her helmet to the ground, she made no effort to control her anger. "Who is this, and where is Holly?"

Fearing too much heat from the battle remained in the woman, Jerrick chose his words carefully. "This is Evar, a friend. I never saw Holly."

Kayra's sword was out in a flash, its point directed at Jerrick's chest.

"Tell me why you brought that thing here and not Holly, and do it quickly."

Her lips barely moved as she spoke, and Jerrick watched her jaw quiver as she fought to contain herself.

"When I recognized Evar—"

"Damn you, patroller!" Kayra inched her blade closer. "Holly is *my* responsibility. You were supposed to retrieve *her*, not this *thing*!"

"He is no 'thing.'" While uncomfortable staring down the length of Kayra's blade, Jerrick was also losing patience. "He is Evar, Eldest of the Elders."

"I don't give a damn who he is! You should have—"

"Enough!"

Murik appeared next to them. With a gesture, the point of Kayra's sword fell to the ground like a leaden weight. The sudden motion nearly ripped the sword from Kayra's grasp, but she managed to hold fast to the hilt, but only barely. Through clenched teeth, she said, "Release—my—sword—wizard!"

Murik stepped back and crossed his arms. "Perhaps when you've come to your senses."

Try though she might, Kayra could not lift the sword's point from the ground. As her brow tensed with exertion, even her grasp on the hilt began to falter. Then, the weight finally too much, she let go. The weapon hit the ground with a thump.

"Jerrick could not have brought your friend back to you," their mysterious benefactor said, "for your friend is no longer with the monsters."

"How do you know that?" Kayra asked. "Who are you?"

The woman threw back the hood of her cloak, revealing dainty features, ivory skin, and, most striking of all, hair and eyes the color of dark emeralds. "My name is Aliah Starbough."

CHAPTER THIRTEEN

THE CIRCLE

THE WITCH LED HOLLY ALONG a dark, circuitous path neither visible nor marked. Though the way was littered with spidery outcroppings of roots and clumps of jagged rock, the witch never once hesitated, her rapid pace both deliberate and unrelenting. Holly found the going difficult; the one and only time she said so, the witch threatened to rip her tongue out if she spoke again. Holly decided to remain silent after that.

Not long into their journey, the weariness of the night's events caught up to Holly. Muscles ached, her head swooned, and she felt herself succumbing to an overwhelming need for sleep. Thereafter, it was all she could do to keep from falling to her knees as the witch forced her onward by way of the rope between them. Keeping the line from growing taut became a constant struggle. When it did, Holly was punished with a swift tug which jolted her from her fatigue-induced trance and, more often than not, catapulted her to her knees. She regained her feet each time, though, refusing to allow the witch to drag her through the woods like a laden sack.

As the night wore on, the mist thinned before them, and Holly saw pinpoints of stars shining above. They were dim in comparison to the moon, though, which shone near full now, only the smallest sliver remaining dark. The forest landscape changed from the flat terrain Holly had grown familiar with into shallow, undulating hills which formed small valleys with each rise and fall. The two descended into one of these shallow valleys, picking their way through shrubs and thorny bushes that snagged and tore Holly's clothing at every step. The witch, for all her size and voluminous robes, passed through unobstructed, the foliage seeming to shrink from her person.

Holly lost track of time as the witch forced her deeper and deeper into this new part of the Simarron. Eyelids drooped of their own accord, but fear of the witch and sharp pricks from the bushes kept her awake. Finally, when the bard's bare hands, forearms, and face bled from a score of small cuts and she felt as if she might finally collapse from exhaustion, the witch stopped.

Holly's concentration was fixed on the ground before her, and so at first she did not see the great, gaping maw cut into the earth before them. When she did see it, she could look nowhere else. Blacker than blackest night, the dark pit took hold of her, drawing her inside. A chill went down her spine and her knees, of a sudden, felt weak. Holly knew if the rope did not bind her fast to the witch, she would have already turned and fled. Looking from dark pit to witch, Holly asked in a voice which sounded small even to her own ears, "What is this place?"

The great shape of the witch, her face remaining hidden within the darkness of her cowl, turned to her. Holly shrank back in fear, remembering her abductor's threat. She wanted very much to keep her tongue.

"You are a bard, yes?"

Holly's hand went to the neck of her mandolin, which miraculously had remained with her throughout the night's ordeal. She nodded a response.

"Then you shall no doubt appreciate this place, for it is steeped in history." The witch turned to face the pit once more. "It is a dark and evil history, but history nonetheless."

There was something there in that pit, pulling at Holly, hungering for her. The feeling made her tremble.

"Ah, you feel it, don't you?"

Holly wanted to ask what "it" was, but her mouth refused to form the words.

"As long as one remains at a distance," the witch said, "its effects are subtle. Ordinarily, it might take weeks to feel. But this close, for such a small, paltry girl . . ."

Nausea welled up from the pit of Holly's stomach, boiling

over into her throat and mouth, and she clenched her jaw to keep from retching. Despite the chill air, sweat seeped from her pores and her head swam. Her knees swayed and, unable to maintain her balance any longer, she collapsed to the ground. The forest around her spun. From somewhere far off, she heard the sound of the witch's hissing laughter.

"It is too much for you, all of it hitting you at once." She laughed again. "Only give it time, and you shall grow more accustomed to its foulness."

Holly curled up on her side, her entire body awash in feebleness as she drew her knees close. "Let me go." Tears fell from her eyes unchecked. "Please, let me go." She was never meant for this. She should be home in Scilya, protected behind city walls, where others could keep her safe. She was neither knight nor sorcerer nor patroller. She was just a small girl who had foolishly harbored grand, romantic delusions of heroes, and who had mistakenly thought that, perhaps, she might be one, too.

"Get up, girl," the witch said, waiting a moment for Holly to rise. When she did not, the witch said again, "Get up!" Jerking the rope hard, the witch sent Holly sprawling forward. Before the witch pulled again, Holly fumbled to her knees and, still sobbing, rose.

The witch moved closer. Holly thought to pull away, but there was no fight left in her.

"Wear this."

The witch held out a simple talisman, a medallion woven of grass forming two concentric circles hanging from a leather string. Holly took it without thinking, placing it over her head as the witch so motioned.

"It shall protect you from the magic I have cast over this place."

Then, saying nothing more, the witch stepped into the dark pit. Holly hoped—prayed—she disappeared as if stepping over a cliff. To her disappointment, the witch did not. Instead, as the witch took each successive step, she descended farther into the earth, until nothing remained of her. As the rope separating them began to grow taut, Holly knew it was her turn.

She stumbled forward until she stood at the pit's edge. The dark hole lay at the base of a tor whose slopes were covered by a jumble of rocks and loose, sandy soil. Oaks all around it were like simulacra of death, blackened and charred as if burned by fire, though no ash littered the ground. Holly took one last look at the night sky, then she stepped over the threshold and into the hole. Right away, she found solid ground underfoot, which sloped downward the farther she walked. Then, her head sank below the line of the earth and everything turned to black.

The witch did something, and torches embedded in the walls to either side of them flared to life. Holly jumped as one very near her head lit up in a shower of sparks, then she watched as more and more lit up a long, narrow corridor descending deeper into the earth. The walls and floor of the passage were callused limestone, and a fine layer of dust covered all. The witch, who had not halted her progress even to ignite the torches, continued moving forward. Holly followed in silence.

They descended for only minutes before the passage evened out. The air grew warm and stale, and then they were entering a chamber so vast Holly found herself taken aback with awe at the sight of it despite her weariness. Lit by a greenish glow, the chamber was so enormous the opposite wall—if there even was one—lay beyond the range of her vision. The ceiling rose high and irregular before also disappearing. Before them, torches set at eye level marked a byway meandering through a forest of stalagmites. Somewhere in the distance, Holly heard the echo of a drip. Though the air here was cooler than it had been while descending, it remained stagnant and smelled of staleness.

The witch tugged the rope, jerking Holly from her inspection, as she led them down the torch-marked trail. Turning this way and that, Holly became lost almost immediately as stalagmites twice her height enveloped them. Every booted step sent a litany of echoes bouncing off the cavern walls, and she found herself casting glances over her shoulder, half expecting some disturbed cave creature to swoop down and snatch her away. Then, there was a break in the limestone formations, and Holly saw something she was sure was not natural.

The torches ended at a series of steps carved into the cavern floor. The steps encircled a large, raised platform. At the top of the platform, Holly saw more stalagmites. The witch went right up to the stairs and began climbing. As Holly mounted each step behind her, the feeling of sickness and nausea intensified. Whatever was causing her unease lay close. When they had climbed the last of the steps, Holly saw the pool.

Filled nearly to the brim with a turbid liquid which seethed and boiled, it took up most of the dais. Surrounding it were four gray obelisks, ten foot statues Holly had earlier mistaken for stalagmites, which were carved to resemble hooded sorcerers. They faced one another across the bubbling pool, arms outstretched with palms held away as if each pushed against something unseen and, through their concerted effort, contained. Though the steam wafting from the surface gave Holly the impression the liquid was hot, she felt no heat emanating from the pool. Craning her neck upward, Holly just saw pinpricks of stars shining through a wide, slanted shaft which extended all the way to the outside.

"Think of the stories you could tell of this place, the songs you could write," the witch said. "A pity you shall not live to do so, eh?"

Holly had dried her tears on the way down the passage. Now, acceptance of her predicament lent her an odd sense of courage. Like a person drowning, she felt there was nothing worse which could happen to her, and so she asked the witch directly, "What do you mean? What are you going to do to me?"

The witch did not answer as she led Holly around the edge of the pool to a set of manacles fastened to the pool's stonework. She forced Holly to sit with her back to the pool's edge, then fastened one manacle about each of her wrists. The witch then reached into her robe and pulled out a vial filled with a gray liquid. She unstoppered the cork and, without a word, grabbed Holly's throat and forced her head back.

Squeezing her cheeks with long, claw-tipped fingers, she forced Holly's jaw open, poured the contents of the vial into her mouth, then closed her lips, holding her until satisfied the potion had been swallowed.

Though Holly struggled every step of the way, she was physically exhausted and too weak to offer significant resistance. The liquid felt cool as it filled her mouth and throat, but the taste was so awful that, as soon as the witch released her grip, she was overcome by a fit of choking.

"Retch it back up," the witch said, "and I'll only pour more down your throat." The witch started to shuffle off, but stopped after a few steps. Speaking from over her shoulder, she said, "Touch the pool's surface at your own peril." Offering nothing more, she descended just to the topmost step, then turned and fell to her knees. Lifting both hands to the cowl which had obscured her visage since the first moments Holly had looked upon her, the witch pulled it back in one quick motion.

Holly had spent the better part of the night's journey pondering the identity of the witch, and so it surprised her little to discover she was sitheri, that race of reptilians who made their homes in the Grimmere Swamp. Her great size and serpentine voice had been the first clues Holly had gathered. But even with these indicators, something had remained missing. Sitheri possessed great, broad tails that could break a man's legs with the force of their sweep. Holly, even now, failed to see such an appendage sprouting from the witch's posterior. There was, however, no doubt as to what race she belonged. Holly had seen sitheri before in Scilya and elsewhere, but those had always been males, who often left their broods to prove their worth in a barbaric ritual of scalp collecting. Despite her gender, this sitheri was as large as any of those others. Her face was a short, snake-like snout with nostril holes at the tips. Teeth both foul and bent lined her jaw, and her eyes were dark and beady. Jagged ridges ran up from her neck and along either side of her head. Her scales were mottled and gray, with pieces hanging like dried skin from her cheeks and neck.

The witch held an instrument resembling a writing quill. As she went to work with it, Holly heard deep scratching noises, and she realized the sitheri witch was not so much writing as etching into the stone itself. Looking at the dais's edge, she noticed for the first time the presence of engravings. They were strange symbols the bard had never seen before.

Noise from the witch's work became hypnotic. Though Holly resisted, she found herself dozing off. The echo of footfalls scraping across the cavern floor woke her an indeterminate amount of time later. Blinking away sleep, she looked for the source of the noise and spotted a grekkel emerging from the entry passage. The goblin lurched forward on all fours, muttering something unintelligible to itself. It seemed not to have noticed Holly at first. When it did, its expression turned to one of pure delight. Black lips curled back into a devilish grin, pointed ears perked, and its curled chin unfurled to stick out like the blade of a dagger as it scampered toward her. As it drew closer, she saw in greater detail its claws and teeth. Then the grekkel was in front of her, leaning so close it almost pressed its face against hers. The creature's tongue shot out, and Holly turned her face away, disgusted.

"Ah, a tasty human," it said.

As she felt its tongue slide along her cheek, revulsion transformed into anger. Balling her hand into a fist, Holly smacked the grekkel's pointy-chinned face square on. The goblin flew back through the air, landing on its feet just at the edge of the dais where its momentum promptly toppled it over the side. A loud shriek punctuated each impact as its gangly body tumbled end over end all the way to the bottom. Stunned but angry, the grekkel came charging back up the stairs, screeching all the way.

"Leave her, Speck!" the witch screamed from the other side of the dais. "She is not for eating!"

Speck slowed, and then stopped. His teeth remained bared at Holly, and she saw venom in his eyes. "Once my mistress is done with you," it said to her, "you shall be a tasty morsel indeed." Speck took a moment to spit in Holly's direction before joining the witch.

When Speck stood at her feet, it said, "I bring that which you have asked for, O Mighty Harbinger of Death, O Patroller Slayer, O Ruler of the Simarron, O—"

"Just give it to me, you insipid little creature!" the witch hissed.

Speck jumped back in surprise. It took him a moment to regain his composure. When he did, he held out a hand to her and something unseen passed between them.

"You have done well, my slave. Now, return to my house and there await my return."

Speck bowed, shooting one last look at Holly—a look that promised retribution—before he left the chamber. The witch returned to her task, and Holly was wondering if she might fall asleep again when the witch spoke.

"Speck is an annoying little creature, but he serves me well."

It took a moment for Holly to realize the witch spoke to her. Once she did, she was unsure how to respond. Sleep had returned some of her senses to her, though, and she let her inquisitive nature guide her. She needed to know what the witch was doing and, more importantly, what she planned. If there was any chance at all of getting out of this alive, she needed to gather as much information as possible.

"What are you doing?" The question sounded too direct, and Holly was sure the witch meant to ignore her. She was surprised when the witch answered.

"I create a Circle of Power. A Witch's Circle." The sitheri did not look up from her work as she spoke.

"A means by which you can channel power, amplify your spells."

The witch did look up then, but only for a moment. "You are familiar with the ways of witchcraft?"

Holly shrugged. "Only what I know from stories." The bard searched her mind. "In 'The Witch of Ekbar,' an old woman— a witch—creates a Circle, then uses it to cast a charm over all the children of Ekbar. Without the Circle, her spell might not have worked, nor been so effective."

The witch, having successfully created another of the strange symbols, moved along the circumference of the dais to create the next. "This witch . . . What did she do with the children?"

Holly swallowed. "She led most of them over a cliff. They were so ensnared by her magic, they never even saw the edge."

"And those she did not lead over the cliff?"

"She took them deep into the forest and . . . ate them."

The witch hissed a laugh. "Why did she do this thing to the children of Ekbar?"

"Because she wanted to live in their town, but their parents drove her out with pitchforks and threats. She knew a burning stake awaited her if she ever returned."

The witch remained silent, her full concentration upon her work for a time. Then, she picked up the conversation as if there had been no pause at all. "Scorned and feared." She shook her head, and her serpentine tongue flicked out for a moment. "What else could this witch have done? If only the citizens of Ekbar had opened their homes to her."

"Perhaps the witch was the one who should have been friendlier," Holly said, "and not sacrificed innocent children just to satisfy her need for revenge."

The witch shrugged, then held up her quill and said, "'The punishment of the parents shall be handed down to their children.' Such goes the old witch adage."

"That still didn't give her the right to do what she did."

The witch shrugged again, then returned to her etchings. Holly watched her for a time, but after a short while, felt herself succumbing to sleep once more.

A sharp prick at her neck woke her some time later. Opening her eyes, she discovered the witch hunched over her, a dagger held to her throat. Holly tried to back away, the rattle of the chains reminding her of her confinement. The witch leaned closer.

"You will be quiet now, else I will cut out your tongue. Not a sound!" She swiped the air with the dagger for emphasis before concealing it beneath her robe.

Holly breathed a sigh of relief as the witch moved away. But then the sitheri turned, leaning over her and reaching out. Holly shrank back, fearing the witch had changed her mind about cutting out her tongue, but the witch was only reaching for Holly's mandolin, which she took hold of and unceremoniously smashed on the pool's edge. Already damaged from when Holly had fallen on it, a single impact was all it took to finish the job as the witch cracked the instrument in half. The strings were the only thing holding the broken pieces together. The witch tossed the ruined mandolin aside, where it clattered down the dais's steps.

Holly bit her lip as the witch destroyed her instrument. It had been a gift from Brayton, a reminder of all she had accomplished under his tutelage. Seeing it shattered had an equal effect on Holly's resolve, and she sank back, distraught. Though her muscles were stiff and sore from her recent slumber on the hard platform, she felt she had not slept long. Stars still shone through the opening in the ceiling, and torches shone throughout the chamber. At her back, the pool continued to bubble.

The witch, standing at the topmost step just outside of the Circle, turned to face the pool as she bowed her head and closed her eyes. To either side of her, the tall obelisks stood silent watch. Her arms hung limp at each side as she chanted a series of phrases in a language unfamiliar to Holly. Then she lifted her arms high before her, the palms of her hands held down toward the pool. Holly listened as the witch intoned,

"O Spirits of the Dark Earth,

O Denizens of the Night,

I summon thee now.

Bring your unholy blessings unto this place,

Let thy energies be focused with mine,

And this Circle sealed against those who would do me harm."

The witch took one step over the line of sigils and entered the Circle. She walked clockwise around its inner circumference, careful to stay within its boundary. She completed one rotation, then another, and another. Then, when she reached the exact point where she had started, the sitheri turned so she faced away from the pool.

Beneath her, Holly felt the ground shake. Then, all at once, the sigils the witch had so painstakingly carved into the dais's floor began to glow. Subtle at first, they soon shone brighter until they provided an illumination all their own. The witch seemed not to notice as she continued her incantation:

"O Dark Elemental Spirits of the North,

I summon thee now.

Bring your unholy blessings unto this place,

Let thy energies be focused with mine,

And this Circle sealed against those who would do me harm."

The witch repeated the incantation three times, each utterance spoken with identical inflections. Then she walked the inner circumference of the circle, opposite from before. Three times she circled it before stopping to face west. She repeated the identical incantation, altering only the dark spirits she called upon as dictated by the direction she faced. Then, she circled the markings again, walking clockwise this time. She repeated her ritual facing south and then east. Finally, she walked the circumference one last time and was done.

Then the spirits came.

They were like the wind, fleeting and without form, entering through the ceiling chute and coming down to the dais from all sides. Like whiffs of mist, they sailed along the outer edge of the Witch's Circle. Their wailing, a horrible mixture of pain and sorrow, grew so loud Holly covered her ears with her hands. Even then, her head rang from the sound. Pain lanced through her mind, and she felt something warm and moist on her palms. Holding her hands out before her, she saw they were covered in blood. Then, one by one, the spirits joined with the Circle's symbols. Each sigil glowed anew as more of the dark spirit energy gathered there. Soon the symbols were so bright it hurt Holly's eyes to look upon them. She screamed and, somehow above the wailing, shrieking, and moaning, she heard the witch laughing. Closing her eyes, Holly buried her face beneath her arms, praying for it all to end. Mercifully, Holly passed out long before the spirits completed their work.

CHAPTER FOURTEEN

HALLOWED GROUND

THOUGH THEY INUNDATED ALIAH WITH question after question, asking first and foremost about Holly, but also what the woman knew of events in the forest, Aliah adamantly refused to answer any of them right away. Instead, glancing back in the direction they had come, she called an end to their rest, insisting they follow her from the diminishing safety of the thicket back into the woods. She informed them neither of their destination nor how long to get there as, without waiting to see if they followed, she strode away.

There was no discussion between Jerrick, Murik, and Kayra; once Murik had undone the spell on Kayra's sword, they simply followed. Kayra took hold of Aurum's reins, stomping off after Aliah. Murik seemed not to notice the parting glare she cast his way as he busied himself calling S'nar to him. Once the owl had rejoined the eslar, the two followed in Kayra's wake, leaving Jerrick alone with Ash and a still-unconscious Evar. Somewhere in the distance, Jerrick heard a howl he knew came from one of the patroller-fiends. Next to him, Ash whined. Jerrick expected pursuit. He also knew distance was their best —and only acceptable—defense. He'd allow no one to spill more patroller blood this night.

Jerrick knelt before his friend, reaching out to brush an errant strand of gray hair from the Elder's face. Looking upon him, Jerrick was overcome by a strange mixture of disgust, pity, and, worst of all, fear Evar might be trapped in his current condition forever. If there was no solution, if there was no way to change Evar back, Jerrick knew what responsibility fell to him. Better a quick end than a life of dementia and depravity. He knew Evar would expect nothing less of him.

Another howl—this one closer—shook Jerrick from his thoughts, prompting him to scoop up Evar and, led by Ash, set off in pursuit of the others. He settled in behind them, while Ash satisfied himself by running up their line past Aliah, stopping only when he had run too far ahead. As soon as Aliah caught up, he darted off again, repeating the exercise over and over and never tiring of it. Jerrick hoped Ash's renewed enthusiasm was a good sign.

Aliah remained aloof and uncommunicative throughout the journey. Jerrick, for his part, left her alone, though it pained and disappointed him that their reunion happened under such circumstances. Though her only acknowledgment of his presence thus far had been a brief nod following the commotion stirred up by Kayra, Jerrick did not think the distance she kept between them indicative of any ill will she felt toward him. It was this place, and all that had happened.

Aliah was special in many ways. She was a half-dryad, her lineage a mixture of Jerrick's own kind and that of the faeries. Her mother, Vadeya Dawnoak, was a dryad of the Simarron whom Jerrick had always suspected of not really caring for him much. Aliah's father was an enigma. Jerrick doubted even Vadeya knew who he was, for dryads did not cast their wiles upon men for conversation. Some might out of loneliness, but Vadeya's grove was home to many, a sort of commune. Jerrick was shown its general location during his training and informed, if he valued his dignity, to never enter except by invitation. While the dryads never harmed patrollers, their relationship with the Hall remained guarded, for they valued their solitude. Despite these warnings, more than one recruit had been dared into infringing upon the grove's borders in something that became, over time, a sort of ritualistic rite of passage. A warning from the dryads—a wad of prickly thorns in the posterior or a prolonged interval hanging upside down from a tree—usually served as adequate discouragement until the next novice was pressured into entering the grove.

Jerrick had never participated in such games, for he had never had to. By some chance of fate, he became friends with Aliah early on. Accompanied by the half-dryad, Jerrick had been allowed into the grove on more than one occasion. At the time, he'd felt honored. But it seemed so long ago now, as if it had all happened not only in another lifetime, but in someone else's life. So much had happened since those early years when his and Aliah's friendship had bloomed. Even more had happened since they parted company some six-odd years ago. For Jerrick, the last two of those years, since Kendra's death, had been hard ones, and the passage of time had taken its toll. But for all the change Jerrick saw in Aliah's appearance, those six years might as well have been six days. The woman looked no different now than she had then, for even half-dryads reckoned time differently from others, aging slower and marking time distinctively because of it. For Jerrick, it was like stepping back in time. She was still beautiful, still possessed of that fascinating, otherworldly aura. But there was something different about her. For the briefest moment when she had first introduced herself to the others and her gaze had crossed with his own, Jerrick saw something in her eyes the like of which he'd not seen there before: grief and sorrow. He was reminded of the woman's words from that night when he and Ash had crossed the Ugull Mountains. *Dead. They're all dead.* At the time, Jerrick was certain Aliah spoke of the patrollers. Now, he wondered. The patrollers might not be themselves, but they were very much alive. Aliah must have been referring to some other group. But whom? He thought he knew the answer, but it was too terrible to think on any longer on, and so he allowed his thoughts to grow idle for a spell. As the hours passed, he grew wearier and wearier from his burden. At Murik's urging, they tried to place Evar over Kayra's saddle. Aurum, spooked by the smell of the man-turned-fiend, wanted nothing of it, as the destrier sidestepped away from any such attempts. Kayra gave the others a shrug, then offered her steed to them instead. Murik and Aliah shared the saddle for a time, while Kayra, who lightened Jerrick's burden by carrying Evar, plodded along on foot. Despite the weight of her armor and her own obvious fatigue, she uttered no complaints.

They crossed an old game trail which Jerrick remembered hunting along years ago. Aliah's pace allowed no time for reminiscing, though, as she continued to plunge them deeper into the forest. Even still, an inkling of where they were headed formed in Jerrick's mind as familiarity with certain landmarks returned to him. He kept his suspicions to himself, though, and another two hours passed before Aliah finally slowed her pace. It was as if a veil had been lifted, for in this place they saw life once more. Oaks standing healthy and strong rose up all around them, while tufts of shrubbery and patches of wildflowers and grass littered the spaces between them. They heard the songs of night birds and the buzz of insects, and they each wondered if they had somehow been lured to sleep and left to traverse a dream. Fearful of breaking the spell—or of waking—none of them spoke as they followed Aliah deeper into the sudden beauty. When they reached a small glen where a rivulet flowed between sandy shores, Aliah halted their progress.

"The monsters will not venture here," she said. "Here, you are safe."

Kayra set Evar down close to the water. Staring in wide-eyed wonder, she asked, "What is this place?"

"We are within my mother's grove, called Sollin-kel by the patrollers."

Murik's face lit up. "The name means 'grove of beauty.'"

Aliah nodded in affirmation.

Jerrick, his earlier suspicion confirmed, remembered the place well. It possessed such timeless beauty, it was difficult to forget. Much like Jerrick's perception of Aliah, though, something seemed amiss. The half-dryad's words came to him once more then, and his suspicions were confirmed. His face must have betrayed his realization, for Aliah answered his question before he asked it.

"It is true, Jerrick." She spoke softly, her voice heavy with sorrow. "My mother, Vadeya Dawnoak, is dead, as are the other dryads who shared this grove with her. It is them I spoke of the night I contacted you. The life and vitality you look upon," she said, raising her arms to indicate the area around them, "is a fading illusion, for even here the forest's taint does its work, seeping into the earth and killing from the root up. My kin resisted for as long as possible. By the time I arrived, they were already gone."

Jerrick struggled to form words adequate enough to offer Aliah some measure of comfort. But what could he possibly say to alleviate the pain and loss of losing one's entire family? For every one of the dryads had been a sister, aunt, or cousin to her. More than that, her mother had been one of the casualties. "I'm sorry, Aliah." Woefully inadequate, it was all he managed.

Kayra took a few cautious steps toward Aliah. "We are all sorry." Behind her, Murik nodded his agreement. "We also thank you for helping us win free from the . . ." She cast a furtive glance at Jerrick, then left her sentence unfinished. "But I must know what has befallen my friend. You said before she was not with the monsters. Please, if you know where she is . . ."

Aliah wiped the glistening from her eyes, then said, "Your friend has been given over to the witch. *Her* name will not be spoken in this place."

Surprise and puzzlement marked Kayra's expression. "How do you—" The knight paused. More silence before the puzzlement disappeared and was replaced by purpose. "You must lead us to my friend. We must slay this witch before—"

The sadness hanging over Aliah vanished as the woman drew herself up, cutting off Kayra in mid-sentence. "If slaying her were such an easy task, do you not think I would have already done so?" Aliah's hands clenched into fists and her face became a mask of annoyance and anger. It was a display Jerrick had never witnessed before in the woman. "Do not presume to dictate my course or issue me orders, knight. I regret your friend's abduction, but there was no help for it. I tried to reach you all at the Hall of the Wood, but I was . . . delayed. By the time I realized where you had gone, you were already root-deep in trouble." Aliah stopped to take a breath. The pause melted the tension from her, and her voice became softer. "Dawn is only a short while away. Your friend will be safe enough for the time being, for the witch will not perform her ritual until the light of the full moon shines high over the forest tomorrow night. We have until then."

"What is this ritual you speak of?" Murik asked. "Can you tell us naught of her plans?"

"I can tell you much, but first I must rest. For now, though, know that the witch is responsible for everything: the corruption of the forest, the morphing of the patrollers, the death of my ilk. There is more, but it will have to wait. The trees are weak. I am only a half blood, but still I share in their weakness." She was intent on a quiet corner of the glen when Jerrick's voice halted her.

"Aliah, wait. What of Evar?" The patroller's gaze strayed to his friend, who lay sleeping where he had set him down.

"The witch's magic does not hold sway here," the half-dryad answered. "Not yet. Given time, the Elder should return to his old self. Until then, he will sleep as his body and mind regain themselves."

"If that is so," Jerrick said, "then surely hope remains for the others as well."

Aliah met his gaze. For a moment, Jerrick thought she might say something to ease his fears, but she simply shrugged, then made for a corner of the glen. Unclasping her cloak, she wrapped it about her as she lay down with her back to the others.

Murik, whose sorcery had exacted its own toll upon him, excused himself as he moved off to find his own place to recuperate. Once the eslar was settled, S'nar perched on a low-hanging branch where both old and new masters were well within sight. Kayra saw to Aurum, leaving the horse free to feed on the grove's wild grass or simply to stand amidst it while he slept. Then, still adorned in her armor, the knight propped her back against a tree and laid her naked blade across her outstretched legs. Jerrick knew the group's idleness was driving her crazy; he saw it in her eyes and in the way she fidgeted with the hilt of her sword. But some part of her must realize they—herself included—needed rest if they were to be of any use saving Holly or anyone else. As Jerrick settled to the ground near Evar, he saw the knight's eyelids already drooping.

As for himself, the lingering effect of the poison was gone from his system now. In its place was exhaustion. Unlike Kayra, Jerrick surrendered to it. Next to him, Ash pressed against his side. Somehow, peculiar though it seemed, Jerrick felt reassured by Ash's presence, as thoughts of the patrollers, Evar, and, most of all, Aliah's brief comments concerning their enemy—this witch—flooded his mind. At last, he knew the fate of the patrollers. More than that, he knew who was responsible. If Aliah was right and this witch's malediction was lifted from Evar, then perhaps there was hope after all.

When Jerrick woke, he felt as if he had slept the whole of

the day away. The position of the sun said otherwise, though, for it was still early morning. Despite the brevity of his sleep—he gauged it had been no more than a few hours—he felt well-rested. Some part of Sollin-kel remained magical even if Darkness dwelt but a stone's throw away.

Jerrick spied Aliah kneeling at the nearby stream. He watched her in silence for a moment as she splashed water on her face, then as she toweled herself dry with one end of her cloak. He wanted to announce his presence, but he found himself lost in his inspection of her. She was a dainty woman, slight of shoulder, with slender arms and legs. Her skin was neither soft nor rough, but somewhere betwixt the two, weatherworn from a life spent in the outdoors. Beneath the cloak she had removed, she wore leather breeches and a short-sleeved jerkin tied at the waist with a leather belt. Her hair—green like the leaves of a tree—hung long and loose, and she ran wet fingers through the tresses as she glanced sidelong at Jerrick and said, "I'm sorry if I woke you."

"You didn't." Jerrick rose, ignoring the amused smile Aliah threw his way as he took quick stock of his surroundings. Evar still lay next to him, as did Ash, who currently was busy stretching his body out full length. Jerrick shot a quick glance up at S'nar, who remained perched far too close for Jerrick's liking. Stooping over his old friend while keeping one eye on the bird, Jerrick found the Elder looked markedly better already. His skin had shed the sick, yellowish tinge, and his chest lifted with even, restful breaths. Jerrick let him sleep. The Elder needed it. Kayra, her chin resting on her armored chest, still slept as well. Murik was nowhere to be seen.

Ash padded down to the stream for a drink. Jerrick followed. While the patroller took his turn refreshing himself, Aliah sat back and crossed her legs.

"I was surprised to find your eslar friend already up and about," she said. "He must have expended much energy casting his magic last night. We spoke briefly while you slept. I hardly know him, but already I like him." She paused for a moment, then gestured at Kayra. "Your knight friend, on the other hand, I don't like. She's not very pleasant."

Jerrick dried his face, then glanced at Aliah and grinned. "You're not just saying that because she's human, are you?"

"Of course not." Aliah smiled back. "Are you implying I don't like your kind, Jerrick? I like you well enough, don't I?"

"I don't know, do you?" Jerrick smirked as he sat across from her. "It's good to see you again, Aliah."

"And you. You look good, but older. And in need of a shave, as usual."

Jerrick ran his hand across his emerging beard and laughed, momentarily forgetting Kayra, who stirred at the noise. "You look exactly as you did the last time I saw you." Jerrick sighed. "You're not the same, though."

"I'm afraid the person you knew of old is gone," Aliah said. "My journey to the outside world opened my eyes in many ways. Opened them so much, in fact, I no longer wished to see any more of it. It is a wretched place your kind dwells within, Jerrick. Poverty, crime, disease . . ." She sighed. "I came back to the Simarron only recently, thinking to escape it. I came back too late."

They sat in silence for a moment. Kayra stirred once more, but remained asleep.

"Tell me of your friends," Aliah said.

"They're not 'friends.' We're just traveling together."

"I see." Aliah smiled. "Still the loner?"

Jerrick shrugged. "I suppose. We only met recently." He thought about that and almost laughed. It was only recently, though it seemed anything but. "Homewood issued a Call of Heroes, and the knight and her friend, Holly, responded. The eslar is here because . . ." Jerrick stopped to think. "He told me he was looking for a friend." Jerrick shrugged again. "Me, I was just coming back for a visit of sorts."

Aliah nodded, then asked, "And what of your gray friend here?" She reached out, pulling Ash closer. The dog made no show of resistance as he plopped down into her lap and succumbed to her attentions. "As I recall, you never had much fondness for animals." She arched a brow. "Or was it *they* who did not bear fondness for *you*?" Aliah giggled.

Jerrick rolled his eyes. "Ash isn't mine."

"Not yours? Whose is he then?"

With all of the recent events, Jerrick hadn't time for thoughts of anything else, least of all his own guilt. Now, the familiar feelings returned in a rush, and Jerrick groped at the right thing to say.

"I could just ask him, you know."

"Who? The dog?"

"Have you forgotten? Speaking with Ash is no different for me than speaking with . . . oh, for example, you."

"Oh." Jerrick raised a brow. "So talking to me is like talking to a dog? You certainly haven't lost your charm, Aliah."

Aliah flashed him a wide grin, which, not able to help himself, he returned. They both laughed, disregarding any notions of courtesy for Kayra or Evar and suddenly not caring if all the evils of the forest descended upon them. It felt good, just sitting there, surrounded by the beauty of the dryad grove, two friends reunited. Never mind the circumstances of their reunion. It was enough they were together again, and so Jerrick let go of his inner feelings and felt everything returning to the past, when he and Aliah had wandered the woods with only the cares and worries of youths to trouble them. He embraced that feeling until, inevitably, it faded. Like Aliah, Jerrick was not the same person of old. He was in his thirties now, and far too old for idealistic dreams. Now, there was room only for regrets.

Their boisterousness finally woke Kayra. The knight stirred, then screwed her face up as she wiped the sleep from her eyes. "What time is it?" she asked.

Aliah looked at Jerrick and shook her head.

"It is only early morning still," Jerrick said. "Refresh yourself at the stream. In the meanwhile, I'll go find Murik."

"I shall accompany you," Aliah said. She prodded Ash from her lap, then followed Jerrick. Ash decided to tag along behind them.

As the trio left the glen, they settled into a slow walk

paralleling the stream. Jerrick spent his time observing the beauty around him. Birds crisscrossed the way ahead of them. At either side, wild grass flourished and brambleberry vines slithered up elms and oaks. Jerrick stopped a moment to sample the berries—they tasted overripe—and inspect the leaves of the trees, which bore small, gray spots indicative of the wasting disease affecting other parts of the forest. It was as Aliah had indicated: in time, even the beauty of her mother's grove was destined to falter, wither, and finally vanish.

"You still haven't told me who Ash calls master."

Jerrick slowed his pace. "Ash was my wife's . . . before her death."

Aliah's expression transformed into one Jerrick had grown all too familiar seeing in other people when they learned of Kendra's passing. After it had happened, people from all corners of Rell—friends of Kendra's family—had come to express their condolences. For Jerrick, they became more hurtful reminder than comfort, for folk never looked at him the same.

"I'm sorry, Jerrick. I didn't even know you had been married. I was gone far too long." Aliah reached out to touch Jerrick's arm. "How long has it been since she returned to the earth?"

"Just over two years now." Jerrick swallowed. "She died in childbirth, trying to give us a daughter." He turned away to face the stream. Aliah's touch fell away as he did so. Picking up a few pebbles, he tossed them into the water one by one. "Our daughter's name was Anna. The name had been Kendra's favorite. Oh, she made sure I was happy with it, but I think she knew I'd be pleased with any name she liked." Jerrick smiled, a brief, fading gesture. "The baby was stillborn. Kendra died shortly after. There was just too much . . ." He tossed another pebble into the stream. "I was happy without children, but Kendra wanted them. A real family, she said." Jerrick sighed and shook his head. "I should have known better."

Jerrick felt Aliah's eyes on him, studying him.

"You speak of your mother," she said.

Jerrick said nothing.

"Her death—none of their deaths were your fault, Jerrick."

"Weren't they? If not for me, my mother might still be alive. If not for . . ."

"If not for what?"

"Nothing. It doesn't matter."

"Yes, it does matter. What were you going to say?"

Jerrick remained silent, hoping Aliah let things be. He knew she was putting two and two together. He had killed his mother. Anna had killed—

"Surely—" She stopped. "Surely you do not blame the child for your wife's death?"

Jerrick didn't say anything at first. Then, in a whisper, "Why shouldn't I?"

"Because it is . . . ridiculous."

Jerrick scattered the remainder of the pebbles in one toss, and turned on Aliah. Something took hold of him, something pent-up for far too long. His voice was loud, louder than he wished, but there was no longer any control. Just regrets. "We were happy without that child. We were whole. We were fine."

"But," Aliah said, struggling to find the right words, "she was your daughter, Jerrick. Your own flesh and blood. You should be grieving for her, not weighing her memory down with blame. How can you possibly fault an infant for such a thing?"

"My father had no qualms about doing so."

"But—"

"My father watched as I killed his wife. In the end, it was too much for him, and he left." Jerrick started to walk off, but then stopped. "I never really understood the blame he placed upon me until I watched my own wife die. After that . . . I understand him now, at least a little. I'm going to find Murik."

Aliah sighed. "You're a better man than your father ever was, Jerrick. Someday you'll realize that."

Jerrick disappeared into the dense foliage with Ash at his heels. Once out of sight, he stopped. Faint though they were, he heard Aliah's parting words.

You're wrong, Aliah. I am the same as my father.

Taking several deep breaths, he started off into the woods again.

I am the same.

CHAPTER FIFTEEN

PARTHEN

HOLLY WAS LIFTED FROM THE depths of
slumber by a rough scratching at her cheek and
forehead. Cracking lids heavy with sleep, she peered
through her grogginess and saw . . . nothing. There was
darkness but for a small suffusion of light so dim it revealed
naught. Something about the dark soothed Holly: it was warm
here, and quiet. The air smelled musty, but there was a familiar
trace of lavender as well. Beneath her, she felt something not
altogether soft, but comfortable nonetheless. Holly curled
herself into a ball and shut her eyes, losing herself in the still
quiet. She didn't know how long she lay like that, or if she

drifted back to sleep, but she was dragged back to life once more when the rough sensation returned.

Coarse, the feeling was not pleasant. It itched, abrading her skin so that, as if brushing at a fly, she waved her hand about her face to relieve the annoyance. Her hand met resistance. Even more, when she extended her hand, pushing against the barrier, something pushed back.

Holly remembered everything then: the hideous forest creatures, the sitheri witch, the simmering pool and the statues looming over it, and the dark spirits summoned to fortify the Witch's Circle with their energies. The memories brought with them fright and terror. Her environment no longer felt so comforting, the darkness not quite so reassuring. Then she felt something on top of her. Panic seized Holly as she kicked out, thrashing with both arms and legs. Whatever it was remained. Holly renewed her efforts. Then light, like the rising sun, surrounded her, and she looked at her assailant, realizing it was nothing more nefarious than a wool blanket. She lay in a bed, the blanket tangled about her. Beneath her were a mashed pillow and a straw mattress.

"Meow."

The sound came from the floor next to her. Peering over the mattress edge, Holly looked upon a cat she recognized instantly. "Wilbur!"

The brown-and-black cat returned her stare for a moment, then sauntered off toward a bed opposite Holly's, which was neat and made-up. Wilbur rubbed himself against one of the bedposts once, then twice, then padded back to his original position and sat.

"Wilbur," Holly said, calling to him again, "come here."

The cat looked at her with wide eyes, his ears and whiskers drawn back.

Holly sighed. She knew that look. "I didn't know it was you. I'm sorry." Holly patted the mattress. "Come here."

The added motion of Holly's hand convinced Wilbur to leap up next to her. Holly grabbed him and held him close. "Wilbur, such a good kitty." The cat closed his eyes and purred. Wilbur was an old friend, a stray whom Holly had initially bonded with by way of the food she left out on her windowsill each night. "Where have you been? How did you—"

It struck her then, the oddity of the situation. She had been a prisoner, chained to a dark pool in some subterranean cave. Now, here she was, lying in a bed with a cat she had not seen in six—or was it seven?—years. Something was not right. But, for the life of her, as she looked about the room she recognized as the one she'd grown up in, she couldn't figure it out. Nor did she have any inkling as to how she'd gotten here. She knew where here was, though: the orphanage at Scilya, where dear Gracilla had taken Holly in and given her the closest thing to a true home she'd ever known.

Holly glanced out the open window between her bed and the other. Warm sunlight and a slight breeze entered. The drapes, worn thin from age, drifted back and forth, revealing the food dish Holly always found empty each morning. It was, as expected, empty now. Wilbur meowed in protest as Holly set him aside. She swung her legs over the side of the bed so

215

her bare feet touched the cold wood floor. Across from her, the other bed looked like it had not been slept in for some time. It had been like that, roommates coming and going over the years. The first had been Kirsta, the last, Amia. Neither had made it.

The lavender Holly smelled earlier filled her senses again, and she looked to the top of a small, battered dresser, where three stunted candles stood. They were gifts, or payment, for the help Holly had often provided to Lamok the candlemaker, whose old legs no longer carried him to the other side of the city where wild lavender and other plants he handpicked for use in his trade sprouted. She liked the smell the candles gave off; their pleasantness chased away some of the must exuded by her bedding and the staleness always hanging heavy in the small room. Holly especially enjoyed the trips through the city.

Holly stroked Wilbur's back and listened, half expecting to hear Barbadon, who ran the pub next door, shouting outside. The man was always yelling, but only because he was hard of hearing. But there was no Barbadon. Only silence.

Holly ran a hand through her mussed hair. It was short, not long like she had kept it while growing up. She still wore her most recent clothing: breeches with a maroon shirt covered by a leather jerkin. Her socks and boots were on the floor, and she reached for them while Wilbur went to the other end of the bed and sat. Once Holly made her way to the room's closed door, she pressed an ear against the cool surface. Hearing nothing, she took a deep breath, opened it, and peered through.

The hallway outside was deserted. Taking slow steps, Holly left Wilbur behind as she made her way down the bare-walled hall to a spiraling staircase leading down to the foyer. Holly expected to see Gracilla pop her head out in front of her at any moment as she descended the steps, but no one—not even one of her other housemates—materialized. Once she reached the last step, Holly performed a cursory inspection of the ground floor. The playroom, the kitchen, the dining area—all were empty. Not knowing what else to do, Holly went to the front door and walked outside.

The orphanage was located in an older section of Scilya. There was crime, and seedy individuals Holly had learned to avoid, but it was a community where most people looked out for one another. The comforts were not great; everyone wanted for something. But the basic necessities were taken care of as long as one worked hard and stayed out of trouble. For Holly, working hard and avoiding trouble became a sort of mantra. Those times she strayed from either tenet, Gracilla had always been there to keep her on the straight and narrow. "Mind yourself," the portly woman with the gray-and-black hair used to say to her. "Stop for no one you don't already know, and be home before dark." Most of the time, the warnings were unnecessary, for Holly became street smart early on. She had to. It was either that, or end up like her one-time roommates.

Holly looked across the unusually empty street, toward Hannock's butcher shop. The slaughter of the day usually hung in the windows, ready to be taken down and portioned out to the shop's many patrons. The display was bare now, though, and no one jostled for entry. It was the same to either side. Shops, pubs, and other dwellings showed no life, and all was quiet. This was Scilya, though. She was sure of it. Strange that, in a city boasting a population in the tens of thousands, she found herself alone.

Alone.

She hated the word. It sounded so final, so dismal. As a small girl of seven, she'd been left alone by parents who had no use for her. By the time she was eight, and safely living under Gracilla's watchful eye, she made a vow to never find herself alone again. Yet, now, despite all her efforts to the contrary, here she was, alone.

You are not alone.

Holly froze.

The voice had come from all around her. She looked in all directions, but did not see the speaker.

"Who's there?"

Silence answered.

Holly took cautious steps out onto the cobbled street. In many places, the road had fallen into disrepair, and she was careful not to step into a crevice or trip on a chipped stone. A cool breeze blew through her hair.

"Is someone there?" she asked again, this time louder. "I know someone is here." Holly started walking down the avenue. "Show yourself."

If you so desire.

Startled by the voice—behind her this time—Holly spun

around to face its owner. Somehow, she managed to wedge her foot between two rutted stones and, unbalanced, she fell. Her gaze remained glued to the figure all the way down. Wrapped from head to toe in gray robes, the person was marked by long arms and legs and a thin frame. Arms joined together at the hands were lost within the folds of the sleeves, and the cowl concealed his or her features in shadow. The most remarkable aspect of the figure was also the strangest, for Holly saw right through the figure, as if it weren't there.

The realization caught the breath in her throat as she felt her skin go cold. There was a moment of shocked inaction before Holly regained control of her faculties. Struggling to rise, she tried to free her foot, but it was caught fast, the attempt proving futile as she fell back to the street. Fighting to remain calm, she focused her full attention on her trapped foot. Even with both hands on her leg, she still failed to pry it free.

Then she heard the soft rustle of robes, and she knew the apparition came for her.

Frantic, Holly renewed her efforts, memories of another robed figure filling her mind. She had to concentrate! The looming figure was closer now. She had to free herself! Holly gathered all of her strength in one last effort, heaving all her weight backward, but still her foot remained wedged in place. Then the robed figure was over her, reaching for her. Holly shrank from it, scrunching herself against the street and covering her face with her arms. Clenching her teeth, she surrendered herself to whatever happened.

She felt a touch—a physical touch—on her ankle. Her first

reaction was to kick out, but the contact was gentle and non-threatening. It settled on her boot. Then, with a quick jerk, she was free of the rut. Holly peered through squinted lids at the cowled phantom. A ghostly hand—a man's hand—whose skin glowed pink and soft, patted her foot several times as if to indicate all was well. The man then stood and offered the same hand to help her rise. Holly hesitated. His features remained concealed, but—ghostliness aside—he did not seem quite so imposing now as he had at first sight. Studying his outstretched hand, she saw fingers long and delicate, with neatly trimmed nails. Reluctance gave way under the man's non-threatening posture, and Holly extended her own hand to his. A surprisingly firm grip took hold of her, pulling her up from the cobbled street. This close, Holly saw the man's translucent gray robes were of a fine material akin to silk. Despite the obvious richness, they were quite plain, bearing no markings of any kind. He was only slightly taller than she, and even slighter of form than she had initially thought.

My apologies for frightening you.

Panic must have made the voice seem hard and threatening, for now it was soft, inviting, and tinged with an accent the like of which she had never heard before. When he spoke again, Holly realized she was not hearing the words so much as sensing them in her mind.

You have no need to fear me.

"So you say." The fact that she was still alive lent Holly newfound courage. "I've not had the best luck of late with those who conceal their features beneath hoods."

A chuckle resounded in her mind.

You speak of the witch.

Holly's voice betrayed her surprise. "You know of her?"

Yes.

"Do you serve her?" Holly narrowed her gaze, waiting for the apparition's reply. Flight remained foremost in her mind.

No, he answered, distaste plain in his voice.

Holly believed him, inasmuch as she dared. Though questions remained, she wondered if herein might lie an ally. She resigned to tread carefully for now. "Does she know about you?"

The cowled stranger weighed the question. *No. If she did, either subjugation or destruction awaits me. Finding neither choice appealing, I have kept myself hidden from her.*

"Who are you, then? Will you at least show me your face?"

Another pause, this time out of hesitation, Holly felt. He did answer, though.

You may find the sight of me . . . unsettling.

"Why not let me judge for myself?"

The shoulders of the figure rose and fell in a shrug, then both hands rose to the cowl and drew it from his head. A face—translucent and ghostly—which might have been handsome at one time was pockmarked with jagged scars, oozing welts, and deep pits. The dark pink wounds were etched with red; the small sections of skin not affected by such maladies were dry and flecked with bits of flaking skin. His head was hairless; his nose, a sharp point; and his eyes, gray like steel. Swollen lips bearing the same scars as his face were like bloated slugs arranged one on top of the other.

Holly, unable to view the horrible sight even a moment longer, looked away. When she ventured a glance back at the apparition, she saw he had concealed his features once more.

"I—I'm sorry. I shouldn't have—"

Your repugnance is warranted and understood.

"No. No, it isn't. I'm sorry."

The man stood motionless, offering nothing.

"Who are you? What is your name?"

My name is Parthen. Once, long ago, I was priest to a god whose name has no doubt been lost to history.

A god? There were no gods left to serve. "Many of the Immortals' names have been forgotten. They died—destroyed themselves—over five hundred years ago."

Yes, I know.

"Which Immortal did you serve?" Holly asked, reservation in her voice.

The apparition answered without hesitation. *Sarrengrave.*

Holly felt what color remaining in her face drain away, for she knew the name well. Many were the tales which told of the God of Disease, called by his followers the Lord of Rot. Most people believed the stories mere fables, tales told to frighten disobedient children. The Old Gods, as they came to be known, had died a long time ago. Other people, though, believed the tales were more than just stories. Holly was one of them.

She backed away from the ghostly priest. "Sarrengrave?" It was said the mere touch of the Disease Lord's zealots infected a person with sickness so deadly their victims threw themselves on their swords rather than wait for the horrible symptoms to reveal themselves. Holly looked in horror at her own hand, where she had allowed herself to be touched. It looked no different than before, but somehow it felt wrong.

I told you, you have nothing to fear from me.

"I don't understand. How can you say that, if you truly serve . . ." Panic threatened to smother her as she looked about for some escape. There was only the empty city. "What is this place?" Her voice shook and her knees suddenly felt weak.

You know where we are.

She did, as impossible as it still seemed. "How can this be? I was in the cave, in chains . . ."

Where you yet remain. This place is of the mind, a sort of limbo lying somewhere between the waking world and the world of dreams . . . and nightmares. What you see around you is but illusion, a familiar image I found and pulled from your mind. Parthen's head went from one side to the other. *A rather undistinguished place, but one I felt might be of comfort to you while we talked.*

Holly blanched. Pulled from my mind? The thought both confused and sickened her. "What do you want from me?" The feebleness in her legs became too much, and she fell to the ground, sobbing. She felt the priest's presence draw near; she recoiled from it. "Don't touch me!" She lashed out, but Parthen had not moved that close.

My touch has not harmed you.

"You lie!"

I have no reason to lie. Especially regarding this.

"Then what do you want?"

I wish to make a trade.

"A trade?" The words cut through the panic in her mind. They were not what she had expected to hear, and the notion somehow brought reason back to her. "A trade for what?" Holly inspected her person through teary eyes. Except for her clothes, she possessed nothing. Not even her mandolin, which was smashed and worthless now anyway. "What do I have which could possibly be of value to you?"

There is nothing you possess which I want. But there is something you can do for me. I, in turn, am willing to do something for you.

Still holding the hand that had touched the priest close to her chest, Holly pushed herself from the ground so she stood squarely before him. Fighting to control her trembling, she forced her mind to remain focused. "There is nothing you can say or do to make me want to help you. I'm sorry."

Parthen replied without hesitation, as if he had anticipated such a reply. *That is unfortunate, for, even now, events unfold which neither of us can control. A chance remains whereby we may yet effect a solution to our mutual problems, though.*

"You may have problems, priest, but I have none."

Parthen laughed. *You lie chained to an ancient pool of corruption and evil, the prisoner of a witch who will soon empty the blood from your body, and you have no troubles?* He laughed again. *Your friends—*

"What do you know of my friends?" Holly asked.

Only that they will soon be on their way to the temple where we are both held as prisoners.

"You mean the chamber where the witch brought me? They're coming for me?" Hope sprang up. "If my friends come to save me, what need do I have for bargains with you?"

Temper your bravado. If they fail, they doom many more than just yourself. I offer you insurance against that failure.

"How so? Can you help them defeat the witch?"

I can.

"And what do you ask in return?"

Freedom. For five hundred years I have been trapped within the cavern of my god, bound to the Well of Rot. Even outside this illusionary world, I exist as you see me now, for my corporeal form was stripped from me long ago.

Five hundred years? Fathoming such a span was not possible for her right now. A part of her suddenly felt sorry for the priest, living for so long as a mere shade. But she reminded herself of who and what he was, shaking her head as she said, "I will never help free you. Whoever imprisoned you must have had a very good reason for doing so. I can only imagine what heinous deeds you committed to deserve such a fate, but I cannot help but think it justified."

Freedom for me is not what you might think. Long ago, as punishment for the 'heinous deeds' you refer to, my jailers chained my spirit to the instrument of what should have been my greatest triumph. They left me a shade, unable to influence the conscious world around me in any way. They meant for me to exist like this for all eternity, always remembering what I had taken part in and knowing, in the end, it had all been undone.

Holly just shook her head again. "I'm sorry you have been trapped in that awful place for so long, but I won't help release you from it." She meant it too.

When the time is nigh, you may have a change of heart. When lives— when your friends' lives—hang in the balance, you may think twice about spurning my offer. For now, think on it. Fate moves inexorably onward, and we need only wait for all those things we have no control over to come to fruition.

Holly watched Parthen's robed form shimmer, then fade, leaving her standing alone in the middle of the avenue. Moving to a bench situated in front of Barbadon's deserted pub, she sat there for a time, thinking. Parthen had said the others were coming for her. She hesitated to believe anything he said, though. His claim concerning his origin was fantastic: a dark priest from a long-past age, kept alive as punishment for . . . what? It was all too much for her to digest, and Holly found herself wishing one of the others were present to help her. There was no help, though. Whatever she decided— whatever she did—she was on her own.

Somewhere, through the silence of the illusionary city, she thought she heard laughter. Whether witch or priest, Holly didn't know. Still, it rang on in her mind.

CHAPTER SIXTEEN

THE COMING
OF EVIL

"THERE IS MUCH TO TELL," Aliah Starbough said. "So much, I know not where to start."

Murik, Kayra, and Jerrick sat in a half circle before the half-dryad, the whole of their attention riveted upon the emerald-haired woman. Next to Jerrick lay Ash, whose own interest fixed on the procession of birds descending to the gurgling stream. Opposite Ash, at Jerrick's other side, slept

Evar. The Elder tossed and turned every so often, but remained quiet otherwise. Somewhere overhead, S'nar perched amidst the tangled branches, an occasional hoot the only evidence of his presence.

"The beginning," Murik said, offering encouragement, "is always a good place."

Aliah took a deep breath, then said, "I spoke before of a witch. It is she who is the catalyst of the evil come to these woods. The catalyst, but not the source."

The others looked at one another with curious expressions, saying nothing as they waited for the half-dryad to explain.

"Like you, my arrival to the Simarron was only recent. It took little time for me to realize something was wrong, and so I traveled with all haste to Sollin-kel. My arrival was too late. But for the trees, I was alone. It is their counsel I sought first." She paused for a moment, surveying the faces before her. She stopped at Kayra's. "I see the disbelief in your eyes, knight. The notion may no doubt be strange to you, but know that the trees—all trees, not just those surrounding us now—are as much alive as you or I. They think, they speak in their own fashion, they possess their own wants and desires, though these are for simple things like fertile soil, sunshine, and rain. They may stand in silence," Aliah said, as her gaze strayed to the great trees around them, "but they sense everything."

Kayra, who had shed her armor and now wore only the thick, padded gambeson beneath, leaned in closer, intrigued. "What did they tell you?"

"They told me how months or perhaps years ago—time has such different meaning to them—a stranger entered the forest. They knew not whence she had come, nor on what business, but these are not the concerns of trees, and so they troubled themselves little more over it. If only they had been as vigilant as some others," she said, her gaze fixing on Jerrick for a moment before straying to Evar, where it lingered the longest, "perhaps this nefarious business might have been stopped before it ever truly started."

Jerrick didn't like the implication in the woman's stare, especially as she continued to gaze at Evar, but he said nothing.

Aliah finally looked away and went on. "It remains unknown to me even now why the patrollers did not immediately see this woman—this witch—for who and what she was. Whatever the reason, she was allowed to roam the forest unmolested, free to work her evil as she saw fit. The trees and the dryads felt that evil first. It was so subtle, so difficult to ascertain its true nature, that when they finally recognized it for what it was, it was far too late."

"You speak of the decay afflicting the forest," Murik said.

Aliah nodded. "None of them—dryad or tree—understood how soil they had drawn life from for so long suddenly proved anathema to them. Unlike myself, those of my family whose blood runs pure are bound to the trees of Sollin-kel, and so they investigated from within its boundaries only, trying to determine the cause of the malady, even as they drew life—and death—from the tainted earth. By the time they understood what the witch was about, they were too weak to stop her. In the end, they sacrificed themselves, returning their life force unto this grove so its vitality might continue to provide refuge to the creatures surrounding us now.

"The trees told me all of this, and more. Deep in the forest, they said, is a place the witch frequents with growing regularity. The exact details of the place remain unknown to them, for no life—no other trees—exist there to relay information. But it has borders, where life ends and Darkness rules, and so I asked the trees to show me the way. In my grief and anger, I thought to confront the witch, to make her undo all she had done. It was foolishness which guided me, for I was as ignorant of her power as I was her plans. Now, I am ignorant of neither." There was a glimmer of purpose in the woman's eyes. "I get ahead of myself, for you must hear the tale as it unfolded in order to make proper sense of it all. The directions given to me by the trees guided me well, and I reached this secret place of the witch's without hindrance. It was a place of Darkness, a gaping rent in the earth. I almost turned and fled at the sight of it, for it exuded a sense of corruption and decay, the like of which I had never experienced before. It was difficult entering the place. The dryad in me so loves the sky and sun and moon that descending into that pit . . ."

Jerrick saw goose bumps on the woman's arms and neck, despite the warmth of the grove.

"I made myself go on, though. There was a long passage, and then a cavernous room where unlit torches lined a path leading deeper into the chamber. I followed the line of the torches through the half dark to a dais elevated high above the floor. I saw several large obelisks—there were four in all—at the top. They were manlike and swathed in robes of stone. Each held hands outward, toward something at their center. The urge to flee was stronger than ever now, but I had come too far to turn back. I had to see with my own eyes what lay between the statues. Though every step was a struggle, I reached the top of the dais. There, I saw a wide pool brimming with black liquid that seethed and boiled. Looking at its surface, waves of nausea permeated my being and my inner voice screamed at me to flee. My faculties must have left me then, for I only vaguely remember running from the cave and back into the forest. I did not truly regain my senses until the Hall of the Wood hove into view. I thought to find safety there. The notion fled the moment I realized the patrollers had deserted it."

"What about the patrollers?" Jerrick asked. "What happened—I mean, how did they become . . ." Jerrick looked upon Evar, his condition increasingly better with each passing moment. It was a shocking change from the beast of only last night. "How did they become those monsters?"

"The details of their story remain unknown to me," Aliah answered, "but it seems clear they must have fallen under some spell of the witch's. I first encountered them the night I spoke to you through the grove's stream. I don't know if the witch sent them after me, or if they acted of their own volition. The trees gave them such a thrashing, they dare not enter Sollin-kel again." Satisfaction in the form of a smile played out across Aliah's face. "I knew not who or what they were. It was only later, after I had visited the Hall and found it empty, that I guessed at their true identity, for, in all my years in the Simarron, never before had I seen such creatures. The witch wanted the patrollers out of the way, because as her machinations progressed, the ill effects became more and more widespread and recognizable. She knew if the patrollers were left unchecked, they would try to stop her, and so she changed them, making them into her slaves."

"Are you saying they serve her?" Jerrick asked.

"In mind and body, though I doubt in spirit."

Silence pervaded the group then, as each lost themselves in their own thoughts. Murik, who appeared the least fazed of all of them, was the first to start the conversation up again.

"What of this cave you visited?" he asked. "What can you tell us of the pool, and the statues surrounding it?"

"The pool is a Well of Darkness," Aliah said.

"A Well?" Murik said, astonishment in his voice. He paused, lowering his head as he rubbed his forehead. He looked up sharply. "There have been no Wells in existence for over . . ."

"Some five or six hundred years," Aliah said. "The statues are guardians, safe-keepers erected long ago by the ancient druids of the Simarron."

Jerrick straightened. "The druids?" He looked at Murik and Kayra, seeing the confusion in their expressions, and so he explained. "It's said the druids protected the Simarron long ago, though no one has seen or heard from them in so long, many think their existence myth."

"Myth or not," Aliah said, "it was one of their Order, an arch-druid named Delbin Kinkaed, who told me how to stop the witch and undo all she has done."

Murik shifted his staff in his lap. His brow narrowed as his gaze fixed on Aliah. "I know of Delbin," he said, his voice slow and measured. "I also know he died a long time ago. How, may I ask, were you able to communicate with him?"

Aliah answered without hesitation. "With this." She reached beneath her cloak, revealing a fist-sized gem, whose deep cerulean facets glimmered in the morning sun.

"Murik," Jerrick said, looking from the stone to the sorcerer and then back again. "It looks just like yours."

Jerrick had never said anything, but he'd seen a similar medallion hanging from the sorcerer's neck on more than one occasion. Now, Murik pulled the medallion out from beneath his shirt. The stone at its center was the twin of the one held by the half-dryad.

"Aliah," the eslar sorcerer asked, "from where does that stone come?"

"From Sollin-kel. Long has it been kept safe by my family. It is said to have been given unto our ancestors by the druids themselves, in the event their aid was ever needed."

Murik weighed the information. "Tell me what you did with it."

Aliah hesitated, but only for a moment. Something in the wizard's tone demanded she speak, and quickly.

"I took it to Delbin Kinkaed's tomb. It is a secret place known only to me now. There, I used the stone's power to summon the arch-druid back from the dead."

No one said anything right away, as all eyes fixed upon Aliah's medallion.

"What you hold in your hand," the sorcerer said, "is a soul stone. Delbin's tomb must have contained some residual energies or some other mechanism which aided in the summoning process, for it is highly unlikely you accomplished the feat otherwise. Contrary to what you may believe, the stone was not the instrument which allowed you to summon the arch-druid's spirit back from the dead. Rather, the stone is the vessel which contains his spirit."

Though Aliah's grip relaxed, she did not let the soul stone go.

Murik went on. "Summoning the dead is never without a price. What, I wonder, was Delbin's?"

The half-dryad was so enraptured, staring at the amulet in her hand, it seemed at first she had not heard the wizard's words. But then she snapped out of her daze, and said, "There are no debts between us." Whatever price Delbin had demanded, Aliah had already paid it.

Murik studied the woman a moment longer before he said, "Tell us what the arch-druid said."

"Delbin told me of the Well of Darkness." Aliah's gaze strayed back and forth, encompassing them all. "The Well was created ages ago by zealots of an Old God whose name the arch-druid refused to speak. These dark priests thought to use the power of the Well to destroy all life. If not for the druids, they might have succeeded. The druids slew these violators of the earth, then created and enchanted the four sentinels I saw in the underground chamber. Delbin called them 'druid wards.' Then, they sealed off the cavern, it having remained so until the witch somehow discovered it. She negated the wards, whose purpose was to inhibit the power of the Well, and thereby unleashed its evil. This is what I meant when I first began. She is the catalyst, but not the source of the Simarron's woes, for it is the Well which poisons the forest by tainting the very earth beneath us."

Aliah fell into silence. No one said anything for several minutes. Then, one by one, they turned their gazes to Murik. The sorcerer saw their stares, knowing they did not truly look at him, but at the medallion hanging from his neck.

"This also is a soul stone," he said. "Much like the one Aliah holds, it contains the spirit of someone long dead. In this case," he said, fingering the edge of the medallion, "the spirit of my former master, Ushar, who has dwelt within it for some thirty-odd years." He let the amulet fall to his chest. "I told Jerrick when we started this journey I sought a friend. That is not entirely true. I do, in fact, seek someone, but she is no friend. Rather, she is the very same witch who has unleashed the power of the Well upon the Simarron. Her name I will not speak, but for thirty years I have hunted her, following in her steps. Such is her guile that only once have we met in battle." He tapped one end of his staff against his crippled leg. "This is a remembrance of that encounter. It is a testament to her cunning that she has stayed ahead of me for this long. Now, however, she will not flee, not so long as the power of the Well entices her." Murik paused as his gaze met each of theirs. "I have kept this knowledge from you with only the best intentions in mind. My life, my purpose, has been dedicated to her demise for a long time. It is a road I have learned to walk alone."

"How much of what Aliah told us did you already know?" It was the first question which came to Jerrick's mind.

"I learned of that information here and now, just as you did. The only thing I have been certain of is my enemy's involvement, though that certainty came only as we reached Homewood and later neared the Hall."

"If you've known of the witch's presence," Kayra said, "why not just tell us?"

"It was my hope to prevent your involvement. But it is clear the threat has become too far-reaching and grave for that."

"Even still," Kayra said, anger rising within her, "you *should* have told us."

"If I had, would it have changed anything?"

"Yes, it might have. For one, Holly might still be with us."

Murik sighed. "You are right, of course."

The eslar's frank acknowledgement took Jerrick, who found his own anger building, by surprise. Kayra must have felt the same, for her posture relaxed and she remained quiet as they both waited for the sorcerer to continue. Aliah said nothing, though she followed the exchange with interest.

"For not telling you," Murik said, "I am sorry. I miscalculated, and Holly's abduction was the price."

Jerrick heard a rustling next to him, and a soft, raspy voice rose so it was just audible over the other sounds of the grove. "If any of you seek someone to blame, blame me, for it is I alone who am responsible."

Jerrick moved to help his old friend. Evar tried to sit up, but immediately started to fall back, until Jerrick provided an arm for support. The cloak concealing the old man's naked body fell to his waist, allowing all to see the curing effect of Sollin-kel. The yellow pallor was completely gone, his eyes, sane once more. Jerrick offered Evar his waterskin. The Elder drank in great gulps, as if water had not touched his lips in days. With his thirst slaked, he leaned back against one of the grove's trees.

"How are you, old friend?" Jerrick asked.

"Tired, but well. Thanks to all of you." Though his eyes swept over all of them, they lingered the longest on his fellow patroller.

"How much do you remember?" Jerrick asked.

Evar took another pull from the waterskin. "There are images . . . and feelings." He shook his head. "But nothing concrete. The last thing I truly remember is being at the Hall."

Aliah moved so she stood over Evar. "Tell us, Elder, what did you mean a moment ago when you spoke of blame?"

Jerrick glanced sidelong at her, seeing the suspicion written upon her face. "Aliah," the patroller said, "he doesn't know anything about—"

Evar held up a weary hand. "It's all right, Jerrick. I fear I know more than you think."

"Tell us," Aliah demanded.

Jerrick was about to remind Aliah that one did not demand anything from an Elder of the Hall when a sigh escaped Evar's lips and he spoke.

"Deep in the forest," Evar said, his voice old and weary and nothing like Jerrick remembered it, "there is a cave."

"Yes, I know of it," Aliah said. "As well as what lies inside. Do you know how the witch found it?"

Evar took another sip of water. "She found it because I told her where it was."

Seconds passed—seconds used to absorb the old man's words.

"You told her where it was." Aliah spoke with little emotion. The quiver in the line of her jaw, the balling of her fists, and her glare spoke differently. "Why do such a thing?" The color of her cheeks deepened.

"I did it . . ." the Elder said, his voice a whisper. "I did it to save my wife."

The answer caught Aliah off-guard. It seemed the tension building in her lessened, at least for the moment.

"Several years ago, my wife grew deathly ill. The Hall's alchemists and physicians tried everything, but still they had no answers. At that time, we had been together for near forty years. A long time, to be sure, but not nearly long enough. I thought I was doing the right thing by seeking out the witch's help. She'd only been in the forest a short while, and we all thought her harmless, as so many of these woodswomen usually are. She promised a potion to cure my wife's illness if only I provided something of value in return. I offered her every worldly possession at my disposal, even going so far as to offer myself as her servant. I was so desperate, I even thought to kill her and simply take the potion, but I feared bringing down a curse upon my beloved. Finally, I told the witch of the cave.

"I discovered the place by chance when I was a boy. On that day, I traveled farther than I ever had before, for a week of heavy rainfall had kept us cooped up far too long and I was eager to venture out. I wasn't really paying attention to where I was going until I saw it. The rainfall had caused a mudslide, revealing the cave's entrance. I immediately felt something wrong about the place, but my curiosity got the best of me. Oh, when I entered and laid eyes on the Well, I knew instantly it was something terrible, so I returned to the surface and made sure no one found the place ever again. The cave remained undisturbed until I told the witch of it." Evar's shoulders slumped and he looked down, unable to meet any of their gazes. "I thought I had ensured against the witch using the temple's secrets, but I was wrong. For that, and for all of it, I am sorry."

"You're sorry?" Aliah was worked into a fury. "You—*you* brought this down on us!"

"Aliah—" Jerrick started to say.

"*You* slew my mother!"

"Aliah—"

"As surely as if you held the knife yourself!"

Evar looked up, meeting Aliah's rage. His eyes were moist with tears.

"Aliah, that's not fair," Jerrick said. Wasn't it? Jerrick's own thoughts did not agree with his words. How could Evar have done this? He had single-handedly doomed every one of the patrollers.

"I made her swear an oath," the Elder said, his voice a whisper, "a witch's oath, not to use the Well against the Hall or the people of the Simarron. A witch's oath is supposed to be unbreakable, is it not?" He looked at each of them, desperate for confirmation.

"It is true, but only partially," Murik said. "A witch's oath is a powerful binding. Under ordinary circumstances, breaking such a bond is folly, the consequences, dire."

"'Under ordinary circumstances'?" Kayra said. "What about under extraordinary ones?"

"Arrogance can be a powerful force," Murik said. "If the witch has willingly broken her oath to the Elder, then she has grown arrogant indeed."

Evar sank back. There was nothing left for him to say as his hands rose to cover his bowed head.

Jerrick fought to contain the emotions stirring within him as he looked upon the man who had been, in many ways, a father to him. As Evar's brief admission had unfolded, Jerrick felt anger. Evar had condemned every living thing in the Simarron, and possibly beyond. But now, seeing the once-proud man clothed in nothing but Jerrick's own cloak, his frame gone gaunt and his mind only recently elevated back from the stature of an animal's, Jerrick found his anger slipping away. Evar was as much a victim as anyone, for Jerrick had no doubts this witch had manipulated and taken advantage of the Elder's desperation. Evar had made mistakes—horrible mistakes—but Jerrick knew he'd have acted no different were their roles reversed. Jerrick placed a hand on Evar's shoulder. The old man looked up, meeting Jerrick's stare. Though no words were exchanged, Jerrick knew Evar understood at least one person forgave him.

"What is the witch's plan, then?" Kayra asked. "What does she hope to accomplish beyond sickening the forest?"

Both Jerrick and Kayra looked at Murik, whose own gaze had gone to Aliah. The half-dryad continued to stare at the Elder, stewing, oblivious to the question or the stares cast her way. Kayra asked her question again, this time gaining the woman's attention. Aliah tore her gaze from Evar, but only with reluctance.

"Not even Delbin Kinkaed knew the full extent of the witch's plans. He did, however, tell me this much: tonight, when the full moon reaches its apex and the stars align in just such a way, her power will be at its greatest. She has also spent much time of late traveling the forest and even beyond, gathering all manner of strange herbs and such."

"And she has an innocent," Murik added. When the eslar saw the others looking at him in confusion, he explained, "She has all the ingredients for a spell. A powerful one, no doubt."

"What does all of that mean for Holly?" Kayra asked. "What will this witch do to her?"

"I'm afraid that remains unknown," Murik said, "though I doubt the end result will be pleasant."

Kayra stood. "Then our course of action is clear. We must slay the witch and save Holly."

"No," Aliah said, facing the knight. "It is the Well of Darkness which must be dealt with first. If left unchecked—if we do not restore the druid wards—the Simarron Woods and its people are doomed."

"Be that as it may," Kayra said, "I think my friend's life deserves—"

"Aliah is right, but so are you, Kayra," Murik said as he also stood. "It is your task to restore the druid wards. It falls upon me to deal with the witch. We shall have to split up."

There was no immediate reaction from the others. Jerrick didn't like the idea, though, and he gave voice to his concern. "How do we even know the two objectives lie at different locations?"

"I know," Murik said, offering nothing more.

Kayra shifted her weight from one side to another, then said, "I do not like this, either. We are stronger together." Murik had just opened his mouth to speak when she quickly added, "But I bow to your greater wisdom, sorcerer. Your quest to defeat this witch is both admirable and noble."

Murik acknowledged the knight's words with a slight bow.

Jerrick rose. "I think it is foolish for you to go ahead on your own, Murik. At least allow me to join you."

"Your gesture is appreciated, Jerrick. But this contest between me and the witch shall pit sorcery against witchcraft. Conventional warfare and weapons will have no place there."

Jerrick opened his mouth to continue his argument, but then checked himself. He still didn't like the idea, but he also realized Murik's knowledge on this subject was the greater. Also, despite having withheld information from them, Jerrick trusted the sorcerer. The fact he had stayed with them this far said something.

"Only one thing remains to be determined," Kayra said. "How do we restore the druid wards?"

Aliah held out her hand. "With these." Gone was Delbin Kinkaed's soul stone. In its place lay four gleaming emeralds, their color a perfect match with the half-dryad's hair and eyes. "They are the Gemstones of Morann, given to me by Delbin Kinkaed. They contain the necessary enchantment to restore the power of the druid wards, and thereby contain the Well's evil once more. We must travel to the cave and give one unto each of the four sentinels. Only then will the decay of the Simarron be halted."

Quick words of agreement and nods of approval were exchanged, and then there was no further need for talk. Murik wasted no time, readying himself in minutes. One by one, the others offered their well-wishes to him. Aliah's consisted of a simple nod. Kayra voiced a curt "good luck." Only Jerrick's farewell lasted longer.

"Are you sure about this?" he asked.

Ash stood next to the patroller, his gaze fixed expectantly upon the sorcerer. Murik reached out and rubbed behind his ears.

"Yes, I am sure," the sorcerer said.

"But what if you do not succeed?"

"All the more reason for us to split up. At best, I will stop the witch. At worst, she will survive. But by the time she reaches the cave, you will have already restored the druid wards."

Jerrick met Murik's stare. "You told Aliah the dead do not give up their secrets without a price." Jerrick gestured toward Murik's amulet, which still hung outside his shirt. "What price have you paid?"

Murik let the question hang unanswered between them.

"This is farewell, then," Jerrick finally said.

Murik chuckled. "When first we met, I sensed your reluctance in having me join you. Your sentiments seem to have changed."

Jerrick smiled. "I suppose they have." He glanced at Evar, who remained quietly lost in his own painful memories. "A teacher of mine taught me a long time ago that one does not abandon a friend." Jerrick extended a hand to the eslar. "Good luck, Murik."

"And to you also."

With a flourish of his cloak, Murik turned and disappeared into the woods. Jerrick stared after him for a time before he returned to the others. They'd a task of their own.

CHAPTER SEVENTEEN

AMBUSH

J ERRICK HELD UP THE GOBLIN graywood hatchet he
had carried all the way from the Hall for all to see. "There
is one more matter we need to discuss." Jerrick had already
explained to Murik and Kayra about the hatchet and what its
presence implied, and so he had only to tell Aliah and Evar
where he'd found it to convey its meaning to them.

"Then the goblins are coming," Evar said, his voice hoarse
but stronger. "Lord Gral will no doubt lead them himself." The
Elder secured Jerrick's robe around his waist and made an
effort to rise. Jerrick offered an arm, moving away only when
his mentor demonstrated enough strength and balance to

remain standing on his own.

"I feared this," Aliah said, crossing her arms. "But I was more concerned with other matters at the time."

"With the patroller posts and the Hall itself unmanned," Evar said, "the way lies open. Greth can enter the forest at will." Evar looked at each of them. "I know I am in little condition to help, but I need to do something."

"I am glad you have offered, old friend," Jerrick said, "for there is a task I have in mind for you."

"Only say it, and I shall do what I can."

Jerrick laid out his idea. Evar was to wait until after midnight, for if the Elder left Sollin-kel while the witch still lived and the curse still active, he remained susceptible to the transformation. His destination was the lair of the patrollers-turned-fiends. Once they returned to themselves, someone needed to guide and assist them. Most importantly, they needed to return to the Hall to begin preparing for its defense.

"You must also send word to Homewood," Jerrick said. "They must not be caught unawares if any or all of us fail. Greth is coming."

There remained one last arrangement to make. Timing was of the utmost importance, and the Elder's own two feet were inadequate for the task. Jerrick was more than surprised when Kayra, seeing their dilemma, volunteered Aurum.

"He will be of little use inside the cave, anyway," the knight reasoned. "Aurum is a warhorse, not a dwarf." Kayra led the destrier from his grazing to Evar. "As long as he doesn't throw you. Your earlier condition shook him up a bit."

Evar smiled, then he approached Aurum with small steps. When he was within arm's distance, he held out his hand and let the horse get the smell of him. "He may find me more to his liking now." Aurum did allow Evar to approach, and soon the Elder was rubbing the horse's neck and head. "There, now."

Before leaving, Jerrick clasped hands with his former mentor. The two exchanged farewells and promises to see each other once more at the Hall. As Jerrick followed the others from the grove, he wondered if it was a promise either of them would keep.

The clear morning gave way to an increasingly overcast afternoon as Aliah led Jerrick, Kayra, and Ash north. Thunder boomed in the distance, threatening rain, which finally came as tiny droplets fell from the sky to drip from branches and patter on the leaf-strewn ground. The initial excitement of setting off faded rapidly as the group's mood changed to better suit the dismal climate. They walked in silence, exchanging words only when necessary. Aliah Starbough, who purposely stayed ahead of the others, found the situation to her liking.

Evar's deceit troubled her.

More than that, his admission fueled something inside of her she had not thought she possessed. The seed of it had been planted the moment she had returned to Sollin-kel and come to the realization that her mother and the others were gone. Then, as she learned of the witch and the Well of Darkness, that seed began to sprout. The more it grew, the more her anguish faded, until there was nothing within her but this burning need screaming inside her mind, demanding revenge for what had happened to her mother. There was a time in Aliah's life when such a feeling revolted her, but no longer. Her view of the world had changed. Instead of staving it off, Aliah embraced it. The more she did, the stronger she found she became.

When Aliah was very young, Vadeya Dawnoak had told her only daughter about the Hall of the Wood and its people. They were different, she had said. They respect our ways, and can be trusted.

"How are they different?" Aliah had asked, fascinated.

"They are patrollers," Vadeya told her.

Aliah remembered how strong the word had sounded. She was not disappointed when she met her first, discovering the people who laid claim to the title just as resolute as she had imagined. Just as her mother had advised, Aliah did trust them, which is why it came as such a shock to learn of Evar's betrayal.

Realizing she had gotten too far ahead of the others, Aliah stopped to wait. Ash, who padded along beside her, took the opportunity to scratch at his ear. Jerrick caught up quickly. Kayra, however, slowed by the weight of her armor, took longer. Earlier, Jerrick had suggested she remove some of it, if only to reduce the strain on herself, but Kayra had scoffed at the idea.

Aliah didn't particularly care for the knight. Her character seemed all too familiar: full of unmerited bravado and arrogance, as if the world were hers for the taking. It was an attitude Aliah had seen far too often in the world outside the Simarron. There had been worse, though. Ambition, greed, dishonesty. These were the staples of life for some. It was a world of mayhem and chaos, and Aliah, grown sick of it, had fled from it. But her return home was not what she had expected. If only she had come sooner. Guilt swelled within her, and she thought perhaps she understood Jerrick just a little. Blaming himself for things he had no control over seemed ridiculous. But, now, she found she almost felt the same way. There was no way to have known what transpired in the Simarron. No way to know her mother needed her. Aliah didn't feel any less guilty knowing this, but she also had someone to blame in Evar. Jerrick did not have that. For him, there was no villain. For Jerrick, there was only fate or himself. Aliah knew Jerrick held no belief in the former, so that left only the latter.

Despite the storm of emotions brewing within her, there remained room for concern for her friend. In many ways, Jerrick was still the person she had parted ways with those years ago. In others, he was someone new and different. Though at times there had been the hint of something more, they had always been the best of friends. Glancing over at him as they continued to wait for Kayra, who was taking the last few steps to them now, Aliah wondered how things might have turned out for them if they had both stayed.

Kayra arrived with a curse. She was soaked through, as were they all, but hadn't the desire or the self-control to keep quiet about it. Jerrick had pulled his cloak tighter about him, and though he did not join the knight in her complaining, Aliah knew he cared just as little for the rain. Aliah left her own hood bunched loosely upon her shoulders, allowing the cleansing water to dampen her hair and seep beneath the fur of her jerkin. Though it chilled her, she welcomed its refreshing sensation.

Aliah gestured them onward. Soon thereafter she ventured ahead of the others once more, though she did not stray quite so far this time. The trees started to thin here, replaced by massive outcroppings of moss-covered rocks. Aliah altered their course at an animal trail overgrown with shrubbery. The path led them into terrain pockmarked with tree-lined hills and more of the large boulders. The going became more difficult; Aliah was forced to slow her pace else leave Kayra completely behind. Even still, she did so only enough that their line did not become too drawn.

The closer they drew to the Well, the more unsettled the trees became. Aliah reached out to them from time to time, trying to provide comfort, but communicating with them became more and more difficult, as the effects of the Well withered away at their awareness just as it did their roots. In many ways, it was not unlike speaking to an elder person whose mind had waned. Aliah attempted communication anyway, hoping at least some part of her reassurances sank home. It pained her seeing them grown so decrepit. Bark once brown with health was now gray, peeled away to reveal the sick, blackened trunks beneath. Aliah knew the life remaining to them was limited, and so she took comfort in them while they remained.

The trail descended into a wide gorge that sauntered past a formation of rock so high it rose from the valley floor to beyond the gorge's upper edge. The resulting cliff face leaned over the path, providing a temporary respite from the rain, which Jerrick immediately took advantage of once they had descended into the crevasse. The rock here was marked by long, vertical striations, as if a massive cat or other such creature had raked its claws along it. While the patroller moved to study the scorings, Aliah moved out from beneath the protection of the outcropping so rain fell like a mist upon her. She eyed Kayra, who was about halfway into the gorge, then turned her gaze to the opposite side of the chasm, where trees and shrubbery lay thick. Ash stood next to her, also studying the trees. Aliah sensed more unease emanating from them. As before, she reached out, lavishing them with thoughts of reassurance and calm. Only then did she realize something else was in their voices.

Panic. Frustration.

Listen to us!

The words were suddenly comprehensible, as if the trees had gathered all of their strength, focusing so those few words manifested coherently.

Beware!

Next to Aliah, Ash's fur bristled and a growl rose from the pit of his throat. Then searing pain ringed Aliah's neck, cutting off her air. Jerked forward, she fell sprawling to her knees.

Hear me! Help me! Aliah's thoughts rang out, but the trees, their voices gone quiet, remained immobile. *Jerrick!*

Another tug sent Aliah the remainder of the way to the ground. Her hands were at her throat, tugging at the coils constricting the life from her. Already her hands and arms grew light and unresponsive, her fingers numbing just as her mind began to slip away. Spots of darkness encroached across her vision, and she lashed out, a wild jerking motion representing a last surge of effort. Then the gray light shining down from above went black, and Aliah lost consciousness.

Busy inspecting the grooves in the rock face, Jerrick had his back to Aliah when the whip reached out to wrap about her neck. But the whirl of the lash and Ash's growling were all Jerrick needed to hear to know something was amiss. Then the ground shook, and Jerrick had time only to spin around before the forest beyond Aliah exploded. Branches and leaves flew in all directions as the largest gaugath Jerrick had ever seen burst from the woods. The goblin was a staggering mountain of hair and muscle, a juggernaut whose every footfall set the rain-slick earth trembling. In his clawed grasp was murder: a warhammer longer than Jerrick was tall.

Jerrick threw his bow aside. Unstrung because of the damp, the weapon was of no use in a battle such as this anyway. Keeping his eyes on the goblin, Jerrick fumbled for his sword. Ash's barking was a fury of noise as he placed himself bodily between Jerrick and the massive goblin. A snarl erupted from the gaugath's throat as he closed on the canine. Ash reared up, his fangs bared, only to be denied his attack by a sweeping backhand which flung him aside. There was a yelp, and then nothing. Jerrick's sword flashed from his scabbard in those few seconds Ash had bought him. There was no time to strategize, no time to create distance between him and the gaugath. That terrible hammer was coming to pulverize him into mush, and there was no way to avoid it.

But then the gaugath wasn't hurtling at him anymore. Changing direction, he altered course and headed directly for Kayra, who was now running the remainder of the way down the trail and into the gorge. Jerrick thought to pursue, to help her, but then Aliah's attacker revealed himself, and Jerrick knew his fight was here.

Skave sauntered from the woods with slow, even steps. As he neared Aliah's crumpled form, he dropped his whip, the end of which remained coiled around her neck. The creak of black leather mingled with the pattering of the rain as the haurek strode past her without a glance. Stopping less than ten paces from Jerrick, Skave stood stock-still as his black tongue slid out and over his lips. Only when he was finished did his mouth curl into a grin, which set the zigzagging scar upon his face into a pattern of chaos. Gesturing at the graywood hatchet at

Jerrick's belt, he said, "That belongs to me."

Jerrick's gaze remained locked on the haurek as his free hand drifted to the axe's head. "If it's all the same to you, I'd like to keep it. I was thinking of putting it into the gates of Greth someday."

Skave's smile remained. "Keep it then, for now. Once we are through, I shall simply remove it from your corpse."

Jerrick drew his hunting knife. Holding both blades before him, he said, "Come do your worst, stalker."

"Ah," Skave said, his face lighting up, "you know what I am."

Jerrick had known it from the moment he'd laid eyes on him. Only a stalker entered the Simarron without an army at his back. Only a stalker walked to the very door of the Hall and embedded a hatchet there.

"I, of course, know what you are, patroller." Skave spoke the last word with obvious derision. Then he spat, ejecting a great wad of mucus in Jerrick's direction.

Jerrick kept the edges of his vision locked on the stalker's hands. Though the haurek's body had remained still since he had stopped, his hands had not. The motion of his tongue, his sordid grin, and his attempt at conversation all disguised the movement of clawed hands which, inch by inch, went to his belt. The goblin wore a sword there, and a dagger jutted from each boot. Jerrick waited and watched, expecting the attack at any moment. When it came, its speed still surprised him.

Skave's hands went from his belt to back over each shoulder

in a flash before both jutted forward with a quick snap. There was a blur of steel, and then Jerrick was plunging to one side, even as his sword and knife came up for protection. One of the goblin stars whirred by his ear, as another sailed harmlessly overheard. Jerrick caught still another with his sword, flinging it aside mostly by accident. But then a flash of pain seared across his upper arm, and Jerrick knew one of the flying weapons had grazed him, or worse.

Stumbling, Jerrick regained his balance on the slick ground and turned to face the charge he knew was coming. But the haurek just stood there, a look of amusement—or was it pleasure?—reflected in his drab, yellow eyes. Jerrick's arm hurt, but he didn't dare take his gaze off the stalker to inspect it. Already, he felt his shirt clinging to his arm as the blood trickled from the wound.

Skave drew his sword. "It seems first blood is—"

Jerrick spun his knife around so his fingers gripped the edge of the blade. Then he let it fly. The blade twirled end over end toward the stalker's gut. Skave's words caught in his throat as he attempted to dodge the attack. His reaction was too slow, as the blade pierced his hardened leather and sank into the flesh beneath. Skave looked down at the weapon sticking from him. He closed his fingers on the knife's hilt and yanked it free with a grunt.

"You were saying?" Jerrick asked, the edges of his lips turned up in a smirk of his own.

Skave snarled, all traces of amusement wiped from his

257

visage. Tossing Jerrick's knife aside, he raised his blade and charged.

Though Kayra did not see Skave's whip emerge from the woods, she did see the half-dryad fall. It was enough to send her running down the remainder of the trail and into the gorge. The way wasn't steep, but rain and fallen leaves had made it slick, and she was forced to descend with too much caution for her taste. She had made little progress by the time Nohr burst from the concealment of the woods and altered his direction to charge directly for her. One thing was immediately clear: if the gaugath reached her while she still descended the narrow trail, she was dead. The goblin, with or without his hammer, had the advantage in such a confined space. Kayra, her sword and shield held firm, doubled her pace. Her sabatons slid on the wet surface, threatening to send her to the ground, but she kept her momentum up, maintaining her balance long enough to reach the canyon floor. Nohr was no more than twenty paces from her when she did.

The trail widened into an avenue where rocks jutted from the ground like tombstones. Kayra headed for one of these rocks, an idea half forming in her mind even as the looming presence of the gaugath threatened to melt her resolve. She kept herself from thinking too much; thinking too much only fed her fear. Instead she focused on her breathing, just as she'd learned. *Concentrate!*, her weapons master had so often told her while they practiced. *Focus!* She did so now. The half idea suddenly became fully formed, and Kayra knew exactly what to do.

The goblin had both hands on the haft of his hammer, the weapon suspended over one shoulder, ready to swing wide in an arc once he intercepted Kayra. Ten paces separated them now. An immense shadow in the rain, the gaugath grew larger with each step. Kayra renewed her effort, her intention to enter the fringes of the rock garden before her adversary caught her in the open. Five paces. She saw the gaugath's bulk through the leftmost edge of her visor, but she dared not allow her gaze to stray from her goal. Three paces. The goblin was so close now Kayra felt him looming over her. Then the brute was on her, and there was no time left.

A whoosh of air followed by a sharp impact of metal on rock sounded, but that was all. Kayra heard a snarl of frustration, and then her momentum carried her beyond rock, gaugath, and hammer. Turning about, she expected to find the goblin right on top of her. Instead, he remained behind her, trying to turn, but so off-balance he was having a very difficult time of it. Then she saw the reason why as she spied the most ridiculous thing she had ever seen strapped to the gaugath's back: a beer keg, its size proportional to the goblin's own. The gaugath's swing coupled with the keg's weight had spun him around, but also set him teetering dangerously off-balance. Recognizing the opportunity for what it was, Kayra seized it.

She rushed him, her kite shield held before her like a battering ram. There was no subterfuge in her attack, no attempt at concealment. There was only the furious beating of her heart; the short, rapid breaths forced into and out of her lungs; and the noise sounding in her ears, which she finally recognized as her own voice shouting a challenge just as the mountain of muscle and fur loomed over her. Then her shield slammed into him, and her forward motion ground to a near halt. Her whole body jolted from the impact, and she was nearly thrown back. But she pushed forward, doubling her effort. She knew if she failed, if the gaugath regained his balance while she was this close . . . Already, she imagined his oversized paws reaching for her, his fingers flexing in anticipation of squeezing the life from her.

Focus!

Kayra did, and the gaugath toppled.

There was a moment of disbelief as Nohr's eyes and mouth went wide, then he was falling back, his arms flailing outward in a vain attempt to remain upright. A whimper escaped blackened lips right before the entirety of his weight landed on the keg. The barrel creaked and groaned before exploding into wood shards, metal-ring bindings, and honey-colored mead. The rush of liquid streamed all around the goblin, rapidly mixing with pools and streams of rainwater, dispersing until only foam remained.

Kayra stepped back, her lungs heaving. Her head throbbed in time with the pounding of her heart, and she fought to steady herself. She knew she had to strike now, while the goblin was incapacitated. She took two long steps forward, but it was already too late. The audacity of her charge had taken the gaugath by surprise the first time. Not again. Using his great hammer for support, Nohr stood. Kayra took one look at the bestial rage smeared across his countenance and promptly backed away.

"You stupid, puny knight!" Nohr's voice quivered with rage. "That was the last of it! No more beer! No more!"

Kayra shrank back under the goblin's maniacal torrent. She gripped her sword tighter, holding the blade high as a warning. Somehow she didn't think the gaugath found her gesture threatening.

"Now I smash you for good!"

Kayra raised her shield high, as if the device provided any real protection. She watched as the gaugath raised his hammer above his head.

"Now I make you pay!"

Kayra stared in horror as the hammer descended upon her.

Skave closed the distance so quickly, Jerrick had only a fraction of a second in which to raise his sword and turn the haurek's short, broad blade from his vitals. The clang of steel rang out across the rain-soaked gorge, echoing from the overhanging rock above them before disappearing amidst the thickening rainfall. The haurek was strong; a jolt of pain screamed through Jerrick's arm, its last vestiges still fading as Skave's blade worked itself into a flurry of motion. Jerrick had no opportunity for an attack of his own, no chance to do anything but concentrate on staying one step ahead of his opponent. Cursing himself for having surrendered his hunting knife and the advantage of having a second weapon in hand, Jerrick was forced backward under the goblin's assault. He knew scant room remained before he'd find his back up against the rock face. Knowing this did nothing to lessen its inevitability, as Jerrick parried each attack, narrowly avoiding dismemberment or worse. The clang of metal became constant, ringing in Jerrick's ears just as it echoed throughout the crevasse. As a stalker, the haurek was amongst the elite of the goblin legions, and so Jerrick expected to face a skilled combatant. But his proficiency exceeded Jerrick's expectations. Then, through the whirl of blades, Jerrick saw the haurek's rage steadily melt away until it was replaced by that same look of amusement he'd worn just before Jerrick had hurled his hunting knife at him. He was toying with Jerrick, thrusting at him with vigor, but not so much he might deliver a fatal blow. Savoring every moment, the goblin wanted this contest to last. Jerrick wanted it to also, but only as long as it took him to find a way to kill his adversary.

The haurek's attacks came slower now, pleasure gleaming in the goblin's eyes like sparks from a fire. Then he knocked Jerrick's blade aside, reaching out and grabbing Jerrick by his leather vest. Skave pulled him so close they were only inches apart. Jerrick felt hot, fetid breath waft across his face.

"Pity you are the last of the patrollers," Skave said, "for I so wanted to kill more of your kind."

"Save your pity for your own," Jerrick replied, resolution

firming his voice. "They'll be the ones dying if they cross into the Simarron."

Skave laughed, shoving Jerrick back so hard he stumbled into the wall behind. It took him a moment to regain his balance, a moment the haurek took advantage of as he thrust straight for the patroller's gut. Jerrick did the only thing possible as he half staggered, half fell away from the oncoming attack. Somehow, the blade slipped between the side of his torso and his arm, and Jerrick fell to the ground unharmed. Using his momentum to his advantage, he rolled away, just maintaining his grasp on his sword, but causing the waterproof seal across the top of his quiver to come loose. Arrows flew out in all directions. He paid them no heed as he regained his feet and spun around, ready for the next attack. But none came. The haurek still faced the cliff wall, his attack so forceful he'd sunk nearly half the length of the blade into one of the long, deep striations Jerrick had observed only minutes earlier. Skave tugged at it with all his strength, trying to coax the blade loose, but it was stuck fast and refused to budge.

Jerrick lunged at the haurek, indulging in his first real opportunity to press the attack. The haurek caught Jerrick's movement from the corner of his eye, his expression of amusement turning to one of desperation. As Jerrick drew closer, Skave realized his blade was lost, and he turned and ran, spinning about only when he had put some distance between himself and the patroller. Still, Jerrick came on, his blade setting the pace of the battle for a change. Even bereft of his sword, Skave was not helpless as daggers appeared in each of the goblin's hands, the foot-long blades reaching out like wicked tongues as the stalker launched himself at the patroller. Jerrick knocked one arm aside, grabbing the goblin's other with his free hand as he jammed the hilt of his short sword into the haurek's face. Teeth broke with a crack, and blood welled from split lips. Too late, Jerrick realized his mistake in allowing the goblin to close so narrowly with him as the haurek's greater strength came to bear. Skave heaved himself and Jerrick back, toppling them both to the wet ground. Jerrick bore the brunt of the impact, the air knocked from his lungs as, locked together, they rolled across the leaf-strewn mud. Then they pulled away from each other. Jerrick tried to regain his feet, but he slipped and landed flat on his back. Still fighting to regain his breath, he looked up to see the haurek standing over him, a dark shadow in the rain. Clenched in one fist was the graywood hatchet, pulled from Jerrick's belt amidst the struggle. There was no conversation this time. The hatchet fell.

Just as Jerrick expected the goblin to bury the weapon in him, a mass of gray fur and canine teeth whirled across his vision, interrupting the weapon's descent and slamming into the haurek so hard he fell sprawling backward. The hatchet sailed from his grasp, both of the goblin's hands desperately trying to fend off Ash's attack.

Jerrick rose. He didn't remember picking up the graywood hatchet, but somehow it found its way into his hand. The world around him moved in slow motion, and he yelled for Ash to get out of the way. The dog leaped away from Skave, who, no longer held down by Ash's weight, stood. He grinned. Jerrick saw his hand rising, in its grasp Jerrick's own sword. Then the hatchet flew. Jerrick watched the haurek's eyes go wide as he brought Jerrick's sword up to knock the axe aside. Too late. The blur of the twirling weapon came to an abrupt halt as it embedded itself in the stalker's chest. The sword fell away, the haurek's eyes moving downward to spy the cause of his ruin. Then, the life drained from him and he collapsed backward, dead.

Jerrick knees went wobbly, and unable to stand, he sank to the ground. He suddenly felt weak, as if all his strength had been drained from him. Then Ash was there, nuzzling under his arm and whining. Jerrick looked at him with a blank stare until the dog licked his face. Jerrick patted his side and squeezed him close for a moment. There was no need to verbalize his gratitude.

Standing, Jerrick made his way to the dead stalker. He recovered his sword and hunting knife, wiped the goblin's graywood hatchet clean, and returned it to his belt. A distance away, Jerrick heard the bellow of the gaugath as he assaulted Kayra. He and Ash ran to help.

Nohr's hammer was in mid-swing when he abruptly halted its downward motion. Instead he pulled away, stepping back from Kayra. The knight, stepping back herself, looked all around, trying to determine what had given the gaugath pause in his moment of triumph. What she saw startled her.

Aliah stood upon one of the rocks, rain-soaked tresses clinging to her face and neck, her arms outstretched to either side. Behind her and all around them, the trees were coming to life. Trunks swayed and branches reached out. Too far away to assault the gaugath, Nohr was having none of it. Then, beyond Kayra and Aliah, Skave fell, and Kayra knew the gaugath had had enough. Turning, he stomped upon pieces of his barrel as he fled.

Jerrick and Ash joined the two women. Ash barked at the fleeing goblin, but refrained from giving chase. Then the gaugath was gone, and they knew, for now, they had won.

CHAPTER EIGHTEEN

AN OATH
FULFILLED

MURIK SENSED THE PRESENCE OF the witch's house long before he spotted it behind a curtain of trees gone gray with death. The place had stood out like a glaring beacon from the moment he stepped outside Sollin-kel, beckoning him nearer in words spoken for his ears only.

Come to me. Come to your doom.

The words repeated over and over until, finally, Murik closed his mind to them. It was the witch who spoke to him. She knew he was here. She knew he was coming.

Overhead, the afternoon rain had dissipated along with the clouds, and the moon shone full through a sky darkened by night. Four hours hence marked the witching hour, when the deviltry of witchcraft was at its most powerful. Even now, Murik sensed the stirring of eldritch magic, growing stronger by the minute.

Weary of traps, he slowed the closer he drew to the witch's shanty. As he stepped past the last of the deadened trees surrounding the place, he used his sorcery to bequeath his senses with extrasensory perception. Murik discerned the presence about him immediately. Before him and all around— behind him and even underneath—they were there. Patiently, Murik waited for them to strike. Seconds later, they did.

Crawling up from beneath the ground, the first of them broke through the top layer of soil in a thousand places at once. Others streamed from withered, pockmarked trunks, dropping to crawl across the ground, as even more poured forth from hereto unseen nests and hives to take flight. They were the insects of the forest—ants, flies, beetles, gnats, wasps, hornets, termites, stinkbugs, mosquitoes, millipedes, and others— gathered by the witch from every corner of the Simarron to defend her home. Now, they carried out that mandate dutifully, quickly blending into a mass so thick they blotted out the light of the moon and stars and cast the clearing into absolute darkness. Like an undulating sea, those on the ground came for

Murik. In a swarm came those which flew. Words of power, so seldom used when magic was fueled by will alone, flowed from Murik's lips, his voice shouting above the increasing din of mashing mandibles, buzzing wings, and marching appendages. Fire erupted across the length of his staff, flowing to his hands, his arms, and the remainder of his body, until the entirety of his person bathed in its brilliance. Then he lashed out, searing away the ants, beetles, millipedes, and others scurrying at his feet. The flame grew in intensity, billowing out like dragon's breath as it engulfed hornets, mosquitoes, and flies alike. For an instant, the bare patches of vacuum left behind offered Murik a view of the stars and moon. But the moment his magic disintegrated one part of that great mass, more insects moved to fill the gaps, and the light was blotted out once more. The sorcerer's fire illuminated his way as he reached out with flaming death at the insect horde. They came on blindly, flying and scurrying into the path of the flame burning them away to nothingness. Some reached his person. These flared for one brief instant before they also were burned away by the magical energy adhering to his clothes, skin, and hair. Slaughter followed as the wizard killed the witch's protectors by the tens of thousands. His fire stretched out in all directions, so Murik soon saw nothing but bright flame and smoke. Finally, as the pinpricked flares lessened and then ceased altogether, Murik drew the tongues of flame back.

The forest floor all about him was layered in a thick coating of charred insect corpses. Dozens of black, sticky heaps, where masses of the flying bugs had died and fallen to ground as one, poked up from the carpet of dead like hills on a plateau. Smoke rose from those piles as the fried juices bubbled, and Murik held his breath against the noxious smell.

His staff and person still alight, Murik strode across the steaming floor. Branches embraced by his magical flame burned, their glow adding to the full moon's, as he circumvented the blackened piles and moved to within twenty paces of the witch's shanty. Murik let out a deep breath, inhaling air which, even clear of the charred insects, felt rotten to his lungs.

The place looked much like he had expected, for witches were never ones for keeping up their homes. A deserted hunter's lodge, it stood narrow but deep. The structure was old, with rotted timbers covered in moss and a rickety door which appeared ready to fall off at its next use. A chimney exuded black smoke, filling the air with a pungent smell which only added to the reek of the dead insects. Murik concentrated the power of his magical flame into a horizontal pillar which shot out like a battering ram, blasting away the shanty's door. "Come forth, witch!" His voice rose over the crackling of the fires. "Come forth and face me!"

Though silence was the only response, Murik knew the witch was here. He also knew why she did not respond. She waited for him to exhaust himself with his spellcasting before emerging to finish him off. Murik gripped his staff tighter and waited for whatever she threw at him next.

Something moved amidst the dark of the doorway. Something that glistened. Murik watched as two glass bottles shot out from the house's interior. There was a brief glimpse of yellow just before Murik lashed out with his magical flame. The first of the bottles shattered as the fire engulfed it. As it did, to Murik's surprise, the tendril of flame began to simultaneously recede and dissipate. Meanwhile, the second potion hit the ground, exploding. The sorcerer fell back, shielding his face with one hand while his other kept a firm grip on his staff. Small shards of glass cut his arm, face, and neck as the bottle's contents splashed onto his staff and his person. Murik's magical fire and his enhanced senses flickered and died, both spells negated.

Murik tasted blood, and he spat just as a smallish mass of hair and claws bounded from the shanty and loped straight for him. Undeterred by the sight of the lone grekkel, Murik remained where he was, letting the creature come to him. But then the goblin let out a screech, and suddenly others of its kind began piling out from the interior of the shanty like water rushing from a spigot. First ten, then twenty, then fifty, until there were too many to count as the writhing, screaming horde flew straight at the sorcerer. His magic rendered impuissant, Murik drew his short sword. With blade and staff held before him, he waited for the teeming throng to reach him.

Their leader—Speck—reached Murik first. He jumped high, using his momentum to propel himself straight at the eslar's face. Murik glimpsed a long, curved tongue; yellow-stained teeth; and a pair of dark, beady eyes, then he lightly sidestepped the creature and, with a swing of his blade, thought with certainty the grekkel cut in twain. But his attack sliced nothing but air. Murik swore, for his aim had been true, but luck—so elusive even at the best of times—was not on his side, for the mere presence of a grekkel spoiled good fortune. The remainder of the grekkels, slavering for his blood like an incited mob, was practically on him then. Murik raised his sword high, ready to strike at the first of the diminutive goblins when, to his astonishment, the foremost of the grekkels veered off to either side and, instead of surrounding him, kept running right past. Perplexed by their behavior, Murik watched the grekkels' numbers diminish by half. There was no time to contemplate his apparent change of fortune, though, before those remaining attacked. Two lunged for him, rushing him on the side of his bad leg. There was a moment of gnashing teeth and slicing claws, then Murik knocked the pair away with his staff. An instant later another came at him from the opposite side. Murik's sword flashed, and the blade came away black with goblin blood. Claws slashed across Murik's crippled leg, and he bit back a cry of pain as he lashed out with his sword once more, cleaving the creature's shoulder and arm from its body.

Murik spun around, a clumsy maneuver which nevertheless cleared the space around him as he whipped his staff about in a wide arc. Granted a momentary reprieve, Murik sized up the score of grekkels still surrounding him. Their tails waved back and forth as they peered at him with glowering eyes. Tongues slithered from jagged maws, and though several of the goblins made a show of snapping the air before them, none ventured closer. They feared him, which was well, for it bought Murik the time he needed for the potions' effect to diminish and then fade altogether. Exultant, he called forth his magic once more.

As soon as the grekkels realized what he was doing, some turned and bolted. The others let out a shriek and threw themselves at the sorcerer. Murik beat them back, buying himself enough time to will his magic to life again. There was a moment of absolute stillness, and then the air about Murik erupted into a chaos of gale-force winds. The air currents shot one way and then another, lifting a handful of Murik's assailants up as if children's playthings and slamming them into nearby trees, where bones crunched audibly. The wind took on direction, coalescing and twirling around Murik until a whirlwind, visible only by the leaves, broken branches, and grekkels caught up in its embrace, surrounded him. Murik walked forward. One by one, the remainder of the grekkels who did not run away fast enough were swept up by the tumultuous winds. Shrieking, they orbited Murik for a handful of rotations before they were hurled away. Some slammed into trees. Others were cast into the dark of the night. Still others flew to the ground to land, bruised and shaken but still alive. These chose to flee while still able. Soon, the last of the grekkels—their leader—was the only one remaining.

Murik brought the creature's motion to a halt before him. Suspended in midair, the baleful goblin stared at him with hatred in his eyes. "Tell your mistress I'm coming," Murik said. Then he motioned toward the witch's house. Speck was set into motion once more, this time toward Saress's house as the grekkel sailed right through the open doorway. With a grunt of satisfaction, Murik heard the thud he was expecting.

Murik let the air return to calm and, still bewildered by the grekkels who had run past him rather than fight, turned from the house to investigate. Understanding and disgust overwhelmed him all at once as he witnessed the host of grekkels hunkered down to a feast of roasted insects. Some were on all fours, long tongues lapping up the sizzling juices like animals drinking water. Others sat and scooped up great sticky gobs which they shoved into rancid mouths. Murik turned away. He knew once the grekkels had engorged themselves they were more likely to crawl away to sleep rather than pose any further threat, and so he no longer paid them any heed.

Murik walked to the exposed doorway, shouting into the dark interior, "Is this what you send against me, witch? Insects and grekkels?" Murik laughed. It was a mad, hysterical laugh brought about by the power he had wielded and the death it had caused. "Show yourself! Let us end this in the manner Fate has decreed!"

Still, there was no reply. Murik let out a deep breath, calming his nerves. Then he stepped into the witch's house.

Jerrick, Aliah, Kayra, and Ash left the dead haurek behind, walking out from beneath the lee of the cliff and into the drizzle without looking back. Though Jerrick had wanted to examine the red line on Aliah's neck made by the lash of Skave's whip, Aliah brushed him off, reminding them in a voice gone hoarse that time was not on their side.

They followed the same animal trail which had taken them into the crevasse for another hour before Aliah led them into the unmarked, tangled foliage of the woods. They walked amongst oaks and elms, thorny brambles entwined around their trunks as if trying to strangle the life from them. They looked dead, wasted away by the influence of the Well of Darkness. As the group ventured deeper into the untamed forest, the brambles became so thick and prolific they formed dense hedges. Jerrick swore often as thorns snagged his shirt or cloak, attacking him without mercy, and soon his arms, legs, neck, and face bled from numerous small cuts. He used his sword to hack at some, but more often than not pushed them aside and suffered more cuts as they whipped back on him. Ahead, Aliah passed through with little effort, as the brambles seemed to part just in front of her. Ash followed in her wake, bounding a few steps until he caught up to her and then patiently waiting for her to move ahead once more. Occasionally, a thorn snagged his thick fur, but he pulled free with a tug, paying it no more attention. Behind Jerrick, Kayra plunged through the thick brambles with effort, but her armor protected her from any harm.

After some time, they broke free of the tangled foliage, but found the terrain ahead no less forgiving. Sharp hills rose and fell; they scurried down one only to climb, with effort, up the other side. Soon, all of them were sweating despite the cool air. The rain ceased, and the clouds began to break up as night approached. Stars and the full moon lit their way as Aliah motioned them up and over one last hill. Then they saw the cave.

The interior of it was so black it seemed impenetrable to light. Just looking at the place soured Jerrick's stomach, a feeling he had found growing worse the nearer they drew. Ash whined, and Kayra shifted uncomfortably in her armor. Only Aliah seemed unaffected by the cave's presence as she motioned them on. But as they stopped before the opening, the half-dryad turned and met Jerrick's gaze. He saw much of what he felt: trepidation, nervousness, and more than a tinge of fear. Jerrick tried to offer her something, giving her a confident nod, but he felt the gesture fell far short of his intended goal. Aliah, recognizing his intention, smiled anyway. Then, she turned, inhaled deeply, and stepped into the dark opening. Ash, Jerrick, and Kayra followed.

Murik stood within the witch's house. Moonlight streaming through rents in the thatched ceiling provided only partial illumination. A lit stove, its wide, iron surface littered with cauldrons which steamed and bubbled, proved the source of the smoke he had spied earlier. To either side were two long tables, like those found in a hunter or patroller hall. Both were laden with a chaos of bottles and beakers, clay urns and pots, and several open books. At the center of one of the tables was a solitary vial filled with some dark liquid. The back of the room was shaded in darkness.

Murik approached the table, passing close enough to the stove to feel its heat and catch a whiff of whatever stew the witch boiled. The smell induced a shudder as Murik's interest shifted to the single vial and the flame burning beneath it. An open book lay next to it. Though steam rose from the vial, the liquid, pitch-black and thick like tar, did not boil. Intrigued, Murik reached toward it.

"Do not touch that."

The voice came from every direction at once. Murik spun about, his gaze seeking into every shadowed corner. "Show yourself, Saress." Murik's voice echoed from the timber walls. "You cannot escape me this time."

Hissing laughter filled the room. "There is no need for escape . . . this time!"

The rising tone of the witch's voice was the only forewarning Murik had of her imminent attack. One moment he stood alone, the next, she was there, towering over him, black robes fluttering all about her and a crude club, thick enough to smash Murik's skull, held high above her hooded head. Murik raised his staff with both hands just in time to catch the descending club.

Clack!

The staff—hardened alderwood and bound by magic—held. But Saress was sitheri, and possessed strength commensurate with that of a lesser giant or ogre, and so the force behind her blow sent Murik stumbling backward. He expected the witch to press her attack. Instead, she stayed where she was, unmoving. Then, slowly, a clawed hand rose to her hood, pulling back the cloth and revealing a snake face Murik knew well. Time and a life of witchcraft had not been kind. By their first meeting, Saress's delving into the dark ways of her profession had already changed her, corroding her sleek blue and green scales into a sickly, mottled gray and pushing eyes once vibrant back into her skull so her brows jutted forward like some preternatural ancestor of her kind. Once, she had possessed a tail. No longer, for Saress had sacrificed the appendage long ago in some dark ritual. Saress cocked her head, her serpentine eyes regarding the eslar with amusement.

Murik met her gaze without wavering. "I have come to kill you."

The witch's brow ridges narrowed. "Yes, I know." Then, looking about, she said, "I sense . . . another."

Murik touched the amulet at his chest. "Ushar is with me."

"Of course. 'Tis a reunion of sorts, then. Only, this time, you have brought others with you."

"Others?"

"Yes, your allies." The witch smiled, her tongue flicking out from between mottled lips. "Even now, they draw closer to the temple. To the Well. Very soon, they will fall prey to the trap I have laid there for them."

"What have you done, witch? If they are harmed—"

"Of course they will be harmed!" Saress smacked her club into an open palm. "You have wasted your time pursuing me all these years, eslar. Now, you have wasted the lives of your so-called allies. How much longer will you pursue, eh? How many failures will it take?"

"A thousand failures cannot deter me, witch. Since I cannot have what first we agreed upon, I will have your life instead."

"And how does a crippled eslar plan to slay me?"

"My magic has ever been a potent weapon. It is more than a match for your witchcraft."

Saress laughed a loud, long laugh. "Cast your spells, then, mighty sorcerer!" She laughed again. "Bring your power to bear and slay me, if you can!"

The witch was up to something, and Murik thought he knew what. Rather than reveal his hand, though, he took no action, instead waiting for Saress to make her next move. When she saw the sorcerer offered no attack, she groped at her robes with her free hand until she produced a small talisman hanging from a leather cord about her neck. It was a simple thing of straw and sticks, woven into a loop. Tied taut within was something so thin Murik barely saw it. It looked like a hair. She held the talisman up for a moment, making sure Murik got a good glimpse at it before she let it fall to her chest. "Your magic has no hold over me, sorcerer," the witch said, patting the simple talisman once, then twice. She raised her crude club to shoulder level and took a step forward.

Murik's expression remained unreadable. "Does your talisman grant you such confidence you step right into the path of my sorcery? You are mistaken to think it so powerful."

Saress stopped. "It is you who are mistaken, sorcerer." Her

voice was hard now, bereft of all amusement. "While you slept, my servant spirited away a single piece of your hair. From it, I have fashioned this protective charm. Your sorcery cannot harm me." She took another step closer.

Murik smiled. "I fear your talisman shall not prove as effective as you had hoped, witch, for I anticipated your move, and made certain your slave gathered only what I wanted it to. What you weaved into your charm is the hair from a certain horse you'd find yourself admirably protected from if he were only a spellcaster."

The witch paused in mid-step, then let her foot sink slowly to the floor. She advanced no farther. "You lie."

"No, I do not." It was Murik who stepped forward this time. Saress took one backward in response. "I'm surprised you cannot tell the difference between a horse's hair and my own. They are the same color, true, but have completely different textures. I thought to use a piece of hair from the dog we traveled with, but alas, it was not the right color." All levity left the eslar's voice as he continued advancing on Saress, who took one step back for each of his. "Now, witch, it is time to finish this." With a single word, his staff flared into brilliance. Another word shattered the witch's club into a thousand splinters. Saress hissed as the shards flew in all directions. "You should have stayed in hiding, Saress. From the moment I sensed the evil pervading these woods, I knew you were involved." Saress backed past the table with the dark vial upon it. "You made a pact, a witch's pact, with the man Evar, Eldest of the Elders of the Hall of the Wood. You swore to not use the Well of Darkness to harm the Simarron. Have you grown so foolish to risk the consequences of breaking such a sacred covenant? Surely the Spirits will not stand for such a thing."

The witch spat. "They have no hold over me, for they fear my power!"

"Then perhaps they have sent me in their stead, for I do not fear you, witch."

Seeing the witch glance at the turbid potion with wide, desperate eyes, Murik took a quick step toward it, cutting her off from the concoction and any plans she might have had of using it against him. Steadily, Murik forced Saress back, away from the table and toward the rearmost portion of the room. The absence of a bed or other sleeping apparatus did not surprise Murik, for he knew the witch had long ago done away with such base needs.

Murik had nearly backed Saress to the rear wall now. With nowhere else for her to go, he attacked. The magic of his staff leaped out at her like a flaming tongue of death. Too late, though, as Saress bounded aside and simultaneously threw down a vial filled with an olive-green fluid. The container shattered, sending forth great billowing clouds of green smoke which rapidly enveloped the witch and then the entire back of the shanty. Several explosions rang out from behind the smoke screen, the contents of whatever spell ingredients the witch kept on the shelves reacting violently with his magic. Murik stepped away from the encroaching mist. Not fast enough, though, as the witch's fog reached out until he and the remainder of the house were consumed by its embrace.

Expecting the witch to attempt escape, Murik started for the front of the room. Visibility was poor; even the burning light from his staff provided little relief. Instead, he used the noise of the stove's bubbling pots to guide him. He strode past the table holding the dark potion, reaching the open doorway, where the mist drifted out. There was no sign of Saress. "By the Spires of Isia," Murik whispered, worry lining his face, "if she has escaped—"

The sound of a claw scraping on wood rang out from the opposite side of the room. Murik did not react at first, but then he took slow steps toward the sound. When he stood between the two long tables, he stopped. He heard the scrape again, only then realizing what the witch was up to. With a groan and a shudder, one of the thick tables heaved into the air. Its contents—books and glass containers—spilled from it, pummeling the eslar all at once. The table continued to rise, and Murik was just bringing his magic to bear when it fell full upon him. His staff flew from his grasp as, all around him, clay pots and glass shattered. Then there was a jolt of pain, and then nothing.

How long Murik remained unconscious he did not know, but when he awoke, the witch was there, hovering over him. The table lay across his body, covering his legs above the knees and all of his midsection but for one shoulder and an arm deadened by numbness. The eslar's mind swam, drifting in and out of awareness. With effort, he stopped the room from spinning and looked upon his enemy through the dissipating, green mist. The witch's face was marked by a sneer Murik longed to erase.

"Ah, the mighty sorcerer awakens from his slumber," Saress said. "How does it feel to know that, once more, you have failed? I feel your master's disapproval already."

The amulet containing Ushar's spirit was wedged between the table and Murik, and dug painfully into his chest.

Then, as if sensing his discomfort, Saress hopped onto the underside of the table, adding her own sizable weight to the table. Murik's mouth opened wide in agony, but the air had been forced from his lungs and no sound issued forth. The witch shifted her weight. The pressure was pure agony. Already, Murik felt lightheaded from lack of air.

"I go now to Sarrengrave's temple. Once my work is complete there, I will no longer have need for protective talismans, potions, or even witchcraft. The Well of Darkness is a very powerful source of primordial evil. Ancient accountings say it contains the very immortal power of the Lord of Rot himself."

Murik gasped as Saress leaped from the table.

"That power—Sarrengrave's power—shall be mine! Imagine it! The power of a god!" Saress laughed. Reptilian eyes, drunk with lust, met Murik's. "Then you shall serve me!"

"Never." His reply was soft and pitiful, and the witch laughed again.

"Farewell, sorcerer."

Murik barely heard the witch's final words through the pounding in his head. Then she was gone, and everything grew quiet. Murik choked back a sob, for he knew he had failed.

CHAPTER NINETEEN

THE TEMPLE OF THE WELL

ALIAH WAS THE FIRST TO enter the temple chamber. Seeing the accursed place for a second time, she hoped it was her last. Torches—lit now—lined an otherwise invisible path through a myriad of stalagmites. Though their line was not straight, Aliah knew exactly where they led. The four druid guardians, monoliths imbued with the power to contain the corruption of the Well of Darkness but made powerless by the witch's undoing of the wards, stood at their end. They, and the Well betwixt them. Aliah felt for the Gemstones of Morann, nestled safely in the pouch at her waist. They provided no protection from what lay ahead, not until they were given unto the sentinels, but their presence provided a degree of reassurance regardless.

Aliah looked back at the others. Kayra was studying the cavern wall's iridescence. Though the greenish glow provided enough luminosity to see beyond the light made by the torches, much of the chamber's extremities remained cloaked in shadows. Jerrick peered about with guarded curiosity. Ash was close to him, whining softly. Aliah saw the fear all of them felt in the dog's eyes. This place was evil, a burrow of corruption which once, long ago, played host to grisly ceremonies and other abominations. Better for all to leave it far behind. Ash's gaze met Aliah's, and unspoken words passed between them as the half-dryad soothed the canine's nerves. It seemed to help, as Ash grew silent.

Aliah returned her attention to the path, where she picked her way past stalagmites taller and wider than she, and then to the foot of the steps leading up to the Well. The others shuffled behind her. Glancing into the flickering shadows, Aliah half expected a screaming horde of *something* to emerge at any moment. Surely the witch did not leave the Well unguarded. But just as before, when Aliah had previously walked to the foot of these steps, nothing moved against them. Perhaps, with no one to oppose her thus far, the witch had simply grown overconfident. Aliah said a quick prayer to the spirit of her mother, who she knew watched over her, to let it be so. Then she took the first of the steps.

She was halfway up them when she felt her muscles slowing and her mind growing foggy. Two more steps were all she managed. She thought to turn, to warn the others to come no farther, but her body seemed frozen and unable to respond to her mind's direction. The hand holding the pouch containing the Stones of Morann went limp and fell to her side. Some small part of Aliah's mind then realized the witch had not left the Well unguarded. Like fools, they had stumbled right into her trap. A voice—words floating as if on a wind—sounded from somewhere near. Something about the stones. Morann's Stones. Aliah's mind sank into a mire, and then oblivion.

Nohr walked east through the Simarron, back toward his tribe, his family, and his beer-making. He had done what the witch had wanted of him. Not successfully, but he had tried, and now considered himself free of his commitment to her. If the witch saw things differently, then let her journey to Desolation Peak and challenge him there. Nohr chuckled at the thought, for only fools came to a gaugath village looking for trouble. Nohr had agreed to accompany Skave into the woods only because Lord Gral had commanded it. Once the Meat Peddler ruled the Simarron, he'd have no time nor care for what Nohr had or had not done for the witch. Nohr spat, cursing the witch and her buggery beneath his breath. Let the Peddler deal with her, for Nohr planned to never lay eyes on her again.

After their confrontation with the humans, Nohr had run far enough away that pursuit was unlikely, and hid. Then, when he deemed it safe, he returned to the ambush site to gather up Skave's body. He left the stalker's weapons behind, for they were too small for Nohr's own use and not worth much in trade. Gaugaths, even young ones, did not fight with swords and knives, preferring hammer, mace, or morning star. But the haurek's body, even unseasoned, promised a tasty meal on the road home. Nohr had already bitten off one of Skave's hands. The bones were crunchy and the skin was tough, and Nohr had longed for his beer to wash it down. Nohr thought, with anger, of the knight who had spilled the last of his prized mead. It had been a fine brew, and well worth the effort of lugging it down from the mountains and through the forest. Curse the knight for wasting the last of it, and curse the witch for bringing him here!

"By Chaeick's balls," Nohr grumbled, "I'll have Desolation Peak in sight by week's end, or I'm a—"

"Where do you think you're going?"

The witch stepped from the brush, barring Nohr's way and stopping him dead in his tracks. Swallowing hard, Nohr tried to say something, but instead choked on the bile rising from his throat.

The witch, who came only to the gaugath's shoulder,

studied him for a moment, then looked to the body he dragged behind him. "What has happened?" she asked, hissing. "Lie to me, and I shall know it!"

Nohr swallowed again, then gave her a brief recounting of the ambush. When he was through, he fell silent. Thoughts of turning tail and running were just crossing his mind when the witch asked him to bring forth the haurek's body. Nohr obeyed, depositing the corpse at her feet and stepping away. She made no comment about the missing hand as Nohr watched her bare the haurek's chest. Then, drawing forth a knife, she cut into him with practiced precision. In moments, the witch's gruesome work was done, and she held in her hand Skave's heart. She secreted it away into a ragged sack. Rising, she ordered Nohr to follow her. "Your duty to me remains incomplete. Come with me, and you shall have a second chance to fulfill your obligation." She did not wait for him to respond, nor did she look back as she set off.

Nohr thought again of running, but fear of the witch made him think better of it. There were worse fates than lending her assistance. Like death. Nohr hefted his hammer and looked upon Skave's desecrated body one last time. He thought of ripping off an arm for the road, but seeing the witch already disappearing from view, decided to forgo the snack as he lumbered off after her.

Murik heaved in a breath.

He found by remaining still the table's crushing weight had the least effect upon him. Either that, or his body had simply grown numb and he no longer felt the pain. A fire welled within him, though, and he fumbled at the chain hanging about his neck. Using what strength remained, he pulled the amulet out from between him and the table and lifted it before his eyes. He watched the cerulean gemstone at its center catch the moonlight as it spun for a moment. Then, he hurled it from him. The throw was a weak one, and the amulet flew only just past the other side of the upended table.

Physical strength—Murik's physical strength—was of no use here. Even with one arm free, the burden of the table was too much. Though he had drawn heavily upon his staff's energy to cast his magic, his life force had also been consumed. Fueled by adrenaline, he had pushed himself beyond his normal means. Now, that high had fled from him, leaving his mind foggy and his body drained. Lifting the table from him was beyond his power. But moving something smaller was not. Murik lifted his head to search for his staff. He spotted it a short distance away. Concentrating, the staff budged only an inch at first, then slid erratically toward him, until, finally, he closed a hand upon its polished surface. Murik closed his eyes and allowed its power to soak into him. Focusing, Murik used that power to replace his failing strength. Another moment of concentration and the spell needed to free him solidified in his mind. With his eyes still closed, he exerted his will. The table trembled, but did not move. Then, one corner lifted. The eslar's brow furrowed with effort as he urged the table from him. Sweat glistened on his brow. There was risk in what he did: the staff's energy was great, and in his weakened state, drawing too much of it into himself might cause more harm than good. Murik was no apprentice, though. He drew what he needed, maintaining control. As quickly as the power came into him, he dispersed it into his spell. The one corner to lift soon became one whole side, and with a sense of triumph, Murik scurried out from beneath the table's weight. Relieved, he discovered his legs numb but not broken. His concentration melted away, and a loud crash resounded throughout the room as the table fell back to the floor.

Murik leaned his back to the wall, letting the blood flow painfully back into his legs. Then, using his staff for support, he rose. The effort created a roiling sea in his mind, and he nearly fell back to the floor. Sweat streamed down his face, chilling him despite the heat emanating from the witch's stove. But, finally, the dizziness passed enough for him to stumble a few steps, and then a few more. He circumvented the overturned table, stopping when Ushar's amulet lay a few feet from him. He didn't bother picking it up, as his eyes locked on it and he began the spell of summoning. He'd invoked the spell so many times in the past its formulation came unbidden. He coupled his will with energy from his staff, and then again with his own life force. Collectively, the energy surged from Murik's person and into the amulet. The sigils surrounding the soul stone flared to life, and then the spell was completed. A momentary flash lit the room. Once Murik's eyesight returned to him, he saw the spirit of Ushar, gray and without life, hovering just above the amulet. Ushar's demeanor was dour, his face, unreadable. Gray robes and his long, braided beard hung still and lifeless as eyeless sockets studied Murik.

Why have you summoned me this time?

Murik licked dry lips. He hesitated for a moment, then blurted out, "I need your help."

Silence, and then the expected laughter. *So it comes to this. I would tell you to go rot if I thought it made any difference.*

It did not. Ushar was bound to the stone, and thus to Murik. Anything Murik asked, Ushar was compelled to do, as long as it was within his power. He had no choice. That the spirit hated him bothered Murik, but not so much he was ready to let go of the old sorcerer or his knowledge.

"I am weak. It was a wonder I had the strength to even summon you."

It's a pity, is what it is. A pity you did not expend yourself. A pit you did not burn yourself to nothingness.

Murik ignored the comments. "I need your help mixing a potion. A witch's potion. One to rejuvenate me. I do not know how to concoct such a thing with the witch's ingredients, but you do."

You know a witch's magic has costs.

"All too well. But I've no choice."

You also know I will attempt to deceive you at every turn.

"You will do as I say, as you must. You *will* help me."

Perhaps, in this, I am not helping you, but harming you. It is enough for me.

Murik sighed. "Tell me what I must do."

The apparition said nothing else except that which Murik wanted to hear.

Kayra felt the mild sensation of warmth beneath her gambeson the moment she set foot within the great cavern. Unused to magic and its indicators, she passed it off as nerves, tightening her grip on sword and shield as she examined every flickering shadow leading up to the temple's raised dais. Once they stood at its base, she looked with silent reverence upon the towering sentinels standing guard in this place of evil for untold centuries. Though excitement was in her heart, it was an excitement tempered by a sense of humility and caution. This temple, evil though it was, was a monument to a time when Immortals walked Uhl, when evil followers of evil gods bred war and carnage, and when druids and those of the Order—Kayra's predecessors—had risen to stop them. Though the Gods of Light and Darkness were no more, the good and evil they had cultivated with such careful purposefulness lived on. Here and now, in this temple, evil had risen again. But good, just like in the stories of old, had come to chase away the shadows and drive Darkness back to the Great Pit from which it had been spawned.

Now, with nothing rising to challenge them, victory seemed

all but assured. Following behind the others, Kayra mounted the first of the steps. Her chest, for some reason, felt afire. Kayra sheathed her sword in a quick, practiced motion and then removed her helmet. Taking hold of the leather string hanging about her neck, she revealed the simple talisman given to her by young Jezebel of Homewood. The blue gemstone, ridiculously small, blazed with fierceness. She held it to her face, feeling the heat emanating from it, then let it drop so it lay outside her surcoat.

"Something is wrong."

Kayra's words quickly faded into the gloom. Though Ash looked at her, neither Jerrick nor Aliah did. Kayra repeated herself. Neither of them even turned to acknowledge her. Kayra dashed up the few steps separating her from Jerrick, who was closest. "What has happened?" she asked, walking around to face him. Looking into his eyes, she saw glassy unawareness. Kayra repeated the exercise with Aliah, finding the woman similarly cataleptic. Only she and Ash seemed unaffected. "Give me the stones," Kayra said to Aliah, whose glassy expression remained unchanged. Aliah made no reaction. The duty was hers, then. She took the pouch from the woman, then ascended to the top of the dais. Ash, who seemed reluctant to leave Jerrick at first, followed. There, Kayra's gaze fell upon the black, bubbling surface of the Well of Darkness. Around it stood the great druid sentinels, but Kayra hardly noticed them as her gaze remained fixed on the churning motion of the Well. Only the sight of Holly, who lay bound by chains at its other side and seemed not to have noticed Kayra's arrival, distracted the knight from it. Kayra felt a renewed sense of resolve at seeing her friend whole and unharmed. A moment later, a serpentine voice sounded from behind.

"What transpires here?"

Kayra spun around. As she did, the pouch containing the druid stones flew from a gauntleted hand more suited to grasping the hilt of a weapon than thin fabric. Kayra ignored the stones, narrowing her gaze at the sight of the sitheri witch and her gaugath lackey as the pair emerged from the flickering shadows down below. The witch's hood was pulled back, revealing a reptilian snout, beady eyes, and ashen head ridges. Both witch and goblin started coming up the stairs.

Kayra swallowed hard as she held shield and sword before her. "Come no farther, or—"

"How is it you were not affected by my spell, hmm?" The witch's reptilian voice slithered from her mouth in a near whisper as she stopped and glanced at the knight. Serpentine eyes locked on the glowing gemstone at the knight's chest.

Kayra met the witch's stare despite the shiver it sent down her spine. Next to her, Ash snarled.

The witch shrugged. "No matter." Looking at Nohr, she said, "Kill this fool. When you've finished with her, kill the rest."

The gaugath chuckled, obeying instantly as he continued his climb. His presence, drawing near, forced Kayra to move away from the Well. She had no choice but to leave the druid stones where they had fallen. The steps encircled the dais, so Kayra descended the other side even as Nohr completed his ascension. Meanwhile the witch drew closer to Holly. Kayra knew what purpose the witch had in mind.

Sacrifice.

No one had so much as come out and said it plainly, but Kayra knew what had been implied when she had asked what fate the witch meant for her friend. Now, with the others stricken by paralysis and the sorcerer dead—what else could the witch's presence here indicate but Murik's failure?—Kayra was the only one capable of saving the Simarron Woods and its people. Of equal importance, she was the only one able to save Holly.

Knowing she'd never get around the gaugath to confront the witch, Kayra continued to back away while searching for a suitable strategy. Ash was lost to view, though his growling and occasional bark told her the dog remained with Holly. Before, when they had been ambushed, there was no time to think, no time to contemplate the danger. Now, there was too much time. The gaugath was in no hurry; each step of his was slow and measured. He knew there was nowhere for her to go or to hide. This was his time with her, to maim, torture, and, finally, kill. His devilish grin told Kayra he planned to cherish every moment.

The smirk set her on edge, and Kayra was suddenly reminded of her nightmare. In it, just as now, she had stood alone. Only then, her adversary had been an ogre. Tit for tat, she thought, her eyes moving up and down with the rhythm of the gaugath's hammer as he slapped it into his open palm. Beads of sweat ran down the back of her neck, and something in her stomach, faint at first, rose up to clench at her heart. The goblin was a colossus of strength—one fist darted out, breaking off the top of one of the stalagmites in a cloud of dust, as if to demonstrate—and she but a knight-errant. As the enormity of the situation sank in, the strength in Kayra's arms melted away, leaving them feeling spongy and lifeless. The tip of her sword wavered, nearly touching the cavern floor. A chuckle—boisterous and mocking—snapped her back to attention, and she shook her head, raising her blade high once more. Her gesture of defiance was not enough to drive the fear from her, though, as she fought to keep from trembling. Somewhere from within, a voice screamed at her to turn and run. Remembering thoughts of victory and glory, Kayra laughed. She choked from the effort, though, and her body started to tremble. Nohr, sensing her terror, grinned as the sharp impact of his hammer's head slapping his open palm rang out.

Try though she might, Holly was unable to wake herself from the place Parthen had taken her. The priest claimed she was in Scilya; Holly's every sense seemed to confirm it. Yet her mind refused to accept it for anything but the illusion it was, and so, except for trying to wake herself, Holly spent all of the time between the priest's departure and his return in idle thought. When Parthen did return, it was in a flourish of gray, silken robes.

Your friends have arrived.

Holly, startled at first by the priest's sudden appearance, jumped up, her face alight. "I knew they'd come!"

And so it is time to choose.

Parthen's hood was pulled back and folded at his shoulders, exposing his pockmarked cheeks and the horrible scars plaguing his face. The enormity of his announcement had the effect of momentarily dispelling Holly's revulsion.

They have already entered the temple chamber.

"Then I shall be freed any moment!"

Unlikely. They have fallen under the spell of the witch.

Holly's excitement wavered.

Their lives hang in the balance. I have felt the witch's dweomer; it is an assiduous thing which shall reach deep inside of them, forcing them to confront that which they most fervently deny. Should they surrender themselves, their minds will be destroyed from the inside out. It shall not be pleasant, nor survivable. Will you allow this to happen?

Dejected, Holly said, "You mean, will I help you?"

They will live if you do.

Holly had spent much time trying to rationalize all which had happened. Questions had filled her mind, and she thought to pose them to Parthen upon his return. Now, however, thoughts of her friends in danger caused the questions to fade from her mind. In their place was panic—a sense of helplessness—which threatened to unravel her. Holly looked away, her mind's eye searching for something—anything—to help ground her emotions. Then she heard Parthen's voice in her mind. To her surprise, his tone was soothing. His words, encouraging.

We often walk through life facing things larger than ourselves. At those times, choices are given to us. Do we flee? Do we compromise? Do we refuse to yield no matter the cost? What we choose and how we choose comes from who we are. You are young and still new to the world. But I sense within you devotion which, once set, will not sway easily. Help me, Holly. Help me, and I will do everything in my power to help your friends. I swear it on my god's—

Though Holly did not look at his face, she felt she sensed his smirk.

I swear it.

She did look up at him then, and for an instant saw something she never expected. So fleeting, she thought perhaps she had been mistaken. But it had been there. Concern had been etched in his face, and compassion, perhaps mitigated by a lifetime spent trapped beneath the earth in a lonely, deserted temple with nothing but regrets for company. Holly let out a deep breath. She knew her mind had been made up the very first time Parthen had made his proposal to her, for she refused to sit by while her friends suffered.

"Save them, and I will help you."

Parthen's ghostly head nodded as his bulbous lips curled into a smile Holly knew she'd remember for the rest of her life.

CHAPTER TWENTY

ATONEMENT

DARKNESS, COLD AND NUMBING.

A flash, and a room—Jerrick's room—stood revealed. The light faded, immersing the blood-red walls in shadow once more.

You did it!

The voices combined into something physical, hitting Jerrick like a hammer. White-hot pain seared his mind, and he almost crumbled to the ground, if only he could move. Memories came to him. The cavern. The Well of Darkness. He and his allies had fallen into some bewitching concocted by the witch.

Another flash chased away the dark, and Jerrick saw his dead wife nestled in their bed. Their baby—stillborn—was swaddled at her side.

You did it!

It was only one voice now.

You killed her!

Images of a faceless mother Jerrick had never known filled his mind. A shadow—his father—hung over the dead woman.

You killed all of them!

The voice was his own.

"I know what I did," Jerrick said, spacing each word so that each and every one sank in.

Another flash illuminated the room. This time, it stayed lit, revealing all Jerrick had done. Immobile, he tried to close his eyes and failed. His dead wife and child were the only things he saw. Them, and their blood. *I did it.* Grief and anger rose within him. He seized the latter until a rage boiled within him. With it came mobility. "I did it!" Though no one was there to hear him, Jerrick screamed the words, over and over. He yelled them at the walls, the furniture, the open window. "I did it!" Let the world know. It didn't matter. Jerrick stormed the place, toppling everything in his path. The revolving mirror given to Kendra and him as a wedding gift from her parents was the first piece to fall, the glass shattering on impact. Candles set upon Kendra's vanity were knocked away. The vanity itself— handcrafted by his own poorly skilled hands—tumbled over after them. Kendra's hairbrush and a small collection of hand-mixed lotions and powders crashed to the floor along with it. Jerrick cried out, knocking his own dresser to the floor. Finally, with nothing left to topple, he stopped. His gaze fell on Kendra and Anna, and he went silent.

You know what you must do.

The voices again. But this time a foreign, serpentine one joined their litany. It didn't matter. He saw the sword—his sword—the naked, bloodstained blade lay across the foot of the bed, and he knew what to do. What must be done. Picking it up, Jerrick held the blade before him. Slowly, he dipped his forehead so it just touched the weapon's edge. Then he turned the blade upon himself. Jerrick's eyes met his wife's lifeless ones for one instant. Someday, somehow, she might forgive him. But he'd never forgive himself. Jerrick leaned against the tip of the blade.

There is another way.

Jerrick paused. The voice was new and unrecognizable.

Silence, but only until the other voices returned. *No,* they said, a snake's hiss ruling them, *there is only the one way. Do what must be done, and be done with it.*

Jerrick's grip on his sword hadn't relaxed. "I killed them," he said to the room.

Did you? The solitary voice again. *See for yourself. Judge for yourself.*

Jerrick felt faint, and he swooned, unable to keep his legs beneath him. The voices left his mind, and his sword fell from his grasp, clattering to the floor as he went to his knees. Leaning heavily against the bed, he buried his face in the softness of it. The world was like a sea, with him dipping and rising with each wave. Nausea set in, and Jerrick clenched folds in the sheets as if holding a lifeline. Then the motion stopped. Jerrick lifted his head and was dumbfounded.

The room was gone. In its place was another. It was a simple affair: a small dresser and foot chest to one side, and a bed whose sheets Jerrick continued to clench. There was a woman in the bed. Jerrick did not recognize her lifeless face. The room shimmered, and Jerrick braced himself for another wave of nausea, but the effect lasted only a moment. When it faded, Jerrick was not alone.

At one side of the bed stood his father.

Jerrick had been a child of six when the man had abandoned him. Still, he recognized the hard, chiseled face, elegant moustache, and steel-gray eyes. Jerrick's father gazed upon the woman. Gently, he leaned over her and kissed her cheek. Then he straightened and looked at Jerrick.

"I killed her."

Surprised, Jerrick found the voice his own, the words, his. He had been six years old when they had had this conversation. But this wasn't right. His mother had died giving birth to him, six years before he and his father had spoken thus.

"No, Jerrick. You did not do this." His father's voice was strong but weary.

Memories, so gray and dim Jerrick was not certain they were

even his own, passed through his mind. He remembered their last conversation, when his father had looked upon him and said the words that had haunted him since Kendra's death. Yet, now, Jerrick realized for the very first time, those words had not been his father's, but his own.

"It is because of me she is gone." Jerrick's voice sounded flat and hollow to his ears. As a child, had he truly sounded so empty? "Do not tell me it is Fate, beyond my control, like the midwives in town do." Heady words for one so young.

"Fate played no part in this, son." Jerrick's father stared deeply into his eyes. There were none of the accusations Jerrick remembered. Only sorrow and regret. "There comes a time, Jerrick, when a man must admit to his mistakes. I did not do so in time, and your mother paid the price. Your mother's death is no one's fault but mine." This conversation had never happened! Or had it? The words sounded so familiar, but their memory was like reading tattered and torn paper, some of them sounding more familiar than others. "I must leave, Jerrick. I will return. But it may be some time before I do."

His father's voice started to fade. The room swirled again.

"No! Wait!" Desperation seized him. "What do you mean? To where do you—"

Darkness returned.

Then, lightning flashed overhead and the coolness of rain pelted him. Wind whistled through thick stands of trees, and the ground felt soft and fertile beneath his booted feet. He took steps not his own. Something was ahead.

See for yourself.

Jerrick strode forward, pushing through dense brush to emerge into a place he had never seen before.

It was a place of evil.

A grove surrounded by elms and oaks, the ground rising so it peaked at its center. There, at the grove's cusp, was a flat, jagged rock. Lying atop it was a woman, bound and screaming. Another, wrapped in dark robes, hunched over her with arms raised high. Through the howl of the wind, Jerrick heard chanting.

Witchcraft!

There was no hesitation as Jerrick ran toward them. Somehow, a knife appeared in his throwing hand. Seconds later, he was close enough to see the prone woman writhing against her bonds in a futile struggle while, above her, the hooded figure gesticulated and flailed arms too thin to be a man's. Then, abruptly, the chanting ceased. The witch's hands—withered and dry from age—reached down to pull away her captive's clothing, revealing a belly swollen with life. A scream filled the grove as both hands gripped the woman's stomach tight. Then the chanting began anew. The witch paid no attention to Jerrick's approach.

Confused but cognizant of the helpless woman's need, Jerrick acted. The knife left his hand in a practiced motion, hurling end over end to sink into the witch's chest. She fell back from the impact, releasing her captive. Then, her chanting silenced, she collapsed to the other side of the great rock.

Jerrick made his way up the remainder of the slope, stopping when he reached the bound woman. She looked upon him with frightened eyes. Her face was pale and delicate, and looked somehow familiar. Her hair was dark like his own. Jerrick undid the ropes binding her, covering her nakedness with his cloak. Then, taking her hand, he knelt.

"I fear I am too late." Jerrick bowed his head, unable to meet the woman's stare.

"Oh, Jerrick."

The woman's voice was familiar.

Jerrick looked up and his breath was taken away. "Kendra?" The auburn hair and chestnut eyes were hers. Jerrick struggled to sift through a jumble of words. "How is this possible?"

Judge for yourself.

Again, the voice.

Jerrick ignored it. He squeezed his wife's hand tighter, one hand smoothing the tresses from her forehead. She smiled a weak, slight smile, but one which set his heart ablaze.

A shadow fell over her, and the witch was there once more. Impossibly, the knife remained embedded in her chest. With a howl, she leaped up, smothering both Jerrick and Kendra in a swaddling of black robes.

Aliah sank to her knees amidst the blackened ash and burned-out husks of the tall and proud oaks of Sollin-kel. But for the wail of the wind, the grove was silent. Foulness ruled here: a reek of soot and ash and smoke and death. The air hung heavy with it, making it difficult for Aliah to breathe. Holding her arms close, she tried to still her trembling as tears slid unchecked down her cheeks. Far worse than when she had returned home to find her mother and the other dryads wilted and dead, this nightmarish scene left Aliah unable to speak, think, or react in any way other than to cling to the hope that somehow none of it was real. Her home was gone. More so, the Simarron had been razed to the ground.

This cannot be.

But she knew her senses were true. She saw the charred trees, smelled the acrid air. The sounds of the forest were muted, the forest's denizens gone. Even the grove's stream flowed no more; its bed was dry, the earth, a network of spidery cracks. Though a shrinking isle amidst a sea of Darkness, Sollin-kel had still contained life. Her people's strength, which lingered on even after their deaths, had seen to that, shielding the grove from the worst of the Well's sickening taint. It should have been months, perhaps years, before this came to pass.

What is this then? The future?

Aliah closed her eyes, steadying her breathing as she tried to remember how she had gotten here. She had been in the cavern with Jerrick and the others. The Well of Darkness had been just ahead. She remembered ascending the steps leading up to it, then nothing. She opened her eyes. Nothing made sense. Nothing had since her return.

The woman who had left the Simarron behind was not the

same one who returned. Just as the forest had changed, so had she. Only when she had learned of her family's demise did she realize just how much. Initial grief had quickly given way to a newfound sense of rage, and she swore revenge on whoever had murdered her ilk. Delbin Kinkaed told Aliah of the witch and the Well, but not of the person truly responsible for unleashing both upon the Simarron. The arch-druid had not told her of Evar, Eldest of the Elders. If not for him, the witch would never have found the Well of Darkness. If not for him, her mother and the others would still be alive. Aliah looked upon the forest and all Evar had done, and anger and rage mounted.

The wind blew in a fierce gust, whipping Aliah's hair all around her face, blinding her. Parting the strands from her eyes, Aliah found her thoughts become reality, as Evar was there before her. Clad in simple patroller leathers, he was unarmed. Arms hung at his sides, and his shoulders had none of their usual proud bearing. His eyes spoke of sadness and regret. Aliah was moved by none of it.

She looked upon him with distaste, seeing in him an outlet for the emotions threatening to boil over within her. A club—a gnarled and blackened thing—was in her hand. Without thought, she used it, striking him across the cheek. It opened the skin, jarring his head to one side. Then she jabbed the knotted end into his stomach, doubling him over. Despite the force of her blows, Evar remained silent, crying out neither in pain nor for mercy. Aliah circled to one side, shoving the Elder so he toppled to the ground. In obvious pain, he lay like that until Aliah shouted for him to rise. His movements were mechanical and slow, but he managed to regain his feet just long enough for Aliah to knock him back to the ground.

"Get up!"

Evar, like an automaton, rose on unsteady legs. Aliah laid into him again, hitting him across the face once, then twice, driving him back amidst a sparse tangle of charred branches hanging nearly to the ground.

Finish him.

Aliah, club raised, stopped. The words, whispered by a multitude of voices, faded as quickly as they had come, leaving her unsure if she had heard anything at all. Chest heaving, she watched with interest as the stiff and lifeless branches swayed. Is there life still here? Then the wind howled, stirring the branches and dispelling curiosity and hope along with it. Aliah returned her attention to Evar. The Elder's mouth bled. The side of his face was swollen and bruised.

Aliah stared at him. Is this what I have wrought? Pity welled within her. Is this what I have become?

Finish him, sister.

Aliah spun around, fully expecting to find herself surrounded. "Who's there? Show yourself!"

Has it been so long you no longer recognize us? Perhaps another form shall suit your senses better.

Aliah gasped, taking a step back as, one by one, dryads—members of her family—emerged from blackened tree husks. There was a pushing at the bark from the inside, a bulge, and then they were there. Stooped and twisted, they were pale shadows of their former selves. Gone was the grace of their step, the elegance of their standing. Dead like the trees they had come from, these creatures—there were twelve in all—had no claim to calling her sister. Smooth, green skin hung rotting from desiccated bones; lustrous, emerald hair was blackened and missing in tufts; and supple hands were stained with blood—red blood—which was not their own. With shambling gaits, they encircled Evar, leaving a place in their ring for Aliah so their number was now thirteen. Their stench—the stench of the dead—nearly caused Aliah to retch. One of them— Aliah did not recognize her for the rot of her face—motioned for the half-dryad to join them. Aliah only looked on in horror.

They closed on Evar, who backed away from one only to find himself in the clutches of another. They shoved him, much as Aliah had just done, smacking him hard with skeletal hands, forcing him to stagger into the waiting arms of another. Aliah squeezed her eyes shut for a moment, then opened them, half expecting—hoping—that what she saw was illusion. But nothing had changed. Then, just for an instant, her eyes met those of Evar, and she saw something in them which shook her. She had seen that look before while on her journeys. In what city, on what street corner, it mattered not. It was a pleading look of desperation. A cry for help.

"Leave him alone." Aliah's voice was weak and barely heard. She wanted revenge, but not at this cost. She repeated herself, louder this time. Several of the dead dryads looked her way.

Leave him? Come, sister, they said, a serpentine hiss amongst them now. *This is the time for vengeance. Strike back at the one who took us from you. Strike back, and feel whole again.*

Whole? Aliah remembered the cities and the bullies and braggarts who ruled their streets. Thieves, murderers, and brigands, all of them. I am not like them! But revenge, revenge for the death of her family, called to her in a voice demanding satisfaction.

Come, sister. Join us, they said, hissing the words. *Do not forget what he has done.*

Images came to her: the Simarron, Sollin-kel, the Hall of the Wood, all brought down by the actions of this single man. Aliah's blood simmered once more, and she knew there was nothing for her to do but join her sisters. Their ways had always been the same.

Is there nothing left, then?

The voice halted her, somehow diminishing the bloodlust roiling within her. "Nothing left of what?" Aliah asked in a whisper. Sudden exhaustion hit her, and the world went silent save for the single voice. Aliah hung her head, not bothering to turn to address this newcomer.

"Compassion. Forgiveness."

Aliah sighed. "I want there to be, but it's so hard." The fingers gripping the club relaxed. "How can I forgive him after what he has done?"

The voice did not answer. But then Aliah felt a light touch at the back of her shoulders. Gently, the hands turned her so she looked into the eyes of her mother. At the same time, the club fell from her grasp.

Vadeya Dawnoak was radiant, a shimmering light in a fog of dark. Tears came to Aliah's eyes as she embraced her, burying her face in her mother's emerald tresses. The smell of the forest clung to Vadeya; Aliah inhaled deeply, losing herself in the memories the scent rekindled. Tender hands moved to stroke Aliah's head.

"The path of revenge is a long and lonely one, my daughter." Her voice was cool and comforting, just as Aliah remembered it. "Once you start down it, there is no turning back."

Aliah sighed and said nothing.

"You must make a choice. Choose revenge, and finish what you've started here. Choose forgiveness, and . . . begin anew."

Aliah pushed herself back just enough so her eyes met those of her mother. "Begin anew alone? I don't know if I can. Without you and the others, I am alone."

Vadeya smiled. "You will always have the forest. As sure as your name is Aliah, Branch of the Stars, you will never be alone." Her mother's hands fell from her. "Choose wisely, my daughter." Her body grew translucent, fading like morning mist.

"No! Mother, wait!" Aliah's plea went unheeded, as Vadeya Dawnoak disappeared. Aliah was left staring into the dark of the forest, alone.

The sounds of the world returned, and she once more heard

the monsters who called themselves her kin having their fun with Evar. Once again, they urged her to conjoin with them. Aliah took in a deep breath, wiping the tears from her eyes with the back of her hand. She stooped to pick up her fallen club. Her gaze downward, she walked toward the ring of phantasms. Her mother had been right. There was a choice, two paths diverging before her. Neither short nor easy, but for better or worse, a decision had to be made. Aliah took a deep breath and made hers.

She gripped the club tighter as she drew closer to the group. Standing at their center, arms held up to shield his face from his tormentors, was Evar. His defenses were paltry; both arms and his face were marked with a dozen or more bleeding cuts. Just like when Aliah had assaulted him, he made no move to counterattack or flee. Spying Aliah's approach, several of the dead dryads' eyes lit up. They waved grotesque hands her way, gesturing her forward.

Yes, yes! Come, sisters, open a place for dear Aliah. Let her hand strike the killing blow.

Their line parted, allowing her to walk to the center of the ring they had formed around the Elder. Stopping within easy range of him, Aliah did not raise her weapon, but instead dropped it. Aliah had thought for a time if she visited the same death upon the perpetrator of her mother's murder then she might attain some sense of satisfaction. She realized now how wrong she had been. Nothing was going to bring her mother back to her, least of all more death. Now was the time for new beginnings and forgiveness.

Evar's face came out from behind his arms, allowing Aliah's eyes to meet his. Despite the physical hurt he had endured, the look of regret and grief remained. Evar knew what he had done. Such knowledge was punishment enough. Something unspoken passed between them, and Aliah saw in his eyes the understanding that she had forgiven him.

A terrible, high-pitched shrieking sounded all around them. Aliah instinctively clasped hands to ears, trying to muffle out the sound. Her effort was in vain, though, her mind sent spinning as she spiraled to the ground. She kept her eyes fixed on the dryads who were not dryads, watching as they faded, but not like her mother had. Instead, they melted away. Already, their legs were gone. They fought it every step of the way, clawing at the earth and wailing in protest. Looking to Aliah, they beseeched her to help them.

Seek your revenge, sister! Slay the one who has harmed us!

Aliah didn't need to look for Evar to know he was already gone. Aliah closed her eyes. Gradually, the pleas and wailings subsided. As they did, Aliah felt the last vestiges of her desire for revenge against the Elder disappear. Opening her eyes, she wasn't surprised at all to find herself back in the temple of the Well.

Fear.

It rose like bile at the back of Kayra's throat, choking her as she backed away from her adversary. The gaugath was herding her, driving her deeper into the farthest recesses of the cavern. Kayra knew this as surely as she knew there was nothing else to do about it. The ground was uneven and rough here, and she stumbled too often. Fear ruled her. Kayra kept her jaw clamped; it was the only way to keep her teeth from chattering. The trembling in her limbs was more difficult to contain. Only by tensing her muscles and holding tight to her upraised sword and shield was she able to keep them steady. Still, the dread coursing through her had drained much of her body's strength, leaving only her diminishing resolve to keep her from shriveling into a simpering mass of cowardice.

Cowardice.

She repeated the word in her mind, hating it and herself, but knowing full well what it meant for her future as a knight—for her very life!—if she let it consume her. Though Kayra had participated in dozens of battles and trained to fight against such monsters as trolls and giants, none of those mirrored her current situation. Those times, she had fought alongside others: fellow knights, experienced soldiers, mercenaries. But here, she stood alone, bereft of allies and doomed unless she controlled her fear and *did something*.

Indecision added fuel to her trepidation, and though cool air drifted in through her helmet's eye and breathing slits, the remainder of her body felt as if it baked within an oven. Sweat soaked her gambeson; drops ran down her front, back, arms, and legs. Her breathing, already labored, grew more rapid. Once more, a voice inside her mind screamed at her to throw down her sword, tear off her armor, and run away before it was too late. Another voice, rising to drown out the first, told her escape was impossible, that surrendering herself to the goblin and hoping for a quick death was the only remaining option. Kayra tried to shake both voices from her head, but it was no use. Without realizing it, she allowed her shield to droop and the tip of her sword to fall. In that moment, the gaugath struck.

He kept his hammer in plain view the entire time while he forced Kayra back, punctuating what fate he meant for her by methodically swatting his hammer's head into his open palm. But then, instead of letting it fall to his clawed hand, he cocked the weapon back, letting it swing from over his shoulder like the arm of a catapult. Kayra watched that terrible hammer arcing toward her. The sight of it shook something within her, forcing her mind back to alertness. She realized the gaugath had trapped her, corralling her so that a wall was at her back, and to either side, an insurmountable screen of stalagmites. No time to think, Kayra reacted by instinct alone. Her shield was useless. There was no hope of parrying such an attack, either, and so Kayra chose the only option left to her: she rushed her assailant. With no time to position sword or shield, her entire effort went into avoiding the killing blow hurtling toward her. Just as she closed with her enemy, she felt and heard the impact behind her, and she knew she had escaped the hammer's touch. Hot breath and a nauseating scent greeted her as she found herself face-to-face with the gaugath, whose swing had hunched him forward. Kayra struggled to raise her sword, but the weapon was knocked aside. Then the gaugath struck, rapping her with a backhanded swipe so forceful it hurled her into the air and up and over one of the stalagmite walls. The cavern became a spinning haze of jade as Kayra cried out. Her shield had taken the brunt of the blow; fiery pain lanced through her shield arm and into her shoulder, and then she was falling. Armor grated on rock as she slammed into the cavern floor, landing flat on her back. There was a moment of gasping as she fought to regain her breath, then her training took hold. Though her armor was heavy, it was not so awkward it prevented her from rising on her own, even when prostrate. She did so now, using her weapon arm for assistance. Somehow, she had managed to hold on to her sword. Her other arm and shoulder were ablaze with pain. Heaving herself up, Kayra scanned through blurred vision for the goblin. She spotted him not circumventing the wall he had just tossed her over but leaping right over it! All eight-odd feet of him hung suspended in midair for an instant, then he was falling, both feet aimed directly at her, ready to smash her back to the ground.

Kayra shook the fog from her mind and leaped away. An audible thump sounded behind her, but she dared not risk a glance back. Desperate, Kayra ran. No act of cowardice this time; she knew what she was about and what she needed to do. Heavy footfalls sounded behind her, Nohr's cadence suggesting he was in no hurry. Somewhere in a distant part of the cavern, Kayra heard the echoes of a reptilian chant. Time was running out for Holly.

Kayra slowed her pace, catching a quick glimpse of the gaugath's shadowed form from over her shoulder. Like a harbinger of doom, he advanced slowly, his hammer dangling at his side as he flashed her a wide grin full of jagged teeth. Kayra shuddered, knowing full well his kind's reputation as omnivores.

Stumbling, Kayra skirted stalagmites grown thick over time. Her shield arm and shoulder—no longer in pain—had gone numb. Looking ahead, she noticed how the ceiling narrowed to meet the floor. She was running out of room to run. Kayra stopped and turned. She steadied her breathing, watching as the great shadow of the gaugath approached. His path meandered through the cavern's obstructions, buying Kayra time. Letting out a deep breath, she let her shield fall from her numb arm and waited.

She was scared, but not like before. Scared of failing her friends, scared of tarnishing her family's name, scared of dying. But, on her oath as a knight, she refused to let fear rule her. Pushing it down, she buried it beneath the anger her father always said she'd been born with. Sometimes, Kayra felt there was little else inside her. She didn't know why. Perhaps because of the persistent need to prove herself, to show her family she was never meant to fit the mold of a prim-and-proper lord's daughter. They made her so angry sometimes, dictating her life as if it were a minstrel's script, all laid out and already decided. Her protests always fell on deaf ears, and her anger only grew. She learned early on the extent of its power, its ability to push her past limits she scarcely thought surmountable. Her liege, Sir Devon, had always thought her anger would result in her undoing. Her weapons master offered a contradictory assessment, believing it provided her great strength, but only if she learned to control and channel it properly. She thought both of them correct to some degree. Now, she embraced it. She had come too far, sacrificed too much, to let fear conquer her now, and she'd be damned if any goblin—regardless of its size—was going to slay her without a fight. Let this goblin come. Let him come and know he'd fought a knight of the Order. A knight who had met him in single combat, pitted her sword against his hammer, and put all on the line in defense of honor and duty.

Kayra's limbs quivered anew, this time from the berserk fury building within her. The gaugath remained a good ten paces away still. Removing her helmet, Kayra tossed it aside and shook the sweat from her brow. She positioned herself between and just behind two massive stalagmites towering even higher than the gaugath. She made an effort to control her ragged breathing, but the furious pounding of her heart made it difficult. The gaugath was only a handful of steps away now. Kayra raised her sword, the blade glimmering in the cavern's glow like the magic swords of Holly's tales. Then the gaugath was on her. Limited by the narrow space created by the twin stalagmite formation, the gaugath's hammer stroke was short and ineffective. Kayra took advantage, scoring a hit on her adversary's leg before his hammer came back around. When it did, Kayra had already retreated out of range. Nohr let out a roar and rumbled forward, using his sheer size to drive Kayra back. Kayra let him, moving so she circumvented one of the towering stalagmites. Not bothering to follow her around it, the gaugath simply took his hammer to the thick formation. His first stroke sent a shivering of cracks up and down the stalagmite's limestone surface. Bits and pieces crumbled away, and a smattering of dust rose up and into the stale air. His second blow sent shards and chunks of the rock sailing. In that instant, Kayra completed her circumvention and attacked him from behind.

She came in quickly, stabbing into the goblin's leg once more. Her thrust was shallow. Even still, the jab drew blood and another enraged howl from its victim. Before the wounded goblin retaliated, Kayra's sword whipped up to slash across his side. The razor-edged blade sliced leather hide, fur, and flesh alike before Kayra stepped away.

Incensed, Nohr snarled a challenge and, despite his wounded leg, leaped toward Kayra. He raised his hammer high above his head while still in midair, the tip of it just scraping the craggy ceiling and knocking loose a multitude of dagger-like stalactites before both gaugath and hammer landed hard on the ground. Kayra, sidestepping the attack, was nearly knocked from her feet as the goblin's impact sent tremors through the floor. She maintained her balance, though, recovering enough to come within striking distance. But the gaugath slashed a backhanded, bear-like paw at her, driving her back. Kayra heard the tips of his claws scrape across her armor, and then she was out of range. But only for an instant as the gaugath pressed the attack again. His hammer came at her in a sidelong, swiping motion she just managed to duck beneath. Coming up within the arc of his weapon, she drove her sword at him. The gaugath, fearful of the blade's sting, backpedaled away, using the haft of his hammer to block several blows meant for his midsection. Kayra surrendered the advantage almost immediately, forced back by the sheer size of the goblin as he renewed his assault. Somewhere in the distance, nearly forgotten, the witch's chanting was reaching a crescendo. Kayra needed to act now. Then, as she looked to the cavern's ceiling, an idea struck her.

She avoided a blow which instead struck a stalagmite, halving the structure and sending chips of limestone flying everywhere. The resulting dust acted as camouflage as she slipped away. Her ruse was short-lived, as the goblin spotted her and pursued. She ran back toward the twin stalagmites where her stand had started, probing the floor for her salvation. Then she saw it. Stooping, she let go of her sword and picked up her shield. Behind her, the pounding of the floor told her the gaugath was close. No time! Holding tight to her shield, she spun around and let it fly toward the ceiling. Just as she did, the gaugath sent his hammer at her. She saw the initial arc of the gaugath's swing, but not the hammer's head as it glanced from her shoulder, spinning her around like a child's top. Her shoulder blazed with pain, and so many stars spun across her vision, she was momentarily blinded by their brilliance. The next thing she knew, she was laid out on the floor.

The darkness of unconsciousness rose up. She might have welcomed it if not for the laughter sounding from somewhere above. Blinking back the dark, Kayra rolled to her side, seeing the outline of the gaugath towering over her and the glint of her shield lying just behind him. If the shield had knocked free any of the stalactites, none had found a home in him.

Kayra managed to push herself to her knees. Somehow, her hand found her sword. She tried lifting the weapon, but it was a futile effort, and the blade fell back to the ground with a clang. Another spate of raucous laughter sounded from the gaugath. Kayra looked up, locking her blurred vision with the gaugath's. The goblin's laughter faded.

"Time to die, knight."

Kayra scarcely heard the words through the ringing in her ears. Understanding was unnecessary; Kayra knew what the gaugath intended. In affirmation, she watched as he lifted his hammer high. One last blow to pulverize armor, flesh, and bone. Death. An ending. *Her* ending.

Not while I still draw breath.

The hammer was so far back the gaugath's elbows pointed ceiling-ward, leaving the gaugath completely exposed to attack. Kayra's eyes never left the gaugath's. She gathered every bit of strength remaining, funneling everything into one last effort. The goblin's eyes were telling. When she saw the delight in them which told her his hammer was about to fall, she raised her sword and lunged forward. Her head swam, her dazed vision showing three enemies. She hoped she aimed for the right one. Thrusting, she felt her blade sink home. The sword plunged upward through thick hair, skin, muscle, and fat, into the gaugath's chest. Kayra didn't see the gaugath's eyes go wide in surprise, nor did she see them dim until only a dead stare remained. She somehow rose, stumbling away as she watched his ponderous bulk sway for the slightest moment before toppling backward. The goblin crashed to the floor and did not rise again.

Kayra sighed in relief, the only gesture of triumph she was able to summon. She had faced the gaugath—and her fear—and won. The honor of the battle was hers. Behind her, the witch chanted on. Holly and the others still needed her. Her sword, embedded deep in its victim's body, was beyond her strength to remove. She left it. Dizzy and weak, she stumbled back through the forest of stalagmites.

CHAPTER TWENTY-ONE

ENDINGS

MURIK ENTERED THE CAVE, HIS person ablaze with magic. His staff glowed like the very sun; his body, suffused with fire. Gone was his limp, healed by the potion drawn from the witch's stock of components and concocted under Ushar's guidance. The potion had done far more than just heal his leg, though. He felt more alive than ever, energized with power previously unknown. This power had its price; no witch's potion was ever a cure-all. But Murik saved consideration of such things for later. Now, it was enough to have one more chance against his enemy.

Midway along the torch-lit path and just as the sacrificial dais came into view, Murik stopped. He spotted Aliah Starbough and Kayra at the lowermost steps. Aliah knelt over something, or someone, while Kayra stood, the knight's gaze fixed upward at Saress's Circle of Power. Gray and shifting like mist, it formed a wall of energy about the entirety of the dais. Sequestered behind that impenetrable barrier was the witch, the sound of her chanting echoing from the cavern walls. The ritual whereby Saress joined the power of the Well of Darkness with her own was not complete yet. There was still time.

Murik strode toward the two women, both seeming apprehensive at his approach. He moved close enough to be heard and that was all. Gesturing at Jerrick, who lay unconscious upon the floor, he asked, "What has happened?"

Aliah stood. "The witch left a trap for us. Only myself and Jerrick were afflicted. Its effects . . . wore off on me." Aliah looked down at Jerrick and shook her head. "I have done all I can, but still he will not wake."

Murik had felt the tingle of Saress's trap when he first entered the chamber. It had been nothing to shrug its effects off. Now, Murik noted the soft glow of the talisman about Kayra's neck and guessed at the woman's own immunity.

"He is not asleep," Murik said, "though to him it may seem so. There is nothing any of us can do for him." Murik shifted his gaze to the witch's magical barrier. "Saress thinks herself invulnerable behind her Circle."

Kayra's gaze joined his. "Can you get us through it?" she asked, holding up Jerrick's hunting knife. The topmost section of the blade was missing, a black, jagged line marking the separation. "Our own attempts have not been successful." She let the weapon fall to the floor. Her shield, helmet, and sword were all missing. Limestone dust and sweat marked her forehead and cheeks, and her hair had come mostly unbraided and hung haphazardly about her shoulders.

"She has the druid stones," Aliah said matter-of-factly. The witch had scooped them up when Kayra dropped them.

"And Holly," Kayra added.

Murik nodded. "Never mind the Gemstones of Morann. Sealing off the Well is the least of our worries now." Above them, the witch chanted on. It was only a matter of time before she completed her ritual. "Stay here," Murik ordered. "I will see to the Circle. Be prepared, though. A Circle of Power is a potent source of magic. When it collapses"—Murik gestured toward Jerrick—"pull him as far away as you can. Stay with him until it is safe to approach."

"What of you?" Aliah asked.

Murik looked at each of them. It was a quick look, but one which spoke volumes. "Best you go."

"What about Holly?" Kayra asked. "You mustn't—"

"Holly will remain unharmed. The same cannot be said for Saress. We must hurry. She must not be allowed to complete her spell."

Murik moved away without looking back, taking the dais's steps in twos and threes until he reached the wall that was the witch's Circle of Power. The ruins etched upon the floor—the source of the Circle's power—were aglow with yellow interlaced with ebon. Peering through the magical barrier, Murik spotted Saress, her scaly arms outstretched over Sarrengrave's Well. One hand was open, palm facing down. The other gripped a small, dark vial. Her hood was thrown back and her eyes closed. The Well's viscous fluid seethed and boiled, its foul energy beckoned forth by the chanting of the witch. Holly was there too, off to one side, chained and unmoving but for a hand absentmindedly stroking Ash's side. The dog was draped across her legs like a lifeless doll, the marks of Saress's claws raked across his side. Murik's gaze moved from Ash back to the girl. Her features were contorted in pain; her skin, tinged with green from her prolonged proximity to the Well. The great druid sentinels, cold and lifeless, witnessed the entire affair in silence. From somewhere high above, moonlight shone down through the ceiling to bathe all upon the dais in an eerie luminance.

Murik gathered his magic, concentrating all of his energy into his alderwood staff right before he plunged it into the Circle of Power. The wall crackled, spidery tendrils of magical energy bursting forth in all directions as half the staff's length pierced it. His action attracted the witch's attention, as she halted her chanting and centered her gaze upon him. Murik dared not meet her stare else his concentration falter, but he imagined the look of disbelief and annoyance stamped there. It gladdened his heart and imbued him with new resolve.

Saress must have felt it, too, for she moved into action, walking around the Well so it stood between her and the sorcerer. Murik watched her with interest. Using her free hand—the other still clutched the black vial—she pulled forth a heart, shriveled but purple-red with lingering vitality. Long, scaled fingers wrapped around the organ as if it were a child's ball as she extended it out over the Well. Then she squeezed. One. Two. Five. Nine. Twelve. One more—a total of thirteen drops of blood—fell from the heart and into Sarrengrave's Well before Saress tossed the crumpled organ aside. A vial appeared in her hand, this one filled with a fine, red powder, which she unstoppered with a practiced motion of her thumb. Sprinkling its contents over the spot where the drops of blood had mixed with the black murk of the Well, she mumbled the words to a spell. Once she finished the incantation, she continued on her way around the Well and toward Holly. She did not give Murik a second glance.

Murik's eyes followed the witch for a moment before his gaze returned to the Well. He neither sensed nor saw any change in its simmering surface. But blood and a witch's component had been mixed with the unwholesome power of a god long dead. Murik expected nothing good to come of it. Redoubling his efforts, Murik focused on breaking down the Circle before the witch's latest spell came to fruition.

There!

Murik perceived the first minute cracks forming in the Circle's essence as, all around him, lightning-like energy flared and crackled. He seized on several of the cracks, forcing his own energy between them like a wedge. Slowly, the chinks widened.

Then a hand emerged from the Well.

The Well's liquid clung to it like sludge, as the hand fumbled at the pool's edge closest to Murik. It found purchase, and another hand followed. Arms, head, and shoulders appeared next, as the creature clambered over the side and stood. It was unclothed, its skin sickly and rotted. Bone poked through in places where gray-white flesh was missing; those areas of skin remaining were pockmarked with welts, blisters, and other scarring indicative of one afflicted with the rotting diseases of Sarrengrave. But for the sucking noise of its feet lifting from the floor, it was silent as it advanced on Murik. Behind it, others rose from the Well.

In all, there were thirteen, one for each of the drops Saress had squeezed from Skave's heart. As one, they moved toward Murik. Unwilling to abandon his efforts, he hesitated. Discretion ultimately won out as he withdrew his staff from the Circle of Power and backed away. The cacophony of magical energy engulfing him faded until only a shimmering of its radiance remained. As Murik turned to descend the stairs, the first of the creatures to rise from the Well stepped across the Circle's threshold. The abomination passed through unharmed. Its fellows followed.

"What are they?" Kayra yelled as she neared Murik.

"Victims of Sarrengrave's priests. Made whole again, and now in service to Saress."

"How do we stop them?" Aliah asked.

Murik answered by concentrating the flame still blazing across his staff into a burning finger which reached out to touch the lead creature. That single touch was enough, as its decaying form burst into flames. Its advance slowed, and then it toppled, collapsing into a desiccated, burning mass. Even still, the command of the witch was strong, and melting, rotted fingers groped the floor, trying to pull the creature forward. Then even those were consumed, leaving only a charred husk to mark its passing. The others came on without hesitation, passing their burning fellow without a glance.

"There is no time for me to deal with them all," Murik said. "I have succeeded in weakening the witch's Circle, but must be given the opportunity to complete its negation."

"Do what you need to do, sorcerer," Kayra said, flourishing Jerrick's sword. "We'll do what we can."

Murik nodded. "Whatever you do, do not let them touch you. They carry with them the Well's potency." Then he leaped forward, blazing a path through the creatures' ranks with his sorcerer's flame. Two fell, and then another, and then he was through. Just behind him, Kayra headed off a trio which turned to pursue Murik back up the stairs, while Aliah used her dagger to hold off several more.

The moment Murik reached the edge of the Circle, he plunged his staff back into it. Once more, sorcery battled witchcraft as he probed for, and soon found, the small cracks he had chiseled there already. Wedging the power of his magic into them, he exerted his will and the power of his staff.

Within the Circle of Power's protection, Saress had unchained Holly and now held her suspended over the Well by the neck. Murik saw the terror in Holly's eyes. Though she struggled, choking out pleas for her life, her resistance was ineffectual, her words falling on deaf ears. The witch said nothing as her other hand—still clenching the black vial— came up and then poured the vial's contents into the Well of Darkness. There was no immediate effect as she tossed the empty vial aside and pulled a curved dagger from her robes. She held the blade to Holly's throat.

Murik was driven into a fury. He attacked the Circle, pouring every last bit of his strength into his effort. His magic grew so bright it obscured his vision. Shutting his eyes, he sensed the small cracks widening into chinks, and then fissures. One last push, and then he had it. The Circle shattered, and all around him, the world exploded.

Catching only a glimpse of the witch hurtling at them, Jerrick used his own body as a shield to cover and protect his wife. The witch landed on his back, her unwashed stench overwhelming his senses as her nails raked his skin. Jerrick threw an elbow at her, knocking her aside enough for him to stand right before she was on him again. A fist across the jaw knocked her back. She seemed a frail thing, her hooded head reaching only to Jerrick's shoulder, but moved with such quickness she'd closed again and, using a sharpened nail, drew a fine line across Jerrick's cheek all in the span of a breath. Jerrick seized the witch by the arm. Pulling her closer, he slammed his fist into the aperture of her hood, hitting her squarely in the face. The blow stunned her, and she went limp in Jerrick's arms. Holding her at arm's length, he ripped her hood away. The face he saw was no face at all, for there were no eyes, nose, ears, or mouth. Like a blank slate of flesh, it was hairless but for gray, wispy tendrils sprouting from her head. Jerrick took hold of her shoulders and shook her. "Tell me who you are!" Some part of Jerrick's mind recognized the witch had no mouth with which to answer him, but he didn't care. He shook her again, rage and frustration guiding him. Then a chain, a gold chain which hung about her neck, slipped out from beneath her robes. Jerrick seized it without thinking, lifting it so he saw, dangling at its end, a medallion whose face depicted a clawed hand grasping at a circular disk.

The witch came back to consciousness and, with surprising strength, shoved Jerrick backward. Still holding firm to the medallion's chain, it ripped free from her neck. If the woman had eyes or a mouth, Jerrick imagined both opened in horror, for as the medallion separated from her, her body was rocked by a fit of spasms. She stumbled away, tripped, and tumbled down the grove's slope. Arms and legs kicked out as her body flopped end over end. Finally, the mass of robes came to a stop and moved no more.

The medallion dangled from Jerrick's grasp. He lifted it to eye level. The symbol, a clawed hand grasping a solid disk, was unfamiliar. Jerrick dropped his arm to his side. Looking to the night sky, he thought of the voice which earlier had prompted him to learn more. Then, holding the medallion up again, he thought of his father.

The world swirled again, and Jerrick, too weak, collapsed. Darkness and light became one. Kendra was gone, the grove replaced by the room where he had seen his father. But now, the woman—his mother—was the place's only other occupant. The fragrance of her—rosewood mingled with traces of neroli—overpowered the smell of death, and Jerrick closed his eyes, basking in the scent he somehow remembered as hers. He clung to it, finding solace in the gentle fragrance. Then he opened his eyes. Rising, Jerrick took careful steps to the side of the bed, where he looked upon her. She had died in childbirth, so he had never seen her face. Or had he? As an infant, he had seen her. But the memory was so distant, so buried beneath layer upon layer, he'd no conscious memory of her. Now, he recognized her face as one he had known all his life. More than that, he realized the woman he had first spied upon the stone altar and the one now lying before him were one in the same. But the actions I took, the words I spoke, neither had been mine. Whose then? Thoughts of his father returned, and he suddenly realized the swelling of his mother's belly—her unborn infant—had been him. Jerrick swooned, lowering himself to the floor before he fainted. The instant he settled his back to the bed, he heard her frail whisper.

"Jerrick? Is that you?"

Turning, he went to a knee and took Kendra's hand without wondering why or how she was suddenly there. Her eyes, always so beautiful and full of life, were half-closed; her hair, matted to her forehead with sweat. The bulge of her stomach was absent, their stillborn daughter gone. Their eyes met as her eyelids fluttered open. "I'm here, Kendra." He gripped her hand tighter, seeing in the paleness of her face that the end was near. His presence was the only comfort now.

"This isn't your fault, Jerrick," she said, her voice a whisper.

Jerrick wiped the sweat from her forehead and shushed her. Isn't it? Jerrick thought of the grove, of his mother, and of the witch who had clenched her belly with obvious deliberateness. But to what purpose? A hexing. A malediction. A curse. One which had been passed through the womb to Jerrick. But what did his mother do to deserve such a fate?

"Fate played no part in this," Jerrick's father had told him. "Your mother's death is no one's fault but mine." Jerrick's mother had done nothing. It was his father. It always had been. Jerrick had spent years blaming himself, wondering what he had done to bring Death's scythe down upon those he loved, when it had always been his father's doing. Somehow, the man had crossed paths with a witch, and Jerrick's mother, Kendra, and their baby daughter had paid the price.

Jerrick thought of Anna, and his heart sank. He had spent two years trying to share the blame for his wife's death with an infant who had never enjoyed so much as a moment of life. All because he had thought his father had done the same to him. Jerrick sank his head into the blankets, unable to stomach the guilt.

Then he felt a squeeze at his hand. Lifting his head, he stared into his wife's eyes. "None of it is your fault, Jerrick."

Jerrick reached out to stroke her hair. Then why do I still feel it is? He kept his thoughts to himself, smiling slightly. Then, as Jerrick clasped the chain of the witch's medallion tighter, his smile faded. Questions, and never enough answers.

Jerrick was sick and tired of them. Just once, he wanted his questions answered.

Jerrick felt the trembling first. Then shock washed over him. It was deafening, like a clap of thunder, and the room quaked from the force of it. Furniture—upright once more—tumbled, and the bed lifted from the floor, hurling Kendra's body into the air. Jerrick flung himself at her, reaching out and catching her and just managing to bring them both back down to the mattress, unharmed, as the bed fell back to the floor. Jerrick took hold of the headboard with one hand as the bed lifted again. As if caught in an ocean's swell, it rose up and, with a crack, smashed back down. Only Jerrick's grip kept them grounded. The room shook again, blinding light—emerald light—flaring up all around them. Jerrick buried Kendra's face in his chest, using his arm to shield his eyes from the light's brilliance. "Kendra, come." Cradling his wife in his arms, Jerrick made to rise. "We must leave. I will carry—" Jerrick took one look at Kendra's face and stopped. It was too late. Jerrick raised his hand to her cheek, hesitating to touch her for fear of confirming what his eyes already told him. Then he did touch her, running his finger along her cheek in gentle brushes and feeling the coldness of death there. Jerrick leaned back with her still in his embrace, pulling the blankets close and wrapping their warmth about the both of them.

Then Kendra's body began to fade.

"No!" Jerrick held her tighter. "Stay." His wish went unheeded as she continued to dissipate. "Stay!" His hands fumbled for her, but it was no use. He cried out again, but then she was gone.

Jerrick shot up, rising and feeling the cold chain of the witch's medallion wrapped about his wrist. Untangling it, he looked at it one more time. Then he hurled it from him. The room was gone. There remained only shadow now, and the medallion sailed through the air and disappeared into the dark.

Lightning flashed, and Jerrick was back in the starlit grove where a witch whose identity remained unknown had cast a dark curse upon his mother. The hillock with the altar stone rose up ahead. Lightning changed the scene again, showing him the cavern he had never left, the hill replaced by the raised platform of the Well of Darkness. He walked toward it. Somehow, his bow and several arrows were clutched in one hand. Jerrick nocked one as he passed Kayra and then Aliah, both lying unconscious upon the floor, without a glance. Charred heaps of—something—littered the space around them. Jerrick reached the foot of the steps, finding Murik similarly comatose. The eslar lay on his back, his arms and legs spread wide, as if he had been hurled down from above. As Jerrick stopped next to the sorcerer, he peered toward the druid sentinels and saw the witch shamble into view from behind one of them. She was a mass of burned reptilian flesh and smoking robes. One hand clutched a curved knife, whose blade glimmered in the emerald light of the cavern. Jerrick stood transfixed for a moment, watching as the witch leaned over to pick something up. She straightened, and Jerrick saw Holly—disheveled and distraught—gripped at the collar by the witch. Though the girl beat at her captor with both fists, her struggles were ineffective. The witch moved the blade to her throat.

Jerrick held his bow up, drawing the string back to his ear. The motion was natural and quick, and he had only to aim the arrow's head before he let it fly. The missile took the witch in her weapon's arm, piercing flesh and bone and lodging fast. She recoiled from the sting, her blade clattering to the floor. There was a moment of surprise, and then she hurled Holly from her and turned to face Jerrick. Jerrick nocked and released another arrow, hitting the witch squarely in the chest. She stumbled back, but remained on her feet. Nocking another arrow, Jerrick took the first of the steps toward her. The witch, wounded and stunned, swayed. She took one step toward Jerrick, but no other. Before Jerrick loosed another arrow, a chain materialized from behind her. It rose over the witch's head, looping around her neck once, and then twice, before the metal loops grew taut. Jerrick saw her eyes go wide as her feet shuffled backward, and then the back of her leg hit the edge of the Well and she was falling, her arms flailing in circles. Weakened and stunned, with no tail to counterbalance her weight, the witch fell over the Well's edge and into its brackish liquid.

Jerrick took the remainder of the steps in threes, reaching the top in seconds. Walking between two of the massive statues, he saw Holly on her knees, both small hands holding tight to one end of a rusted chain whose length extended from one side of the Well to the other. It sank in the middle, where it remained looped about the witch's neck. Jerrick peered over the edge. The Well was empty, a cup-shaped pool filled only with blackened sitheri bones laid out in perfect order. Robes, pouches of components, and even flesh and his own arrows had been disintegrated away to nothingness. All had happened in an instant, with not a single sound to mark the occurrence.

"It was what . . ." Holly said, taking in a deep, ragged breath. "It was what he told me to do. He said . . . the Stones . . ."

Jerrick saw them then. Four gemstones, the druid stones, lying near the witch, the pouch containing them dissolved away just as everything else had been. No longer emerald green, they were a drab black and no longer reflected light at all.

Jerrick's eyes drifted back to the witch's bones. Then he saw that the Well had not claimed everything. A slender chain lay across and between the witch's rib cage. Probing with one end of his bow, Jerrick lifted it and the medallion at its end. A clawed hand reaching out, grasping at the moon. Jerrick just stared at it, not reacting as he let the chain slide back down.

He didn't know long he stared at the witch's bones and the amulet before Murik appeared at his side, the wizard leaning heavily on his staff, but all in one piece. Just as Jerrick had done, Murik leaned over the Well's edge, nearly tumbling over it if not for Jerrick's steadying arm, to study what remained of his nemesis. He looked at Jerrick, then back at the witch. "It is done, then." Murik let out a deep breath and looked away. Spotting Holly tending to a wounded Ash, the eslar moved to assist.

Jerrick stayed where he was. More questions, and never enough answers. He shook his head, uncertain how to feel or what to do. Then he turned to see both Kayra and Aliah ascending the stairs. The two women navigated the steps slowly. Without each other to lean on, they each might topple to the floor. Jerrick met them halfway, helping them to the top. When Kayra's gaze lighted upon Holly, the knight bolted from Jerrick's grasp. Nearly shoving Murik aside, she embraced her friend in earnest. Meanwhile, Jerrick led Aliah to the Well, where the half-dryad saw for herself the outcome of their efforts.

Aliah faltered in Jerrick's grasp, and he tightened his grip around her waist else she sink to the ground. Then she turned, burying her face in his chest. He held her close, hoping she'd gained a modicum of peace. He knew he had not.

CHAPTER TWENTY-TWO

INVADERS

THEY RETURNED TO A DIFFERENT Hall than the one they'd first arrived at. No longer deserted, the place bustled with preparations for war. Evar, who saw them as soon as they emerged from the woods, greeted them with open arms. Wearing patroller leathers now, the elder possessed a renewed sense of strength about him. He quickly explained how, after waiting until midnight as instructed, he'd gone to find the patrollers already waking from the witch's spell as if from a nightmare. He'd then rounded them up and led them back to the Hall. No one was allowed a moment of idleness, for everyone knew the goblins of Greth were coming.

"Do we know how many yet?" Jerrick asked Evar.

"We sent out scouts, though not all of them have returned. But, so far, three full battalions plus at least six vanguard patrols. The vanguards are well into the forest. The core of their invasion force was just entering when our scouts arrived."

Inside and out, patrollers busied themselves donning armor and readying bows, swords, and axes. Cooks fired up ovens and smiths stoked their bellows. A dozen recruits, caught up in the madness the same as everyone else, fletched arrows. Those who had answered the Call and fallen victim to the witch's curse were there as well, reorienting themselves and helping as they could. Most were unwashed, unshaven, and still had the wild hair and hints in their faces and eyes of the creatures they had been, but they all shared in the resolve needed right now.

While Murik accompanied Holly and Ash inside the Hall, Kayra remained close, listening in on Jerrick's conversation with Evar. Only Aliah, saying she needed more time to herself, hadn't returned to the Hall with them.

"Breakdown?" Kayra asked. One of her arms was in a sling. She'd contribute to the upcoming battle, but not with her sword.

Evar let out a breath. "A thousand imps, a scattering of grekkels, maybe a few hundred haureks, and at least fifty gaugaths. Two score or more artillery pieces. Who knows how many shamans. Hard to pick them out sometimes."

Jerrick rolled those numbers around in his head. "Sounds like they emptied Greth."

"They very well might have," Evar said. "That's not all. Lord Gral is leading them."

"The Meat Peddler?" Jerrick said. "He must realize this is a once in a lifetime opportunity. He's never had such an easy path to the Hall before."

"Not only the Hall, but Homewood as well. A quarter of their forces have split off at a fast march for the town. I've already sent a runner with instructions for the town's folk to begin evacuating. We can do little more, for we've no one to spare. We cannot allow the goblins to take the Hall. They'd have the run of the forest if they did."

"We also cannot allow them to slaughter the people of Homewood," Kayra said.

Evar stopped. Jerrick and Kayra followed suit.

"What do you propose, Dame Kayra?" Evar asked. "I ask this sincerely. I do not wish to fail the people of the Simarron again, but I've simply not enough personnel to defend both places at once. Never before have we faced an invading army of this size."

Kayra studied the goings-on around them. Jerrick imagined the gears working in her mind. The gears spun quickly, for she answered right away. "Abandon the Hall."

Evar drew himself up. "That is not—"

"Either that, or Homewood. You said it yourself. You can't defend both places. You'll have to abandon one. If it were up to me, I'd choose the Hall. You've a solid stone structure, but no moat and no walls. You've not even a killing zone around it. The trees growing so close provide more cover for the enemy than anything else. This place is indefensible. At Homewood, we at least might have a chance."

While Evar mustered a rebuttal, Jerrick considered the knight's words. The thought of abandoning the Hall had not occurred to him. Probably hadn't occurred to any of the patrollers, least of all Evar. But there it was. He'd not deny the benefits of the strategy. Evar was right. They hadn't the men to simultaneously defend both places. Not against an army of that size. As much as he hated to admit it, Jerrick knew Kayra was right. He said as much to Evar.

"But that doesn't mean we walk away without a fight."

Evar and Kayra waited for him to explain.

"My suggestion is simple. We meet Lord Gral and his army head-on."

"That sounds like suicide to me," Kayra said.

"I think perhaps we have different definitions of 'head-on.' What I mean is we hit them hard, let them know we're here and in force, then melt back into the woods. But not so fast they don't know which direction we went in. If we're a big enough pain in the arse to them, they'll send troops after us. The artillery will keep on for the Hall, but if we can strip them down to just the barest amount of protection, then the siege engines become easy targets. Without them, we have a chance of saving the Hall and maybe even Homewood."

Evar crossed his arms and nodded. "Lord Gral may want to see the Hall burned to the ground, but once he realizes the patrollers are still here, alive and well, he'll want to kill us as well. Your idea has merit."

Kayra agreed. "As long as your patrollers don't find themselves trapped between Gral's two forces. The goblins already on their way to Homewood will probably be behind you by then."

Jerrick scratched his chin. "Hmm. Hadn't thought of that."

"There's a solution to that problem," Kayra said. "Divide your forces further by sending a contingent to head-off the enemy's vanguard before it reaches Homewood or has the opportunity to turn around and become one end of the pincer."

"This may just work," Evar said. "I'll have to propose it to the others. Jerrick, will you stand by my side when I do?"

"Of course, but you hardly need me to get the men rallied behind you."

"That remains to be seen. I have told the others everything. My tenure as Eldest is coming to a close. Once this crisis is averted, I will step down. I have already informed the other Elders of this and they have agreed it is for the best. The others . . . I'm not sure what they think of me right now. You, on the other hand, are held in the highest regard. Before you'd even returned, your name and stories of how you'd slain the witch had already been bandied about."

Jerrick shook his head. "None of them were there, so how

do they even know I delivered the killing stroke?"

"It doesn't matter. They'll look to you for guidance and strength. If they think you're a hero, let them think it. Encourage it, even. They need your strength right now."

Jerrick found the whole notion discomforting. But he'd go along with whatever was needed if it helped. It turned out it more than helped as the Elders approved the plan by a wide margin only because, when asked, Jerrick backed every detail of the plan and went out of his way to stress the need for extreme action. With the plan approved, it fell to the company commanders to review the details. There were three: Holtz Merritown, Bostan the Quick, and Thomas Drake. While Jerrick knew each of them to varying degrees, he was most acquainted with Thomas, whom he'd trained alongside years ago. Thomas was closest to Jerrick's own age, which was probably a good twenty years younger than either Holtz or Bostan, who were both grizzled patroller veterans.

"The immediate problem I see," Thomas said as he and the other two commanders as well as Jerrick, Kayra, and also Murik gathered in an impromptu circle in front of the Hall, "is that Gral will push the siege weapons harder once we attack. This entire assault of his is for nothing if he can't destroy the Hall. We may lead off a good portion of his goblins, but he won't leave the artillery with no defense at all. We'll need a third force whose sole purpose is to destroy those artillery pieces."

"Maybe that isn't such a bad thing," Holtz said, spitting.

He'd a thick dab of chewing leaf inserted behind his lower lip. "The more they're split apart, the easier they are to pick off."

"Yes," Murik said, "and the clearer each of our own forces' purposes become. One group's mission is to draw away as many soldiers as they can from the main invasion force. The second's is to destroy the siege engines before they reach the Hall. The third concentrates on destroying their advanced contingent already on its way to Homewood. Though I will help in any way I can, I volunteer my services to the second group. I've a few tricks up my sleeve for dealing with their artillery."

"Right," Bostan said. "That'll be my company's task." The patroller leveled a nod at the sorcerer. "Glad to have you."

Holtz volunteered his squadrons for the chore of harrying the bulk of Gral's army and leading it away. That left the advanced contingent already on their way to the frontier town to Thomas.

"My company has four squadrons ready for combat," Thomas said. Looking at Jerrick, he said, "I'd like you to take the Fighting Foxes. What do you say?"

Jerrick had nothing at all to say, as he found the assignment both humbling and overwhelming at the same time. The Fighting Foxes, or Third Squadron, consisted of four squads with ten men to each squad. That meant forty men under his command. Since he'd never commanded more than a single squad, and even that for only a short while, he thought Thomas should know.

"You know my experience, Thomas. Before I left I was pulling solitary rover duty, hiking back and forth across the Ugulls. Leading others has never been my strong suit."

"I don't agree." Thomas remained as direct as he was pragmatic. "Your problem has always been you don't give yourself enough credit, Jerrick. The Third Squadron is yours. If circumstances were different, I might consider your hesitancy. But, we need every patroller in this, making their best contribution. Your best contribution is going to be leading this squadron. Understood?"

Jerrick knew his duty. If it meant stepping up, then that's what he was going to do. He went rigid in a soldier's formal stance and saluted his new company commander. "Yes, sir."

The three commanders split up after that, each seeing to their individual preparations. Kayra, who winced in pain at almost every movement, was assigned the duties of an adjunct to the Council of Elders, where her input would continue to influence their decisions throughout the battle. Jerrick wished both her and Murik well, then he went off with his new commander to meet the other three squadron captains and receive his individual instructions. Introductions were brief due to the nature of their situation, and so Thomas sat them all down and jumped right into the plan. By necessity, the first part focused on Jerrick and his new squadron. Thomas laid out his orders to him.

"You're to take your men to a point ahead of the goblin's advanced contingent. Your job is twofold. First, you need to slow or stop their advance. Second, you need to keep them occupied enough they don't realize the other squadrons are swooping in from behind. Once they're trapped, we cut them down without reprieve. Not one goblin walks away from this. Understood?"

Nods went all around.

Jerrick cleared his throat. "I'd recommend an ambush. That part of the woods, there's a number of ravines and gullies they'll have to pass through."

"How about Arrow Sweep?" one of the other squadron captains said. "You'll have the advantage of the high ground."

"I was thinking more of the ravine at the other side of Potter's Grove," Jerrick said. "Arrow Sweep has an old stream bed leading out and away. If the goblins are smart, they might retreat into it and get away before we can circle round to stop them. The ravine by Potter's gives us the high ground and there's no way out of it except forward or back. Back isn't going to do them any good. Forward, they'll have to run the gauntlet on my archers, which won't do them much good, either."

Thomas nodded his assent. "You've got the right of it, Captain Bur. Anyone disagree?" No one did. "Good. Your men are already assembled in Elder's Grove, captain. Best you get there, take charge, and get them moving. Ask for Sergeant Harsey. He'll get you introduced and knock some heads if anyone questions your authority. You remember him?"

Jerrick chuckled. "Don't reckon anyone ever forgets

Sergeant Hard-arsey, sir."

Thomas smiled. "No, don't reckon they do. Good luck."

Jerrick left with a parting salute and best wishes from the other captains. Elder's Grove was only a short distance from the Hall. There he found the Third making their last preparations. Standing tall amidst them was Hard-arsey. Jerrick was just thinking of how to explain to the sergeant that he'd been given command of the Foxes when, at first sight of him, Sergeant Harsey came to instant attention.

"Captain present!"

Sergeant Harsey's shout sent a lightning bolt through the squadron's men and women as those sitting jumped to their feet and joined the others in a rough assembly. When they were in formation, Harsey stepped forward and saluted Jerrick. The man was every bit the bear Jerrick remembered, right down to the massive shoulders, thick beard, and twin axes hooked into his belt.

Jerrick returned the salute and extended his hand in greeting. "Good to see you, sergeant."

Harsey nodded. "The same. Commander Drake told me he had you in mind for squadron captain, so we've been expecting you. Damn fine choice, if I may say so, sir. Me and the Foxes heard what you did to that gods-damn witch. We're all grateful."

"I did what any one of you would have done," Jerrick said, raising his voice so all heard him. "I'm afraid we don't have much time for introductions. Some of you I remember from my time in service. Others look like new faces." Young faces, Jerrick thought. "I'll meet each and every one of you once our job is done. I have our orders from Commander Drake. We're to head off the goblins making their way for Homewood. Any questions? Good. Sergeant, let's get the men moving. Hard double-file march. We'll spread out once we get closer to Potter's Grove."

Jerrick watched each of his squadron members as they passed, returning their nods. Forty men and women. Forty lives. Every one of them knew what they signed up for when they'd joined. He knew some of them had seen real battle. But many hadn't. Jerrick saw it in their eyes. But he also saw patroller courage and determination. These men and women were not city-bred, but born and raised on the frontier. They knew the way of things and that, right now, the way of things was putting an end to this invasion. Right now, the way of things meant killing goblins. Jerrick waited until the last of them had left the grove before running to take the lead. It was time to kill some goblins.

Past Potter's Grove the landscape dropped off at a steep but not quite sheer angle. At the bottom, an old, long dried-up riverbed cut a path through the crevasse. The path was wide enough to accommodate three or four abreast or maybe a single gaugath. The other side of the crevasse rose up at an even steeper angle than the Potter's grove side. The trail into the gorge was the easiest path. Also, it was an ideal place for an ambush.

At the other side of the crevasse, Jerrick saw Harsey's signal. The sergeant's two squads were in place and ready. Jerrick looked over those he'd kept with him. They'd bows held ready with arrows placed in the ground before them. Knives, swords, and axes were within easy reach. Now, they waited.

The first goblins appeared more or less on schedule as grekkel scouts poofed into view. Two noxious clouds of smoke melted away to reveal a pair of the annoying creatures at the bottom of the gorge. Neither seemed particularly interested in actually doing their jobs as scouts as one found something on the ground and ate it while the other sat and cleaned its claws. The patrollers left them alone. Dead bodies along the gorge's path served no purpose other than to alert the others still coming, so as long as the grekkels remained unaware of the patrollers, they posed no threat. Their presence still caused Jerrick's heart to beat faster, though. He settled down only when the grekkels teleported further down the gorge. Another —poof!— and they were gone from view.

Not long thereafter, the first of the main goblin group came into view. Imps were in the lead. Mean and nasty, they were somewhere between a grekkel and a dwarf in size. Jerrick counted four across and fifteen deep in this first formation, noting also their hodgepodge armor and assortment of flails, axes, and small crossbows. No patroller engaged these first ones, for Jerrick had made it clear they'd wait for the bulk of the goblin troops to enter the gorge before anyone attacked. The next ones came in right behind the imps. These were haurek regulars. Not stalkers like Skave, but skilled combatants nevertheless. Jerrick counted fifty of them. Six gaugaths with hammers resting on shoulders walked amidst them. Another contingent of imps brought up the rear.

—Poof!—

Multiple clouds of vapor appeared all around the marching soldiers as grekkels teleported in. Two were already halfway up the crevasse's slope on Jerrick's side. More observant than the first pair, these two immediately looked up the slope. Concealed behind heavy brush, Jerrick fought the compulsion to drop down further as he kept the grekkels in sight. He trained an arrow on one of them while hoping someone else was targeting the other. Then they both vanished.

The easiest way to kill a grekkel was to hit it before it jumped. The second, less reliable way was to catch it the moment it reappeared. Since a grekkel needed line of sight on its next location, knowing the direction of its stare right before teleportation was key. Jerrick trained his arrow along that path now, waiting for the grekkel to rematerialize. His arrow pointed straight at the sky when the grekkel finally did. Jerrick shot into the telltale cloud of vapor appearing just above a branch overheard. His aim was true as he heard the creature squawk in pain. Another patroller tried to take out the other, but the grekkel's knack for causing bad luck caused the woman's bowstring to snap. Fortunately, another targeting the creature had better luck. The second grekkel fell dead with an arrow through its body. With no more reason to wait, Jerrick shouted the order to engage.

"Now!"

Those around him sprang up and let loose their arrows. The patrollers on the other side did the same until, from both sides of the gorge, arrows fell down on the goblins like rain. The imps took it the worst, for as soon as they realized what was happening their meek sense of order was replaced by sheer panic. Those at the edges forward and back tried to make a run for it, but they only singled themselves out as patroller arrows found them. A few got away, but in such small numbers, it didn't matter. The gaugaths, never ones to take a beating without giving something back, charged up either slope. Despite the steepness, their attempt allowed them to make it almost halfway to the patrollers' position before they fell to the ground looking more like porcupines than goblins. The haureks neither ran nor attempted to climb from the gorge, but instead formed up with shields arranged into a shell-like wall all around them. They managed this after losing only a handful of their number to the initial attack. With their shield wall in place, they showed an uncharacteristic amount of patience and discipline as arrow after arrow bounced off or stuck into their shields. Not a single missile found its way past their barrier.

With the haureks pinned down and out of the fight, the patrollers trained their arrows on anything else still moving. Jerrick dispatched a handful of his men to follow the imps who'd gotten away from the forward section. Those fleeing back the way they'd come had a nice surprise waiting for them in the form of Commander Drake's other three squadrons. That left only the haureks for the Fighting Foxes to deal with. A few more arrows were shot the goblins' way, but these were as ineffective as the others, and so the frequency of such attacks tapered off until no one shot at all.

"Lower your shields," Sergeant Harsey shouted from the other side of the crevasse, "and we might kill you quickly."

The response from the haureks came as no surprise to anyone. "Go shat yourselves, patroller!"

A handful of arrows lodged themselves in the haurek's shield in answer.

Jerrick signaled for his squadron to hold any further attacks as he raised his voice to address the goblins. "Throw down your weapons, agree to leave the Simarron, and we'll let you live! There's no other way out of this for you!"

One of the women to Jerrick's right spoke so that only those closest heard. "Sir, I thought orders called for no mercy?"

She was right. Commander Drake's orders had been specific. Jerrick was all right with such orders most of the time. But not all the time. "We're not butchers," he said to the other, loud enough that others got the hint and passed the word down. "If they agree to surrender, we escort them from the forest. This is on me. None of you will face the company commander for this." Jerrick knew he might be facing the shortest appointment as a squadron captain in the history of the patroller corp. But he'd seen enough death of late. Given the opportunity to avoid more, he'd take it.

Jerrick repeated his ultimatum. This time he received a response.

"Not likely! We throw down our weapons and you'll pick us off one-by-one!" Another insult followed, this time about Jerrick's mother.

Jerrick opened his mouth to shout a reply. He shook his head instead. "This is ridiculous. I'm going down there." Protests erupted from patrollers at either side of him. "Not *all* the way down there." He didn't much like the idea of having to defend against forty-odd haureks all by his lonesome, but he also felt he needed to bring this conversation down to a more amicable level. "Keep me covered, just in case."

Jerrick once more signaled to the patrollers on the other side of the gorge to hold fire as he stepped through the brush and descended the slope. He stopped halfway to the goblins, his bow held ready just in case.

"Send out your leader. I'd like to have words."

Laughter erupted from behind the shields. "How stupid do you think we are?"

Jerrick almost gave an answer to the question. Instead, he said, "You have my guarantee as squadron captain no harm will come to whoever comes out. I only wish to talk."

Still nothing.

"Three other patroller squadrons are on their way here right now. I don't think you'll find them in as talkative a mood as I'm in."

Jerrick heard muttering from the other side of the shields before an opening appeared and a single haurek stepped out. He didn't step out very far.

"I am Captain Zokore," he said with a growl.

"Captain Bur."

"Speak quickly, captain, so we can get back to it."

No wasting time with this one. "My men have the high ground. Yours are pinned down. Surrender your weapons and we'll allow you to leave the Simarron. Don't, and you'll end up like that one." Jerrick gestured with his chin at one of the fallen gaugaths, a score of arrows sticking out of him from every which way.

The haurek captain no more than glanced at the dead goblin before he returned his attention to Jerrick. He made a point of smiling. "I do not know the meaning of this word 'surrender.' Explain it to me."

Jerrick expected but did not appreciate the goblin's mockery. Still, he indulged him. "Surrender is where you throw down your weapons and hightail it back to the Ugulls."

The explanation only elicited a chuckle from Zokore. "You've heard of the Meat Peddler?"

Jerrick nodded.

"He is here in your forest. He has come with carnage and dismay at his side. First, he means to destroy your precious Hall. Then, he will ravage your pathetic frontier town and torture its people. It matters not that the witch has betrayed him and not killed you all as she had promised, for he will find her. Woe to her when he does. Nor does it matter that you patrollers still live. Soon all of the woods and everything in it will belong to Lord Gral. Already he has your roads. Soon he will have the Hall and Homewood as well. There is no escape for any of you. And you come here asking for our surrender." Zokore spat in Jerrick's direction even as the haureks behind the shield wall chuckled.

"What do you mean he has the roads?" It was the only noteworthy thing Zokore had said.

The haurek captain smiled, revealing a row of sharp, yellowed teeth. "The first thing we took was Holden Bridge. No one will escape these woods and no one will come to help. Our finest warriors await anyone coming in either direction. Their orders are simple: no one passes."

Jerrick did his best to hide the sinking feeling taking hold in his stomach. Homewood's women, children, and elderly were walking right into a trap. He spent no further time considering his squadron's options. They had only one.

Nocking an arrow, Jerrick said nothing as he let the missile fly. The arrow hit the haurek captain square in the forehead. His body hadn't touched ground before Jerrick started to scramble back up the slope. Behind him, the haurek soldiers hollered at his back and must have let down their wall to pursue as a volley of arrows flew by over Jerrick's head. Jerrick reached the top of the ridge unscathed. As soon as he did, a patroller horn sounded, signaling the arrival of Commander Drake.

"Corporal!" Jerrick didn't remember the woman's name right now. "Signal to Sergeant Harsey to proceed south along his side of the gorge. We'll meet up and go from there."

The woman did as ordered without hesitation.

To those around him, Jerrick said, "We'll let the others handle what's left here. We've another priority to take care of. Holden Bridge is being held."

That was explanation enough as members of his squadron followed him south along the ridge. They met their other two squads about twenty minutes later. A quick summary of what the haurek captain had said transformed questioning stares into determined ones. No one spoke as they broke into a fast march toward Belkin's Way. They hoped to catch-up to those fleeing Homewood long before they'd even gotten close to the bridge. Instead they found the road empty. When the bridge just came into sight, and still there was no sign of anyone from Homewood, the patrollers knew something was wrong. Before drawing any closer, the patrollers ducked into the woods. Jerrick and Harsey went ahead to scout. Staying low, the two finished their approach on their bellies, settling into a tangle of brush just behind a low rise.

"Nothing there," Harsey said.

He was right. There was the bridge, as wide and solid as Jerrick remembered, but no one was on it. Jerrick knew why, too. "Take a look there," he said, gesturing toward the woods at the bridge's other side.

Movement, and shadows on shadows, which might be the rustle of branches except there was no wind.

"Someone's hiding," Harsey said, confirming Jerrick's suspicion.

"They're waiting for someone to cross the bridge," Jerrick said.

"Doesn't make sense to post sentries on the bridge," Harsey said. "Especially if you're a goblin."

Jerrick eased himself back. "Might scare away the people you're trying to kill."

Once they'd rejoined the others, Jerrick laid out his plan. He was a bit surprised one came to mind so readily, but with so few options available to them, there were only so many courses of action. He crouched alongside his sergeants while patrollers ringed them several deep.

"Chances are we got ahead of the people from Homewood," Jerrick said.

"Or they never left," Harsey said with a sour expression.

Jerrick nodded at that. "Or they never left."

More than a few patrollers shook their heads. Jerrick heard the words 'damn' and 'stubborn' muttered.

"Either way, we've got some goblins to deal with. There's a group of them hiding in the woods at the other side of the bridge. Number and armaments are unknown. We need a way to draw them out. My idea is to—"

"Sir!" A patroller slid his way through the ring to its center.

It was the man assigned to watch the road. Jerrick rose to meet him. "Vrannan soldiers on the other side of the bridge heading this way, sir. About forty of them."

Jerrick swore under his breath. Leave it to Vrannan regulars to show at the worst possible time. Then he realized maybe they were just what they needed right now.

"How long?" he asked the one who'd spotted them.

"Twenty seconds, sir. There's a bend in the road. I didn't see them until just now."

Harsey rubbed at his chin. "I bet the goblins saw them coming long before we did. They'll be ready to pounce the moment they hit the bridge."

"Right," Jerrick said. "We'll be ready to pounce too, the moment the goblins come out from cover. Take two-thirds of the men and position them along the riverbank. Get them ready to lay down fire as soon as the goblins show themselves. I'll take the rest and help get the soldiers across the bridge."

"Shouldn't we warn them?" a patroller asked.

"No time," Harsey said. "They probably won't understand, anyway. Too dense."

While Harsey led his portion of the patrollers toward Stoney Creek, Jerrick took the rest to the road. Jerrick barely had them in position when they heard the raucous bedlam of the goblins unleashing their ambush on the unsuspecting Vrannans. He also heard the distinctive whir of arrows flying and grunts and hollers as the invaders realized they weren't the only ones to fall victim to a trap. What he didn't expect were more goblins streaming out of the forest on their side of the bridge but from the opposite side of Belkin's Way. They ran out onto the road, forming a barricade of steel to keep the soldiers trapped. Only some of the haureks and imps as yet recognized what was happening on the river's other side as their comrades started to topple over from Harsey and his men's initial assault. With the element of surprise still theirs, Jerrick led his patrollers out onto the road. Jerrick dropped to a knee alongside the others. Together they loosed a volley of arrows straight into the backside of the goblin formation.

Jerrick gave the order to drop bows and draw swords and axes as the goblins on the bridge's other side clashed with the Vrannans. The soldiers hadn't had any time to form defensive lines. But most had drawn weapons. The goblin charge smashed through the first two or three lines of soldiers, but then wavered, slowed, and was stopped altogether as the Vrannans joined shields together. The wall, which was only hastily formed, was torn asunder as haureks smashed it aside and smaller imps slipped beneath or between. The larger battle broke into smaller skirmishes all along the bridge.

Jerrick and his patrollers leaped into the fray. Jerrick took down a haurek with a thrust to the back, stepped over the body, and kicked an imp out of his way as he slipped into the throng. Other patrollers did the same, fighting their way through the goblin ranks in an attempt to join up with the soldiers. Captain Zokore had called these warriors Greth's finest. As a haurek rounded on Jerrick, axe swinging to take off his head and then swinging back to disembowel him with the return stroke with nary a pause between, Jerrick had to agree. Knowing if he and the haurek squared off in single combat he'd be hard-pressed to walk away in one piece, he was glad for the presence of the other patrollers, especially the one who came in with a savage swing that knocked the haurek off-balance even as another stabbed it through the side with her sword. Jerrick took hold of the pair before they'd the chance to run off to some other part of the fight.

"You two, advance with me!"

The three of them cut a path through the mass of goblins. Soon, Jerrick faced the captain of the Vrannan company.

"Captain Bur, King's Patrol," he shouted over the din of battle.

"Captain Forsythe, Tenth Infantry."

The press of battle forced them to step back. The pair of patrollers accompanying Jerrick rejoined the fight unbidden, and now stood side-by-side with Vrannan soldiers, holding the line.

"Buggers gotten this far," Captain Forsythe said, "what's it mean for the Hall? Is it . . . ?" His expression froze, waiting for Jerrick's reply.

"The Hall still stands."

Captain Forsythe let loose a sigh of relief. "Damn good to hear. I'd hate to have come all this way for nothing."

"These goblins are only a small contingent of a larger invasion force. The other patrollers are dealing with the rest. If we're lucky, there won't be anything left for us to do when we get back."

"Word back home was you patrollers were all dead. I, for one, am glad to see that's not the case."

Jerrick looked over his patrollers, fighting shoulder-to-shoulder with the Vrannans and toe-to-toe against the goblins. At the bridge's other side, Sergeant Harsey and his men were giving the goblins hell. Jerrick smiled. "That makes two of us."

No more time for talk as both captains got back into the thick of it. The goblins put up a good fight, and while they were a match for the combined Vrannan and Hall patrollers in numbers, they fell short in skill, despite being the cream of Gral's crop. With the last goblin dispatched, the survivors took quick stock of their own wounded and dead. The Vrannans had lost half a dozen, with another score wounded to some degree. The patrollers had lost one and had a handful wounded, but no one seriously. Jerrick took note of the one who'd fallen. He'd make sure his name was entered in the rolls of the honored once this was all over.

Wood and vines were cut and made into stretchers. Able-bodied soldiers were assigned to man them, except for the lone patroller's, whom Jerrick assigned to two of their own. The pallbearers and those more seriously wounded were given instructions to make for the Hall at best speed while everyone else went on ahead. After Jerrick had explained the entirety of the situation to Captain Forsythe, the Vrannan captain had agreed they needed to reach the Hall with all haste. They found the road clear all the way to Homewood. Nor was there any goblin activity at the frontier town. They learned no one had left despite the warning. In fact, the warning had prompted every citizen into action as they prepared to defend themselves. With no time to lose, the Fighting Foxes kept on for the Hall. Forsythe's company was not far behind. As the patrollers drew nearer, they expected to hear the sounds of battle. Instead, they heard nothing. A bit closer, a pair of patrollers stepped out of the woods to challenge them. Fierce stares turned to smiles and the word was passed: The battle was over. They had won.

Jerrick saw Holly standing at the end of the road. Ash, who had a bandage wrapped around his midsection, was with her. The dog, ears perked, looked his way, stayed still, but then came bounding forward. Ash passed Jerrick by as if he wasn't there, bouncing into the throng of men behind him. Jerrick shook his head as he approached Holly, who gave him an embarrassing hug before he thought to stop her as the patrollers streamed past them with Ash now at their lead. Holly and Jerrick followed, though Jerrick paused long enough to take in the Hall one more time. It was good to be home.

CHAPTER TWENTY-THREE

THE ROAD AHEAD

"LORD GRAL ESCAPED, BUT WE all know he will come back someday."

Inside the Hall's great room, an informal gathering of the elders and anyone else who cared to sit, listen, or join in had convened. Smoke hung heavy in the air and beer, brought up from Homewood along with a variety of other, much-needed supplies, flowed freely. The room sang with talk and laughter and the gaiety of victory. But Jerrick, who sat a table with many others, beer in one hand and pipe held between his teeth, knew the patroller who had spoken was right. Lord Gral had gotten away in the chaos of the goblins' retreat. Someday, he'd come back for another try. But not today.

Jerrick got up from the table and went outside. A few called after him, but no one took offense when he continued on his way. He skirted the edge of the main celebration where tables laden with food and drink surrounded an area lively with dancing and singing. The tongues of a central bonfire licked high into the sky. Even at the outskirts of the main celebration, folk stopped Jerrick to shake his hand or offer their thanks. Jerrick rebuked no one. But he did want some time to himself, and so with Ash at his side he chose a path that led to a quiet refuge amidst some trees where an odd assortment of rocks provided plentiful places for him and Ash to sit. He still spied the light from the bonfire and heard the ongoing merriment, but it was all just distant enough it faded into the background. Soon, his pipe was lit and puffs of smoke rose lazily into the cool night air. Jerrick found the usual misty fog strangely comforting for a change.

Digging into a pouch at his belt, he took out the witch's medallion and held it so moonlight cutting through the clouds above just glinted from its polished surface. Jerrick let his hand fall to his lap, where he continued to hold fast to it. Minutes passed before he heard the voice behind him.

"I hope I am not interrupting."

Jerrick glanced over his shoulder at Murik. Ash bounded to

the sorcerer, circling playfully as Murik stepped forward, free of his limp since imbuing the witch potion. Murik's explanation regarding his healed leg had been terse, and he offered nothing on the potential side effects he may have already suffered. Ultimately, no one pressed him on it. Murik's sorcery had turned the tide on the main goblin invasion force. Commander Drake's squadrons had peeled off hundreds of goblins, luring them deeper into the woods and away from the siege artillery, but so many others remained to guard the engines it took the sorcerer's magic to cut a path to them. Then it had been a matter of picking off the gunnery crews and setting fire to the engines themselves. Murik's sorcery had played a role in that as well, his magical fire igniting the wood of the engines with little effort. When the sorcerer's strength had finally begun to fade, strong backs and axes took over, busting axles and demolishing throwing arms. Meanwhile, Commander Drake's squadrons had fulfilled their own mission of destroying the advanced contingent and then, joining up with Holtz's company, had pressed the goblins into a full retreat. Patrollers pursued them all the way to the edge of the mountains. In the resulting chaos, the Meat Peddler had gotten away.

After satisfying Ash's need for attention, Murik nestled himself amidst the rocks opposite Jerrick. Like all the others, Murik had washed and been given fresh clothes. The wizard had opted for the characteristic leather breeches worn by all patrollers, but instead of their hardened leather armor, he selected a soft, long-sleeved shirt with billowed arms. He added his own vest and dark blue cloak, and his staff was ever at his side. His blue-black skin blended well with the night, and his rust-red hair was combed and parted at one side.

"I have recovered those belongings I deemed pertinent from the witch's house," Murik said. "The structure itself is no more." Following the battle, patrols had reported seeing him on his way to the old hunting lodge. On the way back, folk had spotted a wagon rolling behind him seemingly of its own volition.

Jerrick nodded, but said nothing.

"The druid stones I shall take with me. They will be kept safe." He'd had them in his possession since they'd left the caverns.

Jerrick shrugged. "I don't think anyone cares what you do with them, as long as they are taken far from the Simarron."

Murik smiled a faint, brief smile.

"Holly told me you mean to leave soon," Jerrick said. "Where will you go?"

"I intend to take the witch's belongings, including her books and journals, to a place where they will be safe from ill-use. After that? Home."

"Isia?"

"Yes. Long has it been since I have seen my family or walked the lands of my people. It will be a welcome change."

A rustling from one side of the rocky grove caught the pair's attention. Kayra, followed closely by Holly, emerged from the dark. The two women strode up to them, but did not sit. Like Murik, both wore new clothing: dark cotton breeches with blue tunics tied at the waist. Kayra's auburn hair fell freely past her shoulders, while Holly's shorter tresses were decorated with flowers given to her by women of the Hall. Kayra's arm remained in a sling. Nothing had been broken, but she'd bad bruising from her battle with the gaugath. Also, she still wore the charm given to her by young Jezebel of Homewood. In the aftermath, they had located Jezebel's father, who was alive and well despite his ordeal. It remained only to reunite him with his family.

Kayra spoke first. "I do not wish to intrude, but—"

Jerrick waved his hand through the air. "Sit."

Holly made to do so, but hesitated when Kayra remained standing. Jerrick and Murik looked upon the knight with curiosity.

"Something stands between us," Kayra said, directing her gaze at Jerrick. "Something which demands resolution." With one swift motion, and with her one good arm, Kayra drew her sword.

At sight of the naked blade, Jerrick pushed farther back on the rock. "What 'something'?" Kayra's next move both surprised and embarrassed him. She went to one knee, presenting the blade to him hilt first.

"I apologize for drawing my weapon on you, captain" she said, her head bowed. "I acted rashly. For that, and for misjudging you, I am sorry."

Jerrick stood, remembering the incident following their escape through the forest. "I don't think that's . . . I mean . . . Think nothing of it. Heat of the moment and all. Why don't you get up off your knee?"

Kayra remained where she was. "My honor demands I grant you a boon. Assuming you accept my apology, of course."

"A boon?" Jerrick asked.

"That means a favor," Holly said.

"I know what it means." Jerrick glanced at Murik, who seemed amused by the entire affair. "That's really not necessary."

"I must insist," she said, once more offering her sword to him.

"What am I supposed to do with that?" Jerrick asked. "I don't want your sword."

Holly giggled. "You're supposed to take the hilt, then give it back to her. It's the symbolic way of accepting a knight's apology."

Jerrick shook his head. "Very well." He took the hilt as instructed. When Kayra rose, he gave it back to her. "What sort of a boon are you offering?"

Kayra returned the blade to her sheath. "Ask what you will, and I shall do all in my power to see it is done."

Nothing came to Jerrick. With all eyes on him, he started to feel foolish. So he said what seemed the easiest. "How about if, in the future, I need your help, you'll—"

"Done."

There was no hesitance, only immediate acceptance. Jerrick felt he knew Kayra well enough to know she meant it.

"Now," Jerrick said, "will you sit?"

Kayra looked at Holly, who in turn looked back toward the

light of the bonfire. "Holly is eager to return to the festivities. Apparently there are two who wish to dance with us."

Jerrick laughed as he plopped himself back on his rock. "Really? Who?"

"Kren and Marsdan," Holly said, with no attempt to hide her enthusiasm.

Jerrick and Murik both laughed.

"Then by all means," Jerrick said, "don't keep them waiting. Though I'd put the sword away first."

Kayra flashed an annoyed look their way, which quickly turned to a smile, and soon all of them were laughing. When the gaiety subsided, Jerrick said, "We'll join you shortly. Just in case your dance partners are not to your liking." Kren and Marsden were young—Jerrick's juniors by a good fifteen years—but, Jerrick reminded himself, so were Kayra and Holly.

Holly turned and immediately headed back toward the Hall, while Kayra rolled her eyes and followed. Soon, they were gone from sight.

Jerrick looked after them for a time. "Holly's doing well," he said. "She was pretty badly shaken, but she's stronger than she looks." Jerrick kicked at the dirt. "She told you about the priest?"

"Yes," Murik answered. "Parthen. A priest of Sarrengrave, his soul bound to the Well by the druids. An effective prison, I think."

"You believe her story? Or, rather, the priest's?"

"Some of it. Like all things, I venture there is more than

meets the eye there. Before we left, I swept the cavern and the surrounding woods for his presence, but detected nothing. The boon he requested of Holly—freedom from the Well—apparently was indeed fulfilled. What he did for you and Aliah counts for something, I suppose."

"What exactly *did* he do?"

Murik thought a moment. "Provided guidance. Steered you away from that dark place in your mind and heart which each of us possesses in some form. It was a clever spell. I will grant Saress that much. By forcing you and Aliah to fully embrace that dark place, your subconscious minds were at extreme risk. With your minds gone . . ." Murik made a show of situating himself better on the rock. "But enough of that. What are your plans now?"

Jerrick thought a moment. "To stay here for a while. I still have a lot of catching up to do, and I want to help. There will be plenty to do. Thomas wants me to stay on as squadron captain. I have to admit, the thought is intriguing."

Murik nodded. "But you are anxious to be off, to learn the secret of the medallion."

Jerrick had slipped the token away when Kayra and Holly approached. He drew it forth now, holding it so they both looked upon it. "I don't suppose you learned anything about it?"

"Only a little. The witch's journal mentions a coven, twelve other witches to whom she had pledged her loyalty. Given what I know of Saress, this arrangement was likely only a convenience for her. Perhaps she hoped to share in their knowledge, or gain access to forbidden secrets beyond her immediate grasp. Whichever the case, she wrote enough about the Well, without mention of other witches, to convince me she acted alone. However, there was a sketch similar to your medallion on one of the pages. It will take me a little while to decipher the meaning of the text beneath it."

"But you think the witch who cursed my family may have belonged to this coven?"

Murik shrugged. "I don't know. Perhaps."

Jerrick took a long pull on his pipe, sending a drawn-out wisp of smoke drifting into the air before saying, in a soft, subdued voice, "There was a brief moment when I felt relief, like a weight had been lifted from me. Just knowing it wasn't my fault. But now . . ." Jerrick let out a deep breath. In the distance, boisterous singing accompanied by music rose to a fevered pitch. Drunken voices drifted across the treetops. As the sounds faded into the background once more, Jerrick went on. "I miss her. I miss both of them." Silence consumed a few moments before he continued. "I left Rell in hopes of finding answers. Instead, I've found only more questions. What did my father do to bring this witch's curse upon us?"

Murik had no answer to that. "You're angry at him."

"Shouldn't I be?"

Murik sighed. "If the portents you experienced are accurate, he has much to answer for. Perhaps, however, you should wait to pass final judgment. Even your friend Evar, whose intentions were good, made mistakes."

Evar had relinquished his position as Eldest of the Elders.

It remained for the Council of Elders to replace him and to determine his fate. Many, like Jerrick, had forgiven him. Others had not.

Jerrick shook his head. "I may not even be able to find my father. It's been a long time."

"Where does your search begin, then?"

"Cerlin. My foster parents live there. Perhaps they'll have some ideas."

Murik nodded. "I was thinking. I have this business with the witch's belongings to take care of, but perhaps once that is accomplished, I might accompany you on your quest for a time."

Jerrick shook his head. "I can't ask you to do that, Murik."

"It is good you do not ask then," Murik said, smiling. "But still, I offer."

Jerrick sighed and returned the smile. "Thank you."

Murik stood. "Shall we rejoin the others?"

"You go ahead. I'll join you in a little while."

Murik bowed, then disappeared into the trees, leaving Jerrick and Ash alone once more. Jerrick took a draw from his pipe, then touched the dog between the ears. Ash shuffled over and leaned against his leg.

"What am I supposed to do, Ash?"

Ash's ears perked at the sound of his name, then he rested his chin upon Jerrick's leg.

"What are *we* supposed to do?"

Beyond Cerlin, he had no ideas. He patted Ash's head and

stood. There was uncertainty, but, also, there was purpose. For now, it was enough.

Jerrick started back toward the Hall. Ash sprinted ahead, sideswiping Jerrick's legs and nearly bowling him over in the process. Jerrick cursed and shook his head.

"Stupid dog."

But he didn't mean it.

IF YOU ENJOYED THE HALL OF THE WOOD,
PLEASE LEAVE A REVIEW!

READ MORE BY SCOTT MARLOWE

ABOUT THE AUTHOR

Scott Marlowe lives in Bentonville, Arkansas, the Mountain Biking Capital of the World, where he drinks extraordinary amounts of coffee, rides his mountain or gravel bike whenever the opportunity arises, and writes stories that often end in wondrous, explosive mayhem.

You can find more information about Scott online at scottmarlowe.com.

 facebook.com/ScottMarloweAuthor

 instagram.com/ScottMarloweAuthor

Ingram Content Group UK Ltd.
Milton Keynes UK
UKHW040628150623
423495UK00004B/132

9 798201 222079